THE BEAST WHO BOUGHT ME

A DARK MM ROMANCE

CLEMENZA FAMILY
BOOK 1

LEIGHTON GREENE

Cover Design: Natasha Snow

THE BEAST WHO BOUGHT ME

I used to be a mafia prince. Now I'm marked as prey.

Someone is systematically eliminating my Family bloodline, and I'm the last heir standing. No money. No allies. No way out…except one.

An underground auction where the wealthy and the wicked bid on desperate, untouched men like me.

I expect to be sold to a stranger. Used and discarded.

Instead, I'm bought by a man with a two-decades-long vendetta against my dead father.
A beast who drops ten million dollars to own me, then drags me home to a prison he built just for me.

He wants vengeance. He wants to break me.
But I'm not as easy to break as he expects.
And when danger follows me into his territory, he becomes something I never expected.

A protector.
A *possessor*.
He keeps me safe, even while he keeps me caged.

I'm starting to think the most dangerous thing isn't being owned by him.

It's wanting him to keep me...

AUTHOR'S NOTE

This book is a dark romance. The characters are morally corrupt, the power imbalance is intense, and the relationship is the opposite of healthy.

You can find full content guidance on my website.

I hope you fall in love with this book as much as I did.

CHAPTER 1
CALIGULA

I'M RUNNING SO FAST my lungs might burst, but if I slow down, I'm dead. And I'm not going to die like a rat in some dirty alley.

Not tonight.

I was track champion all through high school. Right now, those years of training are the only thing keeping me alive. All those line drills in the August heat…

Worth it now.

I eat up the sidewalk as I sprint toward a bar a block down where there's enough life to offer safety. Or witnesses, anyway.

I've reached full velocity when a colossal figure steps out of a dark alcove directly into my path. I try to dodge, but there's no chance. I clip him hard and head teeth-first toward concrete.

But before I hit, I'm swung around and upright, set back on my feet as though I weigh nothing at all. It's like hitting a wall that decided to help me out instead of letting me face the consequences of physics.

"Careful, pretty boy. You'll hurt yourself."

His voice is warm honey spilled on gravel and broken

glass. Around my biceps, his hands are iron bands holding me effortlessly in place. I look up—up—up to see a face that looks rough, unfinished. As though the artist sculpting him wasn't working with marble but clay, pummeling his face into place with fists, and forgot to smooth it all down before firing. The black hair is cropped short and a shadow darkens his strong jaw.

He's not…unattractive.

And when his dark eyes meet mine, they're *hungry*. Like I'm his next meal and he's debating which bite to take first.

His attention shifts, scanning over my shoulder, and something he sees makes his grip tighten, fingers digging into my arms hard enough to make me gasp. I crane to look over my shoulder and see the hooded figure running toward us, the guy who's been on my ass since I bolted from my grandfather's townhouse.

Since I left my cousin's body cooling on the floor.

The stranger angles himself to shield me. It's such an instinctive, protective gesture that I almost forget to be terrified of him. Almost. The asshole chasing me pulls up short, reassessing. My rescuer—captor?—doesn't move, doesn't speak, just stands perfectly still, silently daring him.

The other guy backs up. Turns. Runs the other way.

Only when he's out of sight does my companion's attention return to me, and that ravenous focus is back, cranked up to eleven.

I pull myself the fuck together. "Let me go," I tell him in my most imperious tone.

He tilts his head, considering. "Should I? Seems like you need someone to keep you safe."

Every impulse I have is a conflicting signal. Run. Stay. Submit. Fight. Lick his neck…

What the hell?

"I can take care of myself," I manage at last.

His lips pull back in not quite a smile—more like a wolf showing its teeth. No, not a wolf. A goddamn grizzly bear, looming over me. "Can you, though?"

With that, he pins me against the wall, one enormous hand flat on my chest, where he must be able to feel my hammering heart, and the other gripping the back of my neck. He leans down as though to kiss me, and I just stand there, speechless.

"You're shaking like a rabbit," he murmurs close to my ear. "Breathe."

He's right, I *am* shaking. And now I'm breathing only because he told me to, pulling air into my lungs with sharp, desperate pants. His thumb strokes across the nape of my neck, and my entire body lights up like a Christmas tree. Heat floods me, making me warm despite the cold, and—

"So," he goes on conversationally. "What did a pretty thing like you do to get chased through my city?"

His city? This city belonged to my Family not so long ago. My grandfather ran half of Manhattan before this jerk could tie his shoes.

And I don't appreciate the victim-blaming, either.

I shove forward, hard, and he lets me go. "Lets" being the operative word—I feel the exact moment he decided to release me, which pisses me off more than anything.

He steps back with his hands raised, that dangerous smile still in place.

"Who the hell do you think you are?" I demand.

He reaches up to adjust his jacket collar. Tattoos pepper his hands, disappearing into his sleeves. But one symbol in particular, just below the webbing of his thumb, makes my stomach drop. The stylized "G" that marks high-ranking members of the Giuliano Crime Family.

The Giulianos are former allies turned hyenas, gorging on *my* Family's corpse. Opportunists who forgot generations of friendship the second my grandfather's body hit the floor.

"You sure you're alright, little Clemenza?" he asks.

He knows who I am. Alarm bells start ringing—and I hear it now, the enjoyment in his voice. He's watching my reactions, relishing them. But then his tone shifts. "You've got blood on you."

I look down. There's blood on my hands, my sweater, soaked into the navy fabric where I couldn't see it in the dark.

"I'm fine," I spit out, backing away. "I'm fine." I hold his gaze until the last possible second, and then I turn and run.

"Run all you want," he calls after me. "I like a chase."

I run faster.

And I absolutely do not think about the way my body responded to his hands on me. It was adrenaline. It was fear.

It was nothing.

The hotel I end up in is a shithole. The guy at the desk doesn't look up from his phone when I check in. Cash only, no questions asked.

My kind of place, these days.

I turn on the TV the second I get into the room for noise cover, and to give the illusion I'm awake and alert. Then I lock myself in the bathroom to survey the damage.

He was right, that giant Giuliano. There's blood all over me. My hands, my sweater, dried rust-brown under my fingernails. Clemenza blood.

Not mine. I found my cousin, Louie, in a puddle of it three hours ago, shot in the back of the head.

Louie was the heir apparent. He'd texted me to meet,

told me he'd figured out who was picking us off. I was desperate enough to go, even though there was no love lost between Louie and me. I found his corpse and the killer still lurking, waiting around for *my* dumb ass to show up.

I tripped over Louie when I turned to run, stumbled through a sticky pool of blood on my way to the door. I was still fast enough to get away with my life. And now I'm the only direct descendant left. The very last grandson of Don Louis Clemenza.

The last of my kind.

I wash my hands until the water runs clear. Rinse out my mouth to quell the nausea. Scrub at my sweater in the sink until the worst of the stains fade, and then hang it over the crooked chrome towel bar to dry.

In the dirty mirror, I take in the face that's always thinner than I expect these days, the smudges under my eyes that make them look darker than their usual amber, the greasy cast darkening the roots of my hair, tarnishing the blond to bronze. It's longer than I've ever worn it, months since my last cut.

I look like shit, but at least I'm still standing. Still alive.

Still a Clemenza.

The eyes of that cold, implacable stranger in the mirror travel down to the marks on my arms. *They're* new. Where —ah. The Giuliano. His fingers closed on me so hard…

I rub my bicep as the memory alone makes it twinge. Traditionally, the Giulianos don't come to this part of town without an invitation. It's not their turf. And they wouldn't come solo, either, unless he was sent alone for a reason.

My attention is snagged by a familiar name coming from the TV in the other room.

…been identified as 26-year-old Louis John Clemenza the third, rumored heir to the Clemenza Crime Family who terrorized

New York through much of the eighties, though their influence waned with the…

My cousin Louie's face comes up on the screen in multiple photos from his social media accounts, followed by his mug shot. Our grandfather and my cousin's namesake, Lou Clemenza, had been furious about that mug shot. *Clemenzas don't get arrested!* Of course, that was before Nonno Lou got put away himself for a few months on some trumped-up charge.

They cut to the live reporter on the street outside the townhouse, but I look past her to a silhouette in the background. Massive. Unmistakable.

The Giuliano.

He turns quickly to avoid the camera, but a flash of blue from the police lights catches his face. It's him. For sure.

Why was *he* there? Was he working with the guy who chased me out of the townhouse, the one I assume killed Louie? But if so, why the hell would he go back to the scene of the crime?

I sink onto the edge of the bed, legs unsteady as my adrenaline crashes. It's not the memory of dark, voracious eyes, the phantom pressure of hands on my chest, at the back of my neck, the way I responded to being pinned down like a—

Maybe I need another shower. A cold one.

To shock some sense into me.

The bruises from the Giuliano develop during the night, so the next morning I'm greeted with indelible fingerprints on my arms that make me feel grubby even after I shower. My clothes, which I washed last night as well as I could in the bathroom sink, are stiff but dry, and the blood doesn't show on my sweater. Good enough.

Today I'll approach one of the last potential allies I have left. Tony Stuccio was my father's oldest friend and the Family lawyer. After the Clemenzas disintegrated, the Feds stuck to "Uncle Tony" like glue. I couldn't tell whether he was cooperating or not, and the cost of making a mistake was too great. Now the cost of staying on the streets is much greater. After Louie's death, there's no more pretending.

I'm next.

Louie was careful. Tough as hell. He made his bones at seventeen and he was deeply embedded in the business. If they got him, they can definitely get me.

I check carefully before I slip out of the hotel, but there's no sign of the Giuliano, or anyone else who seems interested in my movements. When I arrive at the Midtown block that houses Stuccio & Associates on the third floor of an older building, the offices have been open for a while. The receptionist, a woman with a tight face too young for her silvery hair, gives me a quick once-over, taking in my wrinkled clothes. She tells me unsmilingly to take a seat when I give my name and admit I don't have an appointment.

But surely Uncle Tony will make time for me. He and my father went to Princeton together, were members of the same club. He taught me to fish at our lake house upstate when I was eight. On my acceptance to Princeton, he looked just as proud of me as my Dad, gave me a Montblanc pen to celebrate the occasion, told me he expected great things. A few months later, he stood beside me at my father's funeral, his hand steady on my shoulder.

I never went to Princeton. I put it off for a year. And in that year, everything changed. My grandfather was murdered in cold blood during what was supposed to be a peace-talk dinner, and so began the inevitable fall of my Family.

I sit in the waiting area, watching men and women in expensive suits walk past. I know a few faces—people who used to smile and nod at Clemenza functions, who jockeyed for invitations to our Christmas parties. Not one of them acknowledges me now. In fact, as soon as they recognize me, they look away.

Funny how that works. When the Clemenzas were on top, everyone wanted to be seen with us. Now we're poison. I could sit here and build a list of every single turncoat. Names, dates, betrayals. I've got nothing but time and nowhere else to go.

Eventually, the receptionist calls me back over to the desk. "I'm sorry, Mr. Clemenza, but Mr. Stuccio is not available."

"I can wait."

"I'm sorry, Mr. Clemenza," she says again, in the exact same tone. "Mr. Stuccio will not have time to see you."

"Then I'll come back tomorrow. What time would suit him?"

"I'm sorry, Mr. Clem—"

"You know what? I don't think you're sorry at all." A flash of my grandfather's legendary temper.

It doesn't faze her. She gives a small sigh and a false smile. "Would you like to leave a message?"

"As I said, I'm happy to wait. So that's what I'll do. I'll wait right over there until Mr. Stuccio has time for an old Family friend." I put a little emphasis on those last two words.

I do just what I said, and sit in the corner of the reception area, picking up an old magazine to flick through unseeingly. When I glance back at the reception desk, the woman is talking into the phone in quick, hushed tones.

I smile to myself.

A moment later, Tony Stuccio is marching down the corridor toward me with the expression of a man being led to his own colonoscopy.

I stand. I beam. I extend my hand like we're at a cocktail party. "Uncle Tony!" I say loudly. "You look fantastic. Have you lost weight?"

He stops short, ignoring my hand. His eyes dart around —checking for witnesses, the coward. "Cal," he snaps in a low voice. "You can't be here."

I keep the smile on my face. "I understand you're busy, Uncle Tony, and I promise I won't take up much—"

"Cut out that 'Uncle Tony' bullshit," he mutters. "What the hell are you doing here?"

"Didn't you see the news last night? Louie was murdered."

"Keep your voice down," he says sharply, then leans in close. "Where are you staying?"

"Here and there," I say, because there's no way I'm going to confide in a potential FBI informant. "Why don't we have lunch, and we can—"

"Whatever courtesies I might have extended to you and your Family previously, they were done under duress. And that's what I told the FBI and the DEA and the ATF and all the rest of them when they dropped by. Do you understand me?"

I do understand him. Just like the rest of New York, he's turned his back on the Clemenzas. This man, who once claimed he loved me like a son, doesn't care if I live or die.

In fact, it would be more convenient for him if I *did* die.

"I understand completely," I tell him, still with that genial smile on my face. "In fact, Uncle Tony, the only reason I came by was to thank you for your friendship. I hope one day to pay you back for it."

Stuccio takes a step back. "Get out of here and don't come back."

"You have yourself a great life, Uncle Tony. What's left of it, anyway."

He goes a satisfying shade of puce. I turn and nod a polite goodbye to the receptionist before making my way to the elevators. I'm pretty proud of myself. I don't even start shaking until I hit the street again, and then, hopefully, it's from rage, not fear.

Because it was an empty threat. Grandstanding bullshit. The Clemenzas are done and dusted, and someone out there is making sure the line goes totally extinct.

But even at my lowest, I won't show fear. And I swear to God I *will* find a way to pay Tony Stuccio back for his cowardice and disloyalty. To do that, I need to make sure I stay alive myself. Stay far, far away from that Giuliano and his hungry, burning, unforgettable eyes.

Unforgettable? Jesus. I need to get it together.

I need a *plan*. I need *money*. I need someone in this city who still owes me a favor, or at least someone dumb enough to get involved for the thrill of it…

And I think I know where to find them.

CHAPTER 2
CALIGULA

IF I'M GOING to have any chance at this last play, I need to get behind a velvet rope. Which means I need to *look* the part. And right now my clothes stink of mildew and desperation-sweat.

So I head to Bergdorf Goodman, charge a new outfit to Uncle Tony's company account, and take great pleasure in signing my name ostentatiously on the bill.

Stuccio will pay. He won't like it, will make sure I can never do it again, but he'll pay, if only to keep things quiet. And I want "Uncle Tony" to see that he can't sever that Clemenza connection as easily as he'd like, even if he rolls over for the Feds.

While I wait for my new purchases to be tailored to old measurements, I slip into the bathroom and try to nap in one of the stalls, which is about as glamorous as it sounds. But I need a clear head, because tonight really is my last shot.

If it doesn't work, I might as well cut my own throat instead of waiting for that Giuliano to do it.

The line at Kismet snakes down the block, stylish twenty-somethings huddled against the cold, their outfits more suited for Instagram than insulation. It's the most popular gay club in Manhattan, so my target should be here tonight. But I stop dead at the corner when I catch my reflection in a darkened window.

Who *is* that?

Thin cheeks. Too-long hair. The new clothes were tailored, but I've lost weight since last time I shopped there, and I couldn't risk letting them take new measurements. So my outfit hangs a little too loose, hinting at the frame I used to fill out. I look like a ghost wearing a living person's wardrobe.

But the blood of emperors doesn't thin easily, even when the empire has fallen. I tell myself that my sunken cheeks just make my high cheekbones look sharper, more mature. I comb my fingers through my hair, mess it around on purpose. There—now it suggests "bed head" instead of "vagrant."

The Tom Ford herringbone coat I picked out today does most of the heavy lifting as far as image goes. Underneath: black jeans, a black button-down, Hugo Boss boots. I spent a limited time enjoying New York's nightlife a few years back, but I still remember the unspoken dress code. Black is best, and appearance *always* matters, especially when you're faking everything else.

Instead of joining the line, I stroll directly to the head of it, where a slim, well-dressed man stands with an electronic tablet, flanked by security. His eyes sweep over me before I even reach him.

I don't speak when I approach. Don't name-drop. Don't even ask if he'll let me in. I just make eye contact and wait for him to speak first.

If you have to *ask* to get in, you've already lost.

"Hey," he says.

That's my in. "Hey. Looks like a long wait."

"Sure is." He studies me for another beat. "Going to be a packed night," he adds.

It's not a rejection. I shrug one shoulder. "I don't take up much space."

"You with…friends?"

The way he says that word—*friends*—that tells me he's clocked who I am. Reminds me what a terrible idea this is. "It's just me," I assure him.

He touches his earpiece, listens for a beat, and then nods to security. The gold velvet rope is unclipped and a chorus of groans starts up from the line behind me.

"Coat check's mandatory," he says as I step through.

"Sure thing," I lie. There is no way in hell I'm surrendering this coat. Not after I went through all that effort to get it. Besides, it's now the only heavy coat I own, and things have taken a turn for the wintry in New York—not just metaphorically. I can't chance losing it.

And whoever was talking into the ear of that door guy, they recognized me.

So I slip past the coat check while they're busy and head straight for the metal detectors that stand at the inner doors. I'm actually relieved to see the security measures, because it means most of the people in Kismet won't be armed.

Except the Morellis, of course. And they're my top suspect for who's picking off my flesh and blood. Kismet is owned and run by Finch D'Amato, husband of Luca D'Amato: the Morelli Family Boss, *Capo dei Capi*, and the man who murdered my grandfather. I'm in enemy territory, the last place I should be showing my face.

But I have no other options. Tonight is a Hail Mary pass.

I head deeper in and inhale the stifling air heavy with lust, sweat, and expensive alcohol. The sunken dance floor is moving to a slinky, seductive beat that feels hypnotic. The bars on both sides are three-deep with beautiful people, and above us all looms a mezzanine balcony where I assume Finch D'Amato holds court.

I glance up. Is that his silhouette up there near the railings? Is he looking down at me?

Doesn't matter. The man I need won't be up there.

I keep my head down and make my way over to the select seating area. And there he is, just as I knew he'd be: Jesse Foster, gossiping and crowd-watching with a group of gorgeous friends, though he, of course, is fairest of them all.

Jesse has dark hair, sun-kissed skin, and big blue eyes the color of the Mediterranean. He's the kind of guy who spends a lot of time saying "I didn't mean it *that* way" when he absolutely did. I met him a few years ago when I was dipping my toes into the gay scene, terrified but exhilarated. Jesse, already an old hand at nineteen, took me under his wing. I watched him transform from bitchy, scrawny hustler to bitchy, beautiful lapdog over the course of six months. He's still living the high life from what I can see—bottle service in this section starts at a thousand dollars.

Now I need to pray he remembers me before some Morelli-wannabe catches sight of me and tries to make their bones tonight. I make my way closer and closer until he notices me. His eyes go wide, his cheeks cave in as he sucks hard on his straw, and then he slams the cocktail down right at the edge of the table, making one of his minions grab onto it before it spills into their lap.

He leaps up from his seat, waving his arms in the air, and screams my goddamn name for the whole club to hear. "*Caligula fucking Clemenza!* Omigod, I haven't seen you for so fucking long, you little bitch, get over here!"

I started clubbing right after my father died, galvanized by a spirit of seizing the day and all that shit. I quit a few months later when Luca D'Amato took over the Morellis. Partly it was because I could see my grandfather was determined to have it out with the guy, and I didn't want to end up as collateral damage in a mob war. And partly it was because I lost my nerve.

I knew what would happen to me if anyone in my Family found out I was queer.

So I haven't been to Kismet before, but I knew it was where Jesse would be. He loves to be *seen*, and Kismet is where you go to be seen.

I hurry over to him so he'll stop shouting, and suffer his jumping-up-and-down hug before he shoves one of his friends off the sofa and pulls me down to sit next to him. "Where the hell have you *been*?" he shrieks. "I thought you were *dead*. I saw the news about your cousin. It's all over the socials!"

I open my mouth to reply, but nothing comes out, because all I can see is Louie. Blood and brains and those amber eyes, same as mine, staring and blank.

Jesse takes a closer look at me, then turns to the rest of the group and says, "You all need to fuck off." A chorus of complaints goes up. "Jesus Christ," Jesse breaks in. "I can't believe I even hang out with you fucking losers, you're so embarrassing, get the hell away from me—"

The guys leave, more than one with a flip of the middle finger, and Jesse laughs. "These Kismet queers are fucking awful," he says fondly, and then takes my hand. "I've missed you bad, honey. Here, give me your phone so I can take your new number. Last time I tried to text you it wasn't connected."

Trying to play along, I fumble out my burner phone and let him use it to text himself. "Now," he says, pouring out a glass of champagne from the bottle on ice in the middle of the table, "how are you doing?" Those big blue eyes fix on mine. "Really?"

I pick up the glass and drain it. I don't know Jesse Foster all that well, except to know that on top of being bitchy, he's generous. He used to pick up the tab all the time, and he always had the best coke—or so everyone said. I never partook. And since Jesse is the first person in a long time to show a genuine interest in how I'm doing, and since I'm not used to drinking and the champagne is already going to my head, I find myself doing something stupid.

Telling the truth.

"...and so I wanted to talk to you," I finish up, having given him a sanitized version of my current nightmare.

Jesse's manicured fingertips have tightened around his glass. "*Me?* God, Cal, I'm sorry about everything, and I'd love to help, but..." He spreads his hands in a *what can I possibly do?* gesture, diamond bracelets sparkling even in the low lights of the club.

"I just need some cash to get out of the city. Or a place to sleep for a few nights." Somewhere that isn't a park bench or under a bridge.

Jesse bites his lip, his eyes darting around the club. "Fuck," he says softly. "Look, Cal, I really like you, but—"

"Don't worry about it," I say automatically, rising to go. Never show weakness. I should have remembered that. "I'll figure it out."

He grabs my wrist and yanks me back onto the sofa. "I really like you," he repeats firmly, "which is why I'm gonna tell you this. But you can't tell *anyone*. Understand? Especially not in here. So can you keep a secret?"

"I can keep a secret," I confirm, choking back a chuckle of hysteria. Secrecy has been my constant companion since birth—secrecy about my sexuality, about my Family, about the bodies and the blood and the infinite traumas. "But," I go on cautiously, "I don't want to know anything that can get me in more trouble than I'm already in."

Because I know a little something else about Jesse. I know he likes dangerous men. That's why he imprinted so hard on *me*, for the thrill of my last name and the idea that he might meet one of my more infamous cousins. It's also one of the reasons I knew he'd be here at Kismet tonight, soaking up the intoxicating stink of money and power and violence.

As Jesse settles back, the sleeve of his Versace shirt rides up, revealing a ring of mottled purple bruises around his wrist. He sees me looking and doesn't try to hide it. In fact, he *smirks*, tilting his other wrist to show me a matching set of marks under the diamonds.

A strange jolt hits my stomach—revulsion, but it's mixed with something hot and dark that slithers down my spine just like that Giuliano's voice did.

I think about the marks he left on me.

I think about how I *keep* thinking about them.

"It's not dangerous to *know* about," Jesse hedges, voice dropping even as the music swells around us. "It's just—I'd help you if I could, I totally would, but I don't have any money of my own. I'm, uh. I'm owned."

"Owed?" I ask, sure I've misheard.

"Owned," he repeats, emphasizing that little "n" that changes the entire meaning of the sentence.

While I take that in, he pours me a fresh glass of champagne. My throat feels dry, so I take a big gulp and then ask, "What do you mean? You have a sugar daddy, or something?"

He gives that nervous look around again. "Or something."

He doesn't want to chance the Morellis hearing about

this, that much is clear. "But you…you've always covered everyone's costs, so I thought—"

"*He's* paying," he corrects me quickly, words tumbling out now. "It's all on his dime. Whatever I want to drink, eat, wear. Anything I want."

"But—"

"He even lets me buy whatever I want for my friends at a place like this. He just likes to..." He shrugs. "Keep tabs on me."

The implications are crawling through my mind. "Wait—he *owns* you? Like property?"

Jesse grins. "Well, yeah. He's my *owner*, Cal. That's the point." My blank face must read as an invitation, because he goes on eagerly, "So that's one way I *could* help you. I could set you up in a mutually beneficial relationship—"

"Whoa." I hold up my hands. "I'm not looking to sell my ass." It must be the alcohol talking, because under other circumstances, I would have chosen my words *much* more carefully. Jesse's expression turns cool. "Wait—sorry, I—"

"Fuck you." He dips his fingers into someone's abandoned martini and flicks them in my face.

Gin and vermouth, right in the eyes. I deserve it.

And then he laughs as I stammer out another apology. "Listen, Cal, it's really *not* like you think. It's just a kink. I *like* having him in control. It's sexy as fuck, knowing I can have anything I want in the whole world—but as soon as he calls, I go running. And he's hot, Cal. *So* hot. I'd suck his dick for free. Getting paid for it, being owned, that just makes it more fun. Plus I get to live like this." He gestures at the table, the champagne, the club, everything.

My mouth stays dry no matter how much champagne I swallow down, and my heart is clanging in my ribcage. Sweat beads along my hairline despite the club's aggressive air conditioning. The idea is *repulsive*—being owned, controlled, used. Part of me is screaming *no, absolutely not, this is degrading and dangerous and you are a Clemenza and Clemenzas do not kneel.*

But another part is imagining what it would feel like to surrender. To stop running, stop fighting, stop performing. To let someone else make the decisions. Someone who can scare off would-be attackers with a glance, someone with big, rough hands and a voice that makes my spine melt...

"Where did you even meet this guy?" I ask hoarsely.

Jesse leans in. "That's the secret part," he whispers hot against my cheek. "I met him at the Obelisk."

CHAPTER 3
CALIGULA

"THE OBELISK," I repeat, feeling no more enlightened. But something about the word itself—tall, imposing, undeniably phallic—makes me shift in my seat.

"Shh!" Jesse hisses unnecessarily. No one could possibly overhear us with the level of the music, and the way we're huddled together on the sofa, heads close. "It's an underground place. Billionaire bad boys. Invitation only, of course. It's *incredibly* exclusive."

"How did *you*..." I trail off. The alcohol is getting the better of me again. Jesse just laughs it off, though I detect a note of bitterness in the sound.

"How did *I* get an invitation? I met this hot Russian here at Kismet one night. He took me to the Obelisk. Passed me around his friends—God, what a great fucking night *that* was," he interrupts himself with a happy sigh. "Anyway, they told me I could make some easy cash by auctioning myself off—just for a week at first. That's where my owner bought me. And, well," he finishes with a giggle, and I think he's trying to give the impression that he's blushing, "one week led to another, and another, and another...until I signed a ten-year contract."

"Ten *years*?" I practically choke on my champagne.

"I'm not saying *you* should do ten years," Jesse says hastily. "But I mean, a month would be doable. Right?"

"But I'm not—" I stop. Recalibrate. "I'm not very experienced."

I haven't been with *any* guys, not even to kiss. Because, as a Clemenza, I *couldn't* be queer. It was unthinkable. The fear that the Family would find out always overrode my horniness. So I went out, I had fun, but I never…

Never let it go too far.

And then I stopped going out.

Cold panic grips me at the idea of some billionaire paying top dollar, only to discover that the guy with the name that promised ancient Roman debauchery was actually a terrified virgin who didn't know what the hell he was doing.

Jesse's eyes are gleaming. "But that's even better, Cal! These guys, they fucking *love* innocence—even when it's fake. The price goes *way* up. So, like, even if you're not technically a virgin, you should totally say you are."

"Virginity is just a social construct," I say automatically, because that's what I've always told myself. And it's true; it *is* a social construct.

But in my case, it's also a fact. I am a virgin by any conceivable metric. The most action I've seen is my own right hand and a very overworked imagination.

The irony of it all—that I'd be worth *more* for my inexperience. The very thing I've tried so hard to hide, the thing that marked me out as different in the hyper-hetero environment of the Families, could now be my most valuable asset. It never occurred to me that in staying away from sex, I might only make myself more desirable.

I imagine rough hands forcing my legs apart, something blunt and hot piercing its way into me…

I should feel sick about Jesse's suggestion. And I do, I swear on every dead Clemenza that I do, even as I listen to him chatter on about the Obelisk. But under that queasy sensation is something worse, something I can't acknowledge even to myself. A pulsing in my body, a tightening in my chest, a heat at the back of my neck.

I'd be sold off like cattle to some sadistic asshole who would take what I've never given anyone, who would own me, control me, use me…

And for no rational reason, the Giuliano from last night swims up in my memory once more.

No. It's disgusting. Clemenzas don't give up control; we don't submit.

"I can't do it." I stand, desperate to escape these thoughts, this place, my own treacherous body.

With an air of exasperation, Jesse stands too and grabs me by the wrist once more. "Of course you can. You're just freaking out because the idea is new. Let me explain—"

But I yank out of his grip as the hairs on the back of my neck stand up, a primal warning: I'm being hunted.

My body knows it before my mind does—that prickling sensation of being watched. *Stalked.* It's an instinct I've honed during my time on the streets.

Jesse seems to sense my fear, looking around just like I am. "What is it?"

"I need to get out of here."

"But Cal, think about it, will you? The auction—"

"I can't do it," I insist. "But thanks," I add over my shoulder as I start walking as fast as I can back toward the entrance, fighting the urge to break into a run. Running will attract attention.

I'm weaving through the crowd, almost to the exit, when I slam directly into a wall of muscle.

Hands close around my arms. Huge hands. Familiar

hands. And a voice I'd recognize anywhere, because I've been hearing it in my head since last night, tumbling around in the back of my brain.

"You really do need to watch where you're going."

I look up slowly, inevitably, into the face of the Giuliano.

He towers over me—broader, older, harder, making me feel small and helpless despite my athletic build. And those dark eyes bore into mine with an intensity that makes me dizzy.

"Found you," he says, low and intimate, like we're lovers meeting after a long separation. "And this time I won't let you run off."

My body betrays me completely with a rush of blood to the groin. "Let me go," I say, trying to keep my voice steady, trying to act like the man I was raised to be—a Clemenza, a prince of this city, not the frightened rabbit from last night, squeaking and struggling.

His grip shifts, thumbs stroking over my shoulders in a mockery of comfort. "Relax. I'm not going to hurt you." He smiles. "Not here, anyway."

"You're making a scene," I choke out, acutely aware that the other club-goers are pushing past without even glancing our way.

"Am I?" He glances around with theatrical surprise, then leans down until his mouth is level with my ear. "Then maybe we should take this somewhere more private."

Every survival instinct I have screams danger, but my body responds to his proximity with strange eagerness. I can *smell* him—his cologne, expensive and dark, and his own scent beneath, some kind of pheromone that makes me want to lean in instead of pulling away.

My brain finally starts catching up. Two meetings in two days. It's not a coincidence. I try to pull away again. "I need to go."

His expression shifts, frustration flickering across his features. "You're in way over your head with people like Jesse fucking Foster."

"There a problem here?"

I could die with relief. A bouncer has walked up, seeing a potential problem. The Giuliano's grip loosens a fraction. "No problem," he says.

The bouncer's eyes narrow. "Kismet's policies are clear, sir. *All* guests are to feel safe and comfortable in this establishment. This—" he flicks a finger between us "—doesn't look comfortable."

Something passes between the two of them. The hands fall away from my arms. "I'd hate to think I was making anyone uncomfortable," the Giuliano says.

Is that irony in his voice?

I should run. Disappear into the crowd and put as much distance as possible between myself and this dangerous man who's been stalking me through the city.

But I find myself rooted to the spot, staring up at him as he stares back. The blaze in his eyes hasn't diminished. If anything, it's intensified, as though being denied has only made him want me more.

The bouncer leans in to the Giuliano and says, "Why don't you come with me and have a drink on the house. *Sir*." It's not a suggestion. But it's also clear that the bouncer knows exactly who he's dealing with. I get the feeling things would escalate, otherwise.

Reluctantly, my stalker steps back. But his eyes never leave me, even as I melt into the crowd, pushing toward the exit with trembling hands. I can *feel* that gaze burning into my back.

His ghost follows me out of the club, down into the subway as I jump the turnstile, the sound of his voice echoing in my head as I find a shadowy corner off the main platform to collapse in.

The systematic elimination of my Family, the careful way someone's been picking us off one by one—it would take time, planning, resources. It would take the patience of a man happy to stalk his prey for weeks, learning patterns, vulnerabilities, fears.

A man powerful enough that even Morelli-aligned security treats him with wary respect.

The Giuliano looked at me like I *belonged* to him. Acted as though that bouncer was asking him to give up something he'd earned, something rightfully his.

I touch my arms where his hands held me, imagine those bruises deepening. If *he's* the one killing us all, then I'm as good as dead. But another part of me, a shameful part, remembers the dirty promise in his voice when he said we should find somewhere private.

I must be a special kind of stupid to feel drawn to the man most likely to murder me.

I let my head fall back against the tiled wall. Something inside me breaks, and hopelessness overwhelms me.

Everything is gone.

My Family, my home, my safety, my future. And now I'm being hunted by someone who should terrify me but instead makes me feel…

I allow myself exactly thirty seconds of weakness before I straighten my spine against the filthy subway wall. Even here, even now, I'm still a Clemenza. They've taken everything else, but they can't take my name from me.

I won't let them.

I get to my feet, intending to head back onto the platform proper, but the sound of hurried footsteps makes me glance up sharply. A shadow heralds a new arrival on the platform, wide-shouldered and elongated.

He *found* me. My heart jumps right up into my throat as the shadow-owner comes into view.

But it's not the Giuliano.

It's someone else entirely. Hoodie pulled up, face obscured, moving with the head-swiveling alertness of a man looking for a specific target.

And behind his thigh, held low and angled to stay out of sight, a knife catches the light.

CHAPTER 4
DAMIANO

THAT GOLDEN-EYED CLEMENZA prince has led me on quite a chase these last two days.

He's fast. Fast and sneaky and he has something most of his brethren apparently didn't have: survival instincts. Most Clemenzas are too busy tripping over their own egos to know when they're in danger. Not this one. He's quick as a rabbit and just as easily spooked.

But I was ready for him this time. Knew he'd head to the subway, dive underground in search of safety. So as soon as the damn bouncer turned away to order me a drink, I took off after the Clemenza.

I've been keeping tabs on him for years. The last few months, I've been paying Giuliano eyes and ears around the city to tip me off on any sightings. Then I stepped up my own personal surveillance, as the Clemenzas began to dwindle in number.

And recently, to piss me off even more, the remaining Clemenza Loyalists have been looking for him, too.

I don't plan to let anyone get to Caligula Clemenza before I do. Not to kill him. And not to crown him, either.

I pause at the bottom of the station stairs and look

around. The fluorescent lights of the subway station flicker a little, but they're bright enough. I just don't see *him*. My golden-eyed ghost.

He's here. I fucking *know* it. And the train schedule shows the next one is overdue, which means he hasn't escaped. Not yet. He's hiding somewhere. Watching me from the shadows, heart pounding, breath fast.

Maybe I should've stayed in the shadows myself for a few more weeks, kept observing instead of intervening. I followed him to his grandfather's old townhouse last night and hung back as usual, cautious. But I just couldn't help myself when he came tearing down the street. Some devil impulse made me step out and *grab* him.

I wanted to see him up close at last. Touch him. Smell his fear.

Good thing I did, too, since he was being tailed.

I move deeper into the station. A woman talks loudly and drunkenly into her phone, voice echoing around the tiled walls. A business type stands stiffly at the opposite end, briefcase clutched like a weapon as he stares at me warily. Behind me, another couple descends the stairs, heading home from what must have been a romantic dinner, based on how they can't stop making eyes at each other.

The rumble of an approaching train vibrates through the platform, heralded by a rush of warm, stale air from the tunnel. It pulls to a halt, the doors open, and the woman on the phone and the businessman get on. The couple stumble to a seat by the window, where they start eating each other's faces.

And then I see him.

Not my golden-eyed prey, but another hunter.

A bulky figure in a dark hoodie pulled low over his face, heading fast toward the far end of the platform. He circles around, head turning this way and that, then turns to walk back, frustration in the stomp of his feet.

My gut tells me it's the same guy from last night. He's hunting the Clemenza. *How fucking dare he…*

The train is going to close up and go any second now.

A flash of bright hair catches my eye. A slim figure in a dark coat emerges from behind a pillar, darting toward the train.

The Clemenza. Even in this lighting, he's pretty.

Pretty like a poisonous snake, I remind myself.

My fellow hunter has spotted him too, moving forward to cut him off before he can reach the train. I'm too far away to stop him physically, so I do the only thing I can.

"*Hey!*" I holler.

The hooded figure freezes for a split second, long enough for the Clemenza to slip onto the train and the door to slide shut with a definitive hiss. I run down the platform, but the thug is already backing up. He swivels sharply and bolts for the far exit.

He's not what I'm interested in, anyway. Not right now.

I pull up and lock eyes with the Clemenza through the grimy window. He glances toward the exit where the hooded figure disappeared, then back to me, a tiny crease furrowing his smooth brow as the cogs in his head turn.

That's the third time I've saved him. Once from losing those expensive teeth to concrete. Once from Jesse Foster.

And once from what I assume was an assassin.

I raise a hand in a mocking salute. *You're welcome.* A small smile lifts his mouth, transforming him from pretty to a certified heartbreaker. He gives a slight, regal nod.

Nobody smiles at me usually, or not like that. People smile at me the way they might smile at a pet pit bull. Carefully, hoping I won't bite. So much for my previous assumptions. This Clemenza is the same as the rest: no self-preservation instincts at all.

The train accelerates, carrying him away from me, leaving me staring at an advertisement for some bullshit meditation app promising inner peace. There's only one way *I'll* ever get peace.

And for just a second, something in the way the fluorescent lights flicker overhead dredges up that old, dreaded memory. I'm thirteen again, on my knees on the kitchen floor, and the person I'm staring at is leaving me too. A different golden-eyed Clemenza is standing over us both, drenched in blood.

I evaporate the rest of that memory before it can finish. I *never* let it finish, keep it buried so deep it would take a jackhammer to reach it. I shake it off and take the stairs back up into the cold night, the Clemenza's smile still burning in my brain.

CHAPTER 5
CALIGULA

THE SECOND I hit send on my text to Jesse Foster, I think I've made the wrong decision. The screen goes dark. I put down the phone. And then I go into the dirty, doorless attached bathroom and throw up all that champagne I drank at Kismet.

This shitty hotel room cost me the very last of my cash, and I'm out of the protein bars I lifted at a bodega a few days back. So I've made the right call. The *only* call. After getting chased down into the subway by not one, but *two* crazy fuckers, I'm ready to admit I'm out of options.

Sure, one of them saved me from the other—but there's no guarantee he was any safer.

I finish communing with the porcelain, rinse out my mouth, and sit back on the bed. I have no other choice. No. Other. Choice. Not if I want to stay alive. And I do, very badly.

My phone buzzes next to me, and I jump about a foot.

Tomorrow 8pm

A location pin follows.

Panic rises, fast as a freight train. Tomorrow night? I'm not ready. Not emotionally, not physically—

I end up back in the bathroom, dry heaving.

Fantastic.

When the wave passes, I stare into the cracked mirror above the hotel sink as I suck in breath after breath, praying for the nausea to recede. The man in the mirror is a ghost of the person I remember—the one who assumed his Family name was all the armor he'd ever need. But that name has become a stone around my neck, a target on my back.

"You have no other choice," he tells me.

I don't bother arguing. He's right.

My sleep is broken. The next morning, I scrub myself down with cheap hotel soap, comb my hair with my fingers, and pull on the same clothes I wore last night. My stomach cramps hard enough to make me double over. I've missed so many meals lately that my body will have to start eating itself, just like the ouroboros, the tail-eating snake that serves as our Family sigil.

"Just one month," the guy in the mirror tells me this morning. "You can survive anything for a month. And one day, you'll make them all pay."

Every single one of them.

Including whichever motherfucker buys me tonight.

The door is black metal, featureless except for a subtle engraving of a slender obelisk barely visible in the low light of the alley. It seems unlikely that something Jesse insisted was "incredibly exclusive" would be accessed by this Lower East Side back alley reeking of piss and rotting garbage, but that's the Bratva for you. Nonno Lou always hated the Russian mob, said they brought the city down.

Now they're my only hope.

Nonno Lou must be spinning in his grave. Well, he can spin all he likes. I don't plan on joining him there.

The door slides open silently at my tentative knock. Jesse stands there in a deserted hallway, smelling of weed and dressed like he just came from a GQ shoot. "Cal!" he squeals, and then goes on dramatically, "Oh, thank *God* you didn't chicken out. My owner has a good friend who's *very* interested. He's really kind, and *sooo* generous, you're guaranteed a great time..." He trails off as he looks me up and down with a critical eye. "Well, you'll look better when we're done," he says. "I didn't mean it like *that*," he adds at the look on my face.

"Done with what?" I ask suspiciously.

"Preparations." He grabs my arm and starts towing me down the hall. "Come on. We're going to be late if you don't hurry."

We go through an inner door and the world changes. Dark wood panels and thick, deep red carpeting absorb sound. Dim wall lights bathe everything in a Renaissance glow. And it's deathly quiet. "Where is everyone?" I ask halfway down the next corridor.

"You came in via the service entrance," Jesse explains, guiding me through yet another door. "The members come in from the private garage below. They need *discretion*."

And when we get deeper inside, I hear the low rumble of voices. Men's voices. Rich, powerful men discussing their rich, powerful lives. I strain to listen, wondering if I'd recognize any of them. The place might be owned by the Bratva, but Jesse told me it's open to anyone with enough money to pay the exorbitant members' fee—anyone except the Morellis or their allies.

That's the one thing that gives me a little hope. At least I won't be bought by a Morelli. I'd open up my own veins before I allowed them power over me.

I focus on my feet. Left, right, left. Or I watch Jesse's back, wondering what's really going on behind those big blue eyes of his. Jesse is *owned*. Property. And in a few hours, I will be too.

My skin goosebumps despite the perfectly regulated temperature.

The rabbit warren finally ends at a door. Jesse knocks three times, pauses three seconds, enters. The office inside is fitted out in the same dark-red-and-wood aesthetic, lined with books I bet no one has ever cracked open.

There are no windows.

The man behind the desk doesn't stand to greet us. He merely looks me head to toe. "The merchandise, I presume," he says.

Something proud, something Clemenza-born, snarls in my chest. I imagine wrapping my hands around this man's neck, watching those insolent eyes bulge as I squeeze. But I don't. My hands remain at my sides, and I keep my face still.

"My name is Daniel King," he goes on.

His accent, like his name, is upper-crust English, not the slightest Russian tinge. But he's Bratva. I know a gangster when I see one. I bet he was born Daniil Korolyov or something like that.

I don't bother to respond to his introduction. He's beneath me, and he already knows who I am anyway.

He makes an impatient gesture. "Take a seat."

I do, while Jesse stays at the door. I wonder if he's actively blocking it. If I tried to leave, would I be stopped? But I have no more time to think about that as I'm peppered with questions. Cold, clinical questions that strip me of any remaining dignity. Medical history. Allergies. Pain tolerance. HIV status. STI history. Sexual experience.

"I'm a virgin," I mutter in response to the last.

"You're not on the stage yet," King snaps. "I need complete honesty from you so I can—"

"I'm a virgin," I repeat.

Jesse gasps behind me. Sharp. Delighted. Like he just found out his favorite show got renewed.

King's interest sharpens visibly. "Entirely untouched?" he asks, leaning forward. "You've never even sucked—"

"No."

"And no one has ever—"

"*No.*"

He studies me, then writes something down under his other notes. "That significantly increases your value."

Value. Like I'm a fucking collector's item.

One month, I remind myself. One month for money and time off the streets. I can't think properly while I'm exhausted and hungry and afraid for my life. I need time to get my head together, make a plan, find a path.

A contract is placed in front of me and I read key phrases that make nausea rise in me once more.

Merchandise may not refuse any act unless specifically excluded in this contract…

Owner maintains complete control of merchandise's body, including but not limited to sexual access, temporary physical modification, and display to or use by select individuals...

Merchandise must comply with all grooming, dietary, and behavioral requirements...

The "protections" are minimal. No permanent disfigurement, and I'm to be returned to the Obelisk at the end of the contract alive and physically healthy.

Nothing about my mental health, of course.

"Wait," I say sharply. "This contract is for a year, not a month."

"Naturally. Given the amount of money you'll need to disappear from someone who appears to be a professional hitman, I took the liberty of adjusting the parameters to better meet your needs."

How does he know about—

I turn around in my seat to glare at Jesse, who has developed a deep fascination with his cuticles.

"Please, Mr. Clemenza," King says impatiently. "You are wasting time. The preparations for tonight will be extensive. But if you want to back out, if you think you can get a better price for yourself elsewhere, if you prefer to sell yourself on the streets—you are, of course, welcome to try."

I feel numb all over. A *year*? "I can't do a year."

"Cal, sweetie," Jesse says. "Be reasonable." He comes closer, sits on the edge of the desk. "You need the money," he stage whispers.

"I told you that in confidence—"

King sighs, like we don't have time for my outrage. And I'm annoyed at myself, too. I spilled gossip to a gossip queen. What did I think was going to happen? At my age, I shouldn't need a new lesson in keeping my own counsel.

"I told him you needed *protection*." Jesse's voice drops to the same persuasive tone he used at Kismet. "And look what Mr. King is offering—a deal that solves your problem instead of just putting a Band-Aid on it."

King watches this exchange with the detached interest of someone observing lab rats in a maze.

I shake my head slowly. "I will not give up a year of my life."

"Cal. *Sweetheart*," Jesse sighs. "Look at me. *Really* look." He gestures to his designer clothes, his perfect skin, the expensive phone in his hand. "Do I look miserable? Do I look abused?"

My eyes drop to his wrists, but he just gives me a suggestive wink.

"My owner *adores* me," he continues. "I have my own

chauffeur. I live in a penthouse on Billionaires' Row. I go to Paris or Rome or London for the weekend if I feel like it. I have *freedom,* Cal. And I adore my owner. Plus his friend, who's interested in you? *Total* catch. Powerful, rich, protective as hell. You'll live like a prince."

"For a whole year."

"For a whole year that will feel like a vacation, and you'll be *safe*. That's what you want, right? No one will be able to touch you for that year. Whoever buys you, they'll want to protect their investment. And at the end, you'll have a nest egg waiting for you."

What he's saying is too close to the truth for me to ignore. Safety. For a year.

He sees me wavering and his voice softens, becomes pleading. "Cal, *please*. I don't want you to get hurt—or worse. This is your chance. Take it."

"What if I change my mind halfway through?" I ask. "What if I want to leave before the time is up?"

He laughs. "You won't want to."

"But what if I do?"

King cuts in crisply. "That would be between you and your owner. The Obelisk can, of course, provide a mediator if necessary."

Mediator. Right. Like my grandfather was a "legitimate businessman."

But Jesse is right. I need the protection being offered here. The money. The safety. Yet I also need to show Daniel King that I'm not quite the fool he seems to think. "How is the money paid to me—and how much is your commission?"

"The Obelisk retains ten percent commission on the buyer's final price, up front. The rest of the money will be kept in trust for you until the year is over, then paid into an account of your choosing. Any interest accrued will be remitted to you with it. Now, enough talking. It's time for you to leave, Mr. Clemenza—or to sign here." He taps the contract and pushes a pen over.

I pick up the pen slowly. "This can't possibly be legally binding."

"You're a Clemenza. You of all people should understand how the terms of a contract like this might be enforced."

I look up at him sharply. "I don't want you to tell people my name. At the auction. I need to be completely anonymous. I don't even want to show my face."

"Seeing your face and knowing your name will raise the price. Who in this city would not enjoy a little private time with a desperate, virgin heir, fallen so far from grace?"

I put down the pen.

King gives an annoyed tut. "Fine. Anonymity. Now sign."

I pick up the pen again and stare at the contract, wondering if I can really do this. Jesse rests a hand on my shoulder. I can't tell if it's meant to comfort or to keep me in my seat. His grip is tight enough to hurt. "It's only a year," he says. "That's nothing. And think of the money…"

One year to come up with a plan, and at the end of it, I'll have enough to disappear. Enough to start over. Enough to be *safe*.

I picture Louie's sightless eyes once more.

It's an out-of-body experience, watching the pen in my hand scratch my name across the line.

Daniel King smiles at last, revealing perfect white veneers. "Welcome to the Obelisk."

CHAPTER 6
CALIGULA

JESSE LEADS me through back hallways again, this time to a white room so bright it burns my eyes. The prep room, as he calls it, is a horror movie set dressed as a spa: white walls, chrome surfaces, lights bright enough to perform surgery.

Jesse installs himself in a nearby chair, accepts champagne, and tells the team of handlers—two women, three men, all white-clad and Russian-accented—"This one's special. Grisha has dibs."

That must be his owner's friend. "Tell me about this Grisha?" I ask.

"You'll like him," Jesse says breezily, sipping his champagne. "He's sweet. Well, usually. And just between you and me, honey, Grisha loves to *watch*. So you'll have lots of fun with him."

I knew this place was run by the Russian mob. It just never quite clicked that I might be *bought* by one of them. I'd prepared my psyche for billionaires, not Bratva. "He might not win the auction."

Jesse smiles. "Oh, he'll win."

I see then what I should have seen before: this "auction"

is fixed. The winner is predetermined, and no doubt the price has been agreed upon also. I try to conjure up an image of this Grisha, but instead I find myself thinking about the dark-eyed Giuliano again, his hands on my arms.

I shiver and smother the memory. The only thing I should feel when I think about that man is a healthy sense of self-preservation.

"Take off your clothes," a handler says, clipboard in hand.

"Here?" I look around at Jesse watching with amusement, at the team of strangers.

"Merchandise doesn't ask questions."

They'll see the bruises the Giuliano left on me. Not much I can do about that, though, so I unbutton my shirt. Each piece I strip off feels like a further surrender, a betrayal of everything my Family ever built.

Instinctively, I try to cover myself. One of the men pushes my hands aside without expression. "Full visibility is required for assessment."

So I stand there, exposed under the lights, as hands run over me without comment or care. They note the bruises on my arms, but whatever they say about them, they say it in Russian. Jesse gives me a speculative look as my clothes are folded and bagged, along with my backpack.

"Where are you taking those?" I demand. I can't afford to lose the few possessions I have.

"Merchandise doesn't ask questions," the same woman as before tells me.

"*Answer me.*"

There must be something dark in my voice, some echo of my grandfather, because her eyes widen slightly and she does as commanded. "To be returned or disposed of, depending on the buyer's preference."

They lay me out on a padded trolley and begin. Waxing

first. I'm not particularly hairy, but they want me smooth all over, and at times the pain that comes when they rip away the strips makes my eyes water. I clench my teeth tight, refuse to cry out.

Nonno Lou once made me watch as he tortured to death a man who had stolen from us. The man screamed, begged. "See how pathetic weakness is?" my grandfather scoffed.

I was seven. The lesson stuck. I learned to endure, and now I fix my gaze to a spot on the ceiling and try to dissociate as they work on me. Jesse pours himself a second glass of champagne, watching everything avidly.

A hand lands between my legs, and I jerk away with a hiss of warning.

"Measurements," the man tells me. "Just keep still."

It's detached. Impersonal. But my body still responds, because apparently my dick didn't get the memo about dignity. A handler makes a note about it. I stare at the ceiling and fantasize about arson.

One of the men approaches with a nozzle attached to a bag full of water.

"No," I say firmly.

"Non-negotiable," he says. "Merchandise must be thoroughly prepared."

Jesse smiles. "Relax. It's not as bad as it looks."

"Not here," I say flatly. If I'm doing this, I'm not going to do it in front of Jesse, who pouts as the handler relents and leads me into a private bathroom. I'm very careful not to catch my reflection in the mirror. Because if I see myself, this will be real.

After that low point, there's a full-body wash-down that I'm apparently not trusted to do myself, followed by a manicure, pedicure, hair trim—though they leave it longer than I used to wear it—and a makeup job focused on making my eyes look enormous and my cheekbones like razors. Jesse directs from his chair like an auteur. "More mascara. Accentuate the eyebrows. Bronzer."

I hate him. I hate myself more. But beneath the hatred, something else is keeping me afloat: the promise of revenge. The more these people humiliate me, the more they will regret it.

One day, I will pay them all back.

At last, they declare me finished. And then three black velvet cases are brought out, opened with reverence, and the head stylist taps his lips thoughtfully as he contemplates them.

I stare at them in horror as understanding dawns.

"Only premium merchandise earns the gold," he says, selecting the third box.

The cock cage gleams under the lights, deceptively pretty, a filigree sheath. And next to it, a flared plug of the same smooth gold.

Jesse watches from his chair, champagne flute dangling between his fingers. "I got stuck with silver," he says sourly. "You're lucky."

Lucky. I almost laugh.

The fitting doesn't hurt. The handler works carefully, ensuring nothing pinches as he slides the cage onto me and locks the gold trinket around the most intimate part of my body. A tiny key is placed in a sleek black box with the Obelisk insignia.

"That goes to your buyer when we hand you over," Jesse tells me. "Grisha will receive the merchandise and the key simultaneously. Symbolic, you know?"

It symbolizes that even my pleasure now belongs to someone else.

And I think—can't *stop* thinking—about the Giuliano. What if *he* ever saw me like this?

The plug comes next. "For your owner's ease of use,"

someone says. "And visual enhancement during the auction."

I make them take me back into the bathroom for that too. And despite the amount of lube involved, I feel every inch as it enters me. The stretch, the fullness, the strangeness of it. The pressure inside me that somehow makes the cage bite tighter.

They dress me—if it can be called that—in a sheer white toga, a filmy haze that conceals nothing at all.

Daniel King enters and examines me as though I'm a racehorse. I half expect him to lift my top lip to check my teeth. "Use the gold dust," he says after inspection. "This one deserves the full treatment."

Gold dust?

They remove the toga and oil my skin, every inch from my chin down covered in a fragrant, shimmering oil. Then comes the gold dust itself, applied with soft puffs of air. It clings to the oil, covering me from my feet right up to my neck, where they blend it carefully into the makeup.

For the first time tonight, I sneak a look at my reflection in one of the full-length mirrors. I see a golden god. A statue. A *thing*.

Beautiful and soulless and utterly dehumanized.

Jesse stares along with me, awed despite himself. "They've never used the gold dust before. You'll bring in a *fortune*."

I straighten my spine. If I'm doing this, I will *not* do it as a cowering victim. I'll do it like a Clemenza.

A handler notices the shift and smirks. "Look at that. It knows its value."

It.

I smile back, cold and imperial. I'll remember his face. I'll remember all of them.

"It's time," King says. "Not a hand on him, any of you. I

want that gold dust completely undisturbed. Jesse, bring him."

Jesse hands me a gold half-mask shaped like a Roman god—Apollo, or maybe Mercury—and walks me to the stage. Each step shifts the plug inside me; each breath tightens the cage. I'm caged, plugged, painted, and walking on bare feet through a corridor toward the sound of clinking glasses and men's laughter.

But I walk like royalty. Because I am.

Jesse points me to the center of the stage. There's only a red velvet curtain between me and whatever waits beyond. "Remember," he whispers, "the more submissive you look, the higher the price. Keep your eyes down."

He scurries off to the wings.

It's almost kind advice. But I don't take it. I can't—won't—be a shivering flower. I've been stripped of everything except the one thing no one can take: the absolute certainty that I am better than every single person in that room.

I channel my grandfather. His arrogance. His disdain. His iron conviction that the world existed for his benefit.

I *will not* let these motherfuckers beat me.

The music changes, a trumpet fanfare…

And the curtain rises.

CHAPTER 7
CALIGULA

COOLER AIR RUSHES over my gold-dusted skin as the curtain rises. Light blinds me momentarily—harsh spotlights designed to display the "merchandise" to its best advantage. I blink, adjusting to the brightness, grateful for the mask, because behind it, my eyes are watering.

The room comes into view like a photograph developing. At least fifty men sit at individual tables draped in black velvet, each topped with a platinum obelisk statue. Those stares press into me until I think I'll split open.

And to my horror, my cock strains painfully in its golden cage, anonymity making me shameless.

Who *am* I? I don't think I ever knew. Maybe it's just my body's way of protecting my mind. Making the nightmare bearable.

King steps forward. "Good evening, sinners and saints—though we have very few of the latter here tonight." A ripple of appreciative laughter follows his words. "But there is at least one: this lovely *objet d'art* on our stage. Untouched merchandise, my friends. The gold dust tells the story—every fingerprint, every claim will show. And as you can see…" He gestures at my unmarked body. "This is a virgin. Guaranteed."

There's a murmur of interest from the audience and I wonder which of them is Grisha. If Jesse was telling the truth that Grisha could be "sweet." If I should hope and pray that he wins as arranged, or if it would just make everything worse.

"We'll start the bidding at fifty thousand," King announces.

And we're off. The bidding begins slowly, laughter and jibes accompanying some of the offers, and I start to worry. Seventy-five. One hundred. One-ten. It takes a while to get to one-fifty.

I need a *lot* more than that. I won't sell a year of my life for pocket change.

I study the crowd while they study me. Many of the faces are familiar. These men could have anyone they wanted. They're powerful. Rich. Feared. Why even buy someone in the first place when they'd have so many options throwing themselves at their feet?

Jesse told me they want someone submissive. Compliant. But he's wrong. What they really want—what they're willing to pay top dollar for—is entertainment.

They want something they can *break*, and have fun doing it. I know, because my grandfather was exactly the same.

So when the next bid comes in at one seventy-five, I take a step forward, golden light shimmering around me like an aura. "I'm looking for someone who can *afford* me," I announce. "Not someone used to haggling over the price."

A shocked silence follows my words. And then there's laughter—genuine and loud.

The bids resume, higher and faster. And I keep talking.

"Why even show up if you weren't prepared to play in the big leagues?"

"Sir, if you're going to lowball me, at least have the decency to be embarrassed about it."

"If your dick is as small as your bank account, you should save us both some time and drop out now."

Each insult sharpens the room's appetite. The energy shifts from self-satisfied to feral. They don't just want to own me anymore. They want to *shut me up*. And that desire is going to cost them.

I'm enjoying the power this small rebellion brings. It's a valuable lesson, evidence that I still hold a little power despite my situation. I can manipulate these people, make them react to me.

If they want me, they can bleed for me.

There's one bidder who stands at the side, never reacting to my barbs, simply raising his hand regularly. When it reaches three-quarters of a million, I catch him glancing toward the back of the room. He's looking at a slim figure I can barely make out in the shadows, but they give a nod, their long hair shielding their face, and the man bids again.

One bidder at the front with a thick Russian accent has been growing visibly angrier with every barb I aim his way. "Take off the mask," he snarls. "If I'm paying this much, I want to see what I'm getting."

King looks at me, a wordless question in his eyes. Fear spirals through me again. If they see my face, they might recognize me. But then I remember the stranger in the mirror, transformed by makeup into something ethereal, untouchable.

Besides, a part of me—a dark, unfamiliar part of me—*wants* to be seen. Wants to know that I'm desirable and attractive and worth every goddamn penny they'll pay.

Wants to look them all in the eye and show them that they'll never break me, no matter what they do.

I reach up. Find the ribbon. The room holds its breath. I pull the mask off and drop it at my feet.

"Too pretty for you," I tell the Russian. "Save yourself the embarrassment."

"One million," he spits. "And I'll enjoy marking up that pretty face."

That's Grisha. Has to be. I'm already calculating how to manage him after the sale—he's easily provoked, which means he'll be easily handled.

A million for a year. It's the lowest I could possibly accept. But maybe I should try to wind things up now before I provoke this loser too mu—

I get that sensation again. The instinct that I'm in danger. And *of course* I'm in danger. I've been goading a roomful of underworld criminals. What else did I expect? But I look around the crowd again, trying to identify a new expression, a new face—

And there he is.

Right at the back of the room, cloaked in shadows, but I recognize that silhouette as easily as I did when I saw it on the news report about Louie's murder.

The Giuliano who's been stalking me all over the city.

He must have only just arrived, because there's no way I could have missed him before. The bidding continues, but it's background noise. We might as well be alone in the room.

He's not bidding. He's just watching. And God help me, I *want* him to bid.

It's not completely irrational. Out of all the people in this room, he's the only one who has literally proven he'll protect me. So I stare at him, wondering. Maybe *hoping*.

The bidding hits one and a half million. It's enough.

With that much, I could escape to Italy. Find our allies in the old country. Regroup.

Maybe the Giuliano doesn't have the money. He's no blue blood, that's for sure; his clothes are expensive, but it's the body under them, the myriad tattoos, the dead eyes, that mark him out as what he really is. A street thug who climbed the ranks.

The silver-haired man bidding on behalf of the long-haired figure in the shadows has returned to his—or her?—side, after their bid of two million is superseded.

King raises his voice. "Friends, before we close, there's one more thing you should know. Not only is this young man a beauty and a virgin—he is of *royal blood,* one might say."

My head snaps toward him. "*No—*"

"This, ladies and gentlemen, is Caligula Clemenza. The last heir of the Clemenza Family."

A buzz rises up, louder and louder. Some attendees actually stand from their tables and leave the room, too wary to involve themselves. But many others lean forward with renewed interest.

"I told you—" I hiss at King, but it's far too late.

He raises his voice over the noise. "Tell me, friends: what would you like to do with the last Clemenza heir?"

The fantasies they shout back are creative, gruesome, horrifying. But these people don't want to destroy *me.* They want to destroy my name. They want to own a Clemenza, *ruin* a Clemenza. Just once, before we're completely extinct.

The bids surge. Three million. Three-five. Four.

And the Giuliano walks forward. Not fast, not slow. Deliberate. His eyes haven't left me once. "Five million."

The room hushes. Grisha's face goes purple. "Five and a half."

The Giuliano doesn't even hesitate. "Ten." Silence follows his bid. Absolute silence.

"Ten...*million*, sir?" King clarifies.

"You heard me."

Well. I guess he *does* have the money.

"That is a very generous bid," King says at last, brows drawn with concern. Shit. If *King* is worried—

"You hear any higher?" the Giuliano demands. He turns to the crowd. "Well?" No one speaks. He turns back to King. "Call it."

"Going once...going twice..." King pauses, looking directly at the sulky Russian who was so keen to mark up my pretty face. He just shakes his head. King glances around the room again, clearly hoping for a last-minute bid, seeking out the figure at the back of the room. But whoever they are, they remain motionless.

The seconds stretch out so long it's as if time has stopped.

"Sold!"

I watch my stalker—now my owner—mount the stairs at the edge of the stage. The triumph on his face is barely concealed. He doesn't stop at a respectful distance. He steps right into my space, close enough that I can smell him again, spicy and dark and dangerous. Close enough that I can see the complete absence of humanity in those dark eyes.

Close enough that I can hear his soft, shuddering sigh of pleasure as he looks me over from head to toe.

The cage around my cock feels like it might snap from the pressure.

CHAPTER 8
DAMIANO

THE ROOM MIGHT BE SILENT, but blood rushes and sings in my ears. I've never been so focused, so completely present in a moment.

Not for twenty-one years.

Twenty-one years I've waited for this moment. Twenty-one years of rage crystallized into a single victory.

The Clemenza stands his ground as I approach. Objectively, he's a nice-looking thing—the slender frame, the bright hair, the way his shoulders rise and fall as his breathing quickens. He doesn't need all that gold shit they put on him, or the makeup, either. I tower over him, and he has to tilt his head back to keep eye contact. But looking down into that stubborn face—Christ, he looks so much like his father—I find myself entranced by those honey-gold eyes again.

He stares back, trying to be brave. He doesn't understand—not yet—but he will. And I want to revel in this moment, the moment I *won*. I reach out and wrap my hand around his golden throat. He just looks at me with those haunting eyes.

I flex my fingers slightly. "You're mine now, golden boy." Those eyes drop at last, and I have to kill a triumphant smirk.

When I pull my hand away, the print of it remains wrapped around his throat, an absence in the gold dust marking my first claim on him. I turn to the crowd and hold up my hand, showing them my gilded palm.

"Mine," I announce.

None of them speak. They understand now that I'm willing to pay any price to have this prize. The ten million I've paid is nothing compared to the debt I'm collecting.

There's just one problem…but I won't worry about it now. I'll stay in this half-crazed joy tonight and worry about the rest of the world tomorrow.

In silence, the crowd starts to disperse. The most powerful people in this city, used to taking what they want, surrender to my claim. Whoever it was who tipped me off tonight, I owe them.

I got an anonymous text a half hour ago, suggesting I get to the Obelisk fast. I almost ignored it. But Fate is finally on my side.

I turn back to Caligula Clemenza, whose eyes have risen again. "Who—" he begins.

I put a finger over his lips to silence him. His mouth feels soft under my touch. When I take my hand away, the golden print of my finger stays stamped across his lips like a seal. What would it feel like to break that seal? Drive deep into that sweet mouth…

But that's not why I bought him.

"Get this cleaned up," I tell King. "Now."

Daniel King steps closer instead of hurrying to obey. "One year," he says quietly, so that not even the Clemenza can hear him. "No permanent physical injuries or scars. And he is returned alive, Orsini. Those are the terms."

I give a scoff of laughter. "Right."

"Come with me to settle the account." He turns to Jesse Foster, who's lurking in the wings of the stage like the rat he is. King snaps his fingers at him. "Jesse. Take the merchandise to be prepared, then escort it to the private garage." King glances back at me, professional despite the dislike evident in the set of his mouth. "Regarding the ornamentation—it's yours, of course, but if you'd prefer we remove it—"

"Leave it," I cut him off. "Get moving," I tell Foster.

"Yes, sir." Foster, at least, knows his place, jumping to obey.

The idea of keeping Caligula Clemenza plugged and caged until I choose to release him gives me another thrill of pleasure. I want him to feel the humiliation of being trussed up like that.

To begin to understand what it means to be powerless.

King beckons to me. "This way, Mr. Orsini."

I follow him through dark hallways to his office, where he gestures for me to sit not at the desk, but on a small leather couch in the corner.

"Bourbon is your drink, I believe?" he asks, already reaching for a crystal decanter.

"Neat."

He pours it out into a heavy-bottomed glass and brings it to me. "May I congratulate you on your purchase?"

"What you can do is get this process moving so I can take my purchase home."

He inclines his head. "Jesse will hurry things along, I'm sure. But these things take time, Mr. Orsini. We will, of course, take all due care in the preparation of your merchandise. In the meantime, we'll deal with the financial aspects."

I've been staring at my bourbon, paler than the kind I

prefer. It's almost the color of the Clemenza's eyes. But my head snaps up at King's words. "I'm good for the money."

"Of course, Mr. Orsini. Of course. But you must understand, we have a duty of care at the Obelisk. If someone who was contemplating using our services became aware that the contracts and agreements protecting them had been…compromised," he says carefully, "then they might be scared off. I cannot allow that to happen."

"I don't give a shit about that. I bought the Clemenza—for an extortionate fucking price, in case you forgot—and I plan to make good use of my new property." I swallow down my drink and set the glass down on the coffee table. "What I do, how I do it, is none of your goddamn business."

The balls on this fucker, to pretend to give a shit about the down-and-outs who sell themselves here at the Obelisk. I've never come to one of these auctions before because I knew what they were—modern slavery, prettied up with pretenses of consent.

But no one sells themselves at the Obelisk if they have any other choice.

Which tells me a few things about the Clemenza.

King's face has hardened. "No one *forced* you to make such an outrageous bid, Mr. Orsini." I say nothing to that, just let him sit and stew. "One year," he says at last, sliding the contract across the coffee table and flipping through the pages to point out the clauses. "No permanent physical disfigurement or harm. He is returned to the Obelisk alive and well at the end of that year."

I have to force myself to focus, because so many delicious scenes are flashing through my mind. Because the contract isn't a problem. There are a thousand ways to hurt someone without even touching them.

And when the little Clemenza prince sees what I have in store for him…

No. The problem isn't the contract. The problem is much more difficult. But nothing on earth could make me let the Clemenza go now.

King is still watching me. "If you can't agree to these terms—"

I snatch the platinum-plated pen from his hand, yank the contract toward me, and scrawl my signature with enough force to nearly tear the paper. "There," I tell him, throwing the pen down again. "Now, who do I make out the check to?"

"We require payment via electronic funds transfer to a holding account," he counters, unruffled by my display. "And we couldn't possibly allow Mr. Clemenza to leave the premises without that money in trust." He produces a card with the details of the account.

I pull out my phone and make a call to my accountant. "Transfer ten million to this account. Now." I relay the numbers, then tell King to check his balance.

He moves to his desk at last, opening a slimline laptop and tapping a few keys. After what feels like an eternity, he gives a reluctant nod. "It seems everything is in order."

I stand. "I'll wait by my car."

He glides over, blocking my path subtly. "Mr. Orsini, I want to be very clear. If something happens to that young man while he is in your possession—well, I wouldn't want to have to take the matter to a higher power, if you understand my meaning."

For a split second, I feel the old panic of being thirteen again and realizing everything of value can get taken away from you in an instant, just bleed out while you sit there, useless.

And then I want to break Daniel King's jaw.

He knows exactly what my problem is, this motherfucker, and he's stupid enough to try to use it against me. But I'm too close now to lose control.

"You were not the only bidder tonight, after all," he goes on. "There are many other people in this city who would pay a great deal to have power over the last Clemenza heir. You might want to consider that in your dealings with the boy."

King is one of those very people. I can see frustration in his eyes.

"He's not a boy," I grind out. But I'm not about to risk King calling the whole thing off, not when victory is so close. "One year. No permanent physical harm or disfigurement. I return him alive. I understand the terms."

He nods slowly, disbelief written clear in his eyes. But what can he do? The money has changed hands.

The deal is done.

But I'm not so easily rid of Daniel King. He escorts me down to the underground parking garage, where my driver, Vito, is waiting with the car. I jerk my head at him when he gets out to open the door for me, and he disappears back into the driver's seat.

The less he sees, the better.

I pace up and down, checking my watch every thirty seconds. "How much longer?" I snap after five minutes of waiting.

"You're welcome to wait in my office—" King begins.

"Call them and tell them to bring him down. Now."

I catch the sigh from King as he turns to pick up the

discreet phone beside the elevator. He speaks in low tones, then turns back to me. "Very soon now, Mr. Orsini."

Another five minutes of pacing, each passing moment feeding the dark anticipation building inside me. I've been patient for twenty-one years, but these last few minutes are excruciating.

At last, the elevator chimes softly, and the doors slide open. Jesse Foster emerges first, holding a delicate golden chain in his fist that goes taut as he moves forward.

"Come on," he hisses over his shoulder.

Caligula Clemenza steps out of the elevator. I inhale slowly as I look him over. His face is still painted up with all that makeup, eyes rimmed in black and gold, cheekbones dusted with shimmer. He wears a gold satin cloak draped over his shoulders, but it falls open in front, leaving his body on display. The gold dust has been cleaned from his skin, revealing tan perfection beneath. He's a little on the skinny side, but that's how I like my men.

He's *not* my man. I incinerate that thought as soon as it enters my brain.

He's my *property*. And that's signified by the golden cage he still wears between his legs. But from the end of it, a thin gold chain spans from it into Foster's hand, as though he has any claims here.

"Give that to me," I snarl.

Foster gives a deferential bow. "Here you are, sir," he says cheerfully, handing over the end of the golden leash.

I take it, wrapping the cold chain around my knuckles. The Clemenza is watching me with guarded eyes.

"One more thing, sir." Foster reaches into his jacket and withdraws a small ornate box of black lacquer with subtle gold inlay of an obelisk. He presents it to me with both hands, like an offering. "The key."

I grab the box impatiently and shove it into my pocket,

then open the back door of the car and gesture at my new property to get in.

The Clemenza doesn't move. He's staring straight ahead now, his posture rigid, chin lifted in a futile attempt at dignity. As though if he doesn't acknowledge me, none of this is happening.

And I want him to feel every second of his new reality.

I give a tug on the chain and he gasps. His hands fly instinctively to his groin, but he catches himself, forcing them back to his sides.

"In," I tell him, pointing to the vehicle. "There." I indicate the backward-facing seat, wanting him positioned where I can watch him, study him, enjoy his fear.

He steps forward quickly. Guess he learned his lesson. He climbs awkwardly into the back of the car, trying to pull the cloak around himself as he takes the seat I directed him to.

I toss the chain onto the floor of the car, where it lands with a melodic tinkle. It's a symbol, a fragile thing that could be severed easily enough. But over the next year, the chains I'll put him in will be unbreakable.

"Be seeing you," I tell King, who gives a clipped nod and doesn't offer his hand. Foster follows him back to the elevator.

"No permanent physical harm or disfigurement," King reminds me. "You return him alive in one year."

I wait for the doors to close on him before I snort softly, then get into the car. The Clemenza has pressed himself against the far door, as far from me as the confines of the car allow. His head is down, gaze fixed on the floor, hands clutching the cloak around his body like it can protect him somehow.

I say nothing at first. I just watch him, drinking him in.

The car glides forward. Only when we've emerged onto

street level, the city flowing past the dark windows, do I allow myself to fully relax.

It's real. He's here.

He's *mine*.

I study him in the shifting shadows, watch the streetlights illuminate him in flashes—the curve of a cheekbone, the full lower lip, the bronze-gold hair.

"Look at me," I say.

The only response is a brief bunching of his eyebrows, quickly smoothed over. He doesn't look up.

I lean forward, reducing the space between us. "When I give you an order, you obey." I reach out and grasp his chin, forcing his face toward mine. "Look. At. Me."

Those golden eyes finally meet mine, filled with speculation and a hint of fear that makes them almost gleam in the darkness. And there's something else, too. A spark of defiance that revs up my motor just right.

"Do you know who I am?" I ask, still holding his face.

"You've been following me." His voice is surprisingly steady. "And you—you protected me from that guy who was after me in the subway."

Protected him? Sweet that he thinks that. And naive. "And what else?"

"You're a Giuliano," he says, eyes dropping to my hand. "High up, based on how everyone reacts to you—and based on how much you spent back there. A senior Capo. Or..." His eyes travel over me, taking in my chest, my arms. "Enforcer," he says with finality.

So he's observant. Clever. But his mind won't save him now.

"What else am I?" I go on. He shrugs. I slide my hand from his chin to his throat, feeling his pulse racing beneath my palm again. It's almost addictive. "I'm your goddamn savior," I tell him. "And I'm not just talking about that fucker who was following you. I'm talking about tonight. You got any idea who parties at the Obelisk? I'm just about the best of them, and that ain't saying much."

There's that defiance again, as he lifts his chin. "Then this must be fate," he says coolly.

I'll enjoy stripping him of that sarcastic shield. "My thoughts exactly. I'm Damiano Orsini."

He gives a slightly sardonic, "Nice to meet you." No other reaction at all.

"Your father killed mine," I go on, so casually that it takes a moment for my meaning to hit him.

Confusion, followed by understanding…then a flash of stark terror that he tries to hide.

"It was twenty-one years ago. I was thirteen," I tell him, staring him down. "Thirteen years old when I found my father with his throat slit, bleeding out on our kitchen floor, and Cesario Clemenza standing over him with the knife." The memory blazes through my mind again despite myself. Blood spreading across tile, my father's eyes finding mine, his lips moving in a final warning I couldn't hear.

"*I* didn't—" he starts to protest.

I tighten my hand, cutting off his words. "You're his son. Close enough. And now you belong to me."

"For one year," he croaks. "And you can't kill me."

He's trying to be brave. Cute. "One year," I agree. "Do you know what I can do to you in one year, golden boy?"

He tries to pull away, but I grip him harder.

"Everything," I promise. "I plan to do *everything* to you. Break you in ways that will never show. Remake you. Own you." I release his throat at last to slide my hand into his hair, gripping the silky strands. "By the time I'm done with you, you won't even remember your own name."

A small, shuddery sigh escapes him. It strikes something deep inside me, something in the back of my brain, like the perfect harmony to some forgotten tune. I jerk my hand away from him.

What the fuck was that?

It's just physical attraction. Basic biology. The Clemenza is too pretty for his own good, and I haven't touched anyone in months. Of course my body responds.

It wasn't anything more than that.

CHAPTER 9
CALIGULA

THE MAN who bought me for ten million dollars—Damiano Orsini, ruthless Enforcer for the Giulianos and possibly the man who has hunted my Family to the brink of extinction—settles back on the opposite seat. He practically takes up the leather seating, thick thighs spreading wide in that dominant "I own this space" posture that makes me feel like a hamster huddled up opposite him.

The survival instinct that developed in me during my time on the streets makes me watchful and quiet. Because the ghost of his hand around my throat still burns, a phantom reminder that I now belong to this…this human mountain.

I should've taken my chances with the Russian.

I do know the name Orsini, now that I think about it. There's always been talk about the Giuliano Enforcer being queer, but his fearsome reputation kept him safe. But that's *all* I know about the name. Nothing about this father of his, who very well *might* have been killed by mine.

Damiano said his father died long ago, as long as I've been alive. He's spent twenty-one years stewing in his vengeance, but my father is beyond any vendetta. He died soon after I turned eighteen, and it wasn't from a bullet or a hit. It was pancreatic cancer. He was here one month and gone the next.

So now I'm his surrogate. Lucky me.

I take a long breath, force my nerves to quiet down, and observe. The way this Giuliano's dark eyes burn with an almost religious fervor confirms it's deeply personal for him. But there's something else there, too. His gaze keeps dropping to my mouth, my throat, the exposed skin above the cloak's neckline, before he catches himself and his face tightens with what looks almost like…disgust.

No. *Self*-disgust.

He wants me. But he doesn't *want* to want me.

I can use that. Use that desire warring with the darker motives driving him. His hands clench and unclench on his thighs, and I catch him staring at my mouth again.

The plug shifts inside me as the car takes a turn, pressing against nerves I didn't know I had, and the cage grows tighter. Every bump in the road sends dual sensations rippling through my body.

I won't adjust my position. There's no comfortable way to sit with an object violating me, and I refuse to give this bastard the satisfaction of seeing me squirm.

He pulls out a small, flat flask from his inner pocket and holds it out to me. "Have a drink."

"No, thank you." The last thing I need is alcohol clouding what little judgment I have left.

He wiggles the flask in my face. "Go on."

"I told you—" I begin.

He lunges forward and grabs my face again, thick fingers digging into my cheeks. His hand is so large it engulfs my entire jaw.

"You don't *tell* me anything," he growls. "You do what you're told. And I'm telling you to take a drink."

But I notice the way his thumb brushes across my bottom lip as he pulls back—strangely gentle, even lingering.

Like he wanted an excuse to touch me.

I take the flask. I even take a sip when he gives me a warning glare, trying not to choke as it blazes down my throat. And maybe it wasn't such a bad idea after all. It sends warmth flooding through me, dulling the edges of reality. I chance a look out the window, taking in street signs and landmarks. We're coming into Midtown East.

I need to make a plan. I can't let him break my body *or* my mind, so that means I have to find a way into his. I want that ten million waiting for me at the end of this nightmare, and I also want to walk away with my sanity intact.

And my life, of course. According to the contract, he can't kill me. But if this man is as powerful as I think he is, a contract with the Bratva might not stop him. So I'd better start ingratiating myself.

"Ten million dollars." His words echo the number looping through my head as though he's been listening in. "Is that what you think you're worth, little prince?"

"Apparently it's what *you* thought I was worth."

So much for making nice.

He leans in and I catch his scent again. In different circumstances, it might even be appealing. His breathing has changed, become slightly heavier, and when his eyes dart to my mouth this time, his pupils dilate.

"I would have paid more," he confides. "Much more."

"Then I guess you got yourself a bargain."

He seems to enjoy my defiance, a quick smirk appearing and then vanishing. "You really a virgin?"

"Virginity is a social construct."

He laughs. "Oh, sure. And I'm looking forward to

deconstructing it for you. I'm just wondering how much was for show and how much is real. You've never fucked?"

He's so crass it makes my teeth ache. And despite the fact that virginity *is* a social construct, that it's meaningless, that I've never been *fucked* as he so crudely puts it…

Despite all that, it's still embarrassing to admit the truth. Twenty-one years old and never been kissed, let alone anything else.

"Do you think the Obelisk would lie to you?" I counter.

He laughs again, but it has an edge this time, and I catch the way his hands tighten on his thighs. "I think Clemenzas lie as easy as they breathe."

This time I'm the one who leans forward, ignoring the shifting of the plug inside me. His attention snaps to the parting of my cloak. "I *am* a virgin. Which means I can be anything you want me to be."

It's going to happen sooner or later. I'd rather be the one in control when it does. So I slide from the seat to my knees on the floor, letting the cloak gape wide, and rest my hands on his thighs.

"With your permission?" I murmur.

He sits perfectly still but his gaze locks onto my mouth. I think I've won.

Then his hand shoots out, wraps around my throat, and *lifts*. He throws me back into my seat like I weigh nothing. "I don't want your whore tricks, Clemenza. Try that again and you'll regret it."

I'm gasping, more from shock than the brief pressure on my throat. I was sure he wanted me. His whole body went taut when I knelt before him. But he's fighting it, denying himself.

No. Not himself. He's denying *me* power.

This complicates things. A man ruled by his appetites

can be manipulated. A man who can resist temptation when it's literally on its knees before him?

That's a different kind of monster entirely.

He's watching me with amusement. "Did you think it would be that easy?" he asks. "That you could bat those pretty lashes and I'd forget what your father did to mine?"

Carefully, I say, "I thought you might be like the other men who were bidding on me tonight."

"I'm not like any other man. And *you're* not going to whore your way out of what's coming."

Oh, but he *is* like other men. He's just better at fighting it. The bulge in his pants hasn't entirely subsided. He wants me. He just won't let himself *have* me, not if I'm the one calling the shots.

So I'll have to make him think it's his idea.

"We're almost home," he goes on. "So I'll tell you the rules you'll be living by for the next year."

"I'm on tenterhooks," I say before I can stop myself.

He reaches for the window control, lowering it a fraction. The November air rushes in, cutting through the interior warmth and raising goosebumps across my exposed skin.

"Then listen up, golden boy, because I'm only going to tell you once. You break these rules, you'll hurt in ways you never imagined possible. Understand?"

"I'm all ears."

"Rule number one," he says, finger tapping lightly on the window control, "you do what I fucking tell you."

The window drops another inch.

"Rule two: refer to rule fucking one."

Another inch on the window. I start to shiver.

"You do what you're told, we'll get along fine."

"And if I don't?" I manage through gritted teeth.

The window drops all the way down, icy night air

rushing in and all around me. He leans forward to place his palm flat against my bare chest, feeling the tremors I can no longer control.

"Then I'll make you suffer until you're begging me for death—and I won't give it to you."

He raises the window again, cutting off the arctic wind. The return of warmth feels like a reward, and I hate that relief runs through me.

"Any more questions?" he asks with a grin.

I might as well find out now. "*Are* you going to kill me?"

The car turns down a small street and pulls up to the curb. "Home sweet home," he says, ignoring my question.

Damiano Orsini seems very eager to begin whatever he has planned, kicking the door open before the driver can even exit the vehicle.

I consider running. But where would I go? Barefoot and naked except for a thin gold cloak, caged and plugged, in the middle of Manhattan on a November night, with no money, no ID, no allies? I'd be right back where I started—worse off, actually, since the Bratva wouldn't be any happier with me than Damiano would be.

On the other hand, he might kill me if I stay.

But I don't think he will. Not immediately, anyway. He wants me to suffer first. And I certainly haven't forgotten the reason I sold myself in the first place. If I stay with Damiano Orsini—assuming that he won't just kill me as soon as we're inside his house—I'll have one year of relative safety. If I can survive whatever this monster has planned, ten million dollars waits for me. Enough to disappear forever.

Besides, I'm nearly certain now that Damiano isn't the one systematically eliminating the Clemenza line. He's a pro. Whoever killed the others, they were vicious, but they weren't a professional. I've seen enough pro hits to know the difference. Which means the killer is still out there.

If I go back on the streets, I *know* I'll die. As for Orsini…

I think I can survive him. I can study him, learn him, find a way to control him.

He reaches in to grab up the golden leash from the floor and I hurry out of the limo before he can yank my chain again—literally.

A dark brick townhouse looms over me, commanding its corner lot with confidence. The brick shell is studded with tall windows, every one of them shuttered from the inside. Multi-story bay windows protrude from the center of the facade, the lowest level of which has a delicate wrought iron Juliet balcony. The front door, large and black, is set down a few steps from the street and sheltered by a long white stone portico with columns.

So the Beast lives in a castle.

I glance up and down the street, trying to get a lock on where we are. Mature trees line the cul-de-sac, but their branches are bare of leaves, allowing me a view of the East River. I can see the Pepsi Cola sign across the water, and that's the 59th Street Bridge to the left. Yes, it's Midtown East. Turtle Bay, maybe.

Damiano knocks twice on the top of the car and it pulls away, leaving me alone with my new owner. The promise of a bitter approaching winter bites through the thin fabric of the gold cloak, and the sidewalk might as well be ice beneath my bare feet.

Damiano smiles as he watches me shivering.

"Better get you warmed up," he says.

I follow him down the three steps of the portico and watch him open the heavy wooden door with a keypad lock, but I don't catch the code he enters. He pushes the door open and gestures me inside first, as though I'm an invited guest rather than a purchased prisoner.

As I cross that threshold, the warmth inside washing over my frozen skin in a cruel mockery of comfort, it feels like I've just willingly walked into hell. The heavy door locks behind me with an ominous click—the sound of my freedom disappearing.

One year. I just need to survive one year.

But as Damiano's hand comes to rest possessively on the nape of my neck, guiding me deeper into his lair, I wonder if what emerges from this house after a year will still *be* me.

CHAPTER 10
CALIGULA

MY NEW OWNER gives me a little shove with the hand on the back of my neck, directing me to a roaring fireplace right there in the foyer. I give a quiet sigh of relief as the warmth hits my face.

The hand on my neck disappears. "Better?" Damiano stands close enough behind me that I feel his body heat.

"Peachy."

"I always heard you Clemenzas run cold, just like your snake symbol. That was a good choice, whoever picked it."

It's not a *snake*. It's an ouroboros, a mystical and philosophical symbol well beyond this man's understanding.

"I'm warming up," I tell him.

"Good." His fingers trace the vertebrae at the base of my neck, a touch so intimate it makes me flinch. "I want you to feel at home while you're here, golden boy."

I don't believe him for a second.

His hands settle on my shoulders, heavy and proprietary. I brace for violence, but all he does is reach for the chain at my neck, the one holding my cloak. He opens it, letting the golden fabric pool around my feet. And speaking of my feet…

"The floor is warm," I say in surprise. Not just radiant heat from the fire; the whole floor has been warm from the second I stepped in.

"Heated tiles," Damiano says. "I'm sure you had something similar in your Park Avenue place."

We didn't, actually. But I *did* grow up on Park Avenue. Did he know that, or was it a lucky guess? I scrunch my toes on the tile, stretch my hands out to the fire, and look around to take in more of the foyer.

The entryway is cavernous, with soaring ceilings at least eighteen feet high, but the dark wood makes it feel smaller. The tiles beneath my feet are white, inlaid with an intricate pattern of black and gold. Everything screams old money, but there's something slightly *off* about it all.

"What do you think of the place?" he asks. His hands haven't left my shoulders.

"You…have a lovely home?" I try. He seems satisfied with that response. But in asking that question, he's confirmed something about himself without seeming to notice.

This is not a man who grew up with money. People who grow up wealthy don't ask what guests think of the décor, because beauty is *expected*. It would be like asking someone's opinion of oxygen.

"When I bought it a few years back, it was a wreck," Damiano tells me with pride in his voice. "I spent millions restoring it to its 1893 glory. Even tracked down the descendants of the original craftsmen when I could."

"How dedicated," I murmur. "Do all Giulianos have such passion for historical preservation?"

His grip on my shoulders tightens just enough to remind me that those hands of his don't just restore townhouses. They break bones. They wrap around throats. And they own every inch of me for the next year.

If I'm not careful, my mouth is going to get me killed, contract or no contract.

He turns me around, thick fingers sliding to grip my biceps, fitting precisely over the bruises he left there the other night. Up close, he's better looking than he should be. Except for the look in his cold, dark eyes.

"I built this house for *you,* Caligula Clemenza. Every tile, every inlay, every fixture—I chose them with you in mind."

My stomach drops. Not flutters. Drops, like an elevator with severed cables. He doesn't sound exactly…sane. "That's very kind of you," I offer, trying to sound sincere.

Perhaps all my sarcasm in the car was a bad idea. Perhaps I should have been trying to placate instead of defy.

"Kind of me?" He smiles, and I learn something new: his teeth are way too perfect. I bet he's had them fixed after a life of violence knocked the originals loose. "You shouldn't mistake anything I do for kindness, little prince."

Perhaps it doesn't matter what I do. I drop my eyes and keep my damn mouth shut.

"Why don't I show you around?" he says at last. I glance up from beneath my lashes. He looks almost disappointed. Because I haven't said anything more about how amazing his renovations are?

Or because I stopped pushing back?

He lifts up the golden chain, swinging the end of it back and forth. "We can get rid of this now. Right?" For a second I think he means the cage and the plug, but all he does is unhook the chain from the end of that stupid-looking thing on my dick, being very careful not to touch my skin.

At least now he can't lead me around like a dog.

But his hand curls around my arm again, like he can't bear not to keep a firm grip on me, and he turns me to the left, so that I can see into the first room. "We'll start here. They call it a great room," he says, and guides me forward.

Room after room after room. They blur together after a while, and my legs are getting shaky, and the plug is an agony I refuse to acknowledge, and I keep wondering: where is everyone? Because there is absolutely no way this psycho who breaks kneecaps for a living also does his own vacuuming. This place is immaculate. Someone maintains it. But whoever they are, they're invisible tonight.

We troop through the first three levels of ever-so-slightly-wrong grandeur, with rooms that flow into each other in an endless, showy parade of money. The library is lined with leather-bound books with pristine spines. The music room holds a polished grand piano I very much doubt he can play. There are some rooms where I swear the seats have never been sat on. Everything is expensive, top of the line, but chosen like someone who learned about luxury from magazines. It's too coordinated. Too perfect.

And what strikes me most of all is the *emptiness*. Despite the furniture and decorations, there's a hollow quality. This is a stage set rather than a home. No photos, no personal touches. And so much of the artwork he *does* have depicts mythological scenes of abduction, possession, worse. Zeus and Ganymede. Apollo and Daphne. Hades and Persephone. God after god after god, seizing what they want and daring the universe to object.

My stomach drops even further.

"I'm sure you must be hungry," he says at last. "There are three more floors above and two below ground—but we'll get there soon enough."

The plug in my ass is almost unbearable now, and the idea of sitting through a meal sounds *really* bad, but I'm not going to say a word about it. Damiano guides me to the one room we haven't seen yet on the third floor: the dining room.

There's a side buffet set up with an array of silver domes over dishes, and the mouthwatering smells coming from them remind me I haven't eaten today. Maybe yesterday, either. The only thing in my stomach right now is the bourbon this moron made me drink in the car.

"We're gonna have dinner," he tells me. "And we're gonna get to know each other, Caligula."

Caligula. No one calls me that, because it's a ridiculous name that I've always hated. But I just nod. "Sounds…"

I trail off as a wave of dizziness hits me. And for the second time, I'm saved from faceplanting by Damiano Orsini. He catches me easily, hoisting me into his arms.

If I weren't so busy passing out, I'd probably be embarrassed about it.

CHAPTER 11
CALIGULA

WHEN I OPEN my eyes again, I'm in a bathroom. A bathroom that's bigger than the hotel rooms I've been staying in lately, and I'm lying on my side on a divan softer and more comforting than any bed I've slept in since my crib.

My father raised me. My mother had less than zero interest in me, and went back to Italy soon after my birth. My first word was "Da," not "Ma." My earliest memories are of my father throwing me up and catching me, always catching me. I always felt safe with him. Nothing could touch me.

Then he died.

I sit up straight, leaning immediately to favor one buttcheek as the plug inside me pokes hard, and put a hand to my head as things start spinning again. When the world is finally still, I take a deep breath and look up. Damiano is standing well back, watching me closely like I'm a wild animal that might bite him.

"Sorry," I mutter, and then immediately want to punch myself. Why the hell am I apologizing to *this* asshole? He *bought* me. So fuck manners; I'm not going to apologize to him for any damn thing.

"Are you—" He breaks off, starts again. "The Obelisk told me you were in good health."

"I'm fine."

"I didn't pay ten million just to watch you faint after walking up a few flights of stairs." His voice has gone ice cold. "If you're sick, I'll have someone examine you. If you're just weak, I'll have to adjust my plans."

"Look, I just haven't eaten for a while," I snap. And then: "What plans?"

He regards me with those empty eyes. "Get up," he says at last.

I stand, keeping my eyes down. Not from submission, but because there are mirrors everywhere and I don't want to have to see my own humiliation reflected back at me.

Damiano takes me by the arm—again—and pulls me over to the sink set under a mirror. He tilts my chin up, but I resolutely keep my gaze fixed down. "Hey," he says, a world of warning in one syllable.

I look up. Look at him in the mirror. His pants and his shirt are expensive, but it's basically cosplay. Something to make him *appear* civilized, seem like any other man. But he's not a man. He's a monster.

He's taken off his jacket, and the white shirt stretches across his broad shoulders that span significantly wider than mine. In front of him, a head shorter, I'm completely naked except for the gold cage around my cock. He's built from solid muscle and tattoos and scars. I'm leaner, smoother, ink-free and equally unmarked by life's cruelties —at least the physical ones. His hand on my jaw looks huge, capable of snapping my neck with minimal effort.

But I meet his eyes with every ounce of Clemenza disdain I can muster.

"That thing in your ass," he says. "Is it the first thing that's been in there?"

In the mirror, I can see the flush starting in my chest and creeping up to my neck. "Not the first thing, no."

"You played with your hole?"

My cheeks burn now. Even my ears are going red. I hate that I can't hide when I'm embarrassed, not with my coloring. Hate that I'm getting embarrassed at all. "Yes."

"With what? Fingers, dildo?"

"Yes."

His hand slides down to my throat, gripping high under my chin so my head tips back. If I want to meet his eyes in the mirror, I have to look down my nose at him, which would be more satisfying if he weren't the one controlling the angle. His fingers tighten just enough to remind me how easy this would be for him. "Which?"

"Both. I bought a toy online and I tried it out, but…" I squeeze my eyes shut until his fingers dig in, and I open them again. "I didn't like it. It hurt."

"And what you've got in there now, does it hurt?" His free hand slides down my spine.

I swallow, my throat moving against his palm. "Not at all. It's delightful."

He gives a faint huff of laughter. "You Clemenzas. Always lying." He bends me forward, forcing my upper body down until my forehead nearly touches the cold metal of the mirror. "Look at yourself," he tells me. "And open your legs. Wider." He actually kicks my feet open.

I suck in a deep breath and remind myself who I am. Clemenzas don't cry. And we don't show when it hurts.

I stare with unfocused eyes so my face is as unfamiliar as everything else in this house. I force my expression to harden, to show nothing, and open my legs even wider.

"Good boy," he murmurs, and the praise slithers

through me, a warm poison of something shameful but enjoyable unfurling low in my belly. I hate that I respond to it—hate that some broken part of me craves approval from a man like *this*.

His fingers trace down my spine again, slowly, deliberately. I know where he's headed, so I don't flinch when he slides between my cheeks and grasps the base of the plug.

"This thing's been in for hours. So, as much as you might be *enjoying* it, it's time for it to come out." But he doesn't remove it. He twists it, watching my face. "Tell me how it feels."

"Like I've been fucked over by life," I say coolly, even as my cock strains painfully in its cage, the metal biting into sensitive flesh as I harden against my will. What the hell is wrong with me? It has to be physiological. Just a physical reaction to stimulation.

Right?

His smile is dark. "You're real funny. You know that?" He gives the plug a slow, deliberate twist that makes my knees quake, then carefully begins to withdraw it.

The sensation is intense. I hold my breath to keep from making any sound as he pulls it free, stretching me almost unbearably before it pops out entirely. The sudden emptiness leaves me feeling strangely hollow.

He sets the plug aside on a towel, then his hands return to me. "I need to check you're not damaged," he says matter-of-factly, like he's a doctor conducting an examination. One finger traces around my asshole, checking the rim, and I shiver at the intimate touch. "Last goddamn thing I need is to deal with injuries on day one."

His finger doesn't stop. It presses forward, sliding into me with ease, and I swallow hard at the intrusion. It's different from the plug—warmer, more flexible, more…

Human.

But this is no human. This is a beast in disguise.

"Relax," he says when I tense up. "I'm not going to hurt you."

The finger moves deeper, methodical, exploring. His hand stills—just a minute pause, a hesitation so brief I might have imagined it.

And then he touches something inside me that makes my entire body jolt. "Fuck!"

"There we are," he says, and touches that spot again, just a gentle press—but I nearly collapse.

I've never felt anything like this. The toy I bought never got anywhere near this deep. All those times Jesse held court in clubs about how incredibly sensitive his P-spot was, I assumed he was performing.

He was not performing.

And this thick-fingered thug massages me without hurry, watching my face in the mirror like he's reading a manual. I can't stop shaking.

"What—what are you—" I can barely form words.

"I'm learning you, Caligula," he says. "Just like you've been trying to learn me."

Damn it. He's not as stupid as I hoped he was.

"What does it feel like?" he asks.

I just shake my head, no words coming to me. My brain is starting to short out.

His other hand squeezes at the back of my neck. "You answer me when I ask you a question."

"Overwhelming," I gasp out.

But overwhelming doesn't touch it. My legs are trembling, my breathing ragged, and something is building inside me that I have no framework for. This isn't like getting myself off. This originates somewhere deeper, somewhere I didn't know existed, and it's climbing with a momentum I can't control.

"Please." I don't know what I'm asking for. Stop? Don't stop? I can't *think* straight.

He adds a second finger, and it feels *good,* both digits working that same, devastating place inside me. His other hand leaves my neck and flicks at the cage hanging between my wide-open legs, the metal ringing softly as it vibrates against my trapped erection. "You like it, golden boy. Don't you?"

The combination of sensations is too much. The pressure crests. I come, but not like anything I recognize. No release, no relief. Just wave after wave of obliterating pleasure radiating from somewhere so deep inside it feels tectonic. I spasm around his fingers, making sounds I will never forgive myself for, as clear fluid spills through the filigree cage and drips onto marble.

He works me through every second of it until the pleasure flips to agony and I'm begging him to stop, every nerve ending shrieking—

And *finally* he withdraws his fingers.

I'm panting hard, head lowered almost into the sink. The intensity was unlike anything I've ever experienced—terrifying and incredible at the same time. But the way he did it, so detached and methodical, like I'm a specimen to be studied rather than a person…

"Up," he says.

I stand upright and Damiano moves to the sink. He washes his hands like he's just performed surgery. That dispassionate attitude of his makes something hard settle in my belly, even as aftershocks of pleasure still ripple through me.

He dampens a washcloth with warm water and holds it out. "Clean yourself up."

I take the cloth with trembling hands, acutely aware of the clear fluid still leaking from me, pooling on the marble floor between my feet. "What *was* that?" I ask quietly.

"That's the button that turns off your brain, little prince."

I wipe myself clean awkwardly, embarrassed to have him watching me. I'm still trying to process what I just felt. "But why did you…"

"I bought your body. Did you think I wouldn't use it?"

I force myself to meet his eyes. "But you didn't use it. Not for your own pleasure. So try again."

He leans in, but I refuse to shrink back. "You know what?" he asks in a low, intimate tone. "By the time I'm done with you, you'll be *begging* for my cock."

"That's still not an answer," I point out. "So I'll ask again. Why did you do that to me?"

I half expect a backhand from him, but he just gives an unwilling smirk. "What's that thing they say? Knowledge is power." He takes the cloth from me, tossing it over the golden butt plug dismissively. "Come on," he says, taking my arm almost gently this time. "You need to eat. I've got plans for you, Clemenza, and they depend on you being strong and healthy."

He steers me back toward the dining room, and I go, because I have no choice, and because my legs are barely operational.

But my brain is already coming back online. And what it's telling me is this: my new owner just demonstrated that he can dismantle me with two fingers and a few minutes of patience. He found the override switch.

I have a year in this house. Three hundred and sixty-five days with a man who now knows exactly how to take me apart.

I need to find the thing that takes *him* apart.

And I need to find it fast.

CHAPTER 12
CALIGULA

DAMIANO TAKES me back to the formal dining room, where the mouthwatering smells hit me again—roast chicken, herbs, garlic. My belly lets out a loud, embarrassing complaint.

"You sound hungry," he says.

The understatement of the century. But I'm distracted by a recurring thought: this house *definitely* isn't empty, because Damiano sure didn't cook this spread himself, or set it out ready for our return so late at night. And no Giuliano Enforcer would let casual hires roam around his house while he's busy buying the last Clemenza heir at auction.

So he has staff. Trusted staff. Staff who know about me and who will, presumably, *see* me at some point.

See me naked and trussed up.

The thought should upset me more than it does. Maybe I'm already more broken than I realized, or maybe having a roomful of buyers appraising my naked body a few hours ago has lowered my standards for dignity.

I can even guess at who some of those staff members

are. The chauffeur who drove us back here. And a cook, maybe doubling as a housekeeper.

I assume he's going to humiliate me over dinner, make me kneel by his feet, eat off the floor, something degrading. So when he pulls out a chair at the foot of the vast mahogany table and gestures for me to sit, I almost don't trust it. The chair is upholstered in burgundy velvet—expensive, but trying too hard. The chandelier is too modern, too bright, the light too sharp through crystals that haven't yet aged. The silverware is too shiny to be mistaken for anything but brand new.

Damiano spreads a cloth napkin across my lap, the fabric mercifully hiding the gold cage. Then he takes my plate and starts serving me from the buffet spread to the side, heaping portions of everything onto the fine china.

"This enough?"

I can only nod. The plate he sets before me contains more food than I've seen in weeks—roast chicken with crispy skin, vegetables glistening with butter, pilaf studded with herbs and nuts. My mouth waters enough that I might make a different kind of puddle on this man's floors.

"Make sure you leave room for dessert." He gestures at the tower of profiteroles at the end of the buffet, their golden, spun-sugar cage reminding me of my current predicament.

"Thank you," I manage after a pause. I don't want to feel thankful. But it's getting harder and harder not to feel that way.

He takes his own piled-high plate to the opposite end of the table, putting the maximum distance between us. "Dig in."

I'm supposed to follow his orders, so I do what he says. The first bite nearly makes me moan with relief. The chicken is perfectly seasoned, the potatoes crisp and salty on the outside, fluffy and buttery on the inside. I have to force myself to eat slowly rather than wolf it down.

Damiano's gaze stays on me with every bite. It's like being examined under a microscope, clinical but intensely personal, the same way he watched me just before in the bathroom when he was doing…*that* to me. His own fork is mostly decorative. He barely touches his food, too absorbed in observing me.

"The chicken," he says suddenly. "Do you like it?"

"It's perfect."

"Try the rice next."

I take up a forkful of the pilaf, even though it feels like a test. It's like he told me in the bathroom. He's learning me.

As I eat, that gnawing emptiness inside me starts to fill. But with it comes something worse than hunger: a deceptive sense of *gratitude*. The food is delicious, I'm warm, I'm safe in this house with—

No. *Hell* no.

That's a lie my brain is telling me to make this bearable. This new owner of mine wants me to lower my guard, to start depending on him. Dependency starts with small kindnesses, and I won't let him mindfuck me that easily.

But God, the food is *so* good, and I've been so hungry for so long…

"Do you like it?" Damiano's voice carries easily across the expanse of polished table, and his eyes never leave my face. "The rice."

"It's delicious," I tell him honestly. "My compliments to the chef."

"Glad you're enjoying it." He completely ignores my fishing expedition to find out who cooked this incredible meal. "I wanted your first meal here to be memorable."

Something in the way he says that worries me. Is the food poisoned? Drugged? I set down my fork and ask as casually as I can, "Do you have other staff, aside from this talented chef?"

"You don't need to worry about that, little prince. You just enjoy your meal." He chuckles as I look down at my plate. "Suddenly realized it might be spiked? Don't worry about it." He picks up his fork and stuffs his mouth with the same pilaf I'm eating.

He might have done something sneaky. Rubbed poison on the silverware, for example. But if he wanted me dead, he could have killed me as soon as he got me inside his house, could have snapped my neck right in front of the fireplace.

So I keep eating. And as my stomach fills, the knot in my chest loosens. The sheer relief of having food—*real* food, not stale convenience store sandwiches or whatever scraps I could find—makes the tension I've been carrying with me for so long start to bleed away.

After a while, Damiano stops watching me quite so intently and focuses on his own food. The silence isn't comfortable, but it's not threatening either. Just…empty.

Empty like everything else in this beautiful, hollow house.

When I finally push my empty plate away, I feel more human than I have in weeks. Damiano immediately puts down his fork even though he's not done.

"You want dessert?"

"Please," I say, even though my belly is full to bursting. Might as well get all the calories I can while they're available to me.

He leaves his plate to fill a new one for me. But instead of placing the profiteroles in front of me, he stands over me, plate in hand. "Open your mouth."

Something about the way he says it triggers a faint alarm at the back of my head. I keep my mouth shut.

"What's rule number one?" he asks patiently.

"Do what you fucking tell me," I parrot back at him.

He almost smiles. "Well?"

I open my mouth and he feeds me the profiterole, his fingertips brushing my lower lip as I take a bite.

"Slowly," he instructs, watching my mouth work. "Taste it."

The pastry is perfect—light as air, filled with creamy vanilla custard that's rich and silky—but I can barely concentrate on the taste with his dark eyes locked on my lips.

"Messy," he murmurs, swiping his thumb to collect a dab of cream at the side of my mouth. He holds out his thumb, waiting until I lick it clean.

And I'm furious to discover that the cage seems to have gotten a little smaller.

He feeds me two more pastries the same way, each bite a small surrender, each brush of his fingers against my mouth making the cage bite deeper into my flesh. By the time I finish, I'm overfull and flushed with a languid heat that has nothing to do with the food and everything to do with how thoroughly this man has dismantled every boundary I have tonight. I'm comfortable. Satiated. Grateful.

Compliant.

I see what he's doing. I see it clearly. And it's still working.

Damiano puts the plate down and holds out his hand like we're at a restaurant and he's helping his date up from the table. His hand engulfs mine, warm and firm. "There's one more room I want to show you tonight, golden boy."

The rich food in my stomach turns to lead.

"I told you this house was renovated with you in mind,"

he continues, his voice taking on that dangerous quality that makes *all* the alerts in my brain light up, flashing and honking. "But I want to show you our own private space. The place where we'll really get to know each other."

This is it. He's going to take me to his bedroom, hold me down, and fuck me. And I don't know if I'm nervous or…

Eager to get it over with.

My legs feel numb, but I manage to walk with him as he leads me to the elevator, a feature he mentioned during the tour but didn't show me. This time he not only shows me, he pulls me into it.

It's a claustrophobic box, barely large enough to contain Damiano's huge frame, and covered in bronze mirrors on the inside. I have to press my naked back against his chest for us both to fit, and I hate how solid and warm he feels, hate how I welcome his heat after so many cold nights.

There are numbered buttons for every floor of the house, but he reaches past me to press his forefinger against a special brass panel with a scanning square set into it. "This floor I'm about to show you can only be accessed by me," he says. "We'll have complete privacy."

A chill runs over me despite his body heat. The elevator starts a slow downward descent.

"I wanted to make sure you enjoyed yourself when you first came into my house," he continues. "I want you to hold on to the memory of tonight for the next year. Because I want you to remember exactly how *I'll* be living up there—"

The elevator lurches to a stop, and the doors slide open to reveal complete darkness.

"—while *you're* down here."

Damiano shoves me forward. I stumble into a void, one horrible second of certainty that there's nothing beneath me

—but my feet hit solid concrete and I stagger, catching myself.

Dim lights begin to glow around the ceiling's perimeter. Soft gold, rising slowly, a false dawn.

And reality buckles. I'm…*home*.

My grandfather's mahogany desk faces me from across the room. The leather Chesterfield sofa faces it, where generations of Clemenza men sat to discuss business. The Persian rug beneath is the same one I used to play on while the grown-ups talked. I *know* it's the same because I remember that worn patch—it's where I used to drive my toy dump truck over and over until the threads wore down. Even the oil painting of a medieval village hangs on the wall. Dad once told me our Family originated there.

But it's all wrong. The ceiling is too low. The walls are concrete, or covered in what looks like professional soundproofing. The golden light isn't sunshine; it comes from recessed fixtures, casting everything in a soft glow that feels like being sealed inside a beautiful, candlelit tomb.

And Nonno Lou's study is just one area of this enormous basement.

In another, there's a replica of the living room, where Nonna Mellie used to have her friends over to share tea and gossip. And in another, my grandparents' four-poster bed scrapes the low ceiling.

Beyond that is my father's bedroom…

And mine, too.

Every familiar room from the Park Avenue townhouse is represented here. It's like someone dismantled it room by room and laid it out on one level. It's dizzying and upsetting and *strange*, an autopsy of my Family's legacy, a museum curated by my captor.

What kind of hatred burns cold and long enough to fuel such obsession?

I turn away from the uncanny replica, but things only get worse. To the right, against the nearby wall, stands a king-sized bed with pristine white sheets, no pillows and no blankets, a heavy chain snaking from the wall above it, ending in a thick metal collar.

And there are darker things, things that make my bladder clench with apprehension. Shackles mounted to the wall. A metal fucking toilet like the kind I always imagined in jail cells. A glass-walled shower right there next to it.

"Do you like what I've done with the place?" Damiano asks.

"How…" I croak.

"I bought everything at your grandfather's estate sale. Every piece of furniture, every painting, every fucking teacup. And I *kept* buying up everything you Clemenzas were selling, as you started to circle the drain. Amazing the depths people will sink to when they're desperate. But I guess you've discovered that yourself. Right, Caligula?"

I bolt.

Pure animal panic overrides every rational thought as I sprint for the elevator, feet slipping on polished concrete, slamming my palm against the panel over and over while Damiano laughs behind me.

"I told you, golden boy. It only responds to me." His arm comes around my waist, lifting me off my feet like I weigh nothing at all. "Did you really think you could run from me?" He's genuinely amused. *Delighted.* He carries me away from the doors as easily as a child, my feet kicking uselessly at his legs.

He takes me to the bed and throws me down on it. I scramble away, but he grabs a handful of my hair to yank me back, while in his other hand he lifts the heavy metal collar.

It doesn't matter how much I fight. He's stronger than I

am. The metal is heavy as it closes around my neck, the weight dragging my head down. But the psychological impact is much worse than the physical. As the lock clicks shut, reality crashes down.

I am this man's prisoner.

And he's been planning this for a very long time.

Damiano walks to a leather armchair positioned to face the bed. It's the one from my grandparents' bedroom. Now it's Damiano's throne. He takes the silver flask out of his back pocket before settling into the seat.

"Look around," he says after a swallow. "This is your whole world now, golden boy."

I try to slow my breathing, quell the panic. Take in what I can. The chain will allow me maybe ten feet of movement —enough to reach the toilet, the shower.

I can't reach the dissected house. I can only look at it from afar.

I force myself to take in every detail of my surroundings: the chains, the bare concrete floor, the cameras mounted in the corners. The mini-fridge that Damiano reaches out with a lazy leg to kick open, showing me that all it contains are water bottles and vitamins. The dumbwaiter he points out, which is close enough for me to reach for meals sent down from above.

He's thought of everything. Access to food. Hygiene. The soundproofing—I could scream until my voice cracked and no one would hear me. It's the methodical, painstaking approach I'd expect from a serial killer.

"Well?" Damiano asks. "What do you think of your new home?"

I'm finally beginning to understand.

He plans to keep me here in this grotesque facsimile of my Family's history. Keep me down here for the whole year.

Maybe *forever*.

The idea is unbearable.

I meet his dead eyes and give him the truth. "I think you're fucking insane."

His smile is sharp. "Maybe. But you'll join me there over the next year, little prince." He raises his flask to me. "Welcome home, Caligula Clemenza."

CHAPTER 13
DAMIANO

I WATCH the Clemenza for a long time, drinking him in along with the bourbon. I dim the light with the controls on my phone until it lulls the Clemenza into a sleepy state. The shadows dip and swell over the lines of his body as he breathes. For years I've imagined this day, fantasized about all the ways I would make him hurt, mentally and physically.

The reality is very different.

Not *bad* different. Not necessarily.

It'll just take some getting used to, is all. I never thought I'd have him here so soon, for one thing. Everything is in place, has been for months, but he fell into my lap unexpectedly. And I need to find a way to explain this to—how did Daniel King put it?—to a higher power.

I also need to figure out who that kind stranger was who texted me, told me to get my ass to the Obelisk tonight.

But all that can wait. Right now, I just want to enjoy the moment.

Caligula Clemenza is totally shot. I can see it in the way his eyelids flutter and his limbs melt into the bed. He's fighting sleep, afraid of what I might do. He's smart. I noticed that right away, how he tried to play me in the car, the way he observes everything, gives nothing back.

Yeah, he's smart. But he's also human. So, eventually, the eyes blink and close.

"Tell me how you ended up at the Obelisk," I say, to jerk him back awake. "How come the last prince of the Clemenzas ended up selling his virgin ass to a stranger?"

His hand comes up to wrap around the collar. "Does it matter?"

"Everything about you matters to me, golden boy. You're mine now, and that includes your secrets, your fears, every fucking thought in that beautiful head."

The possessiveness in my voice surprises even me with its intensity, and he stares at me for a long moment before responding. "I needed money. And protection."

"Why do you need protection?"

"Someone wants me dead." He gives me an appraising look as he says it.

"I don't want you dead. I want you alive, so you can pay for your father's sins."

He gives a slow shrug. "Someone else, then. They're after my whole Family. Anyone who shared my grandfather's blood. Surely the Commission must have noticed."

So he saw the writing on the wall, the writing that everyone else in this town is so eager to pretend is written in some foreign language that they can't understand. The New York Commission, made up of the heads of the four most powerful Families in this city, has been happy to look the other way. And it figures. Luca D'Amato, Don of the Morelli Family and leader of the Commission, was the one who took down the Clemenzas in the first place.

The amber eyes are narrowing again, not sleepy this time, but sharp. "It's really not you? The one killing us off?"

"No. Was it you?"

"What?"

"You were covered in blood and running away from the scene of your cousin's murder the other night, golden boy. With him dead, the empire's yours."

He scoffs. "What empire? There's nothing left of it. So no, I didn't kill Louie."

No. I don't suppose he did. Those soft hands have never killed anyone. Caligula Clemenza never got made, not like his cousin. Far as I can tell, *this* Clemenza kept out of the business, even though he grew up right there in his grandfather's house.

"So you just found the body?" I ask. He nods. "You didn't go to the cops?"

"Are you serious?"

"Then why not go to the Clemenza Loyalists?"

"There are none," he says flatly. "The Morellis have seen to that."

So he *doesn't* know about that pathetic little movement that creeps around in the shadows. If they'd gotten to him first, I wouldn't have him here with me now. Hell, whoever texted me tonight about the Obelisk might just as easily have texted them. But they didn't.

I need to be careful about that. Figure out why it benefited my anonymous friend to have *me* clean up this particular mess. I should've shown more restraint at the Obelisk, seen the trap laid out for me—because it *is* a trap, I'm sure of that.

But I lost my self-control when I saw the object of my obsession dangled there in front of me, and that fucking Russian bidding on him as though he had any rights to the Clemenzas at all.

"What about friends?" I go on. "You must have some apart from Jesse Foster?"

He smiles bitterly. "Funny thing about my so-called friends. They weren't. Not when it counted."

"Then why not walk the streets and sell your ass the old-fashioned way?" I already know the answer to that, but it amuses me to watch his eyes flash.

"I was being hunted," he snaps. "You think I'd survive half a night out there in the open? And besides…" He trails off.

The silence stretches.

"You're a virgin," I finish for him. He doesn't reply. I lift myself out of the chair and sit on the bed near him. He doesn't shrink away. Doesn't cower when I reach out to him.

Maybe he's not so smart after all.

"Good news," I say, letting my fingers trace the line of his collar, noting his shiver when I brush over his hand. "You got the right buyer. No one will hurt you while you're here." I smile. "Except for me, of course."

"You promise?"

The question catches me off guard. He's supposed to fear me, but there's something vulnerable in the way he asks it, so that for a disorienting second I don't see a Clemenza.

I see a twenty-one-year-old kid who's completely alone in the world, chained to a bed, asking the man who bought him if he'll be safe.

"I promise." It comes out too soft, so I add, "And unlike you Clemenzas, I keep my word." I stand, ready to let him sleep. "Get some rest," I tell him, heading for the elevator. "You're going to need your strength."

"For what?"

I enter the elevator, turning back to revel once more in the sight of him—golden-skinned and chained in steel and *mine*. "For everything I'm going to do to you this year."

The elevator doors close on his sharp intake of breath, and I smile as I rise up again to the land of the living, leaving him there with his memories of the dead.

Because there's another kid I need to keep in mind. A boy of thirteen, also left alone in the world, who deserves to know that justice was meted out in the end.

My rooms are everything the dungeon below isn't: spacious, high-ceilinged, with walls of windows overlooking the East River to let in warm sunshine during the daytime and the lights of both Queens and Brooklyn at night. But there's only one view I'm interested in right now.

It's late, and I'm already drunk on power and half a flask of bourbon, but I pour myself another drink anyway and head to the viewing room that comes off my bedroom. I settle into the chair in front of the wall-mounted monitors. Multiple camera angles give me a complete view of the Clemenza and his surroundings. I can see the shower area, the mock-up of his dead grandfather's house, and my personal favorite: a close-up of the bed, where I can read every expression on his face.

Except right now there's nothing to read. He's curled on his side, chain pooled beside him, and sleep has done what I couldn't—stripped all his armor off. He looks younger with his guard down.

Innocent.

But he's *not* innocent, I remind myself.

He's a Clemenza, and that alone is enough to justify what I'm doing. If I can't kill the man who took my father from me, I'll do the next best thing and break his son.

And he looks *so* breakable lying there. My hands clench

hard until I take a breath and re-center myself. Control. Control is everything.

But fuck if that arrogant, clever, lying little shit doesn't make me want to lose it.

In the early hours, after I've given up on sleep, I go up for breakfast to the sunroom, where I find Rosa setting a second place at my breakfast table like she's expecting company.

"Get rid of that," I tell her.

Rosa purses her lips. "But you have a guest."

"I have a prisoner."

The lips purse harder. The woman could crack walnuts with that expression.

I take my seat, watch her bring over my coffee. "It's the one I've been preparing for," I tell her. "You'll send food down in the dumbwaiter, like we talked about."

I know I'm gonna get pushback here, based solely on the mulish look on her face. "The dumbwaiter is broken." I don't believe that for a second, but her voice carries that edge that means she doesn't like what I'm doing. "So unless you want me carrying food down to your basement—"

"You don't go near the basement. You hear me?" No one knows what's down there except me. And now the Clemenza, I guess.

I plan to keep it that way.

Rosa doesn't look at me, but I can tell she's pissed by the way she clatters a few dishes together. And still she pushes. "Then you'll have to bring your guest up here to eat."

"Get Vito to fix the dumbwaiter today. What the hell am I paying him for?" I grab the extra plate from the end of the table and pile it with food, ignoring Rosa's disapproving stare.

She's been with me long enough to know when to stop pushing. So I'll let it go, this disrespect. She did good last night, when I texted her from the Obelisk as soon as I realized what was happening. She got that meal cooked and set out, just like I asked, despite the late hour.

But I feel her judgment following me all the way to the elevator.

CHAPTER 14
CALIGULA

THE WHIR of elevator machinery jolts me from a light doze. I slept restlessly all night, no better than when I was on the street. I sit up groggily, slowly, strangely weighted down—

Oh. The collar he put on me, heavy around my throat. I'd almost forgotten.

Light floods the basement. I wince, throwing a hand up to shield my eyes.

"Good morning, golden boy." Damiano steps out of the elevator carrying a tray. My first reaction is to make some cutting remark, push back where I can, but my stomach seizes with sudden, desperate hunger as the smell hits me. Eggs, bacon, toast. And coffee. Hot, black coffee.

My mouth waters so hard it actually hurts.

"Thirsty?" he asks.

"Hungry."

He sets the plate on the side table next to his throne and takes out a water bottle from the mini-fridge I've been ignoring all night, cracking it open. "Drink this first."

He hands me the bottle, and I drain half of it immediately, not realizing how parched I was until the cool liquid hits my throat.

"All of it," he commands, settling into his chair with a steaming coffee mug of his own. There's a second mug, too, which I assume is meant for me. I finish the bottle under his steady gaze, but then he gestures toward the metal toilet in the corner. "Go."

Heat stings my cheeks. "I don't need to—"

"What's rule number one?" He's using the tone of voice that I've already figured out means he's not fucking around.

Well, this is a new low. And considering my recent trajectory, that's saying something. Still, I shuffle to the toilet, the chain dragging behind me, acutely aware of his eyes tracking my every movement, and manage the logistics of pissing through the golden cage at last. I take my time washing my hands, trying to slow down whatever is happening here. But Damiano waits patiently until I can't string it out any longer, and then points me back to the bed.

"Now you can eat," he tells me. But when I reach for the plate in his hands, he pulls it away. "Did I say you could feed yourself?"

My stomach clenches with more than hunger this time and I stare at him mutely.

"Hands behind your back."

I link my fingers behind me.

He cuts a piece of bacon and holds the fork out to me. "Open."

I obey, and he slides the food into my mouth, watching me chew with the same intense focus he had last night. I barely taste what's in my mouth, not with his dark eyes locked on my face.

Bite by bite, he feeds me my entire breakfast while I sit with my hands bound behind my back by nothing but his will. When I'm finished, he leans in. For one disorienting moment, I think he's going to swipe his tongue across my lips, and I feel mine part before I can stop them—

But he just wipes my mouth clean with his thumb.

"I want you to know," he says, "that you're only alive because it suits me to keep you alive. Contract or no contract. You hear me?"

Oh, yes. I hear him. I nod my head.

"Go and shower."

"The collar—"

"Stays on." He settles back into his throne, coffee mug in hand. "Now go."

I'm worried the collar will heat up, burn my skin. But I don't have a choice, and using the toilet was *way* worse than this, so I head to the shower, the chain dragging across the floor.

The water is hot at once, but as I step under the spray, I find the collar stays body-temperature on the inside, with a rubber coating to insulate my throat from the hot metal. So I relax a little and let the water wash away the sweat and fear from last night, hyperaware of Damiano's gaze. I try to keep my back turned to him, keep my head under the water where I can pretend I'm somewhere else, anywhere else.

Maybe a nice spa in Tuscany. With significantly fewer chains and threats.

But my thoughts come back to Damiano. His behavior this morning, this whole experience, is designed to be degrading. I should be furious, terrified, anything except…

Except this. My body is responding to his attention, to being watched. To being *wanted*. And he does want me. I feel it in the weight of his stare when I glance through the steamed glass.

I might be a virgin, but I still know when someone is lusting after me.

The Clemenza Family built an empire on finding people's weaknesses and exploiting them. Damiano Orsini wants me—and not just to torture or kill. He wants to fuck me. I can see it in the tension of his shoulders, the way his eyes follow the water streaming down my skin. That want is a weakness I can use.

But how do I use it when I don't know what I'm doing?

On the other hand...how hard can it be? If Jesse Foster could manipulate some billionaire into a ten-year contract, surely I can figure it out. It's instinct, right? Sex is instinctual. Every animal knows how to fuck, how to present itself for breeding.

I reach for the soap with trembling hands. I've never done this before, tried to be... Hell, I don't even know what to call it. Appealing? I've spent most of my life trying *not* to be noticed. But I let my hands linger on my chest as I soap myself up, the way I've seen people do in movies, trying to look deliberate instead of desperate.

When I glance his way again, something has shifted in his posture. He's leaning forward slightly. And he's still watching.

Whatever I'm doing, it's working.

When I finally step out and reach for a towel, Damiano's voice stops me. "Stay there."

He rises from his seat, setting his coffee aside, and approaches, grabbing up the towel. My heart pounds as he stands in front of me.

"Arms up."

I raise my arms, water still streaming down my body, and he begins to towel me down. Not gentle, but thorough. He drags the towel across my chest, down my arms, around my back. And he follows the towel with his own hand, each touch entitled, possessive, like he's making sure his prize poodle is in perfect condition.

His hands linger longer than necessary in some areas. I try to stay perfectly still, to not react, but when he moves behind me to dry my back, his palm slides over the curve of my ass—deliberate, unmistakable.

My breath catches. Blood rushes south, but the cage prevents any real response, creating a dull ache that makes me grit my teeth.

"Turn around."

I face him again, and his eyes drop to the golden cage, noting the way it's grown tighter. A slow smile spreads across his lips.

"You like being caged up, huh?" he asks, voice deceptively gentle as he reaches out to tap the metal with one finger.

Even that light touch sends a jolt through me. "No."

His smile widens. "Your body is more honest than your mouth, golden boy." He tosses the towel aside.

Shame and need are warring in me. Because he's right. My body doesn't seem to care about *should* or *shouldn't*.

"Go lie down," he says.

I crawl back onto the white sheets. I expect this will be the moment, the moment he follows me to the bed, stretches out on top of me, takes that pesky virginity that drove the price up at the auction.

But he doesn't do that.

He returns to his throne, taking up his coffee mug with hands that are perfectly steady, and simply watches me again.

The silence stretches tighter and tenser like a rubber band until I can't stand it anymore. Time to see how much power I actually have here. "Why aren't you fucking me?"

He doesn't reply.

"I thought that was the point. Of the plug." The words feel clumsy in my mouth. "To keep me ready for you."

His eyes sharpen immediately. I prop myself up on one elbow, trying to channel a confidence I don't feel.

"You keep staring. I don't understand why you won't just…" I trail off. I *should* have leverage here, but I don't know how to find it. I don't know how to do this. "Use me?" I finish lamely.

"I didn't buy you to fuck you." His voice is icy. "I bought you to break you."

I study his face as hard as he's been studying mine. The way his pupils dilate when I move. The tension in his shoulders. The careful way he sets down his coffee mug.

Maybe I'm terrible at this, but *something* is working.

"Are you sure about that?" I try like hell to channel Jesse Foster and shift slowly on the bed, hoping it looks intentional. Looks *sexy*. "You put a bed in here. A bed with a good mattress and clean sheets, when you could've made me sleep on the floor. This bed is for fucking."

"You think I spent ten million on you just so I could get my dick wet?" The words explode from him.

What Would Jesse Do?

I force myself to laugh, light and mocking. "You're a terrible liar, Dami." I draw the nickname out, slow and deliberate, *Dah*-mee, so it sounds intimate.

And it's a stroke of fucking genius, because it lands. He sucks in a breath. I roll onto my stomach, making sure he has a clear view of my ass, spread my legs a little to give it definition.

"You're the one who put a bed down here, Dami," I continue. "You don't do that for someone you're not planning to fuck. You don't sit there staring and drooling—"

And just like that, his control snaps. He's standing over me in a millisecond, hand closing on my hair, yanking my head back.

"You think you know me?" he snarls. "You think you can manipulate me with that bitch mouth of yours?"

Triumph and terror war in my chest. I got a reaction. I *do* have power here. But power I can't control might be worse than no power at all.

Up close, like this, he's terrifying.

"I think you're more affected by me than you want to admit," I gasp out.

His grip tightens and I wince, but I don't back down. This is a game I *need* to figure out how to play, even if I'm making it up as I go.

"I think you don't even know what to do with me now that you have me," I pant. "I think you expected me to beg and cry, and instead I'm…" I lick my lips slowly, the way I used to see Jesse doing in the clubs when he wanted a free drink from a hot guy. "I'm offering myself to you."

His free hand traces my jaw, gentle enough to make my breath catch. For a moment, I think he'll *kiss* me.

But he releases me abruptly, and I fall back against the mattress.

"You can't *offer* yourself to me, Caligula Clemenza. I own you already—and if someday I want to use your body, just because it's convenient for me, I will. But you won't ever seduce me. You won't ever make me *want* you, golden boy."

I let out a startled cry as he grabs my ankle, hauling me closer. But he just fishes a golden key out of his pocket and unlocks the cage, tugging it off. My cock springs gratefully free, hardening despite myself.

"You seem to think this is all about sex," he says, pocketing the ornament. "Maybe taking this off will help you understand that it's not." His voice drops dangerously. "This is about vengeance. Nothing more."

"I *know* you want me," I tell him recklessly, shooting my last shot. "Why can't you just—"

His hand closes around my mouth and nose, cutting off my air along with my words. But my traitor dick just gets harder. He leans close to my ear. "One day you'll remember this moment, when you thought you could control me. And you'll understand how very foolish you were."

He releases me and steps back, leaving me panting for breath, hard and aching and completely confused by my own reactions.

"Maybe some time alone in the dark will help you understand your new role in life." He heads toward the elevator again. "And don't you dare touch yourself while I'm gone. That toy between your legs—it belongs to me now."

The lights cut out and darkness swallows the room completely as the elevator starts its ascent. I lie there in the black, heart pounding, cock aching, my body still humming from his touch.

I tried. But I have no idea what I'm doing. Every move felt clumsy, every word uncertain. I'm flying blind, grasping for power I don't understand.

What the *fuck* is wrong with me?

I'm a Clemenza. We don't submit. We don't beg. We certainly don't get aroused by being caged and collared and suffocated.

But my body doesn't care about Family pride. It only cares that Damiano's hands felt good on my skin, that his attention—even cruel attention—made me feel…

I trail my fingers over my aching cock, then jerk my hand away, remembering his words. *It belongs to me now.*

Even my obedience in denying myself sends another jolt of arousal through me. I roll onto my side, chain clinking, and force my breathing back to normal.

I might not know what I'm doing, but I proved something today. I have an effect on him. I can get under his skin, make him lose control. *That's* what matters.

Not the way my pulse races when I remember his hands on me.

Not the way I keep replaying the look in his eyes as he watched me shower.

And definitely not the way part of me—some twisted, shameful part—wants him to come back down here and finish what we started.

CHAPTER 15
DAMIANO

I'VE ALWAYS KNOWN Clemenzas were devious snakes, just like their Family symbol, and Caligula is doing nothing to change my mind. He's a serpent wrapped in human flesh, just as underhanded as his friend Jesse Foster, and I don't know why I thought he'd be any different.

But he *is* getting under my skin. He's too fucking clever for his own good.

And too fucking pretty.

I'm distracted from my musings when I get back upstairs by a text from Sebastiano Conti, the Giuliano Underboss. He's the closest thing I have to a friend—though that's a low bar.

The Giulianos are run by Seb's younger half-brother, Giuseppe—Big Gee to everyone who wants to keep breathing. Seb is smarter. Calmer. And if anything, their father seemed to prefer Seb, the older son he had with his favorite mistress. But in this Family, lineage matters. Big Gee is the Don because he has the name, but Seb was the natural choice as his Underboss.

So I can't ignore a summons from Seb any more than I could ignore one from Big Gee. But for the first time, being called to do something for the Family irritates me rather than interests me. It feels like the whole world is conspiring to steal days away from my time with the Clemenza. But I get my head in the game and get Vito to drive me out to the butcher shop where Seb asked me to meet for lunch. I go in, spare a nod for the guy behind the counter, and head upstairs to the apartment above.

Seb is there already. Like me, he's queer but quiet about it. I don't know if his dad ever knew Seb's preferences before the old man got blown up in Chicago by the Irish, but Big Gee is aware, just like he knows about me, too. He doesn't have a problem with it so long as we don't make it an issue. Maybe that's why Seb and I get along so well. Most Giulianos aren't exactly welcoming, but maybe a little less hostile now that Luca D'Amato is in charge of the New York Commission.

I get the feeling sometimes that Big Gee thinks Seb and I might know something about D'Amato that he doesn't, like there's some secret gay handshake that might come in useful someday.

He's wrong about that. I hate D'Amato just as much as any Giuliano worth their salt.

Seb isn't the only one in the Family who knows just how deep my vendetta against the Clemenzas runs. But he *is* the only one who knows I plan to do something about it.

Unfortunately, he also knows I'm under orders not to.

He rises when I enter, greeting me with a back-slapping hug and kiss on each cheek. He's a touchy-feely kind of guy despite the muscles. In the old days, the real old days back in Rome, he would've done well as a gladiator—or maybe not. He's a little too fair, a little too honorable. He hates playing dirty and he loves being part of a hierarchy, because he knows where he stands at all times. It doesn't bother him that his younger brother is the Boss now, because he never expected any different, since Big Gee was legitimate, and he wasn't.

If not an ancient gladiator, Seb would probably do pretty well in the military, too, with that respect for hierarchy. Lucky for us he chose a life of crime instead. He's good at it, but he doesn't enjoy the work the way I do. He sees violence as a tool.

I just enjoy hitting shit.

The butcher's wife has been busy in the kitchen, because she comes in with a meal for us both. It's tough to get the stink of raw meat from below out of my nose long enough to enjoy it, but it doesn't seem to bother Seb any. As we're eating, he tells me about the job. There's a problem in a dockside warehouse in Red Hook. "Not ours. Not Italian at all," he adds.

"The Russians?" I ask, because they've been on my mind.

Seb shakes his head. "Independent crew. But they're skimming shipments that are moving through our channels, and they need to be dissuaded from doing so."

"When?"

"Now," Seb says. "Before it becomes a bigger problem. Make sure they get the message, but don't go too hard on them. Most of them are kids, got no idea how the world really works."

"I'll handle it."

Conversation turns to other things. The butcher's wife comes in to take the plates away. She replaces them with coffee, and I wonder what's coming next. Seb asks about a crew out on Long Island that needed a little encouragement last week, and then falls silent.

"Anything else?" I ask at last, because I don't like the way Seb is hedging. The man is not a hedger. For a Family man, he's as straight up as they come.

"I heard a rumor."

"Yeah? You shouldn't listen to those."

"This one was crazy," he tells me. "So crazy that I figured it had to be bullshit." He leans forward and drops his voice. "Rumor has it you were at the Obelisk last night. That you bought Caligula Clemenza in one of their slave auctions."

It's not a question. It's a statement he hopes is untrue. But I don't bother softening it for him. "I did."

That fucker Daniel King was not going to let me get away with it. I should've known that. I assumed my membership at the Obelisk granted me certain privileges, such as some goddamn privacy, so that I'd have a few days to figure out a way to break the news to the Boss. But that was my own stupid mistake.

Or maybe King just didn't like me snatching up the Clemenza under the nose of his Bratva pal.

Seb's hand, resting flat on the table, curls slowly into a fist. "Jesus Christ," he says quietly. "You better be joking, Orsini."

I say nothing. He leans back in his chair, dragging a hand down his face. When he looks at me again, there's something like horror in his eyes. "You were ordered to keep your hands off the Clemenzas," he says. "Explicitly."

"I was ordered not to *kill* them."

"That is not the point and you fucking know it."

I shrug. "He was on the block, Seb. The Bratva were circling. You want the last Clemenza heir wearing a Russian leash?"

He stares at me, incredulous. "So you bought him."

"Yes."

"From those evil motherfuckers."

"Yes."

"And now you're keeping him as property?"

"It's for his own good. Maybe no one likes to talk about it, but someone out there *is* picking off the Clemenzas one by one."

"That's not your business. D'Amato is handling it," he says sharply.

He's starting to piss me off now, so I snort, "Don't seem like it to me."

Now I've pissed *him* off. His fist comes down with a bang, shaking the coffee cups. "Because this is way above your pay grade. Just because you don't know about it doesn't mean nothing is happening. And it doesn't matter either way, because Big Gee gave you an order."

This is the problem with Seb. He's so wedded to order, to following the rules, that he can't believe anyone else might see the world a little different. He rises to his feet, and so do I, fast, because I'm not entirely sure he's not going to hit me.

"You don't get to rewrite orders just because they're inconvenient," he growls. "You don't get to decide the rules don't apply to you just because you think you have a prior claim."

"I *do* have a prior claim."

"Big Gee told you you'd get your chance when things quiet down. Things are not fucking quiet right now, Orsini."

"They're never gonna *be* quiet!"

Both of us have raised our voices, and I'm aware that the noise from the shop beneath has hushed considerably.

Seb points at me. "You turn the kid loose. Today."

"I can't do that. He's got no money, no friends, and someone's out to kill him."

He gives a bark of hard laughter. "Don't pretend this is some act of charity, Orsini. You bought a human being at auction. Christ, I knew you were a member of that snake pit, but I never realized how exactly like the rest of those motherfuckers you really are."

That stings, even though I can't deny it. So I try a different tack. "You don't believe me about the protection deal, you can ask the Clemenza yourself," I say, and the sincerity in my tone seems to give him pause.

The truth is, I have no idea what that manipulative little shit would say if I got him face-to-face with Seb. He might claim I'd done it all against his will.

But I don't think he would. The Clemenza knew the Obelisk was his last shot. He doesn't want to go back out on the street any more than I want to let him.

And even if Seb tells me again that I need to let him go, orders me to do it, I'm not going to.

"Caligula Clemenza is mine," I tell Seb. "I bought him fair and square. He knew what he was doing when he got on that stage, and given what you think about the place, you gotta know I was the best he could hope for among the buyers."

"I never took you for such a dishonorable man," Seb mutters, but I can see the conflict in his eyes. He knows what I'm saying is the truth. So I'm starting to feel pretty hopeful until he says, "You need to tell Big Gee about this."

"I was going to." It's a lie.

And Seb can tell. "You go do this job in Red Hook, and then you get on your fucking knees to Big Gee and tell him what you've done," he tells me seriously. "Because if you don't, Orsini, I will. And when he sends someone to kill you for your disobedience, I'll be first to raise my hand."

On top of everything else the Clemenzas have done to me, now they've ruined my only friendship.

"I'll tell the Boss," I grit out. "But you gotta give me a few days to figure out some protections for the kid."

The look Seb gives me suggests he doesn't believe a

word coming out of my mouth. "Hand him over to the Loyalists. They'd be fucking delighted to crown him king and play at power again."

"Those motherfuckers couldn't protect their own ballsacks. And D'Amato wouldn't like it, either. Last thing he wants is a figurehead for the Clemenza leftovers to flock to." I have no idea what Luca D'Amato, the Morelli Don, wants or doesn't want when it comes to his old enemy. But from the look on Seb's face, my wild shot has hit home. "Give me a few days to figure something out," I repeat. "And then I'll talk to the Boss."

All Seb says is, "Get outta here."

I'll take it as a grace period. I have no intention at all of letting Caligula Clemenza leave my house, but I knew the moment I bought him that I'd have to explain myself to Big Gee one way or another. A few days will give me time to come up with a plausible story.

In the meantime, I head down to Red Hook, and despite Seb's orders to keep it light, it's a fucking mess. I'm meaner than usual. Leave one of them unconscious and the rest of them crying. They get the message, but it's a little firmer than Seb wanted, and he'll be pissed when he hears.

But it's not *my* fault. It's the Clemenza's. He's gotten me all riled up, flashing his ass at me so my balls and my brain are mixed up.

So while I figure out how to make my case to Big Gee, and while I cool off and get my dick back in line, I'll stay away from Caligula Clemenza.

Leave him down there alone in the dark.

Let him learn his lesson.

CHAPTER 16
DAMIANO

THREE DAYS LATER, the morning headlines make me smile as I read the newspaper that Rosa set out with my breakfast.

Infamous Clemenza Townhouse Continues to Auction Despite Tragic Suicide.

I refold the paper with a crisp snap and set it beside my espresso cup with a happy heart. Fate has been showering me with her favor lately, and this has to be the cherry on top.

Rosa clears her throat softly from the doorway, her hands clasped tightly around a tray of food. She knows better than to interrupt my mornings unless she has something interesting to say.

"Well?"

"The tray came back full last night." Her voice carries that particular tone—the one she uses when she wants me to know she's not happy. "Same with breakfast this morning." She holds out the tray for me to see. I give a satisfied nod. Everything's lining up.

It's time.

Three days I've left him down there alone.

For three days, Rosa has been sending down three meals a day in the dumbwaiter on my cue. Wherever I am in the city, I take out my phone and open the video feed to watch Caligula Clemenza's reaction as I slide up the lights from off to dim, enough for him to see the food when it's sent down.

Then I send him back into darkness.

No human contact. Not even a voice. Nothing but the darkness and the bones of his grandfather's empire. The Clemenza prince is learning that privilege dies hard, but it does die.

"I'll take something down to him myself," I say, rising from the mahogany table. "Can't have our *guest* wasting away."

Rosa just purses those lips, but she hands over the tray without comment.

I've been watching him on the cameras. More than I should. More than is strictly necessary—but then, I need to monitor my investment. Make sure he doesn't find some way to harm himself and rob me of my revenge. That's the only reason I check the cameras dozens of times a day.

And I watch him shower. After his breakfast each morning, I turn on the shower from my controls, leave it on until he reluctantly gets under the water and cleans himself. I watch the water running over him, the graceful line of his spine as he tilts his head under the spray.

Then I plunge him back into darkness, amusing myself sometimes by cutting the lights before he's reached for the towel, so that he has to grope his way around to find it.

He has become…a distraction. A sweet distraction.

So today I want him to learn that it's not going to be all darkness and solitude while he's here.

Sometimes I'll make him hurt.

The elevator descends and the doors slide open, revealing a void beyond. I stay where I am, standing in the threshold so he can tense up, get scared.

Then I take a step in and turn on the lights.

The illumination isn't blinding by any standards, but I'm pleased to see the Clemenza flinch instinctively, his whole body jerking like he's been struck. One hand flies up to shield his eyes, and the other braces against the mattress as though he's preparing to run.

Christ, he's really pretty.

Even like this—*especially* like this. Sharp cheekbones, those impossible, wide-set golden eyes, the defiant tilt to his chin.

He's a mess. Tangled hair, three days of fine golden stubble softening the angle of his jaw, making him look younger. More fragile. But even like this, there's something untouchable about him. A regal air that three days of darkness hasn't dimmed…

Enough. He's a tool for vengeance, and that's all he is.

I step into the room and let the elevator doors shut behind me, sealing us in together. "Good morning, golden boy."

The Clemenza doesn't answer. Doesn't even look at me. Just keeps one hand over his eyes like a child playing hide-and-seek, as if blocking out the light might make this all disappear.

The vulnerability in his gesture brings an unwelcome memory. My father's body. His blood, everywhere. I threw my hands over my face when I found Cesario Clemenza standing over him in the kitchen, as though if I couldn't see the blood, it wouldn't be real.

My anger returns, that welcome, cold fire of vengeance that I *should* be feeling every time I look at Caligula Clemenza. He might react like a child, but he isn't one. He's not innocent, either.

He's a grown man, and he's a Clemenza, and he deserves what's coming to him.

I walk over and set the tray down on the end of his bed. "You will eat when your meals appear."

He says nothing.

"Eat," I say, settling onto the mattress beside him. "Or you'll regret it."

He doesn't move. Doesn't even acknowledge that I've spoken.

He needs to learn.

I reach out and wrap my fingers around the front of his collar. His whole body goes rigid at the contact. His skin is warm under my knuckles, and I can see the fluttering pulse in his throat.

"I said *eat*." I pull his face up toward mine. "Or I'll feed you myself, and you won't enjoy it."

His lips stay sealed, and I'm close enough to see flecks of gold shining in his amber eyes, close enough to smell his skin. For one insane moment, I want to kiss him. Want to cover that smartass mouth with mine and taste him.

Then he yanks away from me and grabs the fork, shoveling eggs in like he's starving.

"Good boy."

His eyes narrow with anger at the words, but soon enough he'll crave my praise rather than my punishment. He'll see that he's dependent on me. Dependent on me for everything, down to his next breath.

I like that thought. I like it very much.

I stretch out across the end of the bed, leaning on one elbow as I watch him, making myself comfortable. Making it clear that I'm not going anywhere until I'm satisfied with his performance. The position puts me close enough to touch, and I have to actively resist the urge to smooth his tangled hair.

The urge to play with my toy.

"I've been catching up on current events," I say, watching him chew. "Guess what made the front page?"

He stops mid-bite, fork halfway to his mouth, as he looks at the paper I lay out next to the tray. The headline stares up at him in bold black letters.

He puts down his fork and picks up the paper, reading through the story.

"Guess they gave the green light for the sale to continue, since that townhouse is the only thing left that your worthless grandfather owned," I say with a yawn. "Asset forfeiture is a real bitch, huh? Of course, it's a pity about your cousin's 'suicide.'" I add the air quotes. "Guess they got cleaners in to mop up all that blood before the sale."

His head jerks back as though I've struck him.

"Oh, I'm sorry," I say with fake concern. "Were you close?"

"You're an asshole." His voice is raw from disuse.

I arch a brow, encouraging him to continue. To dig his own grave deeper. "Were you fond of him?"

He says nothing.

"I asked you a question."

"He was Family. That's all that mattered."

And now he's just another piece swept from the board. "Touching. Especially since he would have cut your throat himself if he knew you were queer."

He doesn't answer, but his teeth clench. His gaze drops back to the newspaper, to the photo of the townhouse where he grew up, where he learned what it meant to be Clemenza royalty. Where he thought he'd always belong.

"Are you going to buy it?" he asks quietly.

The question catches me off guard. "Why would I buy it?"

"You're a collector. You've collected everything else." There's no accusation in his voice, just weary acceptance. "The furniture. The paintings. The china. Why not the Clemenza townhouse, too?"

"What do I need with the townhouse?" I grin at him. "I've got a real live Clemenza of my very own now. The centerpiece of my collection. The crown fucking jewel."

He doesn't flinch. Doesn't react at all except for the slight quickening of his breath that I see in the movement of his chest. Then he asks, "What if *I* bought it?"

I'll give him this: he's never predictable. "You have no money."

"I have *your* money. The money in trust from the auction," he continues, words coming faster now, desperate. "The ten million. Couldn't I…" He trails off.

I tilt my head. "Why do you want it so bad?"

"Because…" His voice breaks slightly. "Because it's the last thing left. Everything else is gone, like we never existed. But that place…" He swallows hard.

And I have to force myself to stay right where I am. To not reach out and push his hair back from his forehead.

"It's the last connection I have," he finishes quietly. "To the person I used to be. To what I was."

There's something raw in his voice. This isn't manipulation or strategy, not like the last time I was down here with him. This is genuine pain, genuine loss, the kind of grief that hollows a man out from the inside. The kind of grief I understand from personal experience.

And it pisses me off.

I don't *want* his pain to matter. I don't want his losses to be anything more than justice served cold. I sure as hell don't want this twisting in my chest that feels suspiciously like sympathy.

I get off the bed abruptly, putting distance between us. "A property like that won't go cheap," I tell him. "Even with a scandal attached. If anything, that'll make it more interesting to buyers. So you *don't* have the money, little prince. Not even if you paid out every penny of that ten million. You done?" I finish, pointing at the barely-touched breakfast.

He nods his head without looking up.

"I could make you eat it. Could force every bit of it down your throat."

"I know," he says tiredly. "But I'm not hungry."

I study him—this broken prince in my basement, this last scion of a dynasty, with nothing left but his memories. Something about him is different today. Dimmer. The fire that made him so magnetic at the auction—that defiant spark that made a whole room want to pay for the privilege of tearing him apart—seems to be flickering out.

That's the point, of course. I *want* to extinguish that light. That's what revenge means.

I didn't mean it to happen this fast, though.

I should've realized he's no tough guy. He survived on the streets thanks to his Clemenza cunning, but I shouldn't have expected resilience from someone who grew up rich and pampered.

I need to get out of here. I have other things to do today that don't involve waiting hand and fucking foot on a man I consider my property.

His gaze travels slowly up my body until he's looking me in the eye again. He seems cautious. Careful. Like he has something to say.

"What is it now?" I ask impatiently.

"Is there…" He licks his lips in what I assume is a nervous habit, because it lacks even his usual clumsy attempt at seduction. "Is there something I could do? To earn it?"

He sold himself at the Obelisk, so I'm not sure why I'm surprised he's whoring himself out for real estate now. It's a confirmation of everything I've ever believed about the Clemenzas. No honor. No pride. No self-respect.

But even as I think those vicious thoughts, I can't bring myself to believe them. Not really. This is just desperation, a man grasping for the last piece of himself before it disappears forever.

"What are you proposing?" I ask at last.

Those golden eyes are full of resignation. "Whatever you want."

Whatever I want. I almost laugh. "I own you," I tell him. "I can already do whatever I want."

"Then I could…" He thinks, then gives a helpless shake of the head.

With a scoff, I head toward the elevator.

"Please," he calls after me. "*Please*, Dami."

I turn at the elevator doors, unable to ignore the plaintive note in his voice…or the soft way he says that nickname he gave me.

"I'll come back tomorrow," I hear myself telling him, "if you're a good boy and finish every meal between now and then. But you'll have to come up with something. A proposal. Hell, it could be fun, hearing what you think you could possibly offer me."

I reach for the light controls, intending to plunge him back into darkness, but my hand hovers over the switch. He looks pale. Fragile. I dim the lights to a warm amber glow instead—the same color as his eyes. It softens the room, makes his skin look less washed out.

As the elevator doors close on the basement, I see the gears turning in that clever head, trying to decide what he can give me that I haven't already taken.

I almost pity him.

Almost.

CHAPTER 17
CALIGULA

THE LIGHT in the basement hasn't gone off since he left, which should be a relief after three days in darkness.

It isn't. It's worse. So much worse. The light is soft, golden, falsely kind—the eye of a benevolent god. And it shows that mockery of my heritage laid out in a creepy basement. Reminds me of everything I've lost.

I ate every damn meal. Showered more than I probably needed to. And I tried to sleep, burying my face under my arms. Mostly I just sat here staring at the newspaper Damiano left behind, reading the same headline over and over until the words lost all meaning.

Infamous Clemenza Townhouse Continues to Auction Despite Tragic Suicide.

The last stronghold. The last thread connecting me to everything I used to be. And that monster upstairs holds a pair of scissors.

I hear the elevator at last, the hiss of hydraulics, the clink of metal. I sit up, wipe my palms on my thighs. I don't know what's about to happen, but I asked for it.

And I can only hope my offer is a good one.

The doors open and Damiano steps into the room,

phone in one hand, looking me over with a critical eye. The washed hair. The shaved jaw. The empty plate.

The desperate hope I'm trying so hard to hide.

He walks to his usual throne and sets his phone down on the table next to it. "I arranged for my real estate guy to go to the auction for me," he says, as casually as though he's discussing the weather. "*If* I want to bid. It's about to start, he tells me."

My throat feels like it's lined with sandpaper. "Thank you."

He raises an eyebrow, amused. "Don't thank me yet, golden boy. Since the question is, what in the hell do you have to bargain with?"

I know the answer. Have known it since the moment he said that maybe I could earn it. Because I know what a man like Damiano Orsini wants in this life. Aside from vengeance, of course. He has this house, built from obsession. He has all the power he could want. All the money.

And no class.

The words stick in my throat before I can spit them out. "My respect," I say.

"Your respect?" At least he sounds intrigued. He settles into my grandfather's chair again, eyes on me. His phone buzzes, and he casts a glance at the screen. "Bidding started at five million," he tells me. "Okay, then. Show me how much you respect me, Caligula Clemenza."

I force myself to move, get off the bed. My knees hit the concrete, but it's not cold. That's something I've noticed; he keeps me naked down here, but it's always temperate. No chance I'll freeze to death.

Just go slowly crazy.

"You think just kneeling for me is worth five mill, little prince?" He sounds amused. "Come on. How much do you really want that townhouse?"

I rest my hands on my thighs to hide their trembling and lift my chin just enough to meet his eyes. "More than anything."

"Then how, exactly, are you going to show me your respect?"

"I'll suck your dick." There's no point sugar-coating it. Crassness is all this man understands.

He laughs. "If I want you to suck my dick, I just have to tell you to do it."

"That's the point. You'd be telling me to do it. *Making* me do it. But this way, I'm offering. Offering out of respect. And you'd know it, because…" I take a breath. "Because you'd be the first man I've ever asked to let me."

He lets me sweat for a second. Then he says, "Your offer is an amateur blow job and a sweet smile?" I stay quiet, hoping. Praying. "If you've never done it before, it won't even be all that good."

"No. But you could—you could teach me."

"Now you want me to *teach* you?"

I want to kill you slowly and watch you bleed out with the same dead stare you've been giving me since I came here.

"If you would be so kind," I say.

His eyes narrow at my tone. But he just says, "Crawl over here."

I comply, shuffling over on my hands and knees and trying not to glance over at the vivisection of my grandfather's townhouse. The distance between the bed and chair feels infinite, and the chain from the collar around my neck drags along with me. My palms are sweating against the concrete, and by the time I reach him, I can barely bring myself to meet his eyes.

But I do.

He's undoing his belt with one hand while picking up his phone with the other. "Hands behind your back," he says without looking up. "And don't move them unless I tell you to."

He sounds almost bored. But I obey, clasping my fingers together at the small of my back.

Whoever he's calling answers, and he orders, "Bid six million." He looks down at me, moving the phone only a few inches away from his mouth, so whoever is on the end of that line could hear him if they wanted to. "Look how fast you got to your knees. Almost like you want my dick as much as the townhouse." I say nothing. "Open your mouth."

I part my lips, and he traces them with his thumb. The touch is impersonal, testing, examining his property. It reminds me of my first night in his house, when he examined my asshole the same way.

"Wider."

I open my mouth more, feeling foolish and exposed. He presses down on my bottom lip with his thumb, and I tentatively touch it with my tongue, not sure if that's right.

"Now use your tongue. Show me what you plan to do with your mouth."

I have no idea what I'm supposed to do. I've seen things in videos, heard stories from Jesse and his cronies, but actually doing it feels impossible. I try to take his thumb into my mouth, but I'm clumsy about it, unsure of the pressure, the movement. While I try to figure out what he wants me to do, I accidentally bump his knuckle with my teeth.

"Careful," he mutters. But his pupils grow a little larger, and that gives me a flicker of hope.

"Seven and a half million," he says into the phone, but his voice has dropped half an octave. "Christ. People will pay anything for real estate in New York these days."

He pulls out his thumb and slides his hand into my hair, gripping just tight enough to hurt.

"Listen carefully," he says, looking down at me with those empty eyes. "You're going to take me in your mouth. Slowly. And if you gag, you breathe through your nose and keep going. Understood?"

"Yes, sir."

His grip in my hair tightens sharply, even though I'm pretty fucking sure I kept any sarcasm out of my reply, despite what I was thinking.

"No," he growls. "You say my name. I don't want you to forget for a second who you're kneeling for."

Heat crawls up my chest, my neck. "Yes, Damiano."

"Better. And if I feel teeth, you're gonna die with my dick in your mouth. You get me?"

"I get you."

He fishes himself out, and he's already hard, thick and imposing. How is *that* supposed to fit in my mouth? "Come on," he says. "Show me what those pretty Clemenza lips are good for besides lying."

I lean forward, press my lips to the head of his cock like I'm giving it a kiss. He tastes like salt, like the ocean. I pull back, looking up at him uncertainly.

"More," he says. "Open your mouth."

I part my lips and try to take him in, but I gag on just the tip, the strange feeling of having something that big in my mouth. My eyes water, and I pull back, coughing.

"Breathe through your nose," he instructs, his free hand stroking my hair almost gently. "Try again."

The second attempt goes better, but barely. I can still only manage the very tip. I don't know what I'm doing with my tongue, and I keep accidentally scraping him with my teeth.

Despite what he said, he doesn't kill me for that. So I guess I should count myself lucky.

"Relax your jaw," he murmurs. "That's it. Good boy. Don't think so much."

I hate how delicious he smells. I hate how my stomach flips when he calls me a good boy. I hate that I want him to *like* it.

He sets his phone down and puts it on speaker. The auction continues in the background—*eight million, eight and a half.* But all I can focus on is trying not to embarrass myself further. Trying to figure out how to breathe. Trying to understand what he wants from me.

I find a rhythm, taking him a little deeper each time. I figure out that sealing my lips and using suction makes his thighs tense around me. Running my tongue along the underside makes his fingers tighten in my hair.

"Am I doing it right?" I cough, pulling back to look up at him. My eyes are watering. I hope he doesn't think I'm crying.

His teeth are clenched. "Stop asking questions," he says roughly. "Just…keep going."

I get back to it, try to take him deeper like I've seen in videos, but I immediately gag and have to pull back, gasping and choking. Tears stream down my face, and I feel like a complete failure.

"Twelve million!" the voice crackles through the speaker.

I work just the head, using my tongue more deliberately now, and find a spot just under the ridge where he's sensitive. When I press my tongue there and suck at the same time, his hips shift forward involuntarily.

"Thirteen," Damiano spits out, echoed by whoever is on the other end of that phone. But he's not really listening to the auction anymore; he's staring down at me with an intensity that makes my skin burn. His hand tightens in my hair. "Use your hand, too."

I bring my hands from behind my back—he said not to

move them unless he told me, and now he's telling me—and use one to grip him, the angle unfamiliar. I try to coordinate my mouth and hand, and it's clumsy at first, like trying to pat my head and rub my stomach simultaneously. But I do my best to match my strokes to my sucks, and when I look up at him through my wet lashes, something in his expression shifts. His control is slipping.

I have power here. I really do.

I slide him into my mouth again, finding it easier this time, his thick crown weighing down the back of my tongue.

"Look at you, learning so fast," he says. "Natural talent, I guess." The words should sting, not make my cock twitch. I channel my irritation into working him harder, more suction, tighter grip, finding that spot under the ridge again and pressing until he curses.

"*Fifteen million!*" The voice on the phone is getting excited now.

So is Damiano. "Eighteen," he counters, voice strained.

I'm getting better. His breathing is heavy now, his hips jerking in micro-movements. The grip in my hair disappears and his hands frame my face. He brushes away my tears with his thumbs, and the tenderness of that gesture in the middle of this transaction nearly breaks my concentration.

"*Eighteen and a half!*" chirps the phone.

"Twenty," Damiano says unsteadily. "Twenty million for a townhouse that doesn't even have a view of the Park."

I take him deeper than I've managed before—not deep, by any standard, but enough that I feel him hit the back of my throat, and this time I breathe through the gag and hold. His thighs are rigid. The hands around my face are trembling.

"And let's be honest," he says, looking down at me with

pupils blown black, "you're not even worth half that, are you, little prince? Despite what I paid for you."

The casual cruelty barely registers, because I'm too focused on the way his hips are moving, the way his cock feels like it's swelling so much my jaw might unhinge. Because despite my inexperience, despite how clumsy I am, I'm affecting him.

And despite everything he's done to me, I want to be good at this. Want him to lose control…and let me take it.

"Twenty million going once…going twice…"

His balls are tight and hard, the flesh in my mouth impossibly swollen. I prepare myself for what's coming, hope I won't choke—

He pushes me away, his cock falling out of my mouth as I go back on my heels, gasping and confused, saliva and pre-cum gushing down my chin.

He tucks himself away.

"Sold! Twenty million dollars to bidder number seven!"

Damiano reaches out to end the call with a sharp tap.

"But you didn't finish," I say stupidly.

He looks down at me. "Finish? From that pathetic attempt? It's a good thing you never whored yourself out on the streets, Clemenza. No one in their right mind would pay for your skills. Lucky for you I'm—how did you put it that first night? Oh, yeah." He leans forward. *"Fucking insane."*

"I'm sorry," I hear myself saying.

I'm not sorry. He *is* fucking insane.

And he's a fucking liar, too. That might not have been the best blow job he's ever had, but he was *into* it.

"The townhouse is mine," he continues, standing and straightening his pants. "And it could be yours, at the end of our year together. But not with a performance like that." He shakes his head with a disappointed sigh, and then heads toward the elevator. He pauses there, looking back at me still kneeling on the floor. "Maybe next time you'll put a little more effort into showing your *respect*."

I'm left alone once the elevator ascends, kneeling on hard concrete, mouth still wet, a dull throbbing between my legs. And something burning inside me, something close to hate.

But not quite hate.

I wipe my lips with the back of my hand. Twenty million dollars. Twice what he paid for me. For a townhouse he claimed not to want, and hasn't even guaranteed to hand over to me. I paid a high price.

But it was worth it.

Because I know for sure, now. I *do* affect him. I have power over him, even if he won't admit it.

And twenty million dollars says Damiano Orsini is upstairs right now watching me, watching my reaction. For the first time in days, I feel my fire returning.

I look directly at the camera in the corner, the one angled at the bed. I hold its eye the way I held his. And I let one corner of my mouth lift.

He wants to play games?

Game fucking on.

CHAPTER 18
DAMIANO

I GO DIRECTLY to the viewing room in my quarters, where I settle into the leather chair, loosen my pants again, and turn on the monitors. I don't think. If I think, I'll stop, and I don't want to stop.

Didn't want to stop just minutes ago when his mouth was on me, when I had my hand threaded in his bright hair, a prince on his knees for me.

Caligula Clemenza is still kneeling right where I left him, lips wet, looking straight at the camera.

I lean in closer. He's hard.

Even now. Even after everything I said and did.

He shifts slightly, gets to his feet, then walks a few steps to collapse on the bed. He touches himself slowly, wrapping those long fingers around his sweetly curved cock, and starts to slide up and down. He looks right into the fucking camera while he does it.

And I watch.

I shouldn't. There's nothing useful here. No tactical advantage. And worst of all, it makes Sebastiano's accusation correct: I'm no better than the Bratva who wanted to buy the Clemenza. I'm devoid of honor, of anything good.

But that's not news.

So I watch, because the Clemenza belongs to me. Why shouldn't I use my own property? His body belongs to me. Those sounds he's making? Mine. The pleasure coursing through him is mine to give or to take away. It doesn't belong to him, and he knows it. He's doing this on purpose. I told him not to touch himself, and here he is, doing it when he knows it's forbidden.

I should go back down there and punish him. But if I go back down there, he'll know he's won. Besides, my hand is already on my dick. I'm still rock hard, still slick from his spit, and I stroke myself in time with him, watching him twist and strain and press his face against the mattress like he's ashamed of what he's doing.

He *should* be fucking ashamed.

Just like I should be ashamed for wanting to go back down there, shove his hand away, and taste him.

He comes first. I see it in the way his body locks up. The small sound he makes. The tremble.

And then I follow, muffling my gasp against my wrist, biting into myself so that the pain is my punishment.

The post-release spiral hits hard. Shame. Fury. Disgust. What am I *doing*? He's a tool for my vengeance, that's all. An enemy I want to grind into dust, not jack off over him like some horny teenager. This doesn't serve the plan. Using his mouth? That's control. That's different.

Watching him get off while I do the same?

That's weakness.

I wipe myself off. Trash the tissue with more force than necessary, but the rage isn't clearing my head the way it should. Instead, I'm thinking about the way he moved, the way he sounded, the way he tried to hide his face like he had any right to privacy from me.

And then the intercom sounds. I stab the button and snarl, "What?"

"The Big Man is here," Rosa says, and she says it in Italian, so I know exactly who she means.

Well, this is all I fucking need.

Big Gee. In the flesh. At my house.

I guess his brother waited about as long as he could. Seb's never been much good at letting things fester. He's more of a "bring it to a head" man, which I used to like about him.

Not so much today.

Big Gee is sitting in my armchair in my great room, tie loose and eyes blazing, and points at the seat opposite when I walk in as though I need to be told where to sit in my own damn house. Rosa's already poured him a coffee, and she's waiting by the door with a mutinous face.

"Would you like anything—" she begins, and Big Gee cuts her off with a wave of his hand.

"Get outta here," he snaps at her. Yeah, he's pissed. Royally pissed. As soon as the door closes behind Rosa, he turns on me. "You're lucky I don't fucking kill you right now. I heard about the auction at the Obelisk, you sick fuck."

"I was going to come to you—"

"Shut the fuck up, Orsini. You're a fucking perv for buying that kid, but even worse, you're a disloyal shit as well. Did I or did I not tell you to stay the hell away from the Clemenzas?"

"You told me not to *kill* them." I lean back, forcing myself to look relaxed even as fury burns through me. "The Clemenza is alive. Unharmed. And he offered himself willingly at that auction. I'm not some degenerate kidnapping virgins for personal entertainment."

Except that maybe I am.

Big Gee is already thundering on. "You expect me to believe you ain't already put that kid six feet under?"

"You want me to get him in here so you can see him yourself?"

"Fuck, no. I don't give a shit about him. My problem is *you*. You disobeyed a direct order, Orsini. What did you think was gonna happen to you when I found out?"

Pretty much this, actually. But I'm not stupid enough to say that. "I bought him because it was the only thing I *could* do." I've been working on this story, but I'm not sure how convincing it'll be. Still, I need to try. "The Bratva had a lock on him. Did Seb tell you that?"

He just looks at me for a second, and I wish like hell I could take back what I just said. Because I see at once it wasn't Seb who told him. So now I've gotten us *both* in hot water with the Boss.

"Come on, Boss," I say, hoping to bring his attention back to me, "I've done everything you've asked, every time. I haven't touched the Clemenzas, and I'm not gonna kill this one. But you can't blame me for taking what little scraps of justice are left on the table for me. For my father."

Big Gee's silence stretches, thick and grim. He sips my coffee from my cup, studying me over the rim. Then: "You're gonna have to show him off."

"What?"

"You heard me. You're going to have to take him out somewhere public. Soon. Stamp out any rumors that you iced him. Because if D'Amato hears about this, there'll be hell to pay. So you let everyone know that the Clemenza heir is still breathing—and that *you're* still following my orders. You hear me?"

"Where am I supposed to take him to prove all that?"

"The fucking opera. Tomorrow night. D'Amato will be there with all his cronies. Some charity thing he insisted we all attend. I'll send over some tickets."

It's true, Luca D'Amato has been *encouraging* all the Families to attend shit like that, make donations, play nice with the city. But I hate the fucking opera as much as Big Gee does, and I don't want to drag the Clemenza around just to show everyone that I'm behaving myself.

The Boss must see something in my face, because he stabs a finger at me again. "You're on a short leash, Orsini. You so much as twitch, I'll yank it hard enough to break your fucking neck."

I've wondered sometimes what would happen if Big Gee tried to throw down with me. He has a rep built on good honest bone-breaking, just like mine. But the truth is, he hasn't been involved in the grunt work for a long time. He works out at a boxing gym downtown, where his bodyguards all let him punch their lights out to feed his ego.

It's making him soft. Soft in the middle and soft in the fists.

Me, I'm more like Seb. I've got no aspirations. I like where I am, and I like that I don't have to lead a crew. I'm no good at that shit. I've got one talent, and I get to exercise it regularly.

So I just nod my head and tell the Boss what he wants to hear. That I'll show up and parade my prize around like a show pony, make sure the Giulianos stay in good standing with the New York Commission—and Luca D'Amato.

"And one more thing," he says on the way out. "I don't like the way that old bitch of yours looks at me."

"What, Rosa? She looks at me the same damn way. What do you want me to do about it, take her eyes out?"

He brays with laughter. "Make a good match for that

driver of yours then, eh?" He shakes his head, still chuckling hard enough that he doesn't notice I'm not laughing along. "Anyway. You tell her to watch herself."

Big Gee leaves. I go down to the kitchen to find Rosa, who's scrubbing already-clean countertops and pursing those lips again. "That man has no business giving you orders in your own house," she mutters under her breath, as soon as she knows I'm in hearing distance.

There's no love lost between Rosa and the Giuliano Dons. Still, I can't have her disrespecting the Family.

"You mind your damn manners around the Boss," I tell her. "And call Lorenzo Benedetti. Get him over here this afternoon. Tell him I need a rush job."

She scrubs harder and purses those lips until they disappear, but she nods.

I go back upstairs to the viewing room to check in on my property. Part of me wants to leave him down there alone in the dark for the rest of this year, let that flame flicker and die. But I've been given instructions by my Boss, instructions I have to follow.

The Clemenza has curled up on the bed. Spent. Small. Vulnerable.

But Clemenzas are never really vulnerable. I need to remember that.

CHAPTER 19
DAMIANO

LORENZO BENEDETTI ARRIVES that afternoon armed with the weapons of his trade: measuring tape, fabric swatches, and the supreme confidence of a man who's dressed billionaires with more money than taste for four decades.

"Mr. Orsini." He gives a respectful bow as Rosa shows him into the great room. "You said this was urgent?"

"Yeah. I need a tux. For tomorrow night."

Benedetti's eyebrows climb toward his hairline. "Tomorrow night? But sir, you must understand, custom tailoring takes *time*—"

"Then I guess you'll have to work through the night. Money is no object. And it's not for me," I add as he begins to approach me with his measuring tape. I already have one tux from Benedetti. I don't need another. "It's for a guest. You get ready while I bring him up. Rosa will bring you anything you might need."

"As you wish, Mr. Orsini." His eyes gleam with the greed of a craftsman who's just been told to spare no expense, but there's curiosity there too. I don't think his clientele typically have guests who require emergency formal wear.

When I descend to the basement, the Clemenza looks up from the bed where he's been reading that newspaper for the hundredth time. His hair is still a little damp from his shower, but at least he's washed himself after what happened earlier.

He's been behaving himself, ate his lunch when it was sent down, took his vitamins. But there's still the little matter of using my property without permission.

We'll deal with that later.

"You have an appointment," I tell him as I unlock his collar.

He stretches out his neck and gives me a sideways glance. "Appointment?"

"Upstairs."

The wary look in his eyes appears again. I toss him the plain white terry robe I brought down. "Put this on."

"Nothing else?"

I smile. "Well. Almost nothing." I pull the golden cock cage from my pocket and watch his face flush as understanding dawns. "Unless you'd prefer to stay down here?"

He lets me put it on him without further complaint, staring glassily at the wall. I take the cage in one hand and him in the other, soft and warm and growing slightly in my palm as I stand there trying to figure out this stupid device.

I have to be careful. It's in the contract, after all. No permanent physical damage. So I take my time. I slide the cage into place, adjusting him into it with my fingers, because I want to make sure it sits right, that's all. I'm being *considerate*, which is more than he fucking deserves.

At last it's on. And once he's wrapped up in the robe with his golden secret hidden underneath, he gives me a look as haughty as a prince dressed for court.

But that cage is a reminder of his captivity, of who owns his body.

Of who owns *him*.

When we get up to the great room, Benedetti has arranged his tools and is humming to himself softly. He looks up as we enter, but shows no surprise, just the careful neutrality of a tailor who's dressed enough powerful men to know when not to ask questions.

But then the Clemenza steps forward, and everything changes.

"Lorenzo," he says, and his voice is warm. "What an unexpected pleasure."

The tailor's expression morphs into genuine respect, the kind that can't be bought or faked.

"Signor Clemenza!" Benedetti's bow is much deeper than the one he gave to me. "It's been far too long. You look…" His eyes take in the drawn face, the slight frame. "Very well," he finishes, not even blinking at the lie.

"I'm getting there," the Clemenza says.

I wasn't expecting this easy familiarity between them, but of course they would know each other. Caligula Clemenza will have been fitted by the city's most exclusive tailor since he was old enough to wear a suit.

"The new tuxedo is for you?" Benedetti asks eagerly.

The Clemenza glances at me, and I give a stiff nod. He smiles. "The new tuxedo is for me."

"Ah!" Benedetti is clearly delighted. "Maria and I have your measurements on record, of course, but…"

"Yes, I've lost a little weight," Caligula agrees. "Better take some new ones."

Benedetti picks up his measuring tape. "Shall we begin?"

The casual ignoring of my presence, the way they talk around me like I'm hired help in my own house, is an insult.

"Strip," I order the Clemenza, cutting through their friendly chatter.

Benedetti's expression remains perfectly still, and as for the little prince, his smile doesn't falter. "Of course," he says smoothly. "Lorenzo, I hope you'll forgive the informality. My generous host has some specific requirements."

The way he says it—like I'm some eccentric billionaire with strange hobbies rather than the man who owns his body—makes anger bubble in my veins. I take a breath and remind myself that after Benedetti leaves, I'll have all the time in the world to take out my irritation on the Clemenza.

He shrugs off the robe and Benedetti's eyes widen slightly. Not at the nudity; the man has dressed enough powerful bodies to be immune to flesh. But at the golden cage locked around the Clemenza's cock.

But the tailor recovers instantly. "Naturally, Mr. Orsini prefers things to be a certain way," he says with a respectful smile. "For a man is king in his own home." He approaches. "Shall we start with shoulders?"

The easy acceptance, the way Benedetti just incorporates this new information into his professional routine, is somehow more infuriating than shock would have been. And as for Caligula Clemenza, he stands perfectly still as Benedetti works, chin up, shoulders back. When the tailor measures his neck, he tilts his head exactly right. When the tape circles his waist, he adjusts his stance without being asked.

And they talk.

Christ, how they talk.

"How is Maria?" Caligula asks as Benedetti works. "Still terrorizing the apprentices?"

"Worse than ever. She would want me to give you her regards, by the way. She still hangs on to that bolt of Harris tweed you admired."

"The gray? It was divine."

I take in every touch, every casual familiarity, every reminder that they share a world I bought and fought my way into but will never truly inhabit. When Benedetti runs the tape up the Clemenza's inseam—fingers brushing dangerously close to the golden cage—my grip on the arm of my chair turns white-knuckled.

Mine, the beast in me snarls. Other hands don't belong there.

But what pisses me off the most isn't the intimate touching. It's the easy respect in Benedetti's voice. The way he automatically treats the Clemenza as his social *better,* despite the fact that the kid is a third of his age and standing there naked with a golden cage on his dick.

And the Clemenza prince enjoys that world of bespoke tailoring and careful courtesy like he never left it. He belongs there.

Meanwhile, I'm just a barbarian with a credit card.

"*Bellissimo,*" Benedetti murmurs, stepping back to admire his muse. "That posture—perfect. You can always tell good breeding."

Good breeding. I'm going to fucking lose it.

"Your grandmother would be proud," Benedetti adds softly. "You have her carriage."

Caligula's smile falters for just a moment. "Thank you. Thank you very much, Lorenzo."

The genuine emotion in that exchange, the shared history, the kindness offered and accepted—it makes something ugly twist in my chest. The Clemenza was supposed to be humiliated by this, not find some connection to his old world.

"The fabric," I say curtly, to kill the moment. "Show me the options."

For the first time, I get out of my seat as Benedetti lays out the swatches with ceremonial care on the sofa: midnight blacks and navy blues, each one labeled with details I don't understand: mills and weights and thread counts that mean nothing to me, but everything to the two of them.

He's separated out the tuxedo fabrics from the others, but the Clemenza's attention is immediately caught by one particular sample off to the side. Even I can see it's different from the other samples. Special. Black, but not dead black.

"This must be Dormeuil," he says softly, fingertips tracing the fabric. "Surely not their Vanquish II?"

Benedetti beams. "We were fortunate to secure one of the final lengths released—enough for a single suit. Two hundred and fifty grams. Midnight blue, so that it photographs far more richly than black. I had another client consider it recently for his husband…" He hesitates, just long enough. "But he has not committed. So I would be pleased to offer it to you instead, Signor Clemenza."

"Then there's no question. I must have that," he says casually—and then catches himself, mouth snapping shut as he finally remembers his place.

His eyes slide to me, wondering if I noticed.

"You were saying?" I prompt him.

"Nothing at all. I'm just the dress-up doll, right? My opinion doesn't matter." He laughs as he says it, and Benedetti laughs as well.

As though it's a joke.

Benedetti turns to me expectantly. "The choice is yours, Mr. Orsini."

Smooth bastard. I pick up the sample. Imagine it lying over the Clemenza's body, soft and supple.

"It's not traditional," I hedge, because I've just seen the tiny price tag on the back of the sample. "I've never seen a tux made out of something like this."

"It is true, the Vanquish II is more delicate than the heavier cloths usually chosen for formal wear. It drapes beautifully, but it will show wear sooner." Benedetti pauses. "And of course, it is a *very* premium product."

Meaning that it's too good for the likes of me. "Use it," I bite out.

The tailor packs up his tools, but before he leaves, he turns to the Clemenza one last time. "It was truly a pleasure seeing you again, Signor Clemenza," he says, and he fucking means it. He turns to me and gives a slight nod of the head. "Mr. Orsini."

The little prince's smile is radiant despite his nakedness, despite the cage, despite everything. "Thank you for your time, Lorenzo. I've enjoyed myself very much."

After Benedetti leaves with a promise of miracles, the Clemenza leans over to take up the robe once more.

I reach over to snatch it away from him. "You won't need that. It's back to the basement for you."

He just gives an elegant shrug and walks ahead of me to the elevator, still naked, still caged, still carrying himself like royalty even in defeat. I feel my desire and my hatred for him crystallizing into something beautifully vicious.

Caligula Clemenza is desperately in need of correction.

And I am going to take pleasure in providing it.

CHAPTER 20
DAMIANO

IN THE ELEVATOR, I lean in close enough to smell his skin, stinking of the soaps and shampoos that *I've* provided for him. "Enjoy your little reunion?"

"Very much." His eyes meet mine in the mirror. "It's a pleasure to be reminded that there are still civilized people in New York."

When the elevator reaches the basement, I place my hand on his lower back and push him forward—not rough, but not gentle, either. "Now you're back where you belong, golden boy."

"Indeed," he says with a laugh. "Back in this sad attempt to own someone else's legacy."

It's the amusement that gets to me. "Are you laughing at me?"

He turns and gives me a long, insolent stare. "Why, I'd never dare," he drawls.

I step closer. "Did you enjoy your little performance up there? Playing prince for your precious *Lorenzo* while wearing my cage around your cock?"

"That's the difference between us, Orsini. I don't have to

play at being anything. I am who I am. Nothing will change that, no matter how far into the gutter I fall."

I want to drag him down to my level. Make him roll around in that gutter and *enjoy* it. "You think you impressed him with your good breeding and fancy fabric knowledge? All that tailor saw was a whore in chains desperate enough to spread his legs for someone like me."

"I haven't spread my legs for you, though, have I? Makes me wonder if you're having a little trouble downstairs."

I've got no hang-ups about that, so the arrow goes wide. "I don't dip my dick in poison. But since you enjoyed performing for an audience so much, maybe I *should* invite the tailor back. Give him a real show. Let him see exactly what kind of services you provide these days. Give him a turn, too?"

He gives a theatrical sigh. "I'm sorry I wasn't properly humiliated. I'll try to grovel better next time. Can I go back to sleep now, or—"

I cross the room before he can finish, fast enough that he actually backs away—one step, two—before I seize his arm and drag him to the bed. I sit, haul him across my lap, and ignore his startled cry.

"We have unfinished business, Caligula Clemenza."

"What the hell are you—"

"You heard what I said," I tell him calmly, even as my hand comes down hard across his ass and his whole body jolts. The shock of it travels through him into me, so that I feel it in my thighs, in my palm, in the pretty bloom of pink that spreads across his skin. "That little toy between your legs belongs to *me*. Sometimes I might decorate it for company, like I did today."

Another strike, harder, lower, catching the crease where

his ass meets his thigh. He cries out, but his back arches, pushing into it even as he tries to squirm away.

"Sometimes I might even play with it myself."

Another slap, this time across the backs of his thighs, where the skin is thinner and the sting much sharper. He hisses through his teeth.

"But whatever I choose to do with it, it's still mine. When you're alone. When I'm showing you off. It's *mine,* and you don't touch it without permission—like you did this morning." I give him the hardest spank yet, full palm across both cheeks, and he thrashes in my lap. "You need to learn your lesson, golden boy."

"Please—I'm sorry—I won't—" His words dissolve into a moan as I strike again at his reddened flesh. Heat radiates from his skin, and his muscles tense and release with each blow. The sounds he makes are desperate as he writhes around in my lap.

I pause, running my palm over the hot skin of his ass, feeling him tremble. His breathing is fast and shallow, and when I flick hard at a particularly red spot, he whimpers.

"You want to do better, don't you?" I tell him. "And you're learning. Aren't you? Learning to be sorry."

Another sharp slap, and his whole body jolts. This time I don't miss the way his hips grind down against my leg, seeking friction that he won't be able to find, thanks to the cock cage.

"Yes," he pants out. "I'm sorry!"

"Sorry. For. *What*?" I punctuate each word with another spank. His skin is crimson now, hot to the touch, and each impact draws increasingly frantic sounds from his throat. "For touching what's mine without permission? For showing off in front of Benedetti like you still matter? For forgetting that you're my property now?"

His hips are moving now in a rhythm that has nothing

to do with escape. His ass pushes up to meet each blow, red and hot under my palm, and the sounds he's making have changed. Longer. Deeper. Sweat is glistening in the small of his back and his hands twist in the bedsheet as another moan tears from his throat.

He goes rigid across my lap.

And I feel a hot flood soaking into my pants.

For one second, I think he's pissed himself. But then a familiar and more welcome smell rises up…and I'm genuinely shocked. He came. From being spanked. While wearing a cage.

His body took all of that sensation and turned it into an orgasm.

And I'm so hard it's painful.

This is not how it was supposed to go. But underneath the shock, something else rears up—hot, possessive, *proud*. I just pulled sounds out of Caligula Clemenza that no one else has ever heard. His orgasm happened under *my* hand. Whatever that reaction was, it belongs to me alone.

"Well," I say, forcing my voice level as my cock begs for attention in my now-damp pants. "We're making progress. You *are* learning your place, aren't you? Even enjoying the lesson." I run my palm over his hot skin as he shakes in my lap. "You *should* enjoy it, golden boy. It suits you."

He scrambles away from me the instant I release him, flattening himself up against the wall. His shoulders heave as he sucks in air, and his eyes are closed.

Just as well. Gives me a second to pull myself together.

"Nothing to say?" I ask, standing and straightening my clothes, giving a *tsk* of disgust at the mess he's made of my pants. "No clever comebacks?"

The Clemenza doesn't respond, doesn't even open his eyes.

"Look at me."

A sliver of honey appears between cracked lids. His gaze slides over me, up to my face.

"You forgot your manners along with your place," I say. "Now tell me: what are you?"

A long pause. "Your property," he says at last, cold as ice.

"Good boy. And what do you say when someone teaches you a lesson in respect?"

Another pause, even longer this time. But his voice is steady when he finally speaks. "Thank you, Damiano. You've taught me a lesson I won't soon forget."

I should put that collar back around his neck, but there's something dangerous in his eyes that gives me pause. And the smell of him is all over me, soap and sweat and sex, making my head swim. I need to get out of here.

I turn and walk toward the elevator, but each step feels like I'm moving through molasses. My reflection in the polished metal doors looks unfamiliar—disheveled, wild-eyed, my cock an all-too-visible hard line in my pants.

The elevator button is right there. All I have to do is push it. But my hand hovers over the controls.

What the fuck is wrong with me? I *wanted* to punish him. Bring him back into line, remind him of his place. And I did. But watching him fall apart, hearing him moan under my hands, feeling him spill in my lap—

He's a virgin. Every experience he's had so far has been a first for him. Maybe he doesn't know that pain can turn into pleasure. Maybe he doesn't know that what happened to him was perfectly—

No. I won't be manipulated by his inexperience any more than I was by his attempts at seduction.

I punch the button, step into the elevator, and leave him alone.

Anything else would be an unacceptable loss of control.

CHAPTER 21
DAMIANO

THE COMPLETED tux is delivered the next afternoon, and I send it down to the basement in the dumbwaiter along with shoes, shirt, cufflinks, and everything else required to transform my prisoner back into a prince.

I'm tempted to watch him getting ready, but I don't. I've left him alone again since his punishment, unwilling to let him become even more of a distraction. But when I finally go down to collect the Clemenza for the evening, I wish I'd given myself a preview, because I freeze. Just for a second. Because…damn.

He's sitting in his grandfather's study, the first time he's been able to reach the reconstructed rooms since he's been down here, settled on the leather couch like he never left it. He looks bored and irritated, as if he's been kept waiting for a car. He stands only when I start walking toward him, shrugging the satin-lapelled jacket into place with a movement so unconscious that it has to be muscle memory.

Gone is the desperate fugitive. Gone is the arrogant, gold-covered statue who raised the auction price by insulting bidders. Gone, too, is the hostage I spanked into spilling yesterday.

In his place stands a striking young man who might catch my eye in any other circumstances. He's in his element, standing there in the memory of his Family's empire. The tuxedo skims his body, Benedetti's craftsmanship evident in every line. The bronze-gold hair is tamed, combed back from his angular face. And those Clemenza eyes gleam yellow as a jungle cat's.

"You're staring," he says flatly.

"You look…expensive," I reply, because every other word that went through my head was the wrong one.

"I *am* expensive. You established that yourself at the auction." The words might be spiteful, but there's dignity in his voice again. Pride. He *knows* how good he looks, and he's not going to apologize for it. "So, am I being auctioned off again tonight, or hung off your arm like a designer accessory?"

I cross to him quickly, but he doesn't back away this time. I catch his chin between my fingers and tip his face up. "Since you ask, I'll be showing you off. Tonight, *everyone* will see what belongs to me."

He doesn't look away. Doesn't flinch.

And I'm not sure which one of us has the upper hand right now. Time to fix that. "Open your pants."

His hand drifts down slowly, but he does it, opens them up and stands there motionless as I pull out his junk. Only it's not junk, is it? Not on Caligula Clemenza. Not the word to use for a pricey little fuck like him.

I take the cage off and tuck him back in. "Tonight you need to act like a free man," I tell him. "That's my order. Make sure you follow it."

"Where are we going?" is all he asks.

The Metropolitan Opera House is not my favorite place to be in this city. I'm not an opera fan. Neither is Big Gee, but I'm following his orders, proving to New York that Caligula Clemenza is alive and well, proving that I'm still a loyal Giuliano.

Proving that everything's real fucking rosy.

Vito drives us over in the dark-windowed town car, the Clemenza sitting next to me in the back and staring resolutely at the view the whole time. When we pull up, Vito lets me out first, and then I turn and offer my hand to Caligula Clemenza, pulling him out into the flash of cameras and the sharp eyes of the city. And the moment he steps out of the car, I see the shift again. His shoulders square, his hand is firm in mine, and his smile is effortless. Charming.

He's at home here.

It's opening night for the season's run of *The Magic Flute*. Important people are going to be here: the Boss of every major Family, plus their entourages. And aside from them, a bunch of worthless socialites are here too. When we enter the foyer, heads turn. Whispers follow.

"Is that Caligula Clemenza?"

"I thought he was dead..."

"Who's that brute with him?"

I clench my teeth to keep from reacting. But it's true, isn't it? Even in my own Lorenzo Benedetti tux, I can't be mistaken for anything but what I am. A brute. A monster.

A fucking animal.

I keep my hand on the Clemenza's lower back. Guiding. Warning. He walks beside me with that same carriage Lorenzo Benedetti commented on, every inch the blue blood he was raised to be. And the vultures circle.

Salvatore Rossi, head of the Rossi Family, is the first to come over, accompanied by his wife and grandkids, all about the same age as the Clemenza—and they know him. Ask politely how he's keeping, as if they don't all know.

The little prince lies perfectly. "I've made a powerful and generous friend," he tells them. "Damiano has been very kind."

A public endorsement from the Clemenza, offered to important witnesses. And he says it warmly enough that anyone listening would believe it.

I should be pleased.

Instead, I feel the leash slipping through my fingers.

Then we run the gauntlet of the Alessi Boss, and *his* wife and grandkids. Big Gee gives me a nod of approval nearby. Seb's with him. I hoped he wouldn't be, since we didn't leave things great last time we met up, and then I leaned too heavy on those Red Hook fuckers.

He hasn't noticed me yet, so I turn my back on him before he can. Luca D'Amato and the designer dick-sleeve he calls his husband are talking with their flunkies across the room.

The Clemenza's expression changes the instant he follows my gaze and spots the Morelli Don. I know that look. Seen it in the mirror enough times. It's the face of a man haunted by the ghost of a murder.

Of course—D'Amato killed old Lou Clemenza. I actually forgot about that, I've been so focused on my own shit with Big Gee. My hand goes to the Clemenza's arm, wraps around it, and for a second I consider steering him straight over to the Morelli corner.

Now *that* would hurt him. Making him smile and play nice with his grandfather's murderer. Making him shake the hand that pulled the trigger.

Fuck.

I pull him in the opposite direction before I think too

hard about why. He tenses but doesn't break stride, doesn't give those assholes the satisfaction of seeing any weakness.

I'm almost proud of him.

Our box is stuffed full of red velvet and gold filigree that reminds me of the cage I took off him earlier. An elderly couple occupies the box beside ours, the woman dripping in old-fashioned pearls, the man in evening wear that's probably seen a score of opera seasons. The moment they spot the Clemenza coming into the box, the woman gasps audibly.

"Caligula Clemenza! My heavens, child, I haven't seen you since that party at the Pierre. How are you?"

"Mrs. DuPont," the Clemenza replies with charm, his smile warm and genuine. "You look radiant tonight."

They chat with easy familiarity, and the way he slides back into this world like he never left it only makes things worse. I'm the one who told him to act like a free man tonight. He's only doing what I told him. But he's so *easy* with all of it, belongs in a way I never will. These people are *his* people. This world was built for someone exactly like him.

And me? To these folks, I'm new money with a gun collection, and that's all I'll ever be.

"Sit," I growl.

He does as I command, settling into the seat without so much as glancing my way, lavishing all his attention on the old biddy in the next box.

But *I* want his attention. His focus. His submission.

Mrs. DuPont, whoever the fuck she is, continues chattering about mutual acquaintances, charity boards, summer in the Hamptons. The Clemenza says all the right things back, mentioning people I've never heard of.

The lights dim. The orchestra begins to swell. Caligula Clemenza and his new best friend whisper their last whispers. He shifts to face the stage.

And I reach over, slow and deliberate.

My hand finds his thigh first, palm flat against the expensive fabric that's just as soft as I remember. He goes rigid. My fingers find his fly, working the buttons free.

His sharp intake of breath is barely audible over the music, but I hear it. Feel it. He tries to grab my wrist but I catch his hand, pin it against the velvet armrest. "What's rule number one?" I hiss.

He tries to pull free again.

"Don't," I warn softly. "You'll make a scene. And wouldn't that be embarrassing for the Clemenza name?"

I let him go. He doesn't move his hand from the armrest, though his jaw twitches as my hand slips inside his pants. He's not wearing underwear because I didn't send any down with the tux earlier today. I wrap my fingers around his flesh, feel him start to harden despite himself.

"You fucking asshole," he breathes, so quietly only I can hear.

"You should watch your mouth," I murmur, stroking him slow and steady. "What would Mrs. DuPont think?"

Within seconds, he's wet at the tip. His body knows who owns it even when his mind rebels. On stage, some guy begins to sing, his voice bouncing through the place, keeping every eye fixed, every ear occupied.

And in our private box, I work the Clemenza into rock hardness, pulling base to tip, twisting on the upstroke, using his own pre-cum as lubrication.

I ease up at last, let my fingers trace the thick vein on his underside, and he presses his lips together hard. He's trying to stay perfectly still, trying to pretend this isn't happening. But he's leaking in my palm, a flush creeping up his neck. He's fighting a war with himself, and my hand on his cock is becoming the only thing he cares about.

The opera continues. Some lady comes out and starts wailing. The whole room is lost to her.

But not my little prince. His whole world has shrunk to my hand on his dick.

I experiment a little. Rub into his slit and see him shudder. Drag a blunt nail across the sensitive skin underneath the crown and hear his breath catch—pain or pleasure? I think it's both. His head is tipped back against his high-backed seat, showing the long, golden line of his throat, and I want to bite him there. Leave a mark for everyone to see.

"Enjoying the show?" I whisper.

His hips twitch forward, a desperate, involuntary movement. He hates me for it. I feel it in the way he's tensed every muscle in his body, in the way he won't look at me. He hates me, but he can't deny what my touch is doing to him.

And he's close.

"What do you say?" I murmur. "You want to show all these rich folks who you really belong to? Mess up your new tux right here in the middle of the Met?"

His thighs tense. "Not here. I can't—not with—"

"Can't?" I lean close, lips at his ear. "You came across my lap yesterday from nothing but my hand on your ass. Didn't even need to be touched. Just a little pain and my voice, and you gushed like it was the first time anyone ever made you feel good." I twist my wrist slowly. "At least this time you've got a hand on your cock."

The sound he makes—bitten off, swallowed, forced back down his throat—is the hottest thing I've ever heard. I could shoot myself just from the sound of it.

I *could* make him pop. I could bring him right to the brink and then shove a hand over his mouth so no one else hears him while I push him over the edge.

He seizes the velvet armrest, knuckles white. He's breathing in short, sharp bursts, trying so hard not to give me the satisfaction of hearing him moan. The singing on stage has faded to an instrumental break, and the quiet in the auditorium is a weapon in my hands.

I reach down to squeeze his nuts, not too hard—but not soft, either. Just enough to make him jump. "You like that? Getting your balls played with in public?"

He shakes his head, a tiny, miserable movement. "Go to hell."

"My home away from home." I keep fondling that tight little sack, wondering what it would be like to suck on his stones, or have them vibrating under my chin while I eat out that luscious virgin hole…

Fuck. I need to stay in control. I can't lose myself to this. To *him*. I grasp for anger again, find it buried under a haze of lust.

And I keep pushing him. I keep him hard and dribbling all through the first act until the music on stage swells into something dramatic. The audience is captivated, so I work him faster, the sounds muffled by the orchestra. He's trembling, a thin sheen of sweat at his temples, and his hands grip the armrests so tight he might break them off.

"Please," he whispers. "Dami, *please*—"

"Please what, little prince?"

"I'm going to—" The music rises to a climax.

And I stop.

I tuck him back into his trousers, button him back up, and smooth over that fancy fabric he just *had* to have. It's like nothing happened, except that he's still hard.

And so am I.

The first act ends to thunderous applause, and as it dies away, I turn to him and straighten his bow tie. "There we go," I tell him softly. "No one but me will know. Not unless I decide to let New York in on your dirty little secret: that you *enjoy* being treated like this."

He's flushed, trembling, beautiful in his frustrated need. His eyes are glassy with want and humiliation. He's…

Perfect.

The lights come up for intermission. Mrs. DuPont turns to us with bright eyes. "Wasn't that absolutely marvelous?"

The Clemenza's smile is flawless. No one would guess I just spent over an hour edging him. "Breathtaking," he agrees. "I've never had an experience like it."

I smother an unwilling snort of laughter.

"You wanna get a drink?" I ask once the DuPonts have left their box and the house is emptying below. "Or would you prefer I finish you off with the lights up? Let you spray your spunk all over the cheap seats below us?"

The look he gives me could melt steel. "Champagne sounds delightful. And isn't that why we're here? So you can show me off to your betters?"

He barely flinches when I slide a hand into his hair and tug hard, not caring who sees this time.

But he's right, isn't he? These people with their old money and inherited culture, their casual entitlement and generational power—they *are* better than me, in every way that matters to this glittering world.

But they're not better than *him*.

That's his message.

I let his hair go and run my fingers through it, smoothing out the waves. "Sure," I say. "Let's go parade you around."

"Wonderful." He rises, adjusting the gold and diamond

cufflinks I provided for him. "It's been a long time since I've had stimulating company."

I follow him into the hallway outside the box, watch him greet some rich asshole I don't know with a smile that lights up his whole face.

I pull him close and drop my voice as soon as we have a moment alone. "You're showing off again, little prince. And you know what that means."

I feel his shiver and smile to myself. But I hope he keeps pushing. Hope he keeps punching all my buttons, hard as he can.

Because when we get home tonight, I swear to God I will make him pay for every moment he tried to make me feel small.

CHAPTER 22
CALIGULA

I'M POKING THE BEAR.

I suspected it when Sal Rossi approached us and greeted me first, Damiano second. I confirmed it when he got annoyed at my talking to Ambassador DuPont's wife, who gasped out my name with delight but didn't even ask for his.

The Met's chandeliers shine like captured stars above us, and the fabric of my brand-new tuxedo feels liquid against my skin. I haven't felt like myself in years. But right now, surrounded by the glittering elite of New York, I feel…

Dangerous. Alive. Powerful.

And I am going to poke this bear until he roars.

Even if it means he's going to spank me again. Even if it means I can't sit comfortably for a week—and God knows the opera house seats aren't exactly cushiony-soft against my still-smarting skin.

I've *never* been touched like that. And I shouldn't have liked it. God, I *really* shouldn't have liked it. Still can't believe how I responded.

Self-preservation. That's what I told myself it was.

I wish I could believe the lie. But when Damiano's hand

came down on my skin, telling me what I was, who I belonged to—something inside me just...broke open. Or maybe broke apart.

Either way, I came from being spanked like a misbehaving child, and the humiliation of that should have eaten me alive.

Should have.

Instead, all I could think about for hours after he left was the weight of his hand, the heat in his voice, the way he seemed genuinely shocked that my body had responded to him like that.

Which is fucked up on about seventeen different levels.

And the really twisted part is, I want him to do it again. I want to push him until that control cracks, until he puts his hands on me and—

"Caligula, how *wonderful* to see you," a Vanderbilt widow coos, appearing at my elbow with champagne and curiosity. "We heard such terrible rumors. Thank God you're alive!"

Next to me, Damiano's presence is difficult to ignore—but I do my best. I *feel* his fury burning through his clothes as he glares at the white-haired woman, and she smiles at me and me alone, like he doesn't even exist.

These people see my social worth. Half of them see *him* as some hired bodyguard. The ones in the know? They just see the beast who bought me.

And I plan to relish every second of his discomfort.

"Rumors of my demise were greatly exaggerated," I tell Mrs. Vanderbilt with a charming smile.

"But your cousin—?" she asks delicately.

"A tragedy," I tell her, clipped. And I move on, Damiano trailing in my wake now. The crowd parts and flows around me like water, and whispers follow. They're a vicious lot, the New York elite. Few of those whispers are complimentary, toward me or the man shadowing me. But every murmur, every sideways glance, every moment of recognition that bypasses Damiano entirely—I feel it feeding the beast behind me.

And my soul rejoices.

"Cal!"

I turn and see Jesse Foster gliding toward me through the crowd, his arm threaded through that of an older man I also, unfortunately, recognize.

Daniel King.

Jesse's smile is radiant. "You look amazing." His voice drops to an intimate whisper, eyes inquisitive. "How's the arrangement working out?"

It's a struggle, but I keep my expression perfectly pleasant. "I didn't expect to see you here, Jesse. How are you?"

Jesse grins with delight. Daniel King gives me a nod and then stares at Damiano.

I should have realized back at the Obelisk, of course. But I only see it now. *Daniel King* is Jesse's "owner," the one who pays his tabs, the one to whom Jesse signed over ten years of his life. If I'd realized back then, would I still have agreed to the auction?

Probably.

So what does it really matter?

We exchange pleasantries for exactly the right amount of time—long enough to be polite, short enough to avoid running out of small talk. When they drift away toward the bar, I feel rather than see Damiano move closer.

A sense of unreality settles over me as he leans down to speak in my ear. "For such a parasite, Jesse Foster passes well for a human being."

I'm not sure I want to know the answer, but the question comes out before I can think it through. "What do you mean?"

He sounds almost pitying. "Don't you get it yet? Your buddy Jesse gets a commission for every desperate he delivers to auction. He wasn't helping you survive, golden boy. He was selling you out."

I shouldn't be surprised. But somehow, I am.

Still, never show weakness in public. I turn to look Damiano dead in the eye when I respond. "Then you've taught me another valuable lesson, Dami."

"And what's that, little prince?"

"That I have no one left to trust."

Something flashes in his dark eyes. He grabs me hard, and drives me backward.

Shit. I pushed too far. He's lost it; he's going to shove me up against a wall, or drag me into a bathroom and—

But there's a scream. *More* screams, yelling, shouting—

Men are flocking toward us. Bodyguards and security guards and even Luca D'Amato, with cold fury in his strange, pale blue eyes.

For a second I think they're coming for *me*. That this is it: my fate will be appropriately classical. I'm going to be torn apart by a frenzied crowd.

But then Damiano locks his arms around me and hugs me to his chest. We're moving—or he is, anyway, my feet dangling helplessly as he hauls me straight to the entrance, shouldering aside anyone who comes close.

And over that massive shoulder, I see all those men are still occupied, doing *something* to *someone* there on the floor…

"Move!" Damiano roars, and people scatter around us like leaves.

I'm pressed so hard against him that I can feel his heart hammering against mine, can smell his now-familiar scent, can smell something new—something coppery.

We're back in the car before I know it, the driver taking off from the curb like he's in Formula 1.

Damiano's hands pat me all over. "Are you hurt?"

"No?" I look down at myself, bewildered to see dark red smeared across my white shirt. "I didn't see...what happened?"

He's still checking me all over, patting me down, turning me this way and that. "You have blood on you."

"So do you," I point out thickly. "Jesus, you're bleeding—"

"I'm fine."

"You're not fine, you're—"

"I said I'm fine!" He snarls it with such finality that I shut up, but now that I've pointed it out, he's looking at his own arm, at the torn opening in his tuxedo jacket along his bicep, the dark fabric soaked wet through with...

Blood. It's dripping right down his sleeve, sliding down his fingers onto the leather seats.

"You need a hospital—" I begin.

"No."

The car takes the next corner so hard that it throws me back into Damiano's arms, and he wraps them around me at once.

"You're *bleeding*," I say again. I wrap my hands hard around the cut along his arm, since apparently he's happy to exsanguinate in the back of the car. "What happened?"

"Someone came at you," he says, and his arms tighten around me, squeezing hard. "But you're safe."

Safe.

And despite the hot blood seeping out from between my fingers, I believe him. Despite the fact that he was jacking me off in public, despite the creepy fucking basement and the collar and the cock cage...

I actually do feel safe with Damiano Orsini.

When we get home, everything transforms. Literally. Damiano hustles me inside and then activates a setting on the security panel right there in the foyer.

Steel shutters slam down over windows. Locks engage all over the house—deadbolts, security bars, enough reinforcement to withstand a siege. The house becomes a fortress in seconds, sealing us in like a tomb.

Damiano keeps me close as we move through corridors he didn't show me during that house tour the first night. His good arm is wrapped around me, practically carrying me. We hurry down a discreet set of stairs I don't remember seeing before, and then he's leading me into a kitchen that smells like rosemary focaccia.

He stabs his finger at an intercom and barks, "Rosa!"

He strips off his jacket and then his shirt, elbowing me away when I try to help. A woman appears a minute later, steel-colored hair mussed from sleep, robe hastily belted. When she sees the blood, her expression doesn't change. She just comes over to inspect the wound.

"I'll call Darla," she says.

"No."

She simply nods at Damiano's refusal and disappears, returning with a medical kit that looks…comprehensive. This is not the first time she's dealt with something like this.

I sit in stunned silence, watching this "Rosa" inspect the cut. The wound is deep but clean—three inches across his bicep. If it had been higher, across his throat, or lower, slicing open his belly…

Rosa threads a needle and I wince in anticipation. But Damiano doesn't even flinch as she begins sewing him up. He just watches *me* with those dark eyes.

I have no idea what he's thinking.

When Rosa finishes, she puts a large patch over it and winds a bandage around his sizeable bicep. Then she steps back and surveys her handiwork with satisfaction. "We'll clean it twice daily. No heavy lifting for a week."

"My ink'll be all messed up with a scar," he grumbles.

"You shouldn't be disrespecting your body with tattoos in the first place." She pats his uninjured shoulder like he's a wayward nephew, then fixes me with a stern look, taking in my blood-stiffening shirt front. "You need to shower. Come."

It's not a suggestion.

And weirdly, Damiano just troops behind as I follow Rosa, who marches out of the kitchen, beckoning me to hurry. When we reach the stairs, my legs feel unsteady, and Damiano puts his good arm around me again, practically lifting me up the steps. I want to tell him not to, remind him that *he's* the one who's injured, but I don't. I need his steady arm too much.

Someone came at me tonight.

It's still happening. Someone still wants me dead.

We emerge eventually on the fifth floor, Damiano not even slightly out of breath despite half-carrying me the whole way, and then we go down another hallway. In front of a particular door, Rosa gives Damiano one last meaningful glare before disappearing back down the corridor.

We're alone. He pushes open the door, reaches in to snap on the light, and gives me an ironic wave in.

Oh, fuck. This is *his* room. His bedroom.

Dark wood. Thick carpet. A bed so big I could get lost in it, and floor-to-ceiling windows that are currently covered with steel shutters. Damiano sits on the side of the bed, and for the first time tonight, he looks tired. Wrecked, actually.

More human than I've ever seen him.

"Go shower," he says without looking at me. "You're covered in my blood."

I am. It's sticky on my hands, soaked into my shirt, probably in my hair. The metallic scent of it wafts with me into the attached bathroom, where I strip out of my formal wear and step under the water.

But even as the red swirls down the drain, I can't wash away the memory. The way he moved without hesitation. The way he put his body between danger and mine like it was instinct.

Like I was *worth* protecting.

When I emerge with one of his soft, fluffy towels wrapped around my waist, he's settled on the bed, propped against pillows in nothing but black briefs, the white bandage on his arm stark against his inked skin. Brooding and beautiful and bleeding for me.

I stand there dripping. Staring.

"What are you looking at?" he growls.

"The man who saved my life."

He scoffs. "I told you no one would hurt you under my watch. I meant it."

"I know. I know that now."

The silence stretches. And then I drop the towel.

He takes in my naked body—every part of me, and the faint marks he's left on my skin with his chains and his hands.

I cross to the bed, climb onto the mattress, and straddle his hips. He just watches me do it. I brace my hands on either side of his head.

His eyes are black fire, but he doesn't stop me.

I lean down until my breath ghosts across his lips, wondering if he'll let me kiss him, but he moves his head away in mute refusal. But that's all he does, and when I trail my fingers down the ridge between his pecs, down to that oversized six-pack, he doesn't grab my wrist. Doesn't say anything. I let my hand hover right above those black briefs and I keep waiting.

He reaches up and traces my bottom lip with his thumb.

"If you're gonna do it," he says, voice rough as gravel, "then get on with it."

My heart clangs in my ribs as I slide back on his thighs, hands literally shaking as I hook my fingers in the waistband of his briefs. He lifts his hips to help, and then he's bare before me.

Christ.

I didn't really get a good look at him that time before. Turns out he must've been half-hidden by his clothes still, because seeing him in all his glory…

He's huge. Thick and hard and intimidating as hell. And I want to prove something to him. To myself.

I lean forward and take just the head into my mouth. He sucks in a breath and I push down—

It's too much. I gag, pull back, try again. My technique is still clumsy as hell, but I'm persistent. Working my tongue around the crown, fighting my jaw's protests, determined.

Then his hands are on me, lifting, repositioning.

Suddenly I'm turned head to toe, set on my side, his mouth hot against my thighs as he rearranges us in a tangle of limbs and feeds me his cock once more. But then—oh, fuck, he's pulling my legs open, burying his face between my asscheeks, and his tongue is pushing into my hole.

I choke on his cock, my entire body arching like I've been electrified. He doesn't stop for a second, devouring me with tongue and lips and the careful scrape of teeth that has me shaking apart.

He's hurt. He's bleeding. And he's eating me alive like he owns every inch of my skin.

And I—I *want* this. Want *him*. I try to return the favor, to take him deeper, but his mouth is destroying my ability to think. Every swipe, every suck, every insistent stab of his tongue makes my rational mind retreat a little more.

Because he meant it. He really meant it. He'll keep me *safe*. Damiano Orsini took a knife meant for me. He's going to have that scar for the rest of his life.

And that makes me more *his* than anything he's done to me so far.

CHAPTER 23
DAMIANO

HIS MOUTH IS SLOPPY.

Clumsy.

Fucking incredible.

Caligula Clemenza is choking me down as well as he can, all that snotty pride of his stripped away. I've got one hand buried in the sunset mess of his hair, the other gripping his thigh to keep his asshole speared on my tongue. He's panting through his nose, lips stretched wide around my cock, working like he's got something to prove.

I guess he does, after what I said last time. Pretending how bad he was… I mean, he wasn't great. But it didn't matter. It didn't matter one goddamn bit, it was still the most erotic fucking thing I've ever felt.

This time is better. Because this time, it really *does* feel like respect. My royal fucking reward for bleeding for him.

He tries to take me deeper, gagging again, and I bite back a grunt. This…oh, this wasn't the plan. If I used his body, I was supposed to use it *against* him. I wasn't supposed to worship at his asshole like a fucking shrine. But here I am, eating him out like he's the most delicious thing I've ever tasted…

Because he is.

I ease up my hand on the back of his head and let him catch his breath, then push him down again. Slow. Deliberate. His hips twitch as I tongue into him with deep stabs that make him whimper around my cock. He's drizzling all over me, his dick hot as a brand where it's pressed into my chest.

He's got the kind of body made to be used like this, tight in all the right places. And the sounds he makes—*fuck*.

"I didn't say stop," I tell him when he hesitates.

He tries again. More spit, more suction, more of that amateur enthusiasm that makes my balls throb. He's a mess, and I'm getting lost in the wet slide of him, the heat of him.

I want to fuck him.

I focus on eating him out instead. Fingertips digging into the muscle of his ass, spreading him open for me. He's so fucking tight back there, that little knot clenching and unclenching around my tongue like it's begging for something thicker. I drive a finger into him, work him open while I feast on him, licking and sucking and fucking him with my tongue, my fingers. He's writhing against me, hot as a furnace inside, slick with my spit, that tight muscle strangling whatever I put in there. He cries out, a choked, helpless sound that vibrates right down my shaft to my balls.

And pretty soon, I get what I was hoping for when he pulls away, panting into my hip.

"Please." He's flushed and sweaty, voice ragged as he lifts his head to look down at me. "Dami, I want you—inside me. I need it. Please."

A second passes. Then two.

He's trembling—whether from exhaustion or anticipation, I can't tell. When I look down at him, his face is damp, the gold darkening to bronze in the strands stuck to his forehead. I spread a hand over his head and push him back down. "Finish what you started."

He obeys. Caligula Clemenza doesn't know what the fuck he's doing, but he still wants to do it right. Wants to be *good* at it. He's learning to crave what he should fear.

He's also learning that submission can be a kind of power. And I'm the damn fool teaching him.

I pull out of his throat and flip him around right side up, pinning him to the bed under me. He's limp, pliant, submissive. "Say it again."

His lashes flutter. "What?"

"Say it again," I growl. "What did you beg me for?"

He swallows. Licks his lips. "I want you to fuck me." A beat. His voice drops. "Please, Dami."

I chuckle. "Told you you'd be begging for my cock one day."

And there it is. That look. Like I slapped him right across the face, like he's fucking *surprised* at my viciousness. His pink flush of exertion deepens to something closer to shame, and his eyes cut away from mine. The mood shifts fast, glass shattering under pressure. And seeing him flinch away from my cruelty feels like swallowing all those glass shards.

I sit back on my heels and watch him. The rise and fall of his chest. The tremor in his fingers. He's still hard and leaking, that cute toy between his legs crying out for attention. The golden eyes are hazy, his face flushed. His mouth is swollen, lips puffy and red from working my cock. He looks fucking destroyed, and I haven't even started with him. But there's no way I'll give him what he begged for. Not tonight.

Not after what I just said to him.

Anyway, I paid ten million dollars for that virgin ass. As

long as I don't fuck it, I've still got me a virgin. But he needs something from me. And Christ, I want to give him something…

I can't fuck him.

I push two fingers into his mouth and press down on his tongue until he starts to suck. He blinks at me, dazed, but does what I want, sucking them in deep, licking between them. I pull my hand back, and his mouth tries to follow. He's so eager. So *easy*.

He watches my hand drop, a little crease between his brows when I bypass his dick. "Spread your legs," I tell him.

They fall open. *Wide* open. I watch his face as I circle his hole, then push both fingers into him at once, the way slick and easy from all the spit I've worked into him. Those honey eyes go wide, a low moan escaping him.

"Does that hurt, golden boy?" I ask.

"No, no, no." His voice is thin. He shakes his head, and his hands clutch at the sheets. "Don't stop. Please. Don't stop." His cock rolls across his belly, leaving a silver trail that shows me exactly how much he likes what I'm doing to him.

I work him slowly. Teasing. Coaxing. I keep my fingers deep inside him, twisting them, curling them, until he's rocking against my hand. Until he's grinding on them, desperate for more.

It's a beautiful fucking sight. "Look at you," I murmur. "That virgin ass, taking it so well."

"Please. I'll beg if you want me to, I swear to God—"

"Be quiet," I tell him. "You take what I give you. And you're grateful for it. Aren't you?"

He nods frantically. A minute later, instinct takes over, and he tries to reach down and grab himself. I slap his hand away. "Are you fucking serious?" I growl.

"S-sorry," he hisses.

"You touch it without permission, I'll put it back in a cage." He grips the sheets instead. His face twists, and he whimpers. "Shhh." I push another finger inside him. Three now. Stretching him wider. "I'll give you what you need. Just relax."

He's already so fucking close. He's riding my hand, his dick an angry red, his balls tight and high. Usually his face is cold, unreadable, but right now he's wearing a mask of exquisite agony.

"Dami, please," he says, his voice raw.

"Again."

"Please."

"No," I grit out. "My name. Say my name again."

"Dami, please, *please*." He's desperate for it. His voice is broken, and the way he says my name—

"What are you?" I demand.

"Yours," he gasps. "Your property."

Good boys get rewarded. I want him to learn that.

I reach for his dick with my other hand, give it a hard stroke, root to tip, then another and another—and he's done. His eyes roll back in his head, and he shoots, spurting across his belly and chest. His mouth opens in a long, choked groan, and his ass clenches around my fingers so hard my hand could go numb if I leave it in there much longer.

It's not a pretty orgasm. It's messy. Filthy. Loud. His hair is sweat-soaked, his cheeks flushed, his body limp. Totally spent.

And he's never been prettier.

He looks up at me, still panting, and smiles—a slow, sweet smile that doesn't belong on his face right now, and sure as fuck shouldn't be aimed at *me*. I stare back at him, wondering why my heart is pounding so hard.

I roll off the bed and grab the towel he dumped just outside the bathroom door, my dick wagging like a dog tail. It dies down a little as I wipe off my face, and then I turn back to him and clean him up without a word. Wipe away the evidence of what we just did.

He doesn't speak, too fucked-out to do anything much except lie there.

I go wash my hands and face and then come back to bed, settling up against the headboard. He curls into me like a hopeful stray dog who doesn't know if it's welcome or not. I put my arm around him because I've got nowhere else to put it, and the stitch job Rosa did is aching. His breathing evens out, and I swear to God, he's falling asleep in my fucking arms.

I need to return him to the basement. To his proper fucking place.

But…he's still hunted. Still mine to protect. "They won't stop," I say finally.

He gives a little jerk as I yank him off the train to Dreamland, and tilts his sleepy face up toward mine. "Hm?" he mumbles.

"Whoever's cleaning up what's left of the Clemenza mess." I ignore the throbbing pain in my arm as I shift him closer, hold him tighter. "They want you dead, little prince. And they're not going to stop until they finish the job."

I reach up to run my fingers through his hair. It's like damp silk between my fingers. I've enjoyed gathering it up in my fist to hurt him. Now I can't stop stroking it gently, like he might dissolve away if I'm not careful enough.

"You think they'll try again?" he asks at last.

"Yeah." I pause, let him soak in that idea for a minute. "But you belong to me. So I'll stop them, Caligula. I can promise you that."

His eyes flutter closed. "I—" He starts, then pauses.

"What is it?"

"Most people—my friends—they call me 'Cal.'"

"I'm not most people. And I'm definitely not your friend."

He sucks in a breath. "Are you going to put me back in the basement?"

My fingers stall in his hair. Is that what he thinks this is, a reprieve? A temporary escape from his punishment? Maybe he's been playing me tonight, pretending he wanted my dick just so he could sleep up here.

But no one fakes an orgasm like the one he just had.

The basement is secure. Impenetrable. But the thought of him down there alone after what happened tonight…

He's a target. I don't want him anywhere I can't reach him in seconds. "Not tonight," I say. "You're staying here. With me."

His brows lift slightly. "In your room?"

"In my bed." I lean across to grab my phone. It's been blowing up with texts and calls, but they can all wait until tomorrow. I switch into the security app and check every window, every lock, every camera. The house is a fortress around us, and I have enough firepower stashed away to hold off a small army.

"I need to make sure I can protect you," I tell him as I toss it back on the nightstand. "And the best way to do that is to keep you close."

But then I reach out and wrap my hand around his throat. Gently—so gently. Like he's the most fragile porcelain. I could crush his windpipe without effort, but I hold him just firm enough to remind him who owns him. And just soft enough to remind myself that he's priceless.

The last direct Clemenza heir.

"If you think that means you're not still owned…if you think you don't need to obey me at all times…" I apply the barest pressure. Just enough to feel his pulse flutter against my palm. "Or if you think I won't have my revenge, golden boy, you're sorely mistaken."

He doesn't argue. Doesn't test the boundary. He just nods.

"Good boy."

I let go and slide down beside him under the sheets. His breathing's uneven, but not scared. Not anymore. Just alert.

I pull him close and feel him settle against my side.

This definitely wasn't the plan. He was supposed to be my trophy. My victory over everything his Family represented. My gift to my father's ghost.

Now I'm bleeding for him. Letting him sleep in my bed. Giving him orgasms that blow his fucking mind, keeping him warm and fed and wrapped up in soft cotton sheets like he's the final piece of a collection instead of the final piece of my revenge.

Well…I waited twenty-one years for it.

I can wait a little longer.

CHAPTER 24
CALIGULA

I WAKE TO WEIGHT.

A thick arm sprawls over my ribs like a steel beam. A furnace presses tight to my back. And—*oh*—a baseball bat seems to be nestled up against my ass.

Damiano's cock.

He's still asleep, breath slow and steady against my neck. His morning erection grinds lazily into the curve of me with every exhale, like his body already decided what it wants before his brain's online.

I wriggle back just enough to feel the friction, to imagine what it would be like if he woke up and—

Then I remember myself. Remember *him*.

His voice, cruel and mocking. *Told you you'd be begging for my cock one day.*

It was bad enough that he said that. Worse that he proceeded to wring an orgasm out of me I didn't even know my body could provide. Not that intense. Not that *deep*.

I can't even pretend that last night was part of some master plan of mine. I just felt *grateful*, and then a few seconds later, I was…

I hate how easily I gave in to it. Hate how my body betrayed every instinct I have left. And then he didn't even come.

Again.

I pull away from him carefully, turning just enough to see his face. Without the perpetual scowl he wears when awake, he looks younger. Still dangerous, but less like a monster. More like a man who's forgotten how to be one.

Then I notice the bandage on his arm. The gauze is stained through with blood, spreading like spilled red wine across a tablecloth.

He bled for me. No matter what else he did last night, he bled for me.

Of course, he's the one who dragged me out in public and dangled me like bait, so he only has himself to blame in that sense. He said he wanted to show me off, but I didn't get the impression he was enjoying himself.

I sigh out loud. He doesn't stir.

I should be snooping around in his underwear drawer, maybe sneaking out to case a few more rooms so I can find something that will help me find a way to control him. I'm doing okay so far—slept in his bed last night, for example. If only I could make myself believe that attempted blow job was part of my ploy.

The red on the bandage looks bright, which means it's fresh blood. I should wake him and tell him, but I don't move. The guy is an asshole. A dangerous, disturbed, deviant asshole. I should probably be *begging* him to put me back in that basement and just forget about me for the year.

I definitely shouldn't be worried about his bandage.

I slide out from under his arm slowly, careful not to jostle him. My feet hit the floor and I scan the room for something to wear. I can hardly put my tux back on; it's still covered in his blood. I spot his fluffy black robe draped over a chair in the corner and wrap myself up in it. It swallows me up and it smells like him, so that wearing it feels like being claimed all over again.

I have a flash of his fingers in my ass, his hand on my cock, and I give a full-body shiver of pleasure. It gives me pause, though. After last night…am I still a virgin? I don't know what the rules on that are. And I don't care, I remind myself. All I care about right now is doing whatever I need to do to control the dangerous animal currently passed out in bed.

He's still bleeding. There's more red on that bandage now than there was a minute ago.

I don't know how to use all the intercoms and panels that seem to be everywhere in this house, so I guess that just means I'll have to head out and find someone. I can figure out how to get back to the kitchen.

I'm pretty sure I can, anyway…

The hallway stretches before me like a horror movie cliche. To make myself feel less like I'm about to get a jump scare, I check every room that comes off the corridor. They all have the same feeling, the same *look*. Every surface is polished to a mirror shine. Everything is expensive, curated like a magazine shoot. But there are no family photos, no personal touches, just wealth displayed like…

Like armor.

My first impressions were right. This isn't a home. It's a fortress built by someone who trusts no one and loves nothing. Damiano Orsini is a tangled ball of obsession, vengeance, and hatred.

I come across a few locked doors, which are intriguing, and make a mental note to come back to them another time.

But it's actually pretty easy to find the kitchen; I just have to follow my nose. The scent carries me down and down—rosemary, garlic, simmering tomato; sizzling bacon and the suggestion of creamy eggs; fresh-baked bread. It's rich and warm and alive in a way the rest of this mausoleum isn't.

My stomach cramps at the thought of food, too. A sign I should eat something sooner rather than later.

The kitchen feels like the complete opposite of the rest of the house. The steel shutters are still down over the windows, but the lighting is cheerful, warming wooden surfaces and gleaming copper pots. It's lived-in, comfortable—the heart of something that *might* actually be called a home.

A huge pot simmers on the stove, thick red sauce bubbling softly. Steam curls from it, carrying memories of Sunday dinners and family gatherings.

For a moment, I feel almost normal. Like I *belong* somewhere again. Like I'm more than just a prisoner playing house, trying to crack the code on my owner. Caught up in the feeling, I drift toward the stove, grab the large spoon set on the counter, and stir the sauce just to watch it swirl.

It smells divine.

I lift the spoon carefully out of the sauce, raise it to my mouth—

Slap.

The spoon clatters to the floor, sauce splattering like blood.

"What are you doing in my kitchen?"

The old woman from last night—Rosa, Dami called her—stands there like an avenging angel in her robe and slippers. Her scowl could make even Damiano tremble.

"Jesus *Christ,*" I breathe, hand pressed to my chest. "You scared me."

She crosses her arms. "You keep the good Lord's name

out of your mouth, and tell me: What. Are you doing. In my kitchen?"

I flash her my most charming smile. "Looking for you, ma'am. Damiano's bandage bled through. I thought you might want to take a look."

The smile bounces off like she's wearing armor. Her expression doesn't soften one degree. In fact, she gives me the kind of once-over that makes me feel like something she scraped off her shoe. "You made a mess," she says, pointing at the sauce on the floor. "Clean it up."

"I...uh, sure." I grab some paper towels from the counter and crouch down. But as I wipe up the spill, the robe I'm wearing falls open at my chest. When I glance up, she's still watching me. Her face gives nothing away, but she turns abruptly, muttering something under her breath that doesn't sound complimentary.

"Dami's still asleep," I say as I finish cleaning. I use the too-cute nickname to make my story more convincing. "I didn't want to wake him. But like I said, he's bleeding again. So I wanted to make sure someone checked on him later."

She grunts, noncommittal. "Let the man sleep."

I straighten and toss the paper towels in the trash. Rosa has already turned back to the stove, stirring her pot with a new spoon like I'm not worth her attention.

"If you're going to make a nuisance of yourself," she says without looking up, "sit there." She nods toward the counter. "Out of my way."

I slide onto the stool, folding my arms on the cool marble countertop. "Is that for lunch?"

"Dinner."

"It smells incredible." She doesn't respond, but I catch the slight flare of her nostrils. "Can I make an espresso on the coffee machine?"

"No."

I sigh.

She sighs back, grabs a cup, and turns on the machine. The sound of beans grinding fills the silence between us, and then she makes me an espresso, the smell rich and promising.

"Flattery won't work," she says as she slides the cup to me. "Not on me. And not on him."

Damiano, I assume she means. I take a sip of the espresso. It's perfect—strong enough to wake the dead, smooth enough to make me moan. "You say that, but here I am with the best coffee in Turtle Bay."

She almost—*almost*—smiles. She doesn't correct me on the area, either. She goes back to her work and I rest my chin on my hand, watching as she twists off a handful of basil and gets out a new cutting board. She moves as briskly as she speaks, but she hasn't kicked me out yet.

I sip my coffee, trying to find a way through her defenses. "Is Dami a good employer?"

Her knife hits the cutting board hard, chopping herbs like she's got a problem with them.

I try again. "Have you worked for him long?"

Her hands pause. Something vulnerable crosses her face.

"The old Don," she says, "after my husband was killed protecting him, I cooked and cleaned house for him. The new Don…he didn't want to keep me on."

"So Damiano took you in?"

She glares at me. "It's not charity. He gave me *work*. I work hard for him." Her voice drops. "When I had nothing left, he made me family."

Family. Not employer and employee. Not master and servant. Family.

I wonder if Damiano feels the same.

"What about his driver?" I ask.

"What about him?" she returns coldly.

"He's pretty quiet, huh?"

That gets a reaction. Her face tightens, and she sets down the knife. "Vito was the old Don's driver," she says. "The FBI visited him for questioning. They wanted him to talk. About the Family. About the business. He used a razor blade to cut out his tongue."

I recoil. "Are you serious?"

"He was loyal," she continues. "He proved that he would never betray the Family, no matter what."

That's for sure. Good thing the Feds didn't give him a pen and some paper, or he might have started hacking off his fingers, too. Yikes.

I keep prodding. "So…why didn't the new Don keep him on?"

She presses her lips together, hard. Then she says, "Signor Orsini treasures his loyalty. Vito has a home here for life."

I sip my coffee, turning over in my mind what I've learned. This isn't a household, it's a—a *pack*. A pack of stray dogs who learned to work together to survive. And I'm the outsider who's been dragged into their—

Several loud explosions ricochet through the room.

I jump, coffee sloshing as my adrenaline goes through the roof.

"It's the back door," Rosa says calmly. "That's all. When the barricades are down, anyone knocking sounds loud."

That was way more than *loud*. My heart is still racing hard enough to burst. "You can't answer it," I say, voice sharp. "The house is on lockdown."

But Rosa is already at the security console, checking the monitors. "It's just Sammy."

"Who? Wait—"

But she's already disabling the alarm and raising the steel barrier. I grip the countertop hard, trying to remember how to get back to Damiano's bedroom. If I run now, I could make it to the stairs before—

A young man steps into the kitchen carrying a box full of fruit, vegetables, leafy herbs. About my height, lean, maybe mid-twenties with curly dark hair and black gauge rings in both earlobes. His leather jacket is a designer knockoff, and his jeans are tucked into cheap boots.

His eyes go straight to me and then narrow.

"Who's that?" he demands.

"None of your concern," Rosa says, but it lacks the sharpness that's underlined everything else she's said to me so far.

I guess this guy isn't an assassin.

He puts the box down on the counter and Rosa begins looking through it, shaking her head and sighing at what she sees, even though it all looks fine to me. I walk around the island to extend my hand to the newcomer with a polite smile. "Hey. You're Sammy, right? I'm Cal. Cal Clemenza."

He recoils from me, lips pulling up in a sneer. His gaze travels over the robe and down to my bare feet. He turns his back on me to speak to Rosa. "The markets aren't great right now, but I did what I could."

With a sniff at his words, Rosa picks up the box and disappears into the walk-in pantry, leaving us alone.

I search for something to fill in the silence, make him talk. "Are you a friend of Damiano's?"

"I'm a lot more than his *friend*," he mutters, turning on me. He gives me another scathing up-and-down look. "And you're not the first guy he's used for a night. You won't be the last. But I'll *always* be here."

What the actual fuck?

He's glaring at me like I've stolen something from him.

Obviously there's history there—but that's not *my* fault. And hell, based on what he just said, I think we can agree that Damiano's an asshole.

But somehow I don't think we're going to bond over it.

I open my mouth to say something—anything—but the guy goes to the security panel, ostentatiously shielding it from me with one hand as he puts in a code. The barriers outside rattle down once more. Sammy gives me one last glare and slips back down the hallway. From somewhere deeper in the house, I hear a door slam shut.

Whoever Sammy is, he lives here. Just like Rosa and Vito.

Rosa returns from the pantry and doesn't seem surprised to see him gone.

"Who is that guy?" I ask.

"None of your business."

"He seemed…territorial."

She snorts. "So are dogs. Doesn't mean they own the thing they're pissing on."

Something in her tone makes me feel a little better. Not that I care about Damiano's jealous exes. I don't care about Damiano's sexual history at all.

But I can't help wondering how many men might have sat in this kitchen, wearing his robe, having a run-in with Sammy. I slide back onto the stool, a little shaken despite myself. I need to refocus.

"So, do you like working for Dami?" I ask again. She doesn't answer. Just adds basil to the sauce and keeps stirring. "He seems like a good man," I venture.

Her response is instant. "He is not a good man."

I pause, coffee cup halfway to my lips. "Kind, then."

"He is not a kind man, either. But he is loyal. To the death."

Not good. Not kind.

But loyal.

I can work with that.

The voice that cuts through the room from behind me is just as startling as the explosive knocking was a few minutes ago. "Get on with your cooking, woman."

We both freeze.

Damiano stands in the doorway looking like death in black briefs. He's shirtless, pale, and the white bandage is crimson. He looks like he should be in a hospital bed, but he's still menacing, eyes locked on Rosa with dangerous intensity.

"If your tongue gets any looser," he tells her softly, "I'll ask Vito to cut it out."

Rosa doesn't flinch. Just turns back to her sauce like he's commented on the weather.

His gaze travels over me, taking in every detail—his too-large robe on my frame, the coffee in my hands, the way I'm perched on a stool at the counter.

I feel pinned like a butterfly to a board.

"And *you,*" he says, voice dropping to a growl. "Come with me."

I set down the coffee cup and follow my owner like a well-trained dog.

CHAPTER 25
DAMIANO

I LEAD the Clemenza prince back upstairs to my bedroom and I close the door. "What the fuck do you think you're doing?"

Given the circumstances, I think my voice sounds very calm.

Caligula folds his arms. My robe hangs loose on his smaller frame, the front gaping to reveal the golden skin of his throat and chest. And that infuriating, casual confidence radiates from every line of his body like he's still *somebody* instead of *property*.

"I was getting Rosa," he says, and gestures. "Your arm. You're bleeding again."

I glance down. Blood has soaked through the white bandage, a spreading stain I didn't even notice. Like I didn't notice Caligula Clemenza slipping out of my bed and prowling around my house.

My own body was failing me while I slept, weak and vulnerable. The fact that *he* saw it is humiliating. The fact that he went down and shot his mouth off to Rosa is worse.

I don't need *tending*.

"You think that gives you permission to wander around my house unsupervised?"

Caligula shrugs, the gesture making the robe slip off one shoulder. "You were asleep. Rosa and I didn't want to wake you. We decided you needed rest."

We.

The casual suggestion that he and Rosa are a "we," that my household operates by committee, that decisions get made without my authority…

All of it makes me angrier.

"You decided, did you?" Even wearing my robe, wearing my marks, he carries himself like he's doing me a favor by existing in my space. It makes me want to remind him again how far he's fallen. "You stay where I put you unless I say otherwise."

Caligula flings out his arms, letting the robe gape open without shame. "What was I supposed to do? Stay there quiet and awake, staring at the ceiling, while you snored and bled?"

"Someone wants you dead," I snap. "Any time you leave my side, you're in danger. Do you really need reminding?"

"Oh, I don't need reminding that I'm stuck with the Bad Mood Bear for a year. Don't you worry about that."

Snarky little shit. He's got such a mouth on him. And before I can speak again, he tilts his head and narrows his eyes.

"Who's Sammy?"

"Where did you hear that name?"

"I *met* him. In the kitchen." Caligula's voice seems neutral, but there's something underneath—I can't read it. "He wasn't very friendly. Seemed to think I was one of your disposable booty calls."

"Sammy should watch his fucking tongue."

"In case you cut it out? That was mean, by the way, what you said to Rosa. She worships you. You don't need to threaten her to keep her in line."

"You don't talk to my people without permission," I snarl.

The Clemenza's grin is pure provocation. "But Rosa likes me. I can tell."

That's it.

I grab him by the arms, fingers digging into my own robe as I yank him forward until our faces are inches apart. He makes me feel like an animal, like all I am is claws and hunger, ready to rip him apart.

"You will obey me," I tell him, low and dangerous, "or you will be punished."

He doesn't try to pull away. His lashes drop and his voice goes soft, teasing—deliberately pushing me. "Are you going to spank me again, Dami?"

My grip tightens involuntarily. The little viper is getting off on this. On pushing my buttons. On making me want to throw him down and…

"My property has forgotten its place." My fingers dig in even harder, hard enough to make him wince. "I went too easy on you last night, letting you sleep in my bed. Now the little prince thinks he can run my house."

His smile falters. Understanding flickers in those amber eyes. "Wait—"

"No." I squeeze tighter, making him wince. "A few days in chains is what you need."

"Damiano—please," he says quickly, and now I hear real panic threading through his voice. "*Please* don't put me back down there. I was just trying to help—"

"Too late." I shove him toward the elevator doors. "Maybe next time you'll think before you speak."

Inside, the elevator is mirrored on all sides, trapping us

with infinite reflections of this moment—him in my robe, me gripping his arm, both of us breathing hard. He stands rigid in front of me, chest rising and falling rapidly, honey eyes wide and worried. I don't look at him directly, at his pleading expression.

If I do, I might stop.

The elevator stops and the doors open. I drag him to the far wall where another chain and collar hangs from an iron ring embedded in the reinforced concrete. He doesn't get the bed this time. He *deserves* the wall. Cruder. Colder. More degrading.

The chain clinks as I secure the collar to him. He doesn't beg, doesn't fight—doesn't even try to resist. If anything, he helps, bending his head as I secure the lock behind his neck.

And that small submission just angers me more.

"You don't have to do this," he says quietly. There's something in his voice. Not fear—something like disappointment.

I lean over him, letting him see exactly what he's dealing with. "I don't have to. But I *want* to." I straighten, step back. "Think about how you want the rest of this year to go, golden boy. Because it will go like *this* if you don't behave. You'll stay chained there to the wall instead of having the luxury of a bed. Now, when I feel like it, I'll come back down and see if you're ready to apologize."

I leave the light on, a small kindness that he'd better fucking appreciate. I'm almost at the elevator when his voice stops me cold.

"I was *worried* about you, you asshole. That's all."

I don't turn around, but my finger pauses over the elevator button until I have to force myself to push it.

He was worried.

About me.

Or so he says.

I go straight back to the kitchen so Rosa can look at my damn arm, which *is* bleeding. But when I get there, she crosses her arms and gives me a look that tells me exactly what she's thinking.

"You need anything for the boy?"

"He's not a boy." I pour myself out a coffee from the drip machine rather than ask her to make me an espresso like she did for Caligula—judging by the abandoned cup on the counter. But after one sip, I set my mug down. I feel off-balance.

It's the disrespect he showed. It's got nothing to do with how he begged me not to put him back down there. Or the way he said he was worried about me.

Rosa's disapproval wafts over to me along with the scent of her special tomato sauce. "I need to check your arm," she says.

"You need to remember your place!" I snap. "And he needs to learn his."

She shakes her head. "I know my place," she tells me. "And you can get out of it. Go on—get out of my kitchen. Let me get on with my work if you don't want my help."

I dump out the coffee in the sink before I go, just to show her that she can't bully me like she bullies Vito and Sammy. Who the hell does Rosa think she is? She's been pushing back more and more since Caligula got here, acting like a mother who can guilt me into doing what she wants me to do.

Well, she's *not* my mother. And I don't feel guilty. I'd need a conscience for that.

A soul.

I've done the right thing. Reasserted control. Reminded that manipulative little snake who's in charge. I head up to my bedroom, go into the viewing room, and check him on the monitor. He's slumped against the wall, still in my robe —which I forgot to strip from him, damn it—head down, arms wrapped around himself.

So what if he noticed my bleeding? That's not why he was down there in the kitchen pestering Rosa. I'm no fool, though he keeps treating me like one. Still…maybe he wasn't trying to escape. Maybe he was just bored. Curious.

No. He's a Clemenza. They always have an angle. And I confirm it by playing back the video of this morning, watch Caligula Clemenza wandering around *my* house as though he owns it, looking in each room, testing locked doors…

He's looking for a way out.

That's what he wants. Escape.

That's why he offered himself to me last night. And that's why he was down there flirting with Rosa. Buttering her up so he can use her. I bet if Sammy hadn't arrived, he would have persuaded her to raise the shutters and let him walk right out of here.

I catch myself. That, at least, is unfair of me. He was right about that one thing—Rosa is devoted. She would never willingly let him leave the house.

And as for Sammy…

I play the video forward, watch Sammy come into the kitchen and stop dead at the sight of Caligula. He didn't hang around pestering Rosa this morning, when usually he likes to wait until I come down for my coffee. And he barely spoke to Caligula—but that clever little Clemenza picked it up fast, the stupid crush Sammy has on me.

Like all Clemenzas, he was looking for leverage. Sammy gave it to him unconsciously. But…there *was* something strange in his voice when Caligula asked me who Sammy was. Not just curiosity—something sharper.

Or was it calculated?

I need to know. I want to get under his skin. Into his brain. Eat him from the inside out.

My phone buzzes angrily against the desk. Messages have been coming in all night and all morning, news about the attempted assassination, which everyone seems to think was meant for someone higher up the food chain. D'Amato, probably, or Big Gee. They were both nearby. But I know who the target was.

I know because I took the knife for him.

This message, though, can't be ignored: a direct summons from the Underboss. Sebastiano isn't even requesting a response with his terse instructions.

Ristorante Aglio. 12:30.

But as I head into the bathroom to strip off the blood-soaked bandage so I can change it myself, Caligula's words still echo in my head.

I was worried about you, you asshole.

CHAPTER 26
DAMIANO

THE RESTAURANT SEB has called me to is Family-owned—not in the way online reviews like to highlight, but in the way that every server, every chef, even every customer is carefully vetted. Outsiders who walk in and try to get a table will find that the place is fully booked, even when completely empty. The owner who greets me on entry has respect in his eyes. He knows who I am. And everyone here owes the Giuliano Family something—money, information, silence.

Just like Caligula Clemenza owes *me* everything now, whether he wants to admit it or not.

Sebastiano sits alone at a back corner table, already halfway through a glass of red, the bottle waiting on the table. When I approach, he shoots to his feet.

"Jesus Christ, Orsini." He grips me hard, and I have to try not to wince when he squeezes right over the area with the knife wound. "After last night at the opera—and then no replies to my texts—"

"I'm fine." I slide into the booth, and he pours me a glass of wine. I take a few gulps. I never learned how to drink it. Always tastes the same to me, and it's not something I want to savor, just swallow. Get the effects faster. That's the point of alcohol, no matter how wine snobs might talk it up. Booze is to help blunt reality.

"You and the Clemenza boy…" Seb begins slowly.

He's not a boy, I want to say, but I hold my tongue. And before he can find a way to finish his thought, my usual meal appears before me without having to order it—lasagna, steaming and simple. But my stomach churns looking at it, because Seb's relief at seeing me is already shifting into something else.

"Look, I'm sorry about the Red Hook job," I say, trying to deflect further conversation about Caligula. "I know I went too hard on them."

Seb waves his hand, almost irritated. "They got the message. That's not why I called you in. It's about last night. Everyone seems to think that street rat was after D'Amato or his husband—but he was clearly headed for the Clemenza. So why the fuck were you there with the boy in the first place?"

"He's not a boy," I growl, and take another few swallows of wine. I don't want to get into another argument with Seb, but he's sure making it difficult. "I was there because Big Gee *told* me to be there. He wanted me to take the Clemenza to a public place to show him off, show the Families I'm still playing ball." *Still on the leash,* I don't add.

Seb's voice sharpens. "*Big Gee* told you to take him to the opera?" I just nod, my mouth full of meat sauce. When he speaks next, he almost sounds distracted. "You spoke to him?"

I nod again, reaching for the wine to pour myself another in my now-empty glass.

Seb runs a hand over his face. He looks troubled. "Listen. I saw you last night."

He saw me *fondling the Clemenza*? I have to set the bottle down before I spill red wine everywhere.

"When I heard you'd bought him, I…" He looks away with a grimace. "Well, I thought some pretty nasty shit about you—and hell, I know you want to do right by your dad. But a man who wants someone dead doesn't take a knife for them." He looks me right in the face, eyes sincere. "You really did protect him last night. I watched you do it. And I want to believe you, Orsini. I'm *choosing* to believe you, that you acted out of honor when you bought him at the Obelisk. But if I find out that you're hurting that kid—"

"You won't," I say. Because he won't find out.

"I still wish you'd come to me or Big Gee before buying him…but you were right to keep him from the Russians."

I have to drink down a whole glass again while I take that in. Sebastiano Conti is way too good a man for this life he's in. He likes to see the best in others. And now he's convinced himself that the lie I told him was true, that I only bought the Clemenza for the good of the Family, out of loyalty instead of…

"Yeah, well," I say at last, setting down my empty glass again. "I owe you an apology, too. I spilled to Big Gee because he rolled up to my place wanting an explanation, and so I assumed you'd told him. Kinda threw you under the bus without meaning to. I guess he heard about it from somewhere else."

A look of understanding passes through Seb's eyes, and he actually chuckles. "Well, that explains a few of the side-eyes Big Gee's been giving me the last few days. I'll have a talk with him, smooth it over." He extends a hand. "As for you and me—I hope we're good."

I take his hand and shake it. "We're good."

We're not good. Not at all. If Seb knew I had Caligula Clemenza chained to a wall in my basement right now…

Hell, if *anyone* in the Family finds out about that lovingly-crafted torture chamber I put together just for him, they'd put me down without hesitation.

Not because I broke ranks, but because I am, as the Clemenza himself put it, *fucking insane*.

I don't know what this twisting in my gut is and I don't like it. It makes it hard to shovel down the lasagna, but I figure the fuller my mouth is, the less I'm likely to spill something I shouldn't to Seb. Seb still seems troubled, anyway, his fond smile about his younger brother dying away as he toys with his linguine. "Luca D'Amato's been putting the heat on about the Clemenzas."

"Wants them all dead?"

Seb looks up at me with surprise again. "No. That's not how he operates. He's an honorable man, despite what Big Gee might think about him. D'Amato took them down, but he was restrained about it. No innocents caught up in the purge. And besides, you know he put out that order months ago that the Cees are untouchable now. Anyone kills a Clemenza, they answer to him."

I do know. I wasn't happy about it at the time. "Fat lotta good that's done for them," I snort.

Personally, I think D'Amato only ordered that to give his own Morellis a clear run. He wanted to keep the pleasure of eradicating the Clemenzas all to himself.

"Still," Seb goes on, oblivious to my dark thoughts, "maybe it's a good thing the Morellis were there last night to see you protect the kid. Show them that the Gees are playing nice, that these murders have nothing to do with us."

"Any news on the fool who tried it? Shame he got silenced, but there was no other way that was going to end. He was shit at his job." Whoever that moron was who came at Caligula last night, they must have had a death wish to try it in a room full of mobsters.

Seb looks even more troubled. "No ID. Not a Family man. Didn't seem like the Bratva's usual choice, either."

"Maybe not. But the Bratva were pretty pissed when I won the Clemenza from them."

"Mm." Seb is unconvinced. He leans in close, dropping his voice, even though this restaurant is one of the safest places in the city for us outside our own homes. "I want you to look into it."

"Me?" I dump my loaded fork back into my bowl.

"You. You got skin in the game now, after all."

Blood, too. My arm's been killing me all damn day. I should've gotten Rosa to clean it out again this morning. But still… "I'm not your guy," I tell him. "I'm a head-kicker, not an investigator."

He grins in appreciation. "If you need to kick a few heads along the way, have at it. Besides, you're the only one with an inside line." At my blank look, he adds, "You have the Clemenza right there in your home. He must have some ideas about his enemies, surely?"

I just shrug at that. If I refuse again, Seb will start to wonder what's up. "Fine. I'll talk to him. But he wasn't much involved in his granddaddy's business. He was way down the line of succession."

Seb nods. "All the same. Doesn't hurt to ask him. And let's keep this between us, eh?" he says casually.

Too casually.

He doesn't think it's the Russians. Maybe he's suspicious of us Italians. If so, I see why he wants to keep it quiet. If it turns out to be a made man—from *any* of the Families—it's going to cause problems.

I don't go home after lunch.

I don't want to think about Caligula Clemenza chained up in that basement. Don't want to remember how those golden eyes were like warm honey last night when he looked at me, or how that smartass mouth curves when he thinks he's getting under my skin. Don't want to acknowledge that sometimes, in my weakest moments, I think about the way he says my name. *Dami.*

But I need to check on him. Because what I keep saying is true: Caligula Clemenza is my responsibility now.

I have a contingency in place for when I'm out, because no one goes down to that basement but me. Not long after I leave Seb at the restaurant, I tap into the app on my phone and hit the button to release the collar. There, he has his freedom. He'll be able to reach the food I now order Rosa to send down, and he can drink water from the fridge.

Hell, he can even wander around the set I made for him, his Family's graveyard. Reminisce.

I walk around the city for a long time. Well after nightfall, I call Vito to pick me up. On our return, I make him wait a while outside the house with the engine idling.

Caligula Clemenza is in that house. Waiting. Waiting for what he *deserves*.

But those words feel hollow now.

I get out of the car eventually and go into the kitchen, where Rosa immediately points at a tray full of food. "He hasn't eaten."

All the soft thoughts I've been having about Caligula Clemenza evaporate in an instant. Of *course* he hasn't eaten. He's trying to manipulate me. He knows that if he doesn't eat, I'll go down there, give him another chance to drip poison in my ear, to persuade me to take him into my bed again.

I grab the tray. "I'll *make* him eat."

But when I get down to the basement, he's lying on the bed asleep. Even when I put the lights up to full, he doesn't wake. I stand over him, studying the clammy sheen of his skin, the way his breathing seems too shallow.

"Caligula," I say at last.

He starts awake, holding up his hand to shield his eyes from the light. "Dad?" he croaks, and something that had died down roars back to life in my chest.

I seize his wrist, angry not at him, but at the broken, lost sound in his voice. "Your father is as dead as mine," I tell him savagely. "He won't save you."

He's still blinking at me, his eyes clouded. "Sorry," he mumbles at last.

The apology shouldn't affect me, but it does. He looks so young and so lost…

Oh, he's *good*. He's good, this little Clemenza.

"Get up. Why didn't you eat? Or shower? You *will* take care of yourself, or you will regret it. You hear me?"

He looks around as though confused. "I'm tired," he says, and there's something wrong with his voice, with the way he's swaying slightly as he gets to his feet.

"You've had enough sleep. Go and shower."

He gives me a glassy look and then struggles off the bed, heading for the shower stall. I go to my chair and sit there to watch. Once he's clean, I'll feed him. I'll shove the food down his throat if I have to.

He turns on the water and stands under it, leaning forward with his hands on the back wall, head down.

And then he stumbles to the side, slamming into the glass wall. It holds, but he slides down it to land in a crumpled heap on the tiled floor.

He stays there, unmoving.

Fuck.

I bolt over, dropping to my knees beside him. Water

soaks through my clothes, but I barely notice. His skin is burning up, fever radiating from him in waves.

"Hey," I say, gathering him against my chest, and he's so light, too light. "*Caligula.* Wake up."

He doesn't respond, head lolling against my shoulder like a broken doll. Something rises up in me, completely alien. I think it's panic.

I never panic. Not since I was thirteen.

I lift him easily, water streaming from both of us as I carry him back to the bed. His breathing is too fast, too shallow, and his skin is paper-white except for the fever flush on his cheeks. My hands shake as I check his pulse, as I smooth the wet hair back from his burning forehead. He's not faking it. He's sick.

He's very, very sick.

CHAPTER 27
CALIGULA

I WAKE up drowning in Damiano's scent.

The smell hits me before my eyes even open, sending pleasant sparks straight to my balls despite my fuzzy head. And I know immediately where I am—not just in bed, but in *his* bed.

Damiano's bed.

The room takes shape slowly as consciousness returns. I stare at the windows for a long time, taking in the absolute lack of view, before it occurs to me that the shutters are still down. My pulse quickens when I realize I'm not alone—and then just about stops when I see it's not Damiano Orsini.

A woman leans over me. A petite blonde with a messy bun and pink scrubs, holding a digital thermometer. She's got kind eyes, but beneath that, the alertness of a health professional.

"Good, you're awake," she says with a smile. "You gave everyone quite a scare."

"I did?" I rasp.

In the corner of the room, a shadow shifts, and I give a startled jerk.

It's him. Damiano.

"Easy now." She presses a hand against my forehead, and I lean into the touch slightly—her fingers feel nice and cool. "Yeah, you're still burning up. I'm Darla, honey. I'm a nurse. Do you know your name?"

"Cal," I say.

"Very good!" She sounds so pleased with me that I smile back at her. "So, I hear you passed out. When's the last time you had a proper meal?"

I blink. "Yesterday? Maybe..."

Her eyes are still kind, but they narrow as she looks to the side. She's smart enough not to turn around and openly glare. But she seems so nice, I don't want her to do anything that might get her hurt.

So I try to sit up. "I was in the shower—" The world tilts and I collapse back against the pillows.

"Don't do that," Darla says gently. "You need to rest."

Across the room, when it swims back into focus, Damiano looms like a thundercloud, arms crossed, face cold. But his eyes—Christ, his eyes are burning holes through me with the same intensity as the first night I was in his house.

"Do you have any underlying conditions?" Darla asks, following my gaze briefly before refocusing on me.

"Just the usual." I let my voice carry a hint of flirtation. "Apparently I'm irresistible to beautiful women."

She laughs. "Well, that's not in any medical textbook I've read."

In the corner, Damiano's hands are clenching into fists.

"So, are you a real nurse, or is this something you do part-time while you build your career as a supermodel?" I continue.

Darla's smile widens. "You can flirt as hard as you like, it won't change your blood pressure reading." She adjusts the cuff around my arm. "Since you ask, I'm a registered nurse, but I'm also in medical school to become a doctor. I do some freelancing here and there. Off-the-books work, mainly for people who...well. Prefer their privacy."

People like Damiano. People who can afford to keep their secrets buried.

Darla turns to him. "Could you grab me a fresh washcloth, please, Mr. Orsini?"

He hesitates, clearly reluctant to leave us alone together, before turning and stalking from the room. The door closes not much quieter than a slam.

As soon as we're alone, Darla leans closer, all her smiles evaporating. "If you're in trouble, Cal, I can help you. I have friends who can get you out of here."

I let myself imagine it: walking out of this steel-shuttered house, disappearing, breathing fresh air again.

But there's ten million dollars on the line.

And the killer is waiting out there somewhere for me.

I think of the golden cage, the collar. Of Damiano's hands—teasing me with the plug, spanking me until I came, sliding inside me.

I think about him taking a knife for me.

I signed away my autonomy in return for ten million and protection for a year. And he *has* protected me, hasn't he? At the opera. And he didn't leave me lying on the floor of the shower. He got me medical help. I'm not in his basement anymore—I'm in his room, his private sanctuary. Back in his *bed*.

I even have *clothes* on. Pajamas that fit, though the legs are a little short.

A surge of reckless confidence flares within me. He's still controllable. I just need to find the right strings to pull. As for this nurse, maybe she means well, but...

"These friends of yours," I begin, keeping my voice light. "Are they good friends?"

"They're *very* good friends. They're paying for my tuition while I study." Her voice drops to barely above a whisper. "The Morellis."

Nausea rises sharp and fast. There's no way in hell I'll put myself in debt to the Morelli Family. "I'm fine," I tell the nurse. "Damiano and I…we just get a little carried away sometimes. New relationships are intense, you know? We've been so busy getting to know each other that we forgot about little things like eating."

I watch her expression shift from concern to skepticism. "New relationship energy, huh?" She slides a business card onto the nightstand anyway. "Just in case."

The door opens and Damiano returns with a washcloth. The nurse slips straight back into professional mode, taking it from him and dipping it into a bowl of water on the nightstand.

"Cal needs rest and careful treatment," she tells him firmly as she wipes down my hot face. "Meals in bed, plenty of fluids, and gentle handling. Take it easy on the, uh, 'getting to know you' activities for a few days."

He nods curtly, but I catch the way his jaw ticks at her phrasing.

"Dami needs some help, too," I say. "Show her, Dami."

He stares at me.

"Your arm," I say sweetly. "Let the nurse have a look at it."

She turns to him expectantly. "Is there something else I can help you with, Mr. Orsini?"

"It's nothing." She stares him down. After a moment, Damiano strips off his shirt, all the while glaring at me. "Just a cut."

He's tied a new bandage around it, and while this one

isn't stained red, he still hisses when she removes it. "You've pulled your stitches," she says severely, examining it. She glares up at him. "You should have called me in when—"

"Well, you're here now," he snaps. She doesn't cower away from him, just makes him sit on the chair in the corner again while she douses him with disinfectant and then cuts out the old stitches.

"You've been too active," she tuts as she cleans the wound and then sews him up again. Damiano stares at me the whole time, and I watch with pleasure, hoping it hurts like hell.

The bastard deserves a lot more pain than that, but this will do for a start.

"I'll leave you with a course of antibiotics," she says after plastering over the wound again and bandaging him up.

"Thank you," he says shortly. He escorts her to the door as close as a shadow, and I don't miss how he positions himself between us until they leave the room. "Rosa will take you down," I hear him say, and then he comes back into the room, staring at me once more as he shuts the door behind him. The moment the door clicks shut, he stalks over to pick up Darla's card, holding it between two fingers as if it might contaminate him.

"She offered you a way out," he says, voice deadly quiet. "Why didn't you take it?"

I meet his eyes. "Because I signed my name to a contract. And that means I gave my word as a Clemenza. I won't break it."

"Even if it breaks *you*?"

Various feelings rush through me—irritation, arousal, something that might even be pity for this fool standing before me. "I spent months running. Always looking over my shoulder, never knowing if I'd wake up dead. While I'm here, I have a bed and I don't have to worry about an attacker. And you..."

"I what?"

"You gave me your word, too. You said you'd protect me—and you did. I might not like you very much, Damiano Orsini, but I do actually trust you. You proved I could. Besides," I add, "I'd *literally* die before asking the Morellis for help. Luca D'Amato killed my grandfather."

"Did you love the old man that much?"

Whatever medication Darla gave me seems to have loosened my tongue, because the truth spills out unguarded. "I hated him. But love and hate have nothing to do with Family. Family is about loyalty, first and last."

Something shifts in his expression—approval, maybe even respect. "I need you to answer some questions. And no fucking lies."

"Alright. On one condition."

"You don't get to—"

"You haven't even heard my condition."

He glares. "What is it?"

"I won't lie to you, as long as you don't lie to me." I run my hands over the quilt. It's homemade, and the ridges and bumps help soothe me. "Do whatever else you want. We both know you can—and will. Just...don't lie to me while I'm here. I'd rather have the truth, no matter how terrible it might be. And I'll give you the same courtesy."

It takes a second. But he nods. "Agreed." He sits on the edge of the bed and fixes me with that searching stare he gets. "Who is hunting the Clemenzas?"

"You asked me that before. I don't know. Do you?" I study his face right back.

He just shakes his head. "But you don't need to worry. You're safe here."

"How reassuring," I reply. "My very own beast, keeping me safe from all the other monsters out there."

His lips curve slightly. "You must be feeling better. The sarcasm is back." He stands and turns toward the door, then pauses. "Get some rest," he says over his shoulder. "I'll come back later, and I'll have more questions for you then."

When he's gone, I pick up Darla's card, turning it between my fingers thoughtfully. He left it here. Why? Is it a dare?

A test?

I saw approval in those cold eyes when I told him loyalty was the only important thing. I said it partly just to see how he'd react. To slide a suggestion in, see if he'd enjoy it. He did.

But I also *meant* it. I gave my word.

I will keep it.

CHAPTER 28
CALIGULA

"CALIGULA?"

I wake slowly, swimming back up from dreams. I yawn and stretch, blinking up at Damiano. "Hi," I say.

"You need to drink this." He holds up a cup with a bendy straw. "And then you need to take a bath."

"I just showered before. When I—when I passed out."

"That was yesterday. You've been asleep for a long time."

I push myself up a little, looking around, as though the change in day will be observable. Not with the steel shutters still down over all the windows. "What time is it?"

"It's morning. Ten o'clock."

"Oh," I say. "Well, in that case…" I try to sit up, but the dizziness hits right away, sending me back to the pillows with a nausea-inducing spin of the room.

Damiano just stands there looking down at me. "Here," he says at last, offering me the cup again.

I take a tentative suck at the straw and make a face. "What *is* this?"

"It's a protein shake. The nurse left a bunch for you.

Said you had to get nutrients into you and this was the simplest way."

Maybe she's actually the Morellis' assassin, because this shit? Is going to kill me. "Gross," I announce, and try to hand it back.

"What's rule number one?" Damiano asks impassively.

I squint up at him. "Do what you fucking tell me?"

"And I'm telling you to drink it."

Fuck this guy. Seriously. But I drink the toxic sludge down until the cup is empty and he's satisfied. Then he leans down, whips the covers off of me, and slides his arms under me.

"What the hell are you doing?" I demand as he lifts me in his arms like I weigh nothing at all, which is *definitely* not true. I've lost a little weight over the last few months—okay, a lot of weight—but I'm still a grown man, and...

And he's ignoring my protests, carrying me through into his bathroom in a cradling hold that forces me to put my arms around his neck and just *hang on*. Kind of a metaphor for our whole acquaintance so far. Him manhandling me however he likes, while I just hold on tight and *hope*.

He takes me into the bathroom, where he sets me down on the ottoman while he checks the water temperature in the tub.

"Strip," he says over his shoulder, so I do. Weirdly, he doesn't watch me. But then he beckons me over and helps me into the water.

"Oh," I sigh. The water is lukewarm, not hot like I dreaded. I'm so sweaty and sticky all over that it feels *delicious*. I sink right down to my chin and then below, letting my hair soak in the water while I blow bubbles through my nose, resurfacing with a gasp.

"Don't fucking drown yourself," Damiano growls.

I blink the water out of my eyes. "I couldn't if I tried, Dami. Not with you watching over me. Right?"

"Sit still," is all he says. He starts to wash me down with a cloth, starting with my shoulders, my arms, my torso. My nipples are tight buds, and I'm not sure if it's in reaction to the temperature of the water or the attention he's giving them, disguised as washing down my chest.

I guess it doesn't matter. Not right now.

I loll my head back against the tub and enjoy it. But I can't help watching through half-lidded eyes the way his muscles shift beneath his skin, the way the ink dances on his arms as he works.

A few minutes in, I break the silence. "Who's Sammy?"

"We still on that?" he asks flatly.

"We still on that," I confirm.

I don't expect an answer, but I get one. "Few years ago I found him getting beat to death behind a gay club by a group of Clemenzas."

It hurts to hear that—as he intended, I suspect—but I still want to see how much more I can get out of Damiano Orsini while he's in a giving mood. "And now he works for you?"

"He's a runner for me. Carries messages. Does odd jobs, brings in the groceries for Rosa. He's loyal. Good at staying invisible."

"Have you slept with him?" I ask.

He looks at me, long and hard, his dark eyes unreadable. "I would never demand gratitude that way."

The relief that floods through me is so intense, it's dizzying. Good thing I'm already lying down. But why should I care who Damiano Orsini sleeps with?

I home in on his wording to take my mind off disquieting thoughts. "You say you don't demand gratitude that way," I echo him. "But that's not quite true, Dami, is it? When I wanted the townhouse—"

"When you wanted the townhouse, you made me an offer. Not my fault you decided to get on your knees. That was all you."

That's what he says, but guilt flickers across his features like lightning—there and gone so fast I almost miss it. He turns to pick up a sponge this time and lathers it with soap.

"I can wash myself, you know."

"You're mine," he replies. "If I don't take care of you, you'll break. And I hate broken things."

The words are designed to remind me that I'm his property, that I belong to him whether I like it or not. Instead, they send heat spiraling through me, and I have to bite back a moan as he starts to sponge me down.

What is *wrong* with me?

I order my brain to put aside bliss, since my body won't play along. And for a precious moment, rational thought kicks in again—because it occurs to me that Damiano Orsini is *lying,* right after I made him promise not to.

He doesn't hate broken things. If anything, it's the opposite.

Look at Rosa. Vito. Sammy. He gathers up broken things and keeps them in his care.

He runs the sponge all over me, soaping me up. Down my arms, over my collarbone, across my nipples that are too sensitive, too responsive to his touch. When he moves under the water to my stomach, I can't suppress a shiver.

"Cold?" he asks. His hands linger just above my hips, and his eyes are fixed on my face, reading every micro-expression.

"No," I say. "Not cold." I let my thighs part in clear invitation. Let my head fall back again against the marble edge of the tub.

His hand replaces the sponge. Wraps around me under the water, and the touch is sure, maddeningly slow. My breath catches, and I have to grip the edge of the tub to keep from arching into his palm like a cat in heat. We both feel it, my body responding to him.

I close my eyes, but he leans closer, close enough that I feel his breath against my ear. "Look at me."

I force my eyes open to meet his dark gaze, and it's like looking into a storm—dangerous and consuming. His pupils are blown wide. His breath is faster than it should be. But his hand doesn't make another movement.

"You want it, you ask for it," he says.

"Please, Dami," I breathe. "I want it. Touch me."

"You're hard," he says, running his thumb under my ridge until I groan. "And you're my responsibility now, so I guess that means I need to do this for you, too. Right?"

"Right," I gasp out.

His other hand traces my jaw, possessive and gentle. "Remind me who you belong to, Caligula Clemenza."

The words should make me revolt. They just make me harder, and we both know it.

"Say it," he commands.

I stay silent.

He lets me go completely. "*Say it.*"

"I belong to you," I mutter.

"Again. Louder, this time. Make me believe you finally learned your lesson."

"I'm yours, Dami."

"Good boy." He takes me in hand again and moves faster now, so the pleasure builds like a tide I can't fight. When he touches me like this, everything falls away except the sensation. I can't tell what's real anymore except his hand on my cock, the sloshing water, the feel of his breath on my wet skin.

His thumb presses hard into my slit, and I bite my lip to stop from crying out. Then his fingers tighten, a slow, deliberate squeeze. He's so good at this, so sure, that it almost doesn't seem fair. I'm at his mercy.

Almost.

"You gonna come for me, Caligula?" he murmurs, and the use of my full name, usually so hated, sends a jolt straight to my balls, sharp but sweet.

"Yeah," I gasp.

"Not yet." He backs off immediately, loosening his grip, letting the sensation ebb. I groan in frustration, my hips pushing up into nothing. "You come when I say you can come."

The water sloshes as I shift. "Dami—"

"Quiet." His free hand presses on my sternum, a clear command to stay still. "Last thing you need is to get all worked up."

"I'll be good," I promise. "Please..."

He starts again. Slower this time, a maddening, teasing rhythm. He knows what he's doing, the bastard. He knows exactly how to push me to the edge and then pull me back, leaving me hanging. If this is going to end in frustration like it did at the opera—

"Dami," I groan, "seriously—"

He leans into my ear. "You're a greedy little slut, aren't you?"

My cheeks burn, but my dick throbs. I nod, not even caring about the admission.

"Alright," he says, concession in his tone. "Since you're being such a good boy." His grip changes. He's not playing anymore. His thumb finds that spot under the head, rubbing hard, fast circles. My balls draw up tight, and I'm just about there—

"Come on," he coaxes, all traces of teasing gone. "Let it

all out."

The water churns around me as my hips jerk, and I come with a rising, helpless cry as he strokes me through it, the bathwater splashing in a tiny tsunami. When it's over, I sink back, marinating in my own mess.

God*damn* that felt good.

But more importantly, for the first time, I've successfully manipulated Damiano Orsini with my sexuality. Made him see me as helpless. Needy.

Another one of those broken things he instinctively collects and cares for.

He helps me from the tub and wraps me in a soft towel. Leads me back to his bed where he makes sure I sit up gently, arranging pillows behind my back with care.

Food is waiting on a tray beside the bed, so I assume Rosa must have come in while we were in the bathroom. I hope she didn't hear—well, no point worrying about that. I'm too hungry, for one thing, eagerly taking up a bowl of rice and soft chicken in a broth scented with lemon and herbs. The kind of meal that's meant to heal, to comfort.

To help Damiano maintain his property.

I eat, letting it soak into my bones. Damiano watches me the entire time, as usual.

The silence stretches out between us. It's not uncomfortable, but it's also not helping me any. "You could have left me down there in the basement to die," I say at last, deciding to push a little. "Why didn't you?"

"I told you. I don't plan to kill you."

"And why is that?" I raise an eyebrow when he doesn't reply. "Why is that, Dami? You said yourself you don't care about the contract. And you made a big deal out of telling me you wanted revenge for your father when you first bought me. He's dead. So why aren't I?"

Nothing. But I figure my fainting spell has won me a little more leeway than usual. So I keep going.

"And what was that in the bathtub? A reward?"

He gives the tiniest flicker of the eyelid, but I catch it.

"Or was it an apology orgasm?"

"It was supposed to shut you up."

At last I've provoked him to speech. "Was it Darla-sanctioned?"

"Don't be ridiculous."

"Then—"

"Enough," he cuts in, folding his arms over his impressive chest. "My turn. What were you doing at my new property the night your cousin got iced? Your grandfather's townhouse," he adds as I look at him blankly.

Oh, *fuck* this guy. And if we're going into that, I want something back. "I'll tell you if you answer a few questions of mine, Dami."

"We're not bargaining here, golden boy. You belong to me, so—"

"*I* belong to you. My knowledge does not. So if you want to know what I know, Dami, you'll need to give a little yourself, or torture it out of me—but in that case, I *might* just die on you." He says nothing, but it's not a refusal. "Come on, Dami. Two heads are better than one."

He sighs. "Fine."

CHAPTER 29
DAMIANO

THE CLEMENZA PICKS up his bowl again and takes another mouthful, as though rewarding me for giving way. I hope he realizes I could force all that food into him if I wanted to.

The problem is, I know how stubborn this little snake can be. And I don't have time to waste. Seb wants a result, and it'll be hard to keep my investigations quiet once I start poking around.

"So?" I ask. "What were you doing there?"

He pokes around in the bowl while he chews. "Maybe I was visiting my home out of some sense of nostalgia." He gives a bitter smile and looks up before I can snarl again. "Louie texted me to meet him there. Said he'd figured out who was picking us off, but he wanted to talk in person."

"Why didn't you join up with your cousin before then? Safety in numbers and all that shit."

"Louie had no interest in teaming up. He ignored my calls and texts. But then, he always saw me as a weak link."

His mistake. Caligula Clemenza is just as wily as his grandfather was. "*Did* you kill your cousin?" I ask, because I'm still not a hundred percent sure he didn't.

"I keep *telling* you," he says wearily. "He was dead when I got there. I would have checked his phone to confirm that he was really the one who texted me, except right after I saw his body, that guy jumped out and tried to kill me, too. I ran." He gives me a defiant glare. "And then I ran into *you*. Now it's your turn to spill, Dami. Why are you asking me these questions in the first place?"

"I got orders to look into these Clemenza killings."

He stares at me. "Orders from whom?"

"You don't need to know that."

"Not your Boss," he says speculatively. "Big Gee never struck me as someone with much political savvy. Besides, he was happy when the Clemenzas went down. Luca D'Amato let him take over part of our territory."

"Doesn't matter who gave the order. You just tell me what I want to know."

But Caligula is still thinking, and there's a spark in his eyes when he inevitably figures it out. "His half-brother, the Underboss. Sebastiano Conti. He had a reputation as a reasonable man, last time I heard."

"Fine. It was him. Now, whose idea was it for you to go talk to Jesse Foster?"

He snorts. "My own. Not my finest moment, but I was out of choices. I even went to our Family lawyer right before then, hoping he could get me out of the country. But Tony Stuccio had no interest in helping, to put it mildly." He tilts his head to one side. "How long have you been following me, Dami?"

That's a question I don't want to answer. But the longer I pause, the more he'll read into it. "Since your father's funeral."

It hits. It hurts. I see the faint wince though he tries to hide it.

"Who wants the Clemenzas dead?" I ask him, moving on.

He shrugs. "Throw a dart and you'll hit someone. There were personal as well as professional grudges. Just look at the feeding frenzy that happened after Nonno Lou was whacked. At one point, I assumed the Morellis were involved."

"Well, it ain't them. Not to hear Seb tell it."

There must be a note in my voice, because he immediately asks, "You disagree with him?"

Do I? I'm not sure. "Luca D'Amato's priority is stability," I say slowly. "Has been since he took over. He made a lot of money after your grandpa went down, and the rest of us got ours, too. Everyone was happy." Caligula is looking pretty pale. I guess it's not much fun hearing how much his kin were hated. "But a while ago, D'Amato put out an order that the rest of you weren't to be touched."

I meant it as a small comfort. It lands as anything but. The Clemenza gets that red blotchy stain spreading up his neck and his cheeks as he spits, "He *murdered* my grandfather. Now he's trying to take credit for protecting us?"

I'm not used to seeing him so angry. Most of the time he's cold as ice. I watch his color ebb and flow with interest before I say, "You're missing the point, golden boy."

"*What* point?"

"Whoever's doing this is going against the king of the jungle. They either don't know or don't care that D'Amato put a protection order out. Ain't no way they don't know about it, if they've got beef with the Clemenzas. And if they don't care about D'Amato, well, that means they're either powerful enough or hidden enough to get away with it."

It might be the longest thing I've ever said to him. But Caligula takes it all in and then takes a deep breath. "Yes," he says on the breathe-out. "You're right." He's kickstarted his brain, that thinking machine that's always running in the background except when he gets mad, or…when he has an orgasm.

He asked why I jacked him off in the bathroom. It was mostly to dumb him down a little. I was hoping to get the intel I needed without sharing any of my own.

I'm almost impressed how fast he regained his focus.

"The man at the opera who attacked—" he begins, but I shake my head to save him the breath.

"No one knew him. So either he's a ghost—an operative, maybe imported from overseas to do the job—or more likely he was some street guy looking to make a few bucks. Because you'd have to be out of your mind or out of the loop to try something like that in a roomful of the big cats."

Caligula is staring at me.

"What?" I ask, feeling defensive for some reason.

"You're reasonably intelligent when you try to be," he sniffs. "The Bratva," he goes on. "Would they go against D'Amato?"

I think it over. "Maybe. If they thought they could keep it quiet."

"I told King I wanted to be anonymous," he says thoughtfully. "But he didn't honor that. Did they announce I was going to be…you know?"

"Selling your ass? Not that I heard. Those auctions happen on the regular."

"Then how did *you* know I was going to be at the Obelisk? Did you follow me there, too? You turned up right on cue."

I weigh up whether to tell him, since it'll change his mind pretty fast about me being *reasonably intelligent*, as he put it. But I don't give a fuck what the Clemenza thinks about me, and I have a suspicion we both fell for the same play. "I got a text. Told me to show up fast, said it would be advantageous in relation to my, uh. Well, it mentioned the Clemenzas."

The light in his eyes sharpens. "That was the word they used? 'Advantageous'?" I nod. "Louie's text to me used that word, too. I was impressed at the time that he even knew what it meant. But afterward, I realized it must have been whoever was trying to lure me there."

"To kill you, too?" I guess.

"Seems like." He pauses. "Or maybe to frame me. *You* thought I could be the one behind it all."

Not really. He has the smarts to do it, maybe even the stomach. But getting the jump on all his cousins and uncles, that would've been a big ask. Besides, what did he gain from all those deaths? Nothing. He still had to sell himself at the Obelisk.

And then there was the way he was running that night, running for his life from someone looking to do him harm.

No. Caligula Clemenza isn't behind all this. It's someone else.

He's already moved on. "But why did they contact you?" he murmurs aloud, though he's really talking to himself.

"I knew it was a trap," I say. "That text to show up at the Obelisk. But I was willing to take a risk if it meant…" I shrug.

But he's not going to let me shrug it off. "Exactly what did my father do to yours, Dami? Tell me. If I'm going to suffer for it, I'd like to know it was at least earned."

Part of me wants to hold it back. Why give the Clemenza what amounts to ammunition? And I don't like to think about that day more than I have to.

But what he's asked for is fair. If he's going to suffer—which I'll make sure he does, once he's healthy again, and

I've taken out whoever's trying to steal my vendetta from me—then the Clemenza should understand why.

"I was thirteen. At home. Heard a crash. Ran into the kitchen, and your dad was standing there over mine. He'd cut my father's throat…" I have to pause, squeeze my hands into fists so I don't grab the son of that man and shake him until his teeth rattle.

Caligula looks way too much like his dad. He's regarding me with those amber eyes, somber and quiet. "I'm sorry you had to see that," he says at last.

"But not sorry for what he did?" I snarl.

"If my father really did kill yours—"

"What the hell do you mean, *if* he really did?"

"—then he must have had a reason for it."

"I don't give a good goddamn *what* reason he had. He was invited in, came in all smiling and happy—"

"What do you mean?"

I spread my hands. "Your dad and mine. They were friends. Good friends. Right up until…"

His brows, a darker color than his hair, are pulling together. "They were friends? Then how come I never heard the Orsinis mentioned?"

"Because your father was a conniving snake who planned to turn on my dad soon as he got the order, that's why!" The need for vengeance is bubbling just below the surface, that always-present anger at the injustice of the whole world.

"Okay," Caligula sighs in a way that just pisses me off more.

But I can't get hold of him and shake the hell out of him like I want to, because he's fucking sick. So I stand instead and start pacing.

"What happened to your mother?" he asks after I've marched back and forth a few times.

"She's dead. Years ago. Yours?"

"She went back to Italy after I was born. Honestly, most of my life I assumed it was some kind of bloodline arrangement, you know? I can't remember the last time I spoke to her."

I don't really care about his mother. So I ask the question that's been on my mind. "How come you're still a virgin?"

He's lost the red blotchiness of anger that he had before, but my question makes him pink up a little. "I'm not sure how to answer that."

"You were savvy enough to turn a room full of kingpins rabid to get a chance at you during the auction. So how come you never got laid before? There something wrong with you?"

"There is nothing *wrong* with me," he snaps, nose lifting in the air as though I've offended him. "I just…"

"Just what?"

He puts down the bowl. "I'm tired, Dami. I need to sleep."

"You finish that sentence and I'll let you sleep."

It takes a lot of hard eye contact for him to see that I'm serious. "You know why," he says at last, clipped. "Because of my grandfather."

I snort. "You had a thing for him? You Clemenzas *are* sick."

"And you Giulianos live with your minds in the gutter," he says, real anger in his voice. "You said it yourself—about Sammy. What you saved him from. You know my Family would have done it to me, too, if they'd known."

I stop pacing, turn to him, fix him with a stare. "Yeah. I sure do know it. That's another reason I hate them so much. And you fucking should, too."

He smooths his hand over the quilt again, which Rosa made for me a few Christmases ago, the one she shook out and put over the unconscious Clemenza in my bed, just before I sent her off to call the nurse. "I told you before," he says quietly. "Love and hate have nothing to do with Family."

"You loved your father," I point out.

"Yes," he replies. The nose goes up in the air again. "I loved him because he protected me from my grandfather. So did Nonna Mellie. My grandfather sensed that I wasn't the hot-blooded hetero fucking-machine that his other grandsons were. And *I* knew there was something different about me, too. So that's why I stayed away from—from experimenting. I wanted to survive, Dami." He looks me straight in the eye. "I still want to survive. And I'll do whatever it takes."

"Down to sucking my dick?"

"Down to sucking your dick," he confirms.

I laugh. "At least you're being honest about it now. Whoring yourself out for your granddaddy's townhouse."

"You can't have it both ways, Dami. I can't be both virgin *and* whore." He gives a silky smile.

"Somehow," I mutter, "you find a fucking way."

His smile gets wider. "Have I hurt your feelings, Dami? Did you think I *enjoyed* sucking that barbaric club between your legs?"

I take a few quick steps toward the bed before I catch myself. He doesn't even shrink back, just watches me approach with that joyless smile that turns into a laugh when I pull up abruptly.

"For someone who wants to survive," I say, "you're sure doing your best to make me kill you."

"But you can't. Can you, Dami?"

"You think I care about some Bratva contract? If I want to spill your brains—"

"Oh, I think you'd like nothing better. But still...you can't. You won't."

"Oh, yeah?"

"Yeah." He looks up at me from beneath his lashes, eyes gleaming. "You told me yourself, just before—you're under orders not to. From Luca D'Amato, of all people. The irony really is delicious."

"You think I give a fuck what D'Amato wants any more than the Bratva?"

"I think you give a fuck what your *own* Boss wants. And he's D'Amato's bitch right now. Isn't he?"

I could fucking slap myself. Running my mouth to him, all I did was make him see how much my hands are tied. I should have remembered, all Clemenzas are liars, manipulators, *snakes*.

I hear myself laughing. "Your gramps had no idea what a poisonous little viper you are. If he had, he would've paid attention. Made you his direct heir instead of wasting time on all those others."

When I started talking, I could see I was pissing him off, just like I was aiming to. But by the time I finish, he's looking thoughtful again.

"What is it now?" I ask. "What's going on in that twisted brain of yours?"

"Heirs," he says slowly. "Whoever's doing this is making sure to eradicate the Family line of inheritance. They haven't gone for anyone *not* in line of succession. And I'm the last one who could be considered a direct heir." He looks at me, chewing his lower lip as he thinks. "What about those Loyalists you mentioned?"

Shit. Why the hell is he asking about them? For a second I wonder if he actually *does* know about the Loyalist movement, and that he's about to suggest the purge of his bloodline is just a kingmaker move on their part. Because the more I learn about Caligula Clemenza, the more I think he might actually make a decent Boss someday. He's got his grandfather's cunning and he's cool enough to keep his head under pressure. Maybe those Loyalists know Caligula would be a good pick, too.

"What about them?" I ask after a too-long pause.

"Well, *are* they all gone?"

I shrug, still unsure where this is headed. "Far as I know, they're dust—like you said yourself. D'Amato killed them all."

"That's a shame," he continues, almost to himself. "They might've known who's next in line after me."

"*After* you?" I echo. I pause to adjust my thought track, since he doesn't seem to be heading down the Loyalist line. "But why would that be a motive? The money's all gone. You Clemenzas are done."

I didn't mean it to come out so plain, but he takes it on the chin. "Yes," he says after a moment. "But there are more important things than money to some people, Dami. A name. A birthright."

He's not wrong. I think about Seb and Big Gee, and where the Family might be now if Seb was in charge. "I thought you were the last," I say slowly. "The last heir."

"So did I. But we should find out for sure."

It's a smart move. Just one problem. "How do we find out something like that?"

The Clemenza's golden eyes travel over me, head to toe and back again. "Surely a Giuliano Enforcer knows how to make people talk."

"Of course I fucking do," I say, but there's no heat there, just an uneasy sensation that I'm about to get played.

"Then we visit Uncle Tony together, and you apply a touch of persuasion. Like I said, Tony Stuccio was the

Family lawyer. If there's anyone left who knows about the line of succession, it's him."

I don't like the idea that Caligula Clemenza thinks he has the right to aim me at someone and pull the trigger. But his plan makes sense, and I have my orders from Seb.

"When you can stand up on your own again," I tell him, "we'll go visit this asshole."

He nods. We've forged a truce that's about as stable as a seesaw, but it'll do for now.

"By the way, Dami," he says as I rise to leave, "snakes aren't poisonous."

"What?"

"Snakes are venomous. I'm a *venomous* little viper."

I stare at him, at his smug goddamn face, and shake my head. "Yeah. I'll keep that in mind."

CHAPTER 30
DAMIANO

I LEAVE the Clemenza to sleep for a while and go down to get a long-overdue first coffee of the day from Rosa. Sammy is in the kitchen, too.

"What are you doing sitting around?" I ask him.

Usually he's out running errands for Rosa in the mornings. But he's sitting there at the counter, watching her cook.

"Nothing to do," he says, but the way he stares at me makes me think he's been waiting for me to make an appearance.

Rosa, without comment, busies herself making me a coffee. I sit up at the counter next to Sammy rather than take the coffee up top to the sunroom, where I usually have it in the mornings. I don't want to be any closer to the Clemenza than I have to right now. There's something about him that gets my brain clouded. The further I stay away from him, the better.

"Where's the Clemenza?" Sammy asks casually, as though he read my mind.

I'm surprised enough to answer. "I don't know where the fuck you heard that name, but you keep it to yourself."

"The asshole told me himself, said his name like he was *proud* of it." Sammy's eyes flash as he turns to face me.

"It's got nothing to do with you, Sammy." I wish I'd gone up to the sunroom like usual. If I'm not getting harassed upstairs, I'm getting harassed downstairs.

"Are you fucking him?"

I almost spit my coffee back in the cup. "What the hell did you just say?"

"I asked if you're fucking him." There's a cold, obstinate look on Sammy's face when I stare at him.

"You keep out of my business. Don't make me tell you again."

There's silence, blessed silence for a minute, maybe two. Then Sammy keeps on pushing. "If you're not fucking him, why's he here?"

"It's *not your business*," I snarl.

Rosa is glaring at me now. As though *I'm* the one being unreasonable.

The problem is, I understand why Sammy is pushing this. It's not just the Clemenza thing, though God knows that would be enough. The night I saved his life, he was getting beat within an inch of it in a back alley by a bunch of Clemenza thugs.

But that's only part of it.

He's...always had kind of a thing for me. I've never encouraged it. In fact, the one time I was dumb enough to fall asleep in the downstairs lounge, and woke to Sammy's hands sliding up my thighs, I grabbed his wrists and told him to *get*. He ran out and didn't try to speak to me again for a week.

It's just misplaced gratitude, and he doesn't know how to express it except sexually. He grew up real rough, and the only way he ever knew how to pay for things was with his body. So I don't want to come down too hard on him, but he's sure making it difficult.

"But—" he starts again.

I slam down my coffee cup, turning to him. He shrinks back at the look on my face. "You don't get to question what I do in my own house. Do you hear me?"

I'm horrified to see his eyes start to shine with tears. "It's my house, too. You're not the only one who lives here."

"You're here because I'm *letting* you be here."

"You said I was family," he says, the hurt clear in his voice now. And the thing is, when I took him in, that's what I told him. That he'd be like family if he could keep on the straight and narrow, listen to Rosa, do what we told him.

"Family doesn't question the Boss," I growl. "Now get out of here, go do something useful."

He shoves back his chair hard so that it scrapes on the floor, and I roll my eyes as he stomps toward the doorway. Sammy is twenty-six, but his emotional growth stunted around five, probably from the horrific shit he started going through at that age. So when he turns in the doorway again and he's crying for real, I'm not surprised. "I thought I *meant* something to you!"

For fuck's sake, how am I supposed to react to that? "You *do* mean something to me," I tell him, trying to find a way to be gentle. "But…" I shrug, because I'm real bad at emotional shit like this.

And it's exactly the wrong thing to do. There's a fractured look of pain in his eyes, and he turns with slumped shoulders, heading back down the hallway. A second later I hear a door close as Sammy goes back into his room. It's not even a slam.

I'd feel better if it was a slam.

The disapproval on Rosa's face just makes me feel worse. "What are you looking at, woman?"

"A man making everyone miserable, just because he's miserable himself." She shakes her head, muttering more in Italian that I can't catch.

"If you have something to say, fucking say it." I sound more dangerous than I ever have when speaking to her, but I don't regret it. This is *my* house, for Christ's sake. I won't have people disrespecting me in it.

But Rosa is not cowed. She folds her arms, leans back against the counter opposite, and gives it to me. "This might be your house, but you're doing badly by everyone under your roof. That boy upstairs, Sammy, me—and yourself, too. Get your head screwed on straight."

"What do you want from me, Rosa? If you wanted a hero, you're working for the wrong guy."

Rosa snorts. "It's true, you're not a good man. But you're a better one than this. Sammy adores you. He doesn't deserve to be insulted for it. And as for that boy upstairs—"

"He's *not a boy*!" I slam my fist down on the counter next to the coffee cup.

Why does everyone insist on calling him that? He's a grown-ass man who wasn't able to take care of himself, and he should be thankful he ended up with me, the one fucker in New York City with a legitimate reason to kill him who *can't*.

Rosa leans over, takes my coffee cup away, and dumps it out in the sink. "As for that boy upstairs," she goes on calmly, "you should be ashamed of yourself. Now get out of here and let me get back to working for you."

The sarcasm drips off her tongue, and I feel like shit for acting as though she and Sammy are nothing more than staff.

The truth is, I would die for them as well. That's why

I'm so mad at being treated like this, spoken to like this, by people who should know me better.

But if I keep going like this, I'll find myself out of a housekeeper in the next five seconds. I'm pretty sure I've reached Rosa's limit. Vito would probably follow her out the door. And then Sammy.

"I'll be glad to fucking get out of here," I tell her. "Tell Vito to pull around front in the car and wait for me there."

I spend the rest of the day doing the only thing I seem to be good at, which is making people hurt. There are quite a few crews that need encouragement to pull their weight right now, and I'm happy to explain to them the error of their ways.

Once my hands are sore and aching, I can finally think straight again. Rosa was right, even though I don't want her to be. Having the Clemenza in the house is making me crazy. He belongs in the basement. The sooner he gets better, and the sooner we figure out who's hunting his line, the sooner I can put him back there.

That means I need to take good care of him over the next few days to hurry things along.

When I get back home in the evening, I head down into the kitchen. Sammy's there, eating dinner with Rosa, his back to the door. He doesn't turn even though Vito comes in from the side door and gives me a nod, telling me the car is put away for the night. Rosa stands expectantly, wiping her hands down her apron to smooth it.

"Rosa, I need a tray. Two meals."

She nods and starts putting it together. As I go past Sammy, I ruffle his hair exactly the way I always do. "You keep out of trouble today?"

He pulls away with a scowl, but I know I'm forgiven when he says, "Always."

"Good to hear."

Vito happily sits down to the meal Rosa has kept hot for him, sneaking a peek at her as she bustles around. She pretends to ignore it, but her eyes slide his way when he starts eating. Those two have been circling each other for years now. Maybe one day they'll get it together. But it's not my business, and I have enough of my own to take care of.

"Should I send it in the dumbwaiter?" Rosa asks when the tray is ready.

"I'll take it up myself."

It's about as close to an apology as she's going to get, but the look of approval on her face tells me she's accepted it. She puts it into my hands and then turns back to fuss over Sammy and Vito.

At least the air's been cleared downstairs.

Time to face the fog that always comes over me near the Clemenza. I head upstairs slowly, since I don't want to drop the tray. Slow and steady, up all those flights of stairs, instead of taking the elevator. Gives me a few extra minutes to get my head on straight.

I set the tray down on a side table in the hallway near my room and fish out the door key from my pocket. I've kept it with me all day, a reminder of what was waiting for me back home as I beat some sense into my own men.

Big Gee likes to run a tight ship, and I've never complained before. Under the old Don, I didn't get as much of a chance to get my hands dirty. I was proud when Big Gee started calling on me more. Annoyed when Sebastiano called for restraint, if there was any discussion had, since Big Gee ain't much for discussion. Seb does what he can, but the Boss knows his own mind. I guess that's why he's the Boss.

But as I unlock the door and turn back for the tray, see my thick, red knuckles close around the dainty little thing, I wonder for the first time if Seb's right. Sometimes a beat-down isn't the best answer. Sometimes you gotta win hearts and minds instead of break bones.

Because in the end, we're no better than the Clemenzas, if that's our approach.

I lever the handle with my elbow and kick open the door.

Caligula Clemenza is sitting up in bed, staring at me. "*Finally*," he says with a scowl. "I know how we can get to Uncle Tony."

I really thought I'd managed to clear my head today. But there it goes again, that haze in my mind whenever I lay eyes on him.

I thought for a while it was just rage. The need for vengeance. I'm not so sure anymore.

"Eat this first," I tell him. "Then you can tell me your brilliant plan."

He smiles smugly. "It *is* brilliant. But it will require some assistance."

I set the tray down on the bed and hand him a bowl of white bean soup. He takes it—eagerly, I note, since I guess the protein shakes I left with him weren't exactly Rosa's home cooking. He's drunk them all, though, or at least, he's left a pile of empty plastic containers littered on the nightstand.

"We need to do this alone," I tell him, taking my own bowl. "For various fucking reasons."

He eyes me, probably thinking about those reasons like I am.

The most obvious: he's a target. The most important: he's my property, and I don't need him thinking he's anything more than that.

Then he smiles. "It's alright, Dami. You've got the brawn. I've got the brain. All we need now are the right clothes."

I squint at him, wondering if I heard that right.

But I must have, because he goes on, "And for that, we'll need Lorenzo Benedetti."

CHAPTER 31
CALIGULA

"I STILL DON'T SEE why we need Benedetti," Damiano says dubiously, once I've outlined my plan. It's simple, really, despite its genius. There's no way Uncle Tony is going to let me in to see him again. So I'll double down on that, create a scene in the foyer, and make enough of a diversion that Dami can slip right by into the hallway that leads to the offices.

"Because you need to be invisible," I tell him. "So you need to look the part."

"I've got suits. I don't need another one from Benedetti."

I sigh. "Dami, just trust me on this one. I looked through your wardrobe—"

"You *what*?"

I try not to glare at him. "You leave me here all day alone, what do you think I'm going to do? I explored."

He glares back. "You mean you stuck your nose where it don't belong."

"What's behind that door?" I ask, seeing an opening. I point at the door across the room, the one with a fingerprint scanner like the one that lets Damiano down to the basement level of this creepy house. His glare continues. "Okay, look. You *do* have a few suits, Dami." He has several off-rack, ten-year-old suits with shiny elbows—but I don't expand, since he's got that stubborn look on his face. "But you need something different to get into this legal firm. They'll clock you from a mile away otherwise."

He throws his silverware into his bowl and puts it back on the tray, brooding. "I don't like this plan."

I'm pretty sure I know why, too. We might as well get it out in the open. "You think I'm going to run if I get a chance."

His immediate scowl tells me I hit the bullseye. I did wonder how he'd react to the idea of me having the slightest bit of agency. He'll need to trust me to do my part, and then trust that I'll willingly go back into my prison afterward.

"I'm not going to run," I tell him.

"And I'm just supposed to take the word of a Clemenza?"

"I have no *reason* to run," I tell him coldly. "You're currently my only protection, Orsini. Surely you haven't forgotten that. You remind me of it often enough."

He stands to prowl the room. Damiano is the kind of man who likes to be moving while he's thinking. I'm the opposite. My brain is most active when my body is at rest. If he knew that, he'd probably mandate physical exercise all day, every day while I'm here.

"So I get into his office. Then what?" he asks at last.

I almost laugh at that, since it's the simplest part of all. "You're an Enforcer. Enforce."

If I didn't know better, I'd swear I saw Dami smile. But still he paces.

"Well?" I ask at last. I'm getting tired again, and cranky like a toddler with it. But I'm feeling a hell of a lot better than I did down there in the basement, since those protein shakes—despite tasting like depression made liquid—are actually helping.

"I'll think about it," he says. "I need a shower."

He locks the bathroom door. If he hadn't, I wonder if I'd try to press the advantage I have right now and go in after him, stretch my fledgling seduction skills a little more.

I got sick at the right time. It wasn't pleasant, no. But it was useful, since here I am, back in his bed again. I'd rather not be put back in that basement, so I'll need to be more careful in the future.

But when he comes out and heads for the bedroom door to lock it, tucking the damn key into the briefs he's put on, I immediately forget my resolution. There's something about Damiano Orsini that just makes me enjoy needling him.

"Where are you sleeping tonight, Dami? Bed's taken."

He stands next to it, looking down at me. "Shut up and move over."

I blink up at him, taken aback despite myself. The whole time I've been recovering here, I've been sleeping alone. I thought that one time co-sleeping after the opera attack was unlikely to happen again. "Really?"

"You think I'm giving up my fucking bed for you?" he growls. "Move over."

I suppose I should consider myself lucky he's not chaining me to the headboard. I shuffle over awkwardly until he's satisfied, then snuggle down and turn my back on him, my heart beating hard. The light goes out, leaving the room in total blackness, since the metal shutters are still down over the windows, and there are no electronics in the bedroom to give ambient light.

I hear him get into the bed, the mattress dipping under his considerable size so that I find myself rolling back into him despite myself.

His arm goes around me. "You're not going anywhere tonight, little prince," he says, gripping me tight.

I say nothing, just lie there tense and wide awake.

But I must have fallen asleep, because I wake to his powerful grip tightening and *tightening* around me, crushing me hard enough that I fear asphyxiation. "*Hey,*" I wheeze, trying to wriggle my way out. It's no use, and he's talking, muttering—

He's asleep. He's asleep and dreaming, a bad dream. A terrible dream, based on the labored breathing and the plaintive note in his mumbling non-words.

"*Dami,*" I get out, but it's no use. He's deep in his nightmare. So I do the only thing I can, and kick him, hard.

He jerks awake, arm tightening one more excruciating fraction before it relaxes, and I suck in a deep lungful of oxygen. "Jesus *Christ,*" I pant. "It was just a dream, Dami. Just a dream."

He seems to hear me, because he gives a long sigh of what sounds like relief, and rolls onto his back, leaving me feeling strangely cold and unmoored. I guess I got used to the hot iron band encircling me.

I turn over in the bed and curl up close again, wishing I could see his face. I can't see anything at all, only hear his still-ragged breathing. "What were you dreaming?"

"Don't remember," he mutters.

Without getting distracted by trying to read his face, I hear the lie much more clearly in his voice. We made a deal about that. But I'm not going to push. I'm not sure I *want* to know what nightmares a Giuliano Enforcer might suffer. He's certainly willing enough to bring them into the waking world.

I reach out and slide a hand over his shoulder. He doesn't pull away. Doesn't tell me to fuck off. Just keeps breathing, trying to regulate.

I can't see his face. Can't read the warning signs I've learned to watch for. All I have is touch—the heat of his skin, the tension in his muscles, the way his breathing changes when my fingers trace along his collarbone.

His breath catches. Then his hand covers mine, pressing it flat against his chest. I feel his heartbeat, still too fast from whatever horror chased him through sleep.

Neither of us moves. Neither of us speaks.

And then his hand slides up my arm, finds my jaw, tilts my face toward his even though we can't see each other. "This won't mean anything," he says roughly.

"I know."

"I still hate you."

"I know."

I slide on top of him.

His arms go around me and he's already hard against my thigh, but I don't want to rush. I want to really get to know his body this time.

It's different in the dark. More honest, somehow, as though our bodies can tell each other what we really want without all that messy stuff in the background like his father and my father and the auction and the basement…

If I wanted to, I could pretend I was with someone else. But I don't want to. I want to know that this is Damiano Orsini whose arms are around me, pulling my head to one side so he can suck at my neck. He can't help being controlling, even now, even when I'm stretched out on top of him. But I'll let him.

Because I like it.

His lips move up to my ear, my cheek, getting closer to my mouth—but then he stops, pulls my head to the other side, and continues licking down the other side of my neck.

I take a gamble. I pull back and then force the issue, trying to angle my mouth toward his. He pushes my face aside.

He's not going to kiss me.

Well, that's fine. Not where I really want his mouth, anyway, is it? I rock against him, slow, languid, a tease of friction. I feel how hard he is, how hot, how much he wants this.

I want it, too. I start speeding up.

"You like that, don't you?" he mutters against my neck. "You like grinding on my cock like a little bitch in heat."

The words are ugly, but they make me harder. "Maybe," I breathe back. "Or maybe I'm getting bored."

His hands tighten on my hips. Then he rolls me right off him, onto my belly, and pins me beneath him. I gasp at the sudden change in position, at the solid weight of him. In the total blackness, all my other senses are heightened—the shift of our clothes, the smell of him, the hard press of his cock against the back of my thigh.

He shoves my pajama pants down, and I kick them off my ankles. The bed shudders and shakes as he moves about, ripping his own briefs off too, I guess. "Hands and knees," he tells me.

I scramble to comply, my ass in the air. A wave of heat goes through me as I wait for him to move between my legs, slapping my thighs until I widen them, my asshole clenching with anticipation.

This is it. He's going to fuck me. *Finally*.

His hands close around my hips and yank them higher and higher, until I'm almost balanced on my toes. He spreads my asscheeks open and I feel his breath just a moment before his tongue finds my hole.

I choke down a groan, but he keeps licking all over me, his stubble scraping as he rubs his face into me. I push back shamelessly, wanting more, deeper, harder. I've been wanting this again since that night of the opera, to feel his tongue *there* again, to have him work me open with his fingers, too, get me desperate for him.

I'll even beg for it again, if that's what he wants. As long as he gives it to me. This virginity of mine, no matter how technical it might be, has become a burden. Something he can weaponize against me. I want to get rid of it, remove at least one of those pain points he likes to press into.

And maybe I just want to know how it feels. If having this man's monster cock inside me will finally quiet down all my Family's ghosts. Exorcise the ones haunting *him*.

And, hell, maybe I just want to fuck. To know what it's like to have someone else's body filling up my own.

All I know is, I'm in a fever of need. Whatever he does to me, I crave it, need it like oxygen. So I press back against his face, begging silently with my body. His spit runs down between my legs, trickling over my balls and making me moan as much as the sensation of his tongue—

He eases me back down, letting me get my balance on hands and knees again before pulling my back flush against his chest. His muscular thighs bracket mine, keeping my legs locked tight, and this has to be it, right? He's finally going to do it.

I hear him spitting into his palm to slick himself up, and panic zips through me. I assumed there'd be lube, not just—

But then I feel his thick head pressing not between my cheeks, but lower, pushing between my clenched thighs, gliding over the sensitive flesh of my perineum and nudging up against my balls. His cock is a hot, hard bar of flesh sliding back and forth, the friction against my skin maddening. "Stay still," he hisses when I wriggle around, trying to help him find what he must be looking for, because surely—

He reaches up to grab a handful of my hair. Not hard, just a warning. "Stay. Still."

And he keeps doing exactly what he was doing, fucking into the spit-soaked junction of my ass and thighs. I feel every ridge, every bump, as he slides back and forth, his cockhead even teasing my hole now and then, but never more than that.

His fist loosens in my hair, trails down my chest, my stomach, and finds my dick, just as hard as his, and jacks me in the same rhythm as he thrusts. My hips jerk, seeking more of both sensations. His hand. His cock.

"That's better," he pants, and the pride in his voice soothes my disappointment. Because I know, now. He's not going to kiss me. He's not going to fuck me. He's not going to give me a single ounce of power that he doesn't have to.

As if to prove my theory, he murmurs in my ear, "You like being treated like some fucktoy, huh?"

I can only moan in response, pushing back into him, clamping tighter around his shaft. He smacks his hand down hard on my left cheek, the sting sharp and immediate. It brings back the memory of being bent over his lap, coming all over his pants while he spanked me like a naughty child.

And he's thinking of that, too. "Remember how you shot your load all over me," he breathes. "Got off on learning your place?"

I wish I could be angry. Wish I could snipe back at him, but my whole attention is on my dick and the grip he has on it. My body is alight with a raw need as he drives into the tight, wet space between my thighs. His thumb presses into my slit, smearing pre-cum everywhere.

"Yeah, you remember," he chuckles darkly, his rhythm

getting faster. "And you're gonna come for me again. But you shoot that mess into your hand, you hear me? Not all over these sheets that I sleep in."

The dirty talk, the feel of him, the denial, and the sheer reality of being *used* like this—it all coalesces into a storm of sensation that detonates almost before I'm aware. I come with a loud, protracted cry, spilling into my own palm obediently, my whole body trembling, my asshole clenching and unclenching on nothing.

He pulls me close with an arm around my body, his cockhead nestling into my balls, and tugs my overflowing hand up to my mouth. "Come on, golden boy. You need your protein." His grip tightens around my wrist until I have no choice but to open my lips and taste the mess from my own fingers. My face is burning, but a deeper, darker heat swims through me as I lick at it.

He throws me down onto my back and straddles me, his heavy cock resting on my belly. There's a thump beside my head as he falls forward onto one hand. He leans in so close I feel the warmth of his breath on my sweat-soaked face, and I think maybe he's going to finally do it, maybe he'll lean in and kiss me—

CHAPTER 32
DAMIANO

I WANT to kiss Caligula Clemenza.

His chest heaves as he breathes beneath me, harsh and fast as though he's excited all over again.

As for me, I might burst if he so much as lays a finger on me. God, the way he wriggled around while I enjoyed myself between his legs. Felt like wet, hot velvet. I had to exert every ounce of self-control to avoid taking the angle that would let my dick sneak into his tight little knot.

I won't fuck him. I definitely can't kiss him. So I do the only thing I *can* do.

I pull his sticky fingers up to my mouth and start sucking them clean. He tastes so good, so sweet and silky, that I almost groan. I lick right up his palm, chasing the rest.

He makes a strangled, helpless sound beneath me. I stare down at him in the utter blackness while I work my tongue over his hand. I can't see him. But his other hand is sliding coyly up my shoulder, around the back of my neck, trying to pull me down to kiss him.

No fucking way.

I pull my mouth off of his fingers with a wet pop and roll away onto the bed, my dick slapping against my belly, complaining and angry. I ignore it and leave the bed to go clean up in the bathroom. I run a washcloth under water and bring it back to the bedroom for him. "Here," I say, tossing it in the dark.

It seems to land alright, a soggy slap on skin that makes him gasp. I hear him running it over himself.

My dick has finally died down. I need to stop doing this to myself; it's torturing me more than it's humiliating him. Everything I said tonight, he just took as dirty talk, got off on it as much as…

Well. As much as I did.

"What do you want me to do with—" he begins.

"Just throw it on the floor, for Christ's sake. And then move over."

A second later, I feel a breeze past my arm and hear a damp splat against the wall behind. That little fucker balled up the cloth and threw it at me.

But I guess I can't blame him. And I can't prove it, either. There are no cameras in my bedroom that I could review, even if I wanted to.

So I just get back into bed and put my arm back around him.

"Are you going to crush me in your sleep again, Dami?" he needles. "Because if so—"

"Shut up and go to sleep," I mutter, holding him tighter.

I don't plan to give him any chance to get out of bed without me knowing. If that means I have to hold onto him all night like a prickly fucking teddy bear, then that's what I'll do.

I wake the next morning to find the Clemenza gone from my bed.

I sit up, alert and on edge, but I hear the water running in the bathroom. How the hell does he keep sneaking out of bed without me noticing? I've never been a deep sleeper. I usually wake at the slightest sound. But with my greatest enemy in my bed, I'm dead to the world.

I wonder if he drugged me somehow, but then I remember the nightmare, the same one as always, watching my father die. Cesario Clemenza turning on me as well—

And the sex.

I remember the sex, too. The feel of him. The taste of him…

And the aftermath. I look around the room, and yep, there it is. That washcloth, balled up and dry now, lying next to the wall.

Trying to outrun memories before they can take hold, I get up and open the bathroom door. He's there in the shower, just finishing up as I come in, since he turns off the water a second later and opens the door to look at me, slicking back the wet hair from his face. "All yours," he says.

I can't pick the tone. He doesn't sound as cold as he sometimes does, but he sure as hell doesn't sound as open and vulnerable as he did last night when I was—

"Thanks," I say gruffly. "I'll just be a minute."

He slides past me, but his arm brushes mine, and I'm very, very aware that we're both naked. So is my dick, which starts to perk up hopefully, so I lean into the shower and start the cold tap. I find myself trying not to watch him dry off, but why shouldn't I watch? It's my bathroom.

And he's my property.

He feels a little less mine than he did yesterday, somehow. And a whole lot less than when I hauled him down to the basement to punish him.

Once he's back down there, everything will go back to how it should be.

I step into the cold water and try not to gasp too obviously at the shock of it, then lean out to close the glass door behind me, but he catches it with a foot.

"We should call Lorenzo," he says, tucking the towel around his waist.

I'm too busy worrying that he's going to see my hard-on and get the wrong idea to argue about it now. "Sure. Fine. Whatever."

When I get out of the shower, he's bundled up in my robe again, and now I *know* he's doing it on purpose. "Take it off," I order. His eyebrows go up, but he shrugs it off. And then he just stands there buck naked. "What are you waiting for? Get dressed."

"I have no clean clothes in here," he says patiently. "Which is why I took the robe."

I'm tempted to tell him he can strut around naked in front of his precious *Lorenzo*. But then I find my sense. "Whatever." I ball up the robe and throw it into his chest. He catches it, swaying slightly on his feet. "I'll get Rosa to run some laundry later."

He puts the robe back on without comment, and then silently watches me dress. When I head into my walk-in closet I catch sight of one of my old suits.

Okay, I see his point. That suit is not the kind of thing I'd wear these days. I got it back before I was really making any money. "I'll get Rosa to call Benedetti over," I say loudly so he can hear.

"I'm sure he'll be intrigued," says a voice from much closer than I expected. I don't jump, but I turn fast. He's leaning up against the door frame, my robe slipping down one shoulder, and he has a slight smile. "Another emergency call-out so soon."

I'm standing there with one hand on my cheap suit. I have to force myself to keep moving, keep sorting through the clothes, instead of going over to him and yanking the robe right off him.

"I bet he'll be happy to see *you* again," I grunt as I slide a hand through my shirts. "And for Christ's sake, restrain yourself from ordering the most expensive fucking fabric he has this time."

"Why? It's not like you can't afford it." When I glance his way, he's smiling a little more. "You need to learn to dress for the man you are, Dami, not the man you once were."

I shake my head. "I got no time to worry about fashion. I've got a job to do, and I do it well."

"Yes," he agrees softly. "You must do it very well to be living so large."

I can't read his tone, but when I glance his way again, he's disappeared, back to the bedroom. I pull on my clothes, and then fish out the door key from my underwear where I kicked them off in the bed last night.

Neither of us has mentioned it, that fumble in the dark. It was so erotic at the time, but I can barely believe it happened now.

I pause while unlocking the door and look over my shoulder at him. "Let's get this straight, Clemenza. If I could keep you naked and caged, hell, plugged every day, I'd do it. But the nurse said to keep you warm. So I'm gonna keep you warm, make sure you get real healthy again. When we've sorted out this Uncle Tony shit and found whoever is hunting your line, you know what happens."

"Oh, yes. I know what will happen."

He doesn't look as worried about it as he should.

Lorenzo Benedetti arrives later that morning with the same tools and swatches that he brought before. This time, when Rosa brings him into the great room, both the Clemenza and I are there to greet him together. He brightens immediately on seeing Caligula. But I step forward and put out my hand to shake, so he knows who's really in charge.

"Another tuxedo?" he asks Caligula with a beaming smile.

"Not exactly," I say. "I need a business suit."

His eyes stray to me with surprise. "It's for you, Mr. Orsini?"

Caligula steps forward before I can ask Benedetti what's so fucking surprising about that. "I told him we simply had to call you in again. No one cuts a suit quite like you do. Not this side of the Atlantic, anyway."

The old man practically giggles and blushes. I suppose there's something to be learned from Caligula Clemenza, if I wanted to charm and flatter people. I don't think I'd be as good at it as he is, though.

"We'd better take some measurements," Benedetti says, bustling toward me with a measuring tape.

"You heard the man, Dami," Caligula coos. "Strip."

"I don't need to strip—" I start.

"The cut *will* be much superior if I can drape it specifically to your musculature," Benedetti says.

Maybe he just wants my dick in his face or something. But I don't like the grin Caligula has on his face. I know this is intended as payback, but hell, at least *I'm* not wearing a cock cage. Besides, I've got no problem with nudity.

"Just sit down," I growl at the Clemenza. "And put that damn blanket over your knees. Rosa will have my hide if she doesn't think you're warm enough."

She's already been fussing around him this morning, getting on my last nerve. Caligula takes my usual seat, pulling the blanket over his knees obediently. He gives a bright smile and says, "This time you can be *my* dress-up doll, Dami."

I'm about to tell him to shut his mouth when Benedetti lets out a fatherly chuckle and shakes his head at me as though we're sharing a joke together. "Signor Clemenza seems much improved," he confides to me in a low voice. "I am glad to see someone in the city is caring for him. He does not deserve the things that have happened to him."

I don't want to get into a big discussion about that, so I start stripping off, because it usually shuts people up. And it works, as far as Benedetti goes—his eyes widen only slightly, but from him, that's as good as a gasp and a pearl clutch.

The tattoos all over my arms and the scars on various parts of my body are threatening enough as they are, but my muscles are just as impressive. And they should be. I've been working on them since I was thirteen.

Benedetti starts measuring me, and soon he has an air of professional focus. I'm not sure if that's any better, since he has me turning this way and that, and at one point I have to face Caligula full on, arms extended, and watch him gawk at me without shame.

"He really is a remarkable specimen," Caligula says. "Don't you think so, Lorenzo?"

"Oh yes," the tailor murmurs, noting down figures with a small pencil in a tiny notebook. "It is a privilege to dress a man like this."

It's the first time I've ever heard Lorenzo Benedetti say something about me that sounded sincere.

And there's a benefit to playing along with the Clemenza, which is that Benedetti's respect begins to extend to me. By the time he leaves, he's bowed and scraped to me as much as he has to Caligula. Of course, it shouldn't take the golden tongue of a snake to earn me the respect of a fucking tailor, but even so…

It feels pretty good.

When we're done, I walk the man out myself, telling Caligula to stay right there in the chair and save his strength. "Listen," I say to Benedetti at the door. "I know this ain't something you normally do, but Caligula, he needs a whole wardrobe. Not custom," I add hastily. "Bought stuff is fine. But he came to me with almost nothing and—"

"Signor Orsini, it would be my greatest pleasure. You are right, it is not our normal work, but my wife, Maria, is very fond of the young gentleman, and would be delighted to pick out an appropriate wardrobe for him. We have a grandson just a little older than Signor Clemenza, who shares the same taste; he will be able to advise."

"Appreciate it," I tell him. Except I think I'm talking more about his respect toward me than his agreement to act as a personal shopper for my captive. Either way, Benedetti takes it as another sign of my care for the Clemenza. If it lifts my cred with the guy, I guess it'll be worth it.

When I go back to the great room, Caligula looks pleased with himself but tired. He still hasn't fully recovered from his exhaustion, and I guess keeping him up half the night sawing my dick between his thighs didn't help much. "You better go sleep," I tell him.

"I'm not tired." But his eyes are already half-closed as I put out a hand to help him from the chair. "When did Lorenzo say the suit would be ready?"

"I told him it wasn't urgent. A few days, probably. You're still barely able to get out of bed for a couple of hours, so there's no point getting a rush job on the suit if we don't need it yet."

When we get back up to my bedroom, I usher him in, and I stay outside.

He turns to me, somehow surprised that I'm not gonna lock myself in there with him. "Where are you going?" he asks.

"You don't ask questions," I remind him.

He sighs. "Well, I guess I'll see you tonight."

I shut the door on him and lock him in.

I shouldn't be looking forward to seeing him again as much as I am.

CHAPTER 33
DAMIANO

I SPEND the next two nights sleeping in one of the guest rooms down the hallway.

It's helped clear my head to stay away, even though the Clemenza grew more and more cold every time I brought in a meal—or more protein shakes. Having tasted one of those things myself, I can see why he objects.

Frankly, his spunk was a lot tastier.

But he's definitely getting healthier. His skin has that glow to it that caught my eye at his father's funeral. He was eighteen and trembling in the rain under an umbrella, but he still had that rich-kid aura about him.

He lost that sheen over the next few years. But when I saw him on the Obelisk stage, shining with golden dust, it reminded me of that first day I laid eyes on him.

I hadn't considered him at all before that funeral. Hadn't ever seen him in real life. And I hated him the moment I saw him. Made my decision then and there, that he'd pay for his father's sins.

Things have gotten a little complicated since then, so staying away from him is a good way to clear my head, no matter how mad *he* might get.

But today is the day. This morning when I took in his breakfast, the Clemenza's skin had returned to its natural glow, the one that always made me think of him as his Family's golden boy, long before I ever saw him covered in the real stuff.

And just after lunch, a big fucking delivery van pulled up at the service entry, and I had to raise the security system just to let a fashion show troop into my house.

The suit is here. And so are all the other clothes I asked Benedetti to provide for the little prince. Truth be told, I kind of forgot about that. It was a spur-of-the-moment thing. Well, I hope the Clemenza likes them, because he can think about that high-end wardrobe while he's languishing naked in the basement again for the rest of the year.

When I open my bedroom door, he's draped in my robe, walking around the room aimlessly like he's about to lose his mind. He stops dead and folds his arms to glare at me, but says nothing. I know why he's pissed. It's because I haven't given him a chance to manipulate me for the last two nights. Must be frustrating for him.

"C'mere," I say, and crook a finger at him. He approaches cautiously until I back up out of the doorway. "Move it. We're going to visit your Uncle Tony."

At that, he practically shoots out the door.

"Downstairs. To the great room." He follows my orders without complaint, but when we get to the room he stops again to stare.

The minions Benedetti sent over with the clothes spent some time setting up a rolling rack of what his wife bought for the Clemenza, and laid everything that couldn't be hung all over the sofa. "What's this?" Caligula asks suspiciously.

"Looks like clothes."

He approaches them as cautiously as he approached me upstairs, reaching out to touch one of the shirts as though he's not sure it really exists. "What..." He turns back to me, a strange look on his face.

Ah, fuck. I think it's hope.

"Sometimes I'm gonna need to take you out, prove to Luca D'Amato or Big Gee that I ain't killed you yet," I tell him. "You need clothes for that. That's all it is, golden boy."

It doesn't seem to have dampened down his delight in the clothes any. He takes his time running his hands over them, testing the fabrics and holding them up to himself just to see how they fall.

They're all perfect. I guess the Benedettis spent some time tailoring the off-the-rack stuff to fit the little prince as well.

"We gotta make a move," I say at last. "Get across Midtown traffic to see this uncle of yours."

"He's not really my uncle. But yes." He turns to me with an air of business. "The suit?"

I point to a garment bag hanging up at the end of one of the rolling racks. Caligula unzips it and takes out a sleeve of the jacket, nodding. "Perfect. Of course. And these must be for you, too—" He reaches behind to where three plastic-covered shirts are hanging as well. I assumed they were for him, but when he holds up one, I can see it would swamp him.

I frown. "I've *got* shirts. I didn't ask for those."

"You do have shirts," he agrees. "But these are better. Time to play dress-up, Dami." He flicks a finger at me, up and down. "Strip."

I'm already pulling my t-shirt up over my head before I even think about getting pissed at some Clemenza trying to boss me around. But now's not the moment for me to correct him; we need to time this interrogation right. We figured going early evening would be best, when the sun's already on the way down. Caligula said all the lawyers would still be at the office, and it'll be best to do what we need to do with the aid of darkness covering our tracks.

I even let him help me dress, since I figure he knows better than I do how to make it look decent. The tailor included a few ties with the shirts, and Caligula selects one in a deep green. "It will bring out the green in your eyes," he says.

"My eyes are brown," I protest.

"Yes. But they have shards of jade and emerald as well."

Shards of jade and fucking emerald? I just let him tie some complicated knot and adjust it around my neck. He presses a hand down to make the tie sit right and looks up into my face. "There," he says. "Perfect."

He's standing close enough that I swear to God I can feel his body heat, and my robe is sliding down that golden shoulder again. Without thought, my hands come up and close around his biceps, pulling him a little closer so that he has to tip his head back, his throat a long column, his lips falling open as his golden eyes grow heavy-lidded—

A noise in the doorway makes us both turn our heads sharply, but I don't let him go. If anything, I instinctively pull him closer, as though there's any threat in my own house.

It's just Sammy. He's staring at me with big hurt eyes.

"What?" I snap.

"Vito's waiting out front," he says in a quavering voice. "Like you asked."

I nod, dismissing him, but Sammy doesn't immediately turn to go. Those sad eyes travel down my arms to where I'm clutching Caligula against me.

I guess, from where Sammy's standing, it might look like I was about to kiss him.

"Go see if Rosa needs anything," I bark out.

Sammy retreats slowly, walking backward, his eyes on

the Clemenza's face now. And I've never seen such hatred in his eyes before. He turns at last to leave, and I look down at the man pressed up against my chest.

He looks up at me.

"We need to get moving," I tell him, and push him away. "Get dressed."

Vito drives us through Midtown to the building where Stuccio & Associates has their offices, and I tell him to meet us in the side alley. "Won't take long," I tell him.

The Clemenza has barely said a word since we left the house, but he's looking sharp in a caramel-colored turtleneck and brown pants, plus a tailored wool coat over the top. In fact, he looks good enough that every woman in the lobby can't help but turn her head to follow him as we make for the elevator. A few of the men gawk, too. He's walking ahead of me, making it look like we don't know each other. There's no reception in the lobby, so it's easy enough to get to the elevator. But once we get up to the suite Stuccio works out of, that's where Caligula will go to work causing a distraction.

"If you run," I say under my breath to him in the elevator, "I will find you."

He says nothing, watching the numbers light up with a calm expression, acting like he doesn't know me at all.

The doors slide open. I let him go first, and then I pause next to the bank of elevators, checking my phone as though I just got a notification. The offices are still busy in the early evening. I guess lawyers keep late hours, because if anything, the place is humming. More than one of them glances my way, and I tense as they take in the breadth of my shoulders. I don't look like them, not in my physical build. But as soon as they take in the suit, the tie, the shoes, they assume I'm one of them, and go back to their phone conversations or reading the papers in their hands.

Caligula has headed for the woman behind the reception desk like an arrow, and her face tightens in disapproval as she recognizes him. "I need to speak to my uncle," Caligula says loudly.

And then he really goes to town. I always knew the guy was rich and pampered, but hearing the way his voice rises and rises with entitled irritation as the receptionist refuses again and again, I can tell just how fucking privileged he really feels, moving through this world like he owns it…

"Sir, if you won't lower your voice, I'll call security," the lady snaps at last. Every eye turns their way, and conversation lulls. Caligula Clemenza just gets louder.

That's my cue.

I put my phone away and turn left to head down the hallway. Caligula gave me a good idea of the layout, so it's easy enough to find the door stamped in gold: *Anthony Stuccio.*

I walk right in. Stuccio is sitting at his desk, writing notes on a legal pad while he checks something on the computer screen. He looks up with a glower when I come in. "Who are you?"

I reach up to adjust the knot in my tie that the Clemenza put there, angling my hand so the lawyer can see the "G" tattoo in the webbing of my thumb.

He knows what it means. His eyes go wide. And what he says is, "I don't want any trouble."

"Neither do I." I stroll over. "So let's agree to make this easy. Tell me about Louis Clemenza's will."

He's spluttering now as I lean over him. "That's confidential information that I can't—"

"I'll keep it confidential." I lean over and grab *his* tie

now. Mine's definitely nicer. But his makes a good, solid noose around his neck. "After Caligula Clemenza, who's next in line?"

He reaches for the phone on his desk—to call security, I guess—but I pick it up and throw it across the room, all the while keeping a good hold on him.

"Talk," I growl, and I tighten the noose.

His face goes a little red as he fights for breath, grabbing at my wrist with one hand. "I'll call the police—" he manages to get out.

"No you fucking won't. You'll tell me what I need to know, and I'll leave you alive. Or you'll die. No third options, buddy. Make your choice."

I'm already checking out potential exits, because it's only a matter of time before security *does* come in here, or someone else does, to tell the Big Boss that there's a Clemenza out at the desk making a scene. There's a door that I'm pretty sure leads to a private bathroom. And there's a window.

And that's it.

So I'll have to fight my way out, back the way I came. Or just get out of here before the alert goes out.

Stuccio is scrabbling across his desk for something, a weapon maybe. I strangle a little more, and he gives a gurgle. "I—beer—" he says.

"What?" I lean in closer, wondering what the hell he's trying to say, ease up on the necktie a little.

"Ti...berius…" he rattles out.

Tiberius? What the fuck? There's no Clemenza with that name. Although it sounds like it'd fit, given Caligula and his dad, Cesario.

But while leaning in, I took my eye off the ball for a second. Too late, I see what the lawyer is scrabbling for: not a weapon, but an under-desk button. I know when he finds it, because an alarm goes off loud enough to raise the dead.

I'm out of time. But at least I have a name, if it's worth anything. I let him go, and he coughs and wheezes for a second before I punch him hard. Lights out.

I locked the door, but someone is bashing at it, shouting, "Mr. Stuccio? Mr. Stuccio?" I have my Beretta, but getting into a shootout in Midtown feels a little *too* close to my home territory.

I move over to the window and look down. Three stories. But there's an open dumpster down below that I could aim for. And Vito's waiting just up the alley, engine running—I see a faint trail of vapor in the cold night air coming from the exhaust.

I've had worse extractions, that's for sure.

I pull off my suit jacket and wrap it around my arm as a guard, then grab up a heavy bronze statuette from the bookcase and whack at the glass. At least this building is old enough that the glass isn't that durable kind they use in all the new high rises; it smashes immediately, and I try to clean out the frame as well.

The noise gets the guards outside moving, and the heavy thumps now must be hard kicks at the lock. I have about three seconds to judge the jump.

But if there's one other talent I have apart from hurting people, it's this kind of shit. I jump just as the door bursts open, and land ass-first in the dumpster below. I see them all staring down at me.

They won't follow me. No one with an ounce of sense would.

I scramble up and out of the dumpster, barely registering that one of the bags of trash had something hard and sharp-edged in it, and it cut into my shoulder blade. Rosa can deal with injuries later.

The guards above have all disappeared, which means they're running down the internal stairs and will be coming around the corner of the block in half a minute, maybe less. I limp a few steps before I shake it off and charge down the alleyway to the car, throwing myself into the back seat.

The Clemenza is there.

That's the first thing I notice. He's actually here in the car, waiting with Vito.

I didn't know how much I expected him to run until I see him sitting there now, and something inside me gives this weird twist.

Relief, I guess.

By the time I focus on his face, whatever expression he was wearing a second ago has smoothed into oblivion, and he's just staring back at me.

But he's here. He didn't run.

He knows he needs me.

CHAPTER 34
DAMIANO

VITO PUTS HIS FOOT DOWN, throwing us back in our seats as he pulls out into a quieter street with minimal traffic. Vito knows New York like the back of his hand, and he knows the best routes when you're in a hurry. So when I turn to see the security guards appear at the mouth of the alley and rapidly become smaller as we drive away, I grin. "Too slow, motherfuckers."

"What the hell did you do?" Caligula sounds horrified, staring at the shredded jacket wound around my arm, the horror growing as he takes in the rest of me.

I look down at myself. I'm covered in ash and goop. My brand-new shirt is splattered with gunk, there's something yellow smeared down my pant leg, and I'm pretty sure I'm bleeding, judging by the wet warmth spreading down the middle of my back.

"It'll wash out," I tell him with a shrug and a grin.

He doesn't return it. He looks pretty pale, actually. Maybe he's not as strong yet as I thought he was. "You stink," he says bluntly.

"That's what happens when you land in a dumpster. It

was that or cause a major fucking incident fighting my way back out. I see *you* managed to slither away quietly."

He studies my face. "Please tell me the destruction of a Lorenzo Benedetti masterpiece was worth it."

That dampens my spirits a little. "I got a name. But it didn't mean much to me. Tiberius."

"Tiberius?" he repeats, his brows knitting in confusion.

"That's what he said. You got any Tiberius Clemenzas in your poisonous family tree?"

He shakes his head, frustrated—and then freezes. "No Tiberius Clemenzas," he says slowly. "But I have a cousin on my mother's side…Tiberius Vicario."

"Vicario? Shit, I haven't heard that name in years."

Carmine Vicario used to run the whole eastern seaboard. He was the Boss of Bosses, the Big Kahuna, before he got himself scattered into pieces in that infamous Chicago bombing that took out a lot of the fat cats, including Jimmy Giuliano, Big Gee's old man.

"What happened to his Family after he died?" the Clemenza asks, and the way he says it, I can tell he's not asking about the guy's progeny. "They were so powerful—or seemed that way."

"Dead, fled, or assimilated. Just like you Clemenzas. That's how it goes. One empire falls, another one rises, then falls, so another one—"

"Yes. Thank you for the history lesson," he says. "But what about Carmine Vicario's sons?"

It's hard to think when the pain in my back is getting worse with each hard turn Vito makes. "Dunno," I grit out.

"There were three of them. All of them would have been in their sixties when their father died."

"I remember the eldest wasn't worth a good goddamn. Dumber than a box of rocks, and soft along with it." A bit like Big Gee, truth be told, though Big Gee at least has a survival instinct, and he's in the prime of life. "Where does this Tiberius fit in?"

"Tiberius is Carmine Vicario's great-grandson, and my cousin through my mother's sister."

"They really had a thing for the Roman Empire, your mom and her sister, huh? Tiberius and Caligula."

He gives a slight grimace. "Actually, that was *my* grandfather's idea. Nonno Lou thought it would flatter Carmine Vicario, who had suggested my cousin's name to my aunt. Tiberius is a few years older than I am. Anyway, that's how I got stuck with Caligula." He looks down, muttering, "It's ridiculous. That's why I usually go by 'Cal.'"

"I like Caligula," I offer. "Not a name you forget easy."

"It brings with it certain…expectations," he says ruefully, and then his eyes narrow. "You're hurt."

"Just a scratch. Rosa'll patch me up."

He reaches out to my shoulder and nudges me forward in the seat, his eyes going wide. "Dami, you're *really hurt*."

I twist around as though I'll be able to get a look at my back. Of course I can't. But I *can* see the smears all over the seat behind me, and when I swipe at them, hoping it's just more slime from the garbage, my hand comes away red. "I'm fine," I say automatically.

"You're not fine."

"You don't need to worry about it," I snarl at him, wriggling away from the pressure he's trying to apply.

He grabs me by the arm with the other hand. "If you die, I'll have no one to protect me," he says, so cold I feel like my veins are shriveling up—but at least then the blood would stop.

"We're nearly home," I grumble, but I let him press a hand into my back. Vito knows what he's doing; he pulls into the garage ten minutes later, and Caligula hustles me up to the kitchen.

Rosa is in there waiting. I asked her to be prepared tonight. I strip off the shirt, which is pretty much soaked with blood now. And the look on Rosa's face tells me the injury is pretty serious.

"Maybe we should get Darla," Caligula says nervously.

"Yes," Rosa agrees quickly. "We should get the nurse."

"I don't want anyone hearing about this," I growl at them both. "Last thing we need is more cooks in the kitchen. Just patch it up."

She makes me sit backward on one of the tall stools, leaning onto the countertop so she can sew me up. Vito comes in, watching Rosa work, and after a moment, he goes to the coffee machine and starts grinding up beans to make coffee for us all. It's a sign of Rosa's concern that she doesn't chase him away from the machine, her baby.

"This will hurt," she tells me. "A lot."

Caligula leans over the countertop from the other side and holds out his hands to me. "Hold onto me," he tells me, those golden eyes boring into mine.

I want to argue, but the needle begins to drive through my flesh, and I realize how much deeper this cut is than the last one Rosa stitched up for me. I grab onto the Clemenza's wrists and squeeze. His hands clasp my wrists and squeeze back. "Breathe," he reminds me.

He takes in a long breath and blows it out, then does it again, until I do it with him. It does help, a little. Or maybe it's just staring into those pretty amber eyes that distracts me.

There's a shadow in the hallway, and Sammy's frightened face looms out of the dark.

"Get back in your room," I tell him. Of course, he does completely the opposite. He rushes into the kitchen and takes my face in his hands, looking me over for more cuts and bruises. "What happened?" he cries.

I yank my face away. "I'm fine."

"You keep saying that," the Clemenza observes calmly. "But you're clearly not."

Sammy glares at him. "This is *your* fault. Nothing like this ever happened before you came here."

Caligula's eyes don't even move toward him. He doesn't take his gaze from my face. "I'm sorry you feel that way," he says, and it's soft and kind, like he really means it.

"Sammy, go get the iodine," Rosa says.

Sammy backs away, but he's still glaring at Caligula. He comes back with the iodine and passes it to Rosa. "Hey," I tell him. "It wasn't the Clemenza. It was me. I did something dumb, that's all."

He doesn't look convinced, but he backs away to the wall where he stands pressed up against it and just watches the proceedings.

At last the torture is over. I release Caligula's wrists, and I'm a little startled to see red marks ringing them. "You should've told me I was squeezing too hard."

"I'm tougher than I look." He's not as cold as he is sometimes, though nowhere near warm, and yet I find myself relieved at the middling temperature he's chosen. It seems designed to reassure Sammy that nothing is going on between us, although whether Sammy believes that or not, I don't know.

Vito hands out coffees to all of us afterwards, and at least three of us—me, Caligula, and Rosa—have to wash our hands free of blood before we take up our cups.

"What happened?" Sammy asks again. He's not going to let it go.

"What happened," Caligula says, "is that Damiano jumped out of a window, fell three stories, and landed in an open dumpster."

He sounds mad at me again. Like he did in the car. "I told you, we can get the suit cleaned."

"Who cares about the suit!" Sammy breaks in. "That was dumb as hell, Damiano."

"I fully agree," Caligula says.

Vito is nodding as well, and Rosa, giving me an evil little pat on the scar she just stitched into me, says, "You need to take better care of yourself."

I'm about to tell them all to go to hell when I realize that all of them are glancing around at each other with tiny smiles.

"Well," I say, pain and exhaustion coming over me. "I don't plan to do it again."

That actually gets a chuckle out of them. I'm not sure why my misadventure is so funny, but I'll take that over the atmosphere that's been percolating ever since I brought the Clemenza into my house.

We all drink our coffees, and Rosa tells us about her late husband, and a time he had to dive off the Brooklyn Bridge. It doesn't sound very likely to me, but it's a good story, and I find myself grinning along with everyone when she ends that he was sick as a dog for weeks with some bug he picked up in the water.

We're all crowded around the counter, huddled over our coffees, and it feels...*good*. Homey. Like a family. The Clemenza catches my eye, just as he's laughing about Rosa's story, and I'm smiling too, and it feels almost natural.

Like this is how things really should be.

I look away quickly. Unfortunately, the direction my eyes go, I end up glancing at Sammy. He obviously saw the Clemenza and me looking at each other, because he's stopped laughing. His face shutters again, and the moment, whatever it was, is broken.

"Okay," I say, putting down my cup. "I need a shower. Rosa, can you get together a tray for dinner? I'll take our guest back upstairs."

"One or two meals?" she asks innocently.

"Two," I say after a second. The Clemenza and I need to talk more about this Tiberius, whoever he is. Might as well do it over food.

Caligula follows me up the stairs this time and I feel his eyes fixed on my naked back, on the stitched-up skin that everyone's making too much fuss about. When we get to my room, I gesture to the bed. "Get in there and eat while I shower."

"And how exactly are you planning to wash your back without tearing Rosa's stitches open?" Caligula asks, not moving toward the bed. "You can't reach it, you can't see it, and you're covered in garbage juice that's teeming with bacteria. If you take that waterproof patch off accidentally, it'll get infected."

I open my mouth to argue, but he's already talking over me.

"You took care of me when I was sick. Consider this repayment." He's already shrugging off his jacket. "Unless you'd rather call Rosa up here to scrub your back for you."

It's the threat of Rosa that does it. And hell, it's not like we haven't been naked and wet in each other's presence before.

I strip down and start the shower, turning my back to him at the door. I'm glad I'm facing away. He might see the reaction my dick has otherwise. It's the way he's washing me down, all careful and soft, that gets my body thinking the wrong thing. I put up with it as long as I can and then I grunt, "That's fine," over my shoulder.

He doesn't argue, for once, just leaves me alone to finish up my shower.

When I come back out, buck naked, he doesn't look up. And he's had a few mouthfuls of food, which I guess is a good sign, if he's hungry.

"So this Tiberius," I say. "Where is he?"

Caligula pokes at his osso buco in frustration. "I don't know. And I have no idea where to even start looking."

"So that's it," I say. "Another dead end."

He says nothing. I guess he's sulking because he knows what that means. I'll put him away in his underground kingdom while I sniff around for a new lead.

Not tonight, though. He had a rough day. I'll keep him up here tonight, but I'll be damned if I sleep in a bed that's not my own, because I've had a rough day, too.

He's still poking at the food instead of putting it in his mouth. "Eat," I tell him. "Or I'll pour a fucking protein shake down your throat."

I slide into the bed next to him and take up my own bowl. I'm fucking starving after the day I've had. But then Caligula says something that kills my appetite dead.

"We have one last lead. The Obelisk."

CHAPTER 35
CALIGULA

DAMIANO PAUSES with the fork at his mouth. "What?"

"You weren't the only one bidding on me, Dami. The Russian in the front row—I'm pretty sure he's called Grisha—"

"That Bratva fucker?"

"Yes. He was very interested. And there were others, too, a lot of other people with a vested interest in making sure my downfall was complete."

He puts the forkful down in the bowl uneaten. "You think I can stroll up to Daniel fucking King and demand the guest list for that night? He ain't no Tony Stuccio, kid. He's a little tougher than that."

"I think you could handle him." He blinks at me. "But we should try diplomacy first. I got the feeling Grisha goes there a lot. Jesse told me he likes to watch more than participate—he's a voyeur. You could make friends. Drink with him. Get him to loosen his tongue."

"I'm not drinking with some pervert fucking Bratva. And I'm not going back to the Obelisk, not with you in tow."

"It's our only option right now."

"No."

"Dami—"

He grabs my throat, just like he used to do all the time right after he bought me. "If you're looking for an escape by selling yourself to this *Grisha* instead, you got another thing coming."

I don't fight. Don't even flinch. I let him stay there, hand on my throat, until the fire dies down in his eyes a little. "I'm not looking for a new owner, Dami. I'm just looking for answers. Like you."

He drops his hand. "Jumping out a window into a dumpster wasn't a good idea. Going back to the Obelisk? That's unbelievably stupid."

"Then tell me *your* brilliant idea instead. Tell me where we'll find our next lead."

He's silent, eating a few mouthfuls of the food sullenly. "It'd be like throwing chum in the water, taking you back in there with all those sharks," he says at last. "And there's every chance we wouldn't leave alive if the Bratva are the ones hunting you."

"But you'll protect me, Dami," I say as sweetly as I can. "You always do."

I can see he's wavering. I wait patiently.

"If we do this," he says at last. "*If* we do this, we need to convince them we're just there to enjoy the nightlife. You get me? If they think for one second we're there for intel—"

"I will perform my role as chastened slave, Dami. Easily done."

He snorts. "That Clemenza ego of yours is visible from space, golden boy. Did you know that? Nah. It'll never work. You just can't keep yourself from talking back."

He's nearly there. He just needs one more push.

"There's an easy way to tame my ego." I lean in toward him, just a little. "You cage me again. And use the plug."

His eyes travel over my face, my chest, hungry and dark. "Yeah," he says roughly. "That might just do it."

"Then let's go." I slide out of the bed.

Once again, the fork doesn't make it to his mouth. "Huh?"

"We should go. Now. Tonight," I go on, getting more insistent as I see him balk. "Because if Uncle Tony gets the word out—"

"Shit." He throws his fork back in the bowl and pinches the bridge of his nose. "Yeah, yeah. I get it. Everyone'll clam up tighter than your asshole."

I laugh. Mostly from surprise.

"Speaking of which," he goes on, "if I'm gonna shove that golden dildo back in your ass, you should clean out your insides first."

I have a very unpleasant flashback to my night at the Obelisk, to the water flooding into my gut and then flooding back out…

"I haven't eaten since this morning," I tell him quickly. "It'll be fine."

He looks at me, and for a moment I see him contemplating doing what he threatened just before, and pouring a protein shake down my throat.

Then he shrugs. "We'll need the lube."

It's a singularly unpleasant experience to be leaning over a sink and staring at myself in the mirror while Damiano Orsini fingers my asshole, just like the first night he brought me home. Unpleasant not because it hurts—it doesn't, at all; in fact it feels *good*—but because he's so clinical about it. But when he turns away to get the butt plug, I see something that makes it more bearable.

He's hard. He *likes* this. Or his body does, anyway. That's good to know.

Because my body likes it, too.

He already put the cage on me before he ordered me to lean over, and I start filling it out more firmly as he positions the plug at my hole, the tip pressing in. His eyes stray up to my face, and he watches my reaction as the cool metal breaches me, the slight flush that spreads over my cheeks, the way I suck in a breath.

Surely he doesn't need to go this slowly, or twist it around, or pump it maddeningly in and out, a little deeper each time…

"Come on," he says softly. "Open up for it, golden boy."

In the mirror, my lips part, my shoulders drop their tension, and I keep my eyes on his as the plug slides home.

"There you go," he says. "All filled up." He steps back and motions me to stand, which I do, swaying a little as I adjust to the foreign sensation of having something inside me again. "I got that cloak thing they sent you with. That'll do for clothes. As for shoes…"

"I'll go barefoot," I tell him. I'm feeling a little hazy, my voice sounding far away. "Just like I was when you bought me, Dami."

"Yeah," he says after a moment. "Just like when I bought you."

This time my entrance to the Obelisk is much more grand than sneaking down a piss-stinking alley to a back door. Vito drives us down into the underground parking lot, right up to the members' entrance, gets out, and opens the car door for us. I'm relieved that he looks straight ahead, not even acknowledging me as I get out of the car. I think it's respect.

I *think* it's respect.

Even if not, I appreciate him not staring at me. I have the gold cloak pulled tight around me against the cold, but it must be pretty obvious I'm naked underneath. And I'm grateful that Dami doesn't leave me standing there barefoot on freezing cement for long, either. As in the back alley entrance, there's a heavy, black steel door, but the obelisk carved into this one is much larger. Dami buzzes the intercom, gives his membership number when a disembodied voice demands it, and looks up at the camera situated above the door. The door slides open and he pushes me through onto thick red carpet that gives my frozen toes some relief.

Inside, the reception area looks like any high-end members' club in the city. Soft classical music plays over the speakers, and the lighting is low and warm, a few spotlights over the reception desk. Dark walnut paneling lines the walls, punctuated by tall niches displaying Egyptian antiquities, or very convincing reproductions. A few black velvet loveseats are arranged for waiting guests, though nobody's waiting. The place smells faintly of incense.

"Mr. Orsini," says the man at reception. He's mid-twenties maybe, with pale hair slicked back from a beautiful, feline face. "How lovely to see you again. This is your guest for the night?"

"He's not a guest. I bought him here at auction a couple of weeks back."

The blond inclines his head with an understanding smile. "I see. Please go on through."

Dami's hand closes around the back of my neck and he steers me toward one of several doors. I try to remember to keep my eyes downcast, but it's hard not to stare around as we enter the next area. It's bigger than I expected, but wide rather than spacious. The ceilings are still low, and the lighting comes only from the walls or floor lamps. The color scheme is the same as the foyer—black and dark red—which makes everything feel more intimate. Deep booths line the walls, each one curtained for privacy, and clusters of armchairs and low tables fill the floor, arranged so that every group would feel secluded even if it was crowded.

It's not crowded tonight, but it is busy. The clientele are all well-dressed men, drinking and talking in the kind of low murmurs that suggest every conversation is confidential.

"You see this Grisha anywhere?" Dami mutters.

I chance a look around. But then I wish I hadn't, as the conversation in the room lulls, heads turn my way, and a new whisper begins to spread. I hear my name.

And the hatred as it's spoken.

"You don't talk to anyone," Dami tells me in a low voice. "You hear me?" I nod. "And you don't make eye contact with anyone. Either they'll think it's a challenge or a come-on, and I'm not in the mood to get into a fight over it, not after that dumpster jump."

Not after his injury, he means.

"I'll be good, Dami," I murmur. "I promise."

The hand on my neck squeezes just a bit tighter. "You sound like you're enjoying this, little prince."

He sounds strange. Angry. Possessive.

"I'm not enjoying it at all," I tell him truthfully, and the pressure on my neck relaxes.

And then, before I even register it's happening, he pulls the cloak back off my shoulders, so that the whole room can see my nudity—and the cage.

I suck at the insides of my cheeks so I don't gasp or

protest. I should have expected this. Not only because we agreed we had to act the part when we came here, but because it's all part of Damiano Orsini's plan for revenge. He told me when he bought me that he planned to break me. He didn't mean physically. That would be too easy. No, what he wants is to make me suffer psychologically.

What was it that he said just before we left? My Clemenza ego is visible from space. He wasn't wrong. It's something that he and others will be able to manipulate, if I can't control it myself.

Thinking through the problem helps calm my nerves. So when Damiano moves a few steps in front and says, "Follow me," I'm able to do it with suitably downcast eyes and slumped shoulders.

What do I care if the Bratva think he's broken me already? This is a long game, a marathon, not a sprint. The Bratva are not a concern for me right now.

But then I stop dead as I hear a familiar laugh.

In front of me, Damiano keeps going a few feet before he realizes I'm not following, and turns to glare at me.

"What's rule number one?" he says, loud enough for those close by to overhear.

"Do what you fucking tell me," I answer automatically, but my feet won't move.

Because I've seen Jesse. Jesse Foster. He's in a tangle of limbs over in a sunken lounge in the corner of the room, and the look on his face is ecstatic.

Dami comes back and looks where I'm looking. "What?" he asks. "You want to join in?"

"Jesse," I hiss between stiff lips. "If anyone knows where this Grisha guy is, it's Jesse Foster."

I can tell he's about to snarl something back, but he pauses, and sends a speculative look to the mini-orgy going on in the corner. "Well, looks like they're finishing up."

He grabs my wrist and pulls me to a nearby table, where he takes the stool and grips me by the shoulder, pushing me down to kneel at his feet. "Make it believable, golden boy," he tells me, and I swear there's mockery in his tone.

I don't take the bait. I just kneel as comfortably as I can with the damn plug in me, and let him run a hand through my hair. "Knees wider," he tells me. I shuffle to obey, even though I have to grit my teeth.

This will be worth it in the end. And in the long run, every tiny moment like this will be paid back with interest.

Sure enough, the group of men who have been entertaining themselves with Jesse finish up a few moments later with loud groans, slapping him on the ass and laughing, saying something in Russian. Jesse stumbles up and away, but there's a glazed look of ecstasy on his face.

And as he limps away from the men, his eyes fall on me. They go wide with delight. He makes a beeline for where we're sitting.

"Mr. Orsini," he says, swaying a little as he comes to a halt. "And your purchase. I hope you've been very happy with it—not planning to return it?" He laughs after he says it.

Damiano laughs as well. "Not a chance in hell. No buyer's remorse here."

"If you're open to it, there are a number of gentlemen here tonight who would enjoy sharing in your good fortune," Jesse continues. He hasn't even glanced at me since he came up, and my nose is getting assaulted by the various scents of his recent experiences in the corner.

"I don't share my property," Damiano says. "Although…"

I try not to look up at him. I certainly don't want a view from down here of Jesse's spent dick, waving in my face as it is. But I'm on high alert until Dami finishes that sentence he started, because we didn't talk about how far he might go to get information. Maybe that was a mistake.

Or maybe it was by design.

"I'd be delighted to make any introductions," Jesse trills.

Damiano leans on his arms on the tabletop, closer to Jesse as he drops his voice. "Since you mention it, I do feel a little bad about snatching this prize away from that other guy who was interested at the auction. Do you know him? I wouldn't mind sharing a drink. Maybe sharing a little something extra."

I hear the change of tone in Jesse's voice when he says, "Of course I know Grisha. And he's very gracious, I'm sure he'd love a chance to smooth things over."

Jesse Foster can smell a new commission. That's what I'm hearing in his voice. I should have heard it at Kismet nightclub, but it's unmistakable now.

The question now is not what *Dami* is willing to do for information, but how far am *I* willing to go? I already told him I'd do whatever it took to survive.

Perhaps he plans to test that tonight.

"Well, if this Grisha comes in tonight, send him my way," Damiano goes on. "I'd like to buy him a drink, maybe throw him a bone, if you catch my drift."

Jesse laughs as though Damiano has made the funniest joke he's ever heard. "Oh I will, Mr. Orsini. I will. And if you feel like a little something extra for yourself, I'm sure Mr. King would be pleased to offer *my* services to you."

I'm sitting right at knee level, so I notice when Damiano's leg twitches. "That's very generous of him," he says. "But I don't want to push the friendship."

"I'm sure I could persuade him," Jesse says, and now he takes a step closer to Damiano, his sticky thigh just about brushing my nose. I can't help myself; I look up and see Jesse Foster sliding his hand up Dami's bicep.

Damiano glances down at the hand on his arm. At my face beyond. "I'm sure you could," he tells Jesse with a smile. "Let's see how things play out tonight."

Jesse leans into his ear and says something I can't hear. Damiano chuckles. "Would you like a drink in the meantime?" Jesse asks at normal volume.

"I got someone here to take care of that for me," Dami says easily. "I'll send the Clemenza. Let him earn his keep, right?"

Jesse grins. "Yes, sir." And with that, he sets off to find Grisha—hopefully. He better not be finding Daniel King and begging for permission to fuck Damiano.

"Eyes down," the man himself tells me.

He's looking straight ahead. But I'm still glaring up at him. "Have you fucked Jesse Foster?"

He turns his face slowly down to look at me, expressionless. "What does it matter?"

"Just tell me. You said you'd never lie to me, right?"

He snorts. "I'm not stupid enough to stick my dick in a bear trap."

I quickly look down again. Partly to keep up the charade of submission for our audience. And partly because I don't want him to see the relief on my face. "Would you like a drink, Mr. Orsini?" I ask the floor politely, but I'm pretty sure Dami hears the acid in my tone.

"Since you mention it, yeah, I would. Go ask the bartender to make my usual. Bar is down at the end, round the corner." I rise to my feet and he catches me by the arm before I leave. "You go straight there and straight back. You hear me? No wandering off to find a Bratva orgy of your own."

It's my turn to snort. And there's a very tiny smile on Dami's lips as he lets me go.

The bar is, as Dami said, at the bottom of the L-shaped

room, slightly around the corner. I find the bartender and tell him to make Damiano Orsini his usual drink, which apparently is straight bourbon, and half a pint of beer to chase it down.

While I'm waiting, I feel someone slide up behind me. "Hi, Cal," Jesse says.

I turn to look at him. I don't say anything.

"I couldn't say hi before," he goes on, "since you were there with your owner. It wouldn't be respectful for me to talk to you without his permission."

"You don't have his permission now."

Jesse giggles. "Sure, but we're alone now. We can be naughty if we feel like it."

"You were being plenty naughty before with that group in the corner."

He gets a dreamy look on his face. "They're a good time. There's lots of fun to have here at the Obelisk. You'll find out yourself, when Damiano shares you with Grisha."

The bar area is deserted, except for me and Jesse and the bartender. The rest of the patrons of the club are in the long arm of the room, and when I glance over my shoulder, none of them who have a view of us are paying attention.

So I grab Jesse Foster by the throat and shove him up against the opposite wall.

"From now on," I spit, "you keep your hands off Damiano Orsini and your dick out of my face. You wave that thing near my mouth again, I'll bite it the fuck off."

I'm not squeezing hard, but Jesse is gasping for air. I let him go, and turn back to the bar, where the bartender is staring, mouth open, as though he's not sure whether to call security.

"Thanks for the drinks," I tell him, grabbing the bourbon and the beer, one in each hand. I don't bother looking back at Jesse.

I shouldn't have done that. Jesse is likely to get us thrown out, rather than send his friend Grisha over. And I don't even know *why* I did it. Something came over me and I just…lost it.

But it was worth it to see the look on Jesse's face.

I have to walk slowly to avoid spilling the drinks, but eventually I arrive back at Dami's table and give him his drinks. "My Lord," I say with a quick bow of the head.

"You want to watch that sarcasm while we're here," Dami advises me, picking up the bourbon. "It won't go down well with the Bratva."

"About that," I begin, figuring I should give him a heads-up if security suddenly descends on our table.

And in fact, there is someone headed our way right now. But it's not security. It's the Russian who bid on me that night at the auction—Grisha.

And trailing behind him, a vindictive spark in his eye, is Jesse Foster.

CHAPTER 36
DAMIANO

IF I ever have to see Jesse-fucking-Foster's obnoxious little face again after tonight, it'll be too soon. The red-faced Russian he's got with him seems just as annoying as Daniel King's lapdog, too. But I paste what will pass for a smile on my face and take the hand the Russian is extending.

"Grisha Andropov," he says. "And you are the infamous Damiano Orsini, yes? Jesse here tells me you wanted to make amends." He laughs, but it's got no warmth to it. "Of course, there's no need. No need at all." But his eyes hover greedily on Caligula, who keeps his gaze glued to the floor.

"Just wanted to smooth over any ruffled feathers," I say.

"Oh, no feathers ruffled. Your bid was—you must excuse me—quite beyond reason." He laughs again. "Mine was pure curiosity. But Daniel explained the circumstances to me afterward."

I give another smile that feels more like a grimace. Whether this asshole knows it or not, he's telling me how widely known my hatred of Caligula Clemenza must be… and how clear my obsessive behavior was over the years. My weakness has been on display without me even realizing it.

That means *anyone* might have sent the text that summoned me to the Obelisk that night.

"It's been well worth the money," I tell the Russian.

"Jesse said you'd be interested in sharing." The flat eyes gleam.

"And Mr. King says I am also at your disposal, Mr. Orsini," Jesse purrs, putting his hand on my arm again. I have to fight not to shake it off.

The murderous look Caligula sends his way is enough to make me move away from the touch, camouflaged by reaching for my drink. "Actually, I'd prefer a little privacy with my new friend here."

"But—" Jesse begins with a pout.

"Run along, Jesse," the Russian insists. "Book us a private room for an hour."

"An hour?" I say. "Why not two?" The Russian likes that idea, grinning wide. But Jesse doesn't move, obviously trying to find an excuse to join us despite a direct order. "Thanks for the intro," I tell him. "Maybe we can catch up after."

That seems to appease him, although Caligula's clenching jaw doesn't escape my notice. The Clemenza is *pissed*. If I didn't know better, I'd think…

Well, I *do* know better. And I need to keep my head in the game.

Andropov leads me down a hallway to a quieter part of the club, to one of the rooms used for private pursuits. I've been in one or two of these rooms before—with company—although I was just blowing off steam. This one's the same as the others I've seen: a couple of black leather armchairs, a two-seater sofa that's probably seen some action, a coffee table. Low lighting. Private. Soundproofed. The kind of room where you either talk business or get your dick sucked, sometimes both.

There's a small bar cart in the room and the Russian pours us each a vodka, my least favorite drink. I throw it back anyway and accept another. This one I'll nurse.

As for Caligula, I point to the floor next to the armchair I'm sitting in, and he goes to his knees by my feet, head bowed. "I gotta be honest, Grisha," I say before the Russian can steer the conversation. "I had an ulterior motive for getting you in here."

"Oh, yes?" His beady little eyes are all over the Clemenza, and I know exactly what he's imagining.

"Yeah. I wanted some info."

He's all smiles as he looks at me. "And you offer this in exchange?" He flicks one finger, from the hand holding his glass, toward Caligula.

I set down my drink. "You know, Jesse Foster might've given you the wrong impression out there."

"Oh, yes?" he replies again, a lot colder this time.

"The Clemenza is mine." I lay it out clear for him, so he knows not to push. "So if you were hoping to use him..." I give a shrug. "What can I say? I don't share."

The Russian stares at Caligula instead of me, frustration clear in his face. "You expect me to give you information for nothing? You waste my time, Mr. Orsini."

He starts to rise, and I feel Caligula's finger jabbing into my ankle. He glances up at me with a furious, fleeting expression.

The problem is, I knew the second I came into this place that I was not going to share Caligula Clemenza with any other fucker on earth.

I bought him. He's *mine*. And there's not a damn thing any of them can do about it.

But we need that intel.

"Hold on," I say as the Russian turns to leave. "I didn't say nothing."

Andropov pauses, one eyebrow raised. "Then what do you offer? Because I was promised—"

"Jesse promised. Not me." I lean back, keeping my voice easy. "But I get it. You came in here expecting a show. So maybe we can work something out."

The Russian reaches for the bottle of vodka and takes it with him back to his seat, interest rekindled. "I'm listening."

I pause, trying to come up with something. Anything. Caligula shifts slightly, his hand sliding up behind his back where Andropov can't see it, finger and thumb meeting in the universal signal for "OK."

Okay. Go ahead. I trust you to keep me safe.

Fuck.

"Maybe you'd like to watch," I sigh out.

Something shifts in Andropov's expression. I've hit a nerve—the right one.

I reach down and grip Caligula's chin, tilting his face up. Those golden eyes meet mine, unreadable. I tilt his face toward the Russian. "Pretty, right?"

"As you say." He's still guarded. But he's intrigued.

"The Clemenza can put on a show for you. But the only dick going near him is mine."

Andropov's tongue darts out to wet his lips. He's considering it. "And in exchange?" he asks. "What is this information you seek?"

This is it. I have to show our cards now, before we even lay the bet. But no point going through all this if the Bratva has no usable information. "You got any idea who's been hunting down the Clemenzas?"

A slow smile thins his lips. "Why do *you* want to know?"

"Because I wanna shake their fucking hand. And maybe give them a go at this last one, once I've used him up."

"I see. Well…I might have something for you."

"Gimme a crumb. Right now, so I know you're on the up and up."

There's a long pause, and then Andropov says, "He is a compatriot of mine. I can introduce you."

"What's his name?"

"I have paid your entry fee. Now I get my performance, yes? And no rushing."

I look down at Caligula. His hand is still making that "OK" sign behind his back.

"Deal," I say. I unzip my pants, fish my cock out. It's already half-hard at the idea. Because as sick as this fuck across the table from me is, I'm just as sick. Always have been. Always will be.

For the first time, I wish I could be different.

But wasn't this my plan from the start? Humiliate the Clemenza. Break him down bit by bit until there was nothing left of him…

"Is it really true he was a virgin?" Andropov asks, leaning forward in his chair to get a better look at the action.

I slide a hand into the gold-bronze hair of my prize, and Caligula gives a little gasp of pain, even though I'm not even tugging. "He was," I say. "But let me tell you, Grisha, since we're friends now, I didn't take his virginity." I tug Caligula up so that he bends over the arm of the chair, positioning his mouth. "I obliterated it."

My new friend laughs in delight. "So you have had the pleasure of training him. I saw the bruises on his wrists. Has he been difficult to tame?"

Bruises on his…? I glance down at Caligula's wrists and see the marks I left on him from where I grabbed onto him while Rosa was stitching me up. Andropov has assumed they were left over from restraints.

But he's not entirely wrong, is he? Not about me restraining Caligula. And I've done a lot worse to him than just chain him up.

I need to focus.

"He's still learning," I say. "He might choke a little." I take Caligula's jaw in my other hand.

"Let us hope he does," the Russian says. "The Clemenzas were a blight on my brothers. There was much rejoicing after the old man was removed. And they will enjoy my tales of tonight."

Under my hand, Caligula jerks as though stung.

"Well?" Andropov says eagerly. "Begin."

I hesitate.

Because I don't think I can do this. After all my talk at home, telling Caligula that he'd have to play submissive, cower in front of all these fuckers, *I'm* the one who can't play my part. And it should be the easiest part of all for someone like me.

Caligula gives me a quick squeeze on the thigh. The Russian is starting to look impatient. Another thigh squeeze, harder this time.

"Open your mouth," I hear myself say.

He opens it.

And then he swallows me down before I can second-guess my decision.

"There we go, there we go," the Russian encourages, leaning forward. "A little deeper, now."

If Caligula wasn't doing his best to keep me right there in my seat, hands pushing down hard on my thighs, I'd be punching the hell out of this fucker opposite me for talking like that. The Russian doesn't deserve to see this.

But I need to keep it together. Keep Caligula safe while he puts on a show of humiliation for this Bratva asshole—a show I'm supposedly directing. When Andropov leans over like he wants a closer look, I shift my position slightly to block his view.

I thread my hands through Caligula's silky hair. His tongue slides all over my cock, and then he makes a gagging noise.

That sound makes the Russian groan with pleasure.

This is all wrong. But we need that lead.

"Surely he can take in more than that." The Russian grins when Caligula pulls off me to gasp for air. "Don't feel the need to hold back on my account, Orsini."

Caligula's head is bowed, hair hanging in his face, and I feel his fingers curl against my thigh. A silent message.

We started, so we might as well go on. I lift Caligula's face up to look at him, trace my thumb over his wet lips. "You heard him, Clemenza. I'm not going to hold back."

There's an amber flash as he glances up at me through his lashes, and that little bit of eye contact reassures me. He leans forward, mouth open, and takes me in again. His hands grip my thighs, not pushing me away, but bracing himself.

"Harder," the Russian insists. "Make him take it all."

"I don't need a fucking director," I growl at him.

He raises an eyebrow, a clear message. He'll walk if I don't.

I'm about to tell him where he can shove his demands when Caligula moves first. He pulls back just enough to adjust his angle, then pushes forward—hard—taking me deeper, just as Andropov ordered. He gags, chokes, moans in fear.

But his hands on my thighs are steady. Relaxed, even.

He's faking.

He's putting on a show, giving this bastard exactly what he wants to see. My hand is still on the back of his head, so it looks like I *made* him do it. Tears leak from his eyes as he chokes again—and fuck, are those real, or—

No. He squeezes his eyes hard, leaks out a few more. The tears are part of the performance.

"You know," Andropov says, pouring himself another vodka, "I had a son once. Louis Clemenza had him killed over a shipment dispute. Forty thousand dollars' worth of goods. That was the price of my son's life." He drains the glass. "So you see, Orsini, we are not so different, you and I. Seeking justice against these snakes, the Clemenzas."

I want to bark out *Bullshit*, but there's nothing untrue in what he said.

I just don't like hearing it.

As for Caligula, he gives another theatrical choke, pulling up to gasp raggedly before diving back down, making it look like I'm forcing him once more. But he's barely taken half my length, though his hand, wrapped around my shaft, hides the true depth from the Russian.

"That's it," Andropov hisses, leaning forward. "Break him. Make him regret the day he was born a Clemenza."

I spread out my fingers through that soft hair, not guiding, just…anchoring. Letting him set the pace while I play the brutal master for our audience of one. My grip looks punishing, but my fingers are gentle against his scalp, practically a fucking massage.

Caligula Clemenza is completely in control. I just have to let him work.

"Surely you can be rougher than that," the Russian complains, but there's a flush creeping up his neck. He's buying it.

Caligula pulls off with a wet, wrecked sound, gasping for air, spit trailing from his swollen lips to my cock. He looks utterly destroyed.

Then his eyes flick up to mine for just a second—sharp, alert, amused—before he drops back into character.

Christ.

He's magnificent.

And this Russian bastard doesn't deserve to witness a single second of it.

"That's enough." I pull Caligula up and off me, hear him gasp—genuinely this time, I think.

"Don't stop now," the Russian complains. "I want to watch him drown in your—"

"No," I snap. I'm already tucking myself away.

Caligula pinches me on the thigh, hard enough that I squirm. I avoid his eyes, but I don't have to look at him to know that he's fucking furious; he thinks we're not going to get what we came for.

But I will be goddamned if I let some sadistic Bratva motherfucker watch me spill my first load in Caligula's mouth.

"I don't wanna pop yet," I tell Andropov. "This was just a taste. I've had so much fun with him since I bought him, I figured I'd give the whole place a show later. What do you think?" I shove Caligula back down to the floor without even looking at him.

I *can't* look at him. If I look at him, I'm going to fucking lose it.

"A public display?" Andropov taps his lips. He looks at Caligula. I want to tell him to keep looking at me. I want to grab his face and *force* him to see only me. But it would be too late.

He's already seen too much.

In my peripheral vision, Caligula coughs pathetically and wipes at his wet chin, still playing his part perfectly.

"Ah, a pity," Andropov sighs at last. "But you are right; it would be selfish to keep such a delicious humiliation to my eyes alone. There are many people here who will take delight in his debasement."

"Is one of them this guy who's been knocking them off?" I ask desperately. "Because if I could meet him—"

Andropov laughs heartily. "I'm sorry, my friend. I have told a little white lie. I have no idea who killed all those Clemenzas. I, too, would like to shake their hand."

"You lied to me?"

He shrugs, standing to straighten his jacket. "You, too, lied to me. Sent King's pet after me with all those wild promises you never intended to keep. Now we are even. Yes?"

After a long moment, I smile broadly and stand as well. "Sure. I guess that's fair play."

"I have enjoyed my evening very much so far. There's more to come, I hope?"

"Oh, yes. Much more." I grin even wider, putting out my hand. "Here's to new friends."

He takes my hand.

I yank him hard toward me, putting him off balance so that he stumbles, and I sidestep to avoid breaking his fall. I catch his head between my hands before he hits the floor and give a quick, forceful twist. The crack of his neck sounds, and I let him drop to the floor. There's a last, slow hiss of air, and then nothing.

I look over at Caligula, who's crouched down behind the chair as though wanting to avoid getting caught in the crossfire.

He stands slowly, coming around next to me, and looks down at the corpse on the floor. "Oh, Dami," he breathes. "Why in the hell did you do *that*?"

It's a fucking good question.

CHAPTER 37
DAMIANO

WE STAND TOGETHER, staring down at the body. And then Caligula Clemenza steps over it and locks the door. He turns back to me.

"You must be out of your mind, killing a Bratva kingpin in the middle of his own turf," he whispers fiercely. "What were you *thinking*?"

I *wasn't* thinking. That was the problem. Still can't get my mind around it now, so I grope for the one certainty I have. "I said I'd protect you. I wasn't going to let this motherfucker run around crowing about tonight."

I lean down and hoist the heavy asshole up from the floor, then flop him back into his seat. I might've pulled Rosa's stitches, because my back starts to ache again when I'm done.

"I didn't realize your protection extended to my virtuous reputation," Caligula says at last. And for once, I'm glad to hear him being a sarcastic little shit. Means he's calm. He's not going to panic. And if we move fast and careful, we'll get out of this alive.

Maybe.

"The Bratva can get fucked," I announce. "They ain't got the claim on you that I have."

"Ah, yes," he sighs. "Your honorable vendetta."

Okay, he can cut the sarcasm out now. I grab him by the arm and give him a shake. "We need to get out of here."

He looks up into my face. "We need to get what we came for. Information."

"We got a dead Bratva and Jesse Foster with some hard-on to get you punished—what was that about, anyway? He seemed more vicious than usual."

"I physically assaulted him."

It's the *way* he says it that gets me. Cool, calm, collected, and absolutely precise. *I physically assaulted him.* "And what in the hell did you do that for?"

There's the briefest pause before he says, "That's not our most pressing concern right now, Dami. What are we going to do with Grisha?"

We both look at the dead guy. His eyes are open and so is his mouth. "We can't do anything," I say after a glance around the room. There's nowhere to stash him. "We'll just have to leave him here. Hope they figure he died of…a heart attack or something."

I expect the Clemenza to argue. It's a shitty plan and it only gives us a chance to get away, not sleaze around the place looking for someone who knows something. But Caligula just sighs. "Let's move fast."

"Right," I say, relieved he's seen sense.

"We go straight to Daniel King."

"What? *No.*" We're not on the same wavelength *at all.*

But Caligula's already moving to the door, unlocking it, peeking out to check the hallway. He beckons me over. "Do you know how to get to his office from here?"

"No, I fucking don't," I say firmly, but Caligula steps out of the room, fast and slippery like a fish, that stupid silky cloak slipping out of my fingers when I try to grab it.

All I can do is follow and hope we don't run into anyone who might ask where the Russian Bratva went. Caligula is moving fast, and his chin is lifted in that arrogant damn way he has. Even with a cock cage and a butt plug, the guy's ego just leaks out all over the place. If anyone lays eyes on him, they're going to notice.

"Wait *up*," I say sharply, jogging the few steps to catch up, and yank him back to my side. "Remember, you're supposed to be my goddamn property."

"We need to find King," he says obstinately.

"We need to take the L and get out of here with our organs still inside our bodies."

Caligula swerves away down a side corridor before I can pull him through the door back to the main room, and then starts running. I noticed how fast he was that time he was running away from his grandpa's place, and I'm even more impressed by his speed with what has to be a real uncomfortable plug in his ass. It takes me a few precious seconds to catch up with him, go through that same door, only to find him standing at a dead stop a few feet into the room. I run right into him and have to wrap my arms around him to stop him from getting bowled over.

Ah, shit. We're in the auction room, at the side. He's staring at the stage, and I don't like the look on his face.

At least there's no one else in here, because Caligula has chosen this moment to start having some kind of panic attack, his breath getting faster even though he's stopped running. His chest is heaving, and I feel his heart beating where his back is pressed into me. "Calm down," I snap unhelpfully. "We don't have time for this."

And all of a sudden, his breath stops. I let him go, worried he's about to drop dead, but he's just caught his breath in a gasp. "The *proxy,*" he says, like he's solved something.

"Huh?"

"During the auction." He points to his feet. "There was a man standing right here, bidding on behalf of someone else in the room. Someone sitting up there in the dark." He points to the back of the room. "I couldn't see them. They had…long hair. That's all I could see." He looks up at me expectantly. "Who was it?"

"How am I supposed to know?"

"You walked right by them when you marched down to the stage to bid ten million dollars on me."

I don't like the look in his eye or the tone of his voice. I especially don't like the fact that I've got nothing to share, because the only person I noticed in the room that night was Caligula Clemenza, golden and beautiful like some young god, shining in the spotlight.

"I don't know," I tell him. "And we need to get out of here."

"We need to find King's office and ask who that bidder was."

He's got balls, I'll give him that. "We're out of time. We'll find out some other way. Caligula, *listen to me—*" I grab him by the shoulders. "We. Need. To. Leave."

I seem to be getting through to him. Or so I think. Then he breaks away from me again and runs back through the door the way we came. I jog after him again, but I don't think he even knows where he's going, because we end up back where we started, just outside the room where we left a corpse. He seems to recognize it, too, because he finally pulls up and looks around helplessly. "Everywhere looks the same," he mutters.

I seize him by the bicep, determined not to let him go this time.

And then my life gets a thousand times worse as Jesse Foster rounds the corner of the hallway, thunder-faced and pouting. He brightens up when he sees us standing there, evil eyes landing on Caligula for only a moment. "Hel-*lo*, sir," he says to me with a simpering smile. "I came to see if you and Grisha needed anything…*extra*."

He reaches for the door.

I grab him by the arm. "Actually," I tell him, "Grisha's taking a minute for himself. Recovering. You know what I mean?"

Foster casts a disdainful glance at Caligula, taking in his messy hair, flushed cheeks, the dried mix of spit and precum still on his chin. Caligula does his best to look downbeat, eyes to the floor, brows pulled together in an expression approaching sorrow. It's not a great act, but it's enough to fuel Foster's malignant little mind. He smiles in satisfaction.

"I'm *so* glad you were able to find mutual understanding," he coos. "I'll just see if he'd like a warm cloth or—"

I'm still holding both his and Caligula's arms, so I steer them both away with me as I start walking. "You know what, Jesse, you're just the guy I wanted to see. I need a word with your owner. I'd like to make him a—a proposal."

I try real hard to make it sound like something he might enjoy. And as usual with Jesse Foster, personal gain takes precedence over everything else. "That sounds delightful," he purrs. "Mr. King is in his office. I'll take you there right now."

As for the Clemenza, he finally stops trying to fight me.

I try to remember which way Foster takes us, hoping for an easy escape route, but he leads us through back hallways that twist and turn until I'm hopelessly lost. Caligula, when I glance at him, doesn't seem to be paying attention, since his eyes are fixed on Foster and then—when we finally arrive—on the door to King's office.

Foster knocks three times and waits.

"What is it?" sounds a testy voice from within. It's King. And he doesn't get any friendlier when Foster pushes the door open and leads us inside. "What do *you* want, Orsini?"

"He wants me, sir," Jesse simpers. "So we thought—"

"No, I don't," I growl. "I want to talk, King. That's all."

Daniel King looks at me, and then the Clemenza next to me, who isn't bothering to hide his anger now.

"Get out, Jesse," King says. Foster doesn't argue. He just turns and gets. "What is it?" King repeats, standing up from his seat. He stays behind his desk, though. Wants a barricade between me and him.

"We need information," Caligula says, cool and autocratic. It doesn't seem to me to be the right play, but King has kept his eyes on the Clemenza since Foster left, instead of me.

Like Caligula Clemenza is the one in charge.

"I have none to share," King tells him. But I hear the caution in his voice.

"That's a pity," Caligula says, "since I'll take either information or your life."

It would've gone smoother if he'd given me some warning, but I'm fast enough. King reaches for the drawer of his desk, but I slam it closed on his wrist before he can get the gun out. With my other hand, I shove his head down to the desk. Not too hard, just enough to let him know I'm not fucking around.

"You are going to die for this, Orsini," King says calmly.

"You should be more worried about your own life right now," the Clemenza tells him, coming closer. "I want to know who bid on me at the auction—apart from Mr. Orsini, here, and apart from your buddy Grisha."

King says nothing. I grind his head a little harder into the desk, reminding him that I can squash it like a rotten pumpkin if I really need to.

Caligula squats down at the side of the desk, tipping his head to the side to look into King's face. "Mr. King, if you don't tell me what I want to know, I will remove this ridiculous plug from my ass and shove it down your throat. And then, while you're choking on it, Dami here will crush your skull. We'll leave you like that for your pet to find—and your men. Is that really how you want to be remembered?"

King didn't get to where he is by taking risky bets. "How many names do you want?"

"Let's start with the person who had a proxy bidding for him, that silver-haired man at the side of the room. He was taking orders from someone at the back of the room, sitting in the shadows. Long hair."

King chuckles. He actually chuckles.

"Want to share with the class?" I ask, adding pressure until he grunts in pain.

"That was your cousin, Mr. Clemenza. Tiberius Vicario."

CHAPTER 38
CALIGULA

"TIBERIUS VICARIO," I echo. I nod at Dami, who lets King up. "And you didn't think to mention him to me when I came to you desperate and ready to sell myself?"

King, who has been adjusting his jacket with an irritated air, looks wary once more. "Our members' privacy is paramount."

"You wanted the money you could get for me," I say softly. "And you wanted to see the last Clemenza tortured and punished by your Bratva friends. Didn't you?"

At last the mask falls from his face. There's true hatred in his eyes. "Do you know how many of my friends your grandfather had murdered? Yes. We wanted payback. Just like this—this ignorant *oaf* here, who somehow seems to be doing your bidding."

At that, Dami actually snarls, his lips pulling back from his teeth.

"On the contrary, Mr. King," I say lightly. "This ignorant oaf is my legitimate owner. He doesn't like the idea of having his property fondled by others, that's all."

King scoffs at that. "He doesn't even understand your

real worth. Do you have any idea what some people out there would pay to see a Clemenza—"

With a right hook worthy of the world heavyweight champion, Dami knocks him out. I watch Daniel King fall over his desk and to the floor and then I look up at Dami. "What was that for?"

"Tired of his bullshit."

"Why, what did you think he was going to say?"

"Nothing useful. What they'd pay to watch you suffer. Watch you break. You've heard it all before."

"So this time you were protecting my delicate sensibilities?" Dami shrugs. I step to the side, looking down at King on the carpet. "Is this one dead, too?"

"No. I mean, I don't think so." He kneels to check the pulse. "He's alive."

I let out a little puff of relief. "Well, that's one fewer problem at least."

"Might be better if I *did* kill him," Dami suggests.

It's tempting. But I shake my head. "The Bratva will be angry enough about Grisha. Your Boss might be able to smooth that over, but not if you kill Daniel King as well." Dami, who blinked a little at my mention of his Boss, looks worried.

"We better get moving," he says after a moment. "That pet demon of his'll be back any second to cause trouble."

And speak of the devil, there's a knock at the door just as Dami finishes, three hard taps and a three-second wait…

It flings open. "Daniel!" Jesse Foster cries. "Something terrible has—" He sees Dami and me standing over the desk, and then his eyes move to the floor, where King's unconscious body is just visible to him behind the desk.

He clocks the situation fast. Jesse Foster is like me in some ways: he's a survivor. He turns and bolts.

Dami charges after him at once, but I'm faster. I take off

like I've heard the starter pistol and chase him down the corridor. With the cloak streaming behind me, I feel like a superhero, and I gain so fast on Jesse that I'm on him before he reaches the first corner. I push him off balance into the wall, and we go down onto the floor in a tangle of legs and arms. He's like a feral cat fighting to be free, and I get an elbow to the gut that winds me, but a moment later Dami leans down and picks him up, clapping a giant hand across his mouth.

"Get up," Dami orders me. "We need to get out right fucking now."

Jesse is struggling and kicking in his arms, and I'm worried for a nanosecond that Dami might kill him, too.

But I don't have time to waste worrying about a false friend.

"That way," I wheeze, pointing down the other way. "There's a back door into an alley."

"In my pocket," Dami says. "Get my phone. Text Vito to meet us there."

My hands are shaking as I slide a hand into his pocket, and then shaking again when Dami tells me the code to open the phone. But he's patient and calm, even as we hurry down the hallway, even with Jesse Foster wriggling around like a wildcat in his arms.

Somehow I get the text done, and somehow the hallways feel more familiar here. Within a minute we're at the black metal door that I remember closing behind me like the gates of hell when I first came here.

It's locked, a keypad lock. Dami shoves Jesse close to it. "Open it."

Jesse just keeps struggling.

"Jesse," I snarl, and he stops struggling to glare at me. "Do you want to end up like Grisha?"

He stops yanking at Dami's iron embrace, and stabs a

few buttons on the keypad. I hold my breath for a second, hoping like hell there's no alarm code, but the door simply makes a soft clunk as the lock releases. I pull it open, gasping at the cold air outside rushing in, and we hurry out.

Vito's right there in the car, and the door to the back seat is already open and waiting for us. Dami throws Jesse aside, who stumbles to the ground with a pitiful cry, and we pile into the car. It pulls away with a screech, narrowly avoiding Jesse, who flattens himself against the wall, screaming empty threats after us.

I look at Dami. He looks at me. And I feel a grin starting to spread, just as reluctant but inevitable as the one on his face. He shakes his head, trying to get rid of it, and sits back in his seat. "Fuck," he says, wincing as his shoulder blade contacts the leather.

"Let me see," I say at once, pushing him forward and pulling off his jacket insistently. Shit. He's bleeding again—though nowhere near as badly as last time. "Rosa will need to look at this," I tell him.

He shrugs me off. "Let's just worry about getting home first," he mutters.

I sit back as well, content to let him brood. "Whatever you say, Dami. Whatever you say." I'm riding high on adrenaline and satisfaction. We got away. *And* we got intel.

But as I think about that intel, my mood dims a little. My own cousin—trying to buy me. To what end? To save me?

Or to kill me off, so he could inherit?

We get home without further incident. Vito makes sure to slow down as soon as we're a few blocks away, I assume so we won't attract attention. He drives straight into the underground garage I've never seen but now realize must be set above the creepy basement where Dami kept me.

Might keep me again.

But not tonight. Tonight, Dami doesn't even bother to hide the code from me when he punches it in to bring down the garage door, and then the security shields after it.

We troop up a small staircase that opens into a short corridor with several doors coming off it—those must be the bedrooms for Rosa, Vito and Sammy—and into the kitchen. Rosa is already there, first aid kit at the ready, her lips a thin white line.

I pull the cloak around me, shivering. Rosa leaves the room and comes back with a white terry robe to put around me over the cloak, which I gratefully snuggle into. And then she sets about tending to Dami's back.

"It's not so bad," she allows begrudgingly at last. Vito has made some hot chocolate in the meantime, and I curl my hands around its warmth gratefully. "I'll dress it again. And you—" She stabs a finger into the middle of Dami's back. "No more heroics!"

He winces. "Got none planned." I catch his eye, and we both smirk.

Sammy chooses that moment to wander through to the kitchen, rubbing sleep from his eyes. He stops dead when he sees me, as usual. Then he points at me. "That's mine!" he complains.

I look down at the robe I'm wearing. The fact that it's Sammy's explains why it fits so much better than Dami's. Still, I don't want a fight about it.

"Here," I say, shrugging it off. I hold it out to him, and he grabs it from me as though I've stolen his most precious possession. I pull the cloak around me again, ignoring Sammy's expression as he takes it in.

"What's going on?" he demands, looking back to Dami.

"Nothing," Dami replies heavily, and stands, pulling his shirt back on. "Go to bed, all of you. You—" he glances at me "—come with me."

We don't go up to the bedroom, even though I can see Dami's exhausted. I am too, but I'm still humming with adrenaline from the Obelisk. So when Dami leads me into the great room and turns on the gas fire, I'm glad we'll have the chance to decompress.

"I can't believe we actually got out of there alive," I say as he shuts the door behind us.

"Yeah, well, we're still two dead guys walking," he says wearily. "Come here. Let me get that thing off of you." I stand still long enough to let him unlock and remove the cage, but then I go right back to pacing.

"Sit down, would you?" he says.

"I can't," I snap back. "I have a hunk of metal up my ass, and it's really uncomfortable."

He gives a soft snort. "Then come here, like I'm telling you, and I'll take it out for you."

"In a minute," I tell him. I want to calm down a little first. I pull off the stupid gold cloak and throw it down on the sofa. Dami sinks into his armchair next to the fire while I pace around in front of him. It feels completely normal now to be naked in his presence. Naked, even plugged still. None of it bothers me right now, because we have a bigger problem. "We need to think about what you tell your Boss. Killing Grisha was a really dumb move."

Dami is looking at me with an expression I can't read. "You don't need to worry about what my Boss will think. It's got nothing to do with you."

"It does, actually. When we left this house, you were protecting me from one person killing my Family. Now we'll have the entire New York Bratva after us, too. Don't you realize you started a war tonight?"

He leans forward on his knees with an irritated sigh. "I don't need you to be telling me about this business. I'm the fucking Giuliano Enforcer. I know how the politics work."

But something keeps pushing me on. I'm not going to let it rest. "If you knew, then why the hell did you kill Grisha? My reputation is hardly worth a mob war, surely—"

"Because you belong to me," he barks. He catches me as my pacing brings me closer to him, and stands to hold me hard by both arms, even shaking me slightly. "You belong to *me*, and no one else gets to touch you, look at you, fucking *think* about you without my permission. What don't you get about that?"

My euphoria dissolves into frustration. Daniel King was right; this man is an ignorant oaf. "Belong to you? If that's the case, shouldn't you prove it? At least Grisha wanted to fuck me! All *you* do is tease me."

There's a fire in his eyes and I worry that I might have started an inferno I can't put out. "This has never been about sex," he tells me in a low, dangerous voice.

"*Everything* is about sex!" I shout. "Everything in the goddamn world. Money. Power. Cars. Guns. They're all about sex, one way or another. Getting it. Having it. Wanting it. Dying for it. The only thing that's *not* about sex is sex!"

"What in the hell are you talking about?"

"I *know* why you won't fuck me," I hiss at him. "It's because you think it would actually *mean* something. And you're a *coward*."

Dami stares down into my face for a long moment, long enough to make me wish I hadn't said what I just did. Then he spins me around and pushes me over the back of the sofa in front of the fireplace.

In one steady pull, he removes the butt plug and throws it onto the seat of the sofa, pushing my head down far enough that I resist, worried he's going to rub my nose in it. I hear the rasp of a zipper as he opens his pants. "Is that what it will take to shut you up?" he snarls. "My cock in your ass?"

I look back over my shoulder at him. "Like I said, Dami, I just don't think you have the balls."

He grabs my arms, locking one of his forearms under my elbows so they're bent back, my chest rising up. I feel the nudge of his cock at my asshole, and in one stroke, he's deep into me. Balls deep, the warmth of them nestling into my taint.

Well. I guess I'm not a virgin anymore.

CHAPTER 39
CALIGULA

DAMIANO'S free arm wraps around my chest, holding me flush against him as I pant and adjust. He's…he's much bigger than the plug. But having that damn thing in me all night, plus the lube it took to get it in there, means him plunging in like that doesn't hurt.

Oh, it doesn't hurt at all.

But I feel so opened up, so completely filled with him that I can't think.

He thrusts again, testing the angle, and then again, each movement punctuated by an erotic grunt of effort. I arch against him. "This what you wanted, golden boy? This what you needed?"

I can't answer for a second. My mind is shorting out from the sheer, unadulterated pleasure of being so completely possessed.

By a Giuliano.

By *this* Giuliano.

So it takes a second to find my words again.

"Good work, Dami," I grit out at last. "You sure showed me."

He gives an unwilling huff of laughter and slides his

hand up my chest to my throat, wrapping around it. But it's not threatening, not like it usually is. This time it feels…

Caring. Like he's checking my pulse or something, which, honestly, good instinct, because it's going so fast I'm a little worried. He shifts slightly, changing the angle of his thrusts, and then—

Oh, God.

That place inside me, the one I've only ever felt with the aid of his fingers, lights up like fireworks. My entire body spasms, a broken cry tearing from my throat.

And without another pause, he starts to nail it. Again and again. Each thrust is a deliberate, slow strike against that bundle of nerves, pulling sounds from me that I didn't know I could make.

"I know exactly what you need," he murmurs, each word punctuated by another slam against my prostate.

He's right, that's the hell of it. My cock is so hard it feels like stone, trapped between my belly and the velvet of the sofa, and the friction isn't anywhere near enough. I need more. He shifts again, pulling out until his thick head is teasing my stretched-out rim, then slams back in so hard that the force of it punches a gasp out of me.

He lets go of my throat and my arms and wraps me up in a tight embrace, hoisting me higher so I'm up on my toes, impaled on his cock. I'm completely at his mercy, my legs shaking, my whole body focused on the feeling of him filling me, stretching me…

Owning me.

I feel a sharp bite on my shoulder, and then he's nipping at the side of my neck, licking the sweat from my skin as he pounds into me again. I feel like a rag doll. He's right; I *like* being a fucktoy for this beast of a man, and that should be humiliating, degrading. Clemenzas don't like this kind of thing.

But that sense of the taboo just makes it hotter.

And then Dami's arms lift me even higher, right off his cock, leaving me empty and aching. I wriggle around in the hopes that his dick will slip right back in where I want it. But all he does is cross the room, turn my back to the wall, and hike me up in his arms again.

I wrap my arms and legs around him instinctively. He looks straight into my face, lines himself up, and pushes back in, painfully slow. In this position, I can feel every inch of him disappearing inside me, see the sweat beading at his temples, smell the musky scent rising up between us.

He fucks me. *Hard.* Hips pistoning, finding that same spot inside me with unerring accuracy, over and over. He shifts his grip, wrapping an arm around my waist to support me, and uses the other hand to jack my cock. His grip is tight, rough, possessive. He leans in, pressing his forehead to mine, and I breathe in his breath, closing my eyes as I focus on the pleasure building up in me.

"You look at me when I'm fucking you," he growls.

I force my eyes open. He's got that obsessive, intense stare that he used to level at me when he first took me home. I used to hate it. But now it makes me feel like I'm the only person in the world, the only thing he's seeing.

It makes me feel *powerful.*

I'm the only one who has that effect on him. The only one who makes him so helplessly focused that he can't think about anything else. And I stare right back at him.

He lets go of my dick and takes a handful of my hair, not tugging, just guiding my head back so he can slide his tongue up my neck. With his nose tucked just under my ear, he says, "You're mine. You believe me now?"

He pulls out again, and I let out such a noise of complaint that he puts his hand over my mouth, chuckling breathlessly and shushing me. "Okay, okay," he murmurs, and guides his cock back into me again. "Just…hold on, I guess."

He hoists me closer, pulling me away from the wall, and I suck and bite my way across his shoulders as he doggedly makes his way to the door, cursing as each step makes me bounce a little on his dick. He gets the door open at last, and then it's only a few steps over to the stairs. Surely he's not going to carry me up all those flights while buried in my—

No. He's not. He's making for the elevator.

"No," I say as he punches the button. He's still inside me, thick and uncompromising. "*No.*"

I'm not going down to that mausoleum again.

He's already got me into that tiny space, pressed up against the back mirrored wall. "Hey, shh, it's okay," he says, as tender as I've ever heard him, which isn't all that fucking tender. But I keep struggling. "We're going up. *Up*, Caligula. I won't—I won't put you down there again, I promise, *fuck*, I promise—look—" He reaches for the brass panel and hits the button for his bedroom floor, not the fingerprint scanner that goes down to the basement.

I'm so relieved that I slump in his arms, and he has to hoist me back up, grimacing as the movement makes me clamp harder on him. He lets out a pained sound. "If you move too much, you're gonna make me shoot my load right here," he warns me.

He's finally going to come for me. *In* me. I want that. I want him to lose control.

I wriggle again experimentally.

"*Fuck,*" he chokes out, slamming one big palm flat against the mirror above my head. "I'm serious, golden boy. Stop that."

So I stop moving. But I don't stop clenching around him in a slow, rhythmic pulse. His head drops to my shoulder, and I can hear him panting. "You're gonna be the death of me, you know that?" he murmurs.

The elevator doors open. He practically stumbles out, and I wrap my legs tighter around his waist, helping to take some of my weight. We're in the familiar corridor that leads to his bedroom. He doesn't even bother with the light when we get in there, just kicks the door shut behind us, plunging us into the same absolute darkness as before.

Despite the lack of light, he seems to know exactly where he's going, but when I feel him bending over, gravity tearing me from him, I cling tighter in panic. "Easy. It's the bed." He lets me down onto it with a gentleness I didn't anticipate, laying me out on my back, his cock still deep inside me. I feel him moving, shrugging, and realize he's undressing, that he won't even pull out to make it easier.

And then he stretches out over me, covering me with his body, his chest a furnace against my sweat-slicked skin. One hand slides down to cup my ass, pulling me open as he drives in deeper and harder, making me cry out. "Now tell me you belong to me," he demands.

I press my mouth into his neck. "No," I pant out.

With a growl, he slams into me so hard that I slide up the bed. "*Say* it."

I slide my hands down to grip his ass. "No. You prove it."

And holy fuck, does he ever.

He fucks me so hard we move right up the bed, and I have to put my hand out and brace against the headboard to stop our migration. I can't stop the noise I'm making.

"Quiet," he mutters, moving in me with quick, sharp jabs. "Unless you want everyone in this house to hear you getting wrecked."

A wicked thrill goes through me. "Maybe I do," I gasp

out. "Maybe I want everyone to know who owns me, Dami."

"Fuck," he hisses, and gives a hard, deliberate thrust that makes me wail. But I'm beyond caring. My world has narrowed to the feel of him inside me, the stretch and the ache, the overwhelming pleasure…and the delicious promise of having him fill me up.

Because nothing on earth is going to stop Damiano Orsini now. I can tell by the way he's breathing, by the way his hips are moving, by the feel of the sweat dripping off him onto my chest—he's close.

He's close, and it's going to be a torrent.

He arches up, pulling almost all the way out again until just the head of that massive dick is stretching my rim. "You want proof?" he pants. "Fucking take it."

With that, he slams back into me, and I feel it, the flood of him filling me up so completely that I think I might drown. He grunts with every pulse of his cock, marking me as his from the inside out.

He collapses onto me, but I don't want him to move. I want to stay connected to him like this for as long as possible. He's heavy, but I'm willing to suffocate for this. His breath is hot and humid against my neck, and I feel the frantic beat of his heart against my chest, matching my own.

We lie there for a quiet moment, our bodies slick with sweat and cum, the smell of it musky and overpowering in the darkness. I run my hands up and down his back, feeling the muscles there relax, the tension finally leaving them.

I'm still hard and aching, and my ass is sore.

But I'm content.

After a minute, he stirs, pushing himself up on his arms. His cock slides out of me and I feel a hot trickle escape, running down the crack of my ass. I make a noise of protest.

"Jesus," he sighs. He shifts, then I feel his fingers at my hole, tracing the puffy rim, then pushing inside me, into that mess he made. "You're dripping," he says, a note of satisfaction in his voice.

"You filled me up," I manage to say.

"Not even close," he says. "That was round one, golden boy." His hand trails up to my cock, which leaps eagerly into his palm as though it has a mind of its own. I'm so sensitive I feel like I could burst from just the lightest touch. I gasp as he tightens his grip, a slow, deliberate pull from root to tip that has my hips arching off the bed. "Come on," he says. "I wanna taste you again."

I'm still a little disoriented, so when I feel Dami's tongue swirling around the head of my cock, I cry out in surprise. He licks into the slit, then takes the whole head into his mouth, sucking me right down, while those fingers return to my ass again, like he's trying to keep all his spunk inside me. The idea of it, combined with the suction of his mouth and the soft, insistent press of his fingers, is enough to finish me off.

I come so hard it feels like every muscle in my body seizes up, arching into his greedy mouth as he swallows me down. It takes a long, long time for the shudders to stop. When they do, I flop bonelessly against the mattress, exhausted.

He crawls back up to lie beside me, pushing me onto my side. I assume he's going to spoon me, but that's not what he does at all. He tugs at my leg until I let him hoist it up and over his thigh, then he lines himself up again and stuffs himself into me, only half-hard, so soon after emptying into me...but getting harder every second.

It's sore, but it's a *good* soreness. I feel that delicious stretch again as my hole welcomes him back in, and he starts a slow rhythm as he coaxes himself back to full hardness. It's less frantic. Less angry. He slides a hand up my waist to my chest and plays with my nipples for a while. He's only taking shallow little strokes, which I'm grateful for, since I'm still sensitive from my own orgasm.

After a while, his hand moves from my chest to my throat, fitting over it and tipping my head back. He picks up the pace, and I push my ass against him, taking him deeper.

"You wanted proof," he murmurs into my ear. "I gave it to you." The grip on my throat tightens a little, and my pulse hammers against his palm. "Now tell me."

"I'm yours," I choke out. "Dami, I'm yours—"

"Again," he commands, shoving his thigh up under mine so the angle changes. It's deeper. Better.

"I'm yours," I gasp.

"Yeah, you're mine," he spits out, and I feel him swelling up inside me, making me so full I might burst. And just like him, I'm getting hard again, impossibly hard so soon after coming for him. But Dami is stroking inside me exactly right.

He knows me too well.

He knows exactly how to touch me, how to fuck me, what to say to make me so hot I can't think straight. He knows things about me that I'm still not comfortable enough to face, like the fact that I get off on being spanked, or caged, or having a golden dildo stuffed up my asshole. He knows I like it when he holds me down, when he's rough with me, when he makes me submit.

His hand leaves my throat and slides down my chest, my stomach, lower, until he's cupping my balls, rolling them in his palm. I thrust into his grip, seeking more friction, but he just holds them there, a possessive weight that has me whining in the back of my throat.

He's dangerous, but not in the way I thought when he bought me. He's dangerous to my equilibrium, to my self-perception, to my *sanity*.

With a final thrust and a smothered groan, he comes again. I just lie there and take it, my body shuddering with each pulse of his dick, my own cock twitching with sympathetic pleasure. His thumb rubs over the sensitive skin behind my balls, pressing into my taint, and then his hand goes back to my dick. He doesn't even need to do much, just wrap those strong fingers around me and jack me a few times before I convulse in his embrace and start to shoot.

"Come on, golden boy," he says, and I hear the lazy satisfaction in his voice. "Give it up to me again. All of it."

I do.

I come so hard it's almost painful, my ass clamping down on him like a vise, milking every last drop out of his cock. All he does is hold me tighter, murmuring filthy praise into my ear, and then tell me I better get myself ready for round three, because he's not done yet.

He bought me. Chained me. Caged me. But he never really owned me.

Not until now.

CHAPTER 40
CALIGULA

THE NEXT TIME I open my eyes, it's still pitch black, but I'm wrapped up in Damiano's strong arms and I'm in his soft bed and my ass feels a little sore and very thoroughly…

Used.

I grin to myself and have to fight the urge to wriggle around in pleasure. I don't want Dami to wake up and turn back into some surly grump. But he's already stirring, his arms shifting and then tightening, and his nose snuffles at the back of my neck, breathing me in.

"G'morning," he rasps.

"Might be more like good evening," I tell him. "I have no idea what time it is."

"Fuck." He gets out of the bed, which is exactly what I didn't want, and snaps on the light, making me wince. He scrabbles around in his clothes on the floor and comes up with his phone, which starts buzzing like a beehive with incoming messages when he turns it on. "*Fuck*. It's past four in the afternoon!"

"We *were* up all night," I point out.

"Yeah, but I…" He sighs. "I shoulda got in touch with Big Gee or Seb. Given them a heads-up after that business at the Obelisk. They're asking questions…" He turns his attention to the phone again.

I've been ditched for Big Gee and Seb.

"What do they say?" I ask casually.

"Seb wants a meeting. Tomorrow, though, so I guess it's not urgent. Otherwise Big Gee himself would be here, banging on my door—" He breaks off, then adds slowly, "Big Gee's been looking for an excuse for a fight with the Russians, anyway. Doesn't like the way they've been cutting into our profits. Maybe he'll see it as an opportunity instead of a…"

"Catastrophe?" I suggest.

"I was gonna say a fuckin' mess. But yeah. That too. Seb's more restrained. Doesn't want a war with anyone. If he wasn't a Gee, he'd probably be *happy* with the way the Morellis are running the place." He looks at me. "Don't know why I'm saying all this to you."

I prop myself up on one arm. "It's interesting to hear. I knew more about the old Don, Jimmy Gee, than I do about his son."

"His son's more of a thug than Jimmy was," Dami says, and then rubs a hand over his face. "Forget I said that."

Damiano Orsini is not a good man, or a kind man. But he is loyal to the death to those under his protection. I've seen the proof myself.

That sense of loyalty seems to have been tested by his own Boss, though.

"How's your back feeling?" I ask.

"It's fine," he says automatically. "How's your ass?"

I'm busy filing away these little slivers of information about Giuliano business, but when he asks that, I come back to the present with a bump. "Um. Fine. I think. I could use a shower, though. I stink of…well, you."

He nods. "I could use a wash, too. You wanna go first?"

"No." I crawl across the bed. "We can both fit in there."

We can both fit with room to spare, in fact. And it's time to find out where I stand after last night. I'm not stupid enough to think things have completely changed. But maybe I've gained a little ground.

Dami ducks his head, but not before I catch a little smile. "You offering to wash my back again?"

"That and every other part."

He stares at me hard for a second, then grabs the lube. "Come on, then."

As it turns out, we have to be careful of his bandaged wound, so Dami's the one who does most of the washing. He soaps me up all over, gentle and soft between my butt cheeks. And then he pushes me up against the wall, the cool tiles a shock against my hot skin, and drops to his knees behind me to nuzzle into my crack. My hole is still so tender, but when I feel his flat tongue lapping over it, soothing and slow, I'm glad I trusted him. He licks around for a while until I reach back and thread my fingers through his wet hair, pressing him closer in a wordless plea. His tongue wriggles in, a slick, dirty invasion that has me panting.

He knows when I need more without me having to even ask. He stands just before I start begging, spreads my legs wide with one of his, and slicks himself up with the lube. I brace for discomfort when he lines up the head of his cock with my asshole, but he slides right in to the hilt like it's the easiest thing in the world.

And I take it with a deep groan of satisfaction. The water from the showerhead is running between us, down my ass, trickling over my stretched hole where we're joined. Dami starts a slow, easy rhythm, and his orgasm, when it comes, is just as slow, a lazy pulse that makes me feel warm all over.

He stays inside me while he washes my hair, which is nice for a minute, but soon becomes a strange kind of foreplay. By the time we're done, he's hard again, and he starts to fuck me in earnest this time, jacking me off while he does, until I splatter the tiles.

"Messy," he tells me with a grin.

I can only laugh.

By the time we get out, I'm starving. I dress in some of the clothes the Benedettis sent over. "I'll get Rosa to send something up," he says. "We should talk about this Tiberius guy."

I catch his hand. "We need to do that. But let's eat down there in the kitchen. With them."

He looks at me in surprise. "Uh. Sammy'll…be there."

"It's time Sammy and I got used to each other. Besides…" Should I bring this up? "You should warn them. About the Bratva."

His face darkens—but not at me. "Yeah," he says gruffly. "You're right. I don't want any of them blindsided. They need to know the situation."

He lets me keep his hand as we go downstairs, but I release him as we enter the kitchen. I don't want to push too much. Rosa is there as usual and the place smells deliciously of sizzling pancetta and garlic. She glances up as we enter. "I'll send something up," she says.

"We'll eat down here tonight," Dami says.

Rosa's eyes go to me speculatively, but she just nods and sets out a few more places at the round table in the small dining area.

"Sammy and Vito gonna make it to dinner?" Dami asks. "I gotta talk to you all."

"They're always here," Rosa says with a shrug.

Sammy comes in not long afterward, though he stops dead seeing me at the table. "I'm not going to break bread with a Clemenza," he says at once.

"That's fine," Dami says to him. "You can watch the rest of us eat. But you come and sit down, because I need to talk to you all."

Sammy comes to the table. Slowly and angrily, but he comes. He takes the other seat next to Dami and slumps back in his chair so that he doesn't have to see me. Vito comes in soon after, and then Rosa serves up dinner to us all: a creamy carbonara on her handmade pasta to start, followed by chicken saltimbocca with a side of roast vegetables, baked ziti, and two different kinds of bread. At first it's enough food to seem excessive, even for an Italian household, but as I watch Vito and especially Dami start to wolf it down, I can see she knows exactly how much food she needs to make to keep the men of the house happy.

Even Sammy picks up his fork about half a second after Rosa sets the noodles down in front of him. Halfway through the meal, when the atmosphere is more convivial, Damiano starts laying it out to them: that there might be trouble, that they need to be extra careful, that they should stay in the house as much as possible. He points a fork at Sammy. "That means you stay away from the markets, too," he says sternly. "I ain't chancing someone coming at you while you're there. You hear me?"

Sammy looks pleased that Dami singled him out. "I hear you. But what about groceries?"

"We'll get them delivered."

"Won't be as good," Rosa sniffs. "These places get rid of the worst of their stock on delivery orders."

"You'll make it taste as good as it always does," Dami

tells her. "And you, Vito, I want you with Rosa when you're not with me. Just in case."

Vito gives a reassuring smile to Rosa. She flushes a little and busies herself serving out more baked ziti onto his plate.

"I mean it," Dami says. "This is serious shit. And you see anything, hear anything, you come to me right away."

After Dami's pronouncement, an atmosphere of camaraderie seems to settle over us. This little group of strays will pull together, I think.

And me with them.

I have to look down at the second helping of chicken—that Rosa served me without even asking—to hide a sudden prickling in my eyes. I'm not a crier. Learned early that it wouldn't be rewarded in the Clemenzas. But this sense of belonging, of *family,* is exactly what I've been missing since my father died. He and Nonna Mellie and me, we were our own little group. We'd have fun together when I was small, and we'd meet at Bergdorf's for lunch once a week. The three of us were simpatico, my Dad used to say.

God, I miss them so much.

The evening goes on. Rosa brings out dessert—torta della nonna, the custard still warm, pine nuts golden on top—insisting that I take a piece even when I groan that I couldn't possibly. Even Sammy seems to thaw slightly toward me, or at least is less inclined to scowl when he looks my way. And between us, Dami seems relaxed and happy. I've never seen him smile or laugh so much, either at Rosa's stories or my occasional sarcasm, or at Sammy's description of the fishmonger he usually goes to, who knows Rosa personally and is always terrified she'll send back the fish.

Eventually, Rosa says she needs to clean up. I offer to

help load the dishwasher, and Vito helps dry things that need to be washed by hand. Sammy gathers together the trash to take it out, but Dami stops him. "I'll come with you. I meant what I said, Sammy—you keep your eyes open and don't take risks."

I've just finished stacking the dishes in the dishwasher when I find another small trash can under the sink that needs to be taken out. "I'll run this bag out to them," I tell Rosa and Vito, who barely hear me. Rosa's been busy chattering in Italian, and Vito's hanging on her every word.

With a smile, I head toward the back door of the kitchen and find my way after Sammy and Dami. It's easy enough, because they've left the door that opens to the street ajar, and cold air is seeping into the dark hallway.

But I pause there behind the door as I hear my name.

"...glad you're getting along better with Caligula."

"I'm not," Sammy says. There's a rustle of plastic bags. "I hate him. I always will. But for your sake, Damiano, I'll put up with him."

There's a pause. "Well," Dami says at last. "Love and hate ain't got nothing to do with Family. So that's good enough for me, Sammy."

"How much longer will he be here?" Sammy sounds forlorn.

"A while."

"Why are you being so *nice* to him?"

"Hey." There's a warning in Dami's voice. "You don't get involved in business, Sammy. What I plan to do with him—"

"He's a *Clemenza,*" Sammy spits.

There's a silence, and then Dami speaks again, but so quietly that I have to lean closer to the gap to hear. "... keeping him away from some people who are looking for him. A group that calls itself the Clemenza Loyalists. They want to crown him king, put him in as a figurehead, get the Clemenza Family going again. Now, you don't want those fuckers gaining ground again any more than I do, right? Right. So trust me on this, Sammy."

"I always do, Damiano."

The Clemenza Loyalists aren't all dead and gone.

In fact, they're alive and *looking* for me.

Why not go to your Loyalists? Dami asked me, when he was wondering how I'd ended up at the Obelisk. I remember, too, how quickly he changed the subject when I showed no knowledge about them.

And just a few days ago, he looked me right in the eye and told me they were dust.

"Come on," he's saying, "let's get back inside. I don't like the look of that van over there."

I slide silently back up the hallway and make my way down again much more noisily, trash bag in hand. "Oh, hi!" I say when we all run into each other. "You missed one."

I hold it out to Sammy. He takes it with a wide, fake smile. "Thanks," he says, but then Dami grabs it from him.

"You two get back to the kitchen," he growls at us. "When I come back inside, we're going into lockdown again."

"Yes, Damiano," Sammy says, and slides past me, that smile still plastered on his face.

I watch Sammy go on ahead obediently, but I wait there until Dami comes back in. "What did I just say?" he sighs.

"I know. But I wanted to do this."

I wind my arms around his neck and kiss him, press my mouth to those lying lips to find out what deceit tastes like.

Daniel King's cut-off words echo in my head as I do. *Do you have any idea what some people out there would pay to see a Clemenza—*

See a Clemenza what? Suffer, as Dami suggested King

was going to say at the time, before a right hook silenced him? Or see a Clemenza rise again, take control of the Family, resurrect it?

I sold myself at auction because I had no other options —or so I thought.

Damiano Orsini knew I had another option.

CHAPTER 41
DAMIANO

IT'S a new experience to be kissing Caligula Clemenza.

It's our first. I've never kissed him so far. Fucked him, sucked him, ate him out…

Never kissed him.

Didn't want to cross that line. Seemed like the last betrayal of my purpose.

But here and now, it feels…right. It feels *right* to kiss my most hated enemy, the object of my obsession, the target of my vengeance.

Something between us shifted at the Obelisk. Something shifted as soon as I killed that fucking Russian. I still don't know why I did that. Don't know why I'm letting the Clemenza kiss me now, his arms around my neck as he hangs on tight. Don't know. Don't really care.

It feels right.

And the ghost of my father doesn't feel so close as it usually does.

He breaks his mouth away from mine just to whisper, "I want you," in my ear.

I want him, too. Which means we need to get upstairs as soon as we can, away from Sammy—and the rest of them, too. I don't know what any of this means, and I'm not in a mood to examine it. But letting slip in front of the household that Caligula and I are...*whatever*, is not how I want this day to end.

I pull away from his mouth, push him gently back when he tries to kiss my neck, my jaw. "C'mon," I tell him. "We need some privacy for that."

We head back through the kitchen fast, and I pause only to bring down the security doors again. Sammy's already disappeared, and Rosa and Vito are flirting over dirty dishes. "Night," I call over my shoulder, pulling Caligula along with me.

"Goodnight!" he echoes.

We get no response, which is fine by me. The less they notice about us, the better. And besides, I'm being driven by my dick now, the part of me that wants to get back into a part of him. All that fucking we did last night, and then again in the shower before dinner, and I'm still ravenous for him.

I don't know what it means. Don't plan to stop and figure it out.

But when we get back into my bedroom and stripped off, Caligula Clemenza still manages to surprise me. He pushes me back on the bed and climbs on top of me, stretching out carefully. "Put your arms around me," he tells me.

I obey.

Fuck, right now I'd do whatever he told me to. He's the most beautiful man I ever laid eyes on. How did I not see that before? I always knew he was pretty, but he's much more than that. He's a heartstopper. Weak at the knees, launch-a-thousand-ships, drop-dead gorgeous.

He lowers his mouth to mine to kiss me again, and I let him do it. Let him kiss me as much as he likes. Whatever he wants right now, I'll give to him. "Tell me what you need," I say when he finally pulls away again.

"I need you inside me again."

"You're not too—"

"No. I'm fine."

There's something off about the way he says it, but I'm too focused on the idea of getting inside that tight little hole again to take much note. I slap around with my right hand for the lube, which I left sitting right there on the nightstand, until eventually Caligula grabs it himself and pushes it into my hand.

"Like this," he says, rising up to straddle me. "I want to ride you."

"Yeah you do."

My dick is already taking control, but I pause long enough to prep him, to squirt some of the lube over my fingers and then slide them into him. He takes them easily. I can tell he's sore, but he seems to be enjoying the attention anyway. And I like feeling him from the inside, that wet heat that just about sends me crazy.

It's even better when he sinks down onto me, slow and easy, until his asshole is clamped right down at the base of my shaft, my whole dick buried inside him. I reach up and run my hands over his chest, pinching at his nipples as he starts to rock, just a gentle back and forth that makes me groan.

He hasn't taken his eyes off of my face.

I can't take mine off of his. How did I not see it before, such rare beauty? Or was it always there and I was just too blind to see it? I reach up to trace the line of his jaw, and he turns his head to kiss my palm. Such a sweet, small gesture, but it makes my cock jump inside him.

He leans down to brush his lips over mine, and I need to kiss him again. I grab the back of his neck, angle his head just right, and plunder his mouth. There's no gentleness in it, just raw need, a hunger so sharp it borders on violence. It's a stark contrast to the slow, languid way he rides me. But he meets me kiss for kiss, his tongue dueling with mine, hands gripping my shoulders hard.

I know this is wrong.

I know it.

But I can't stop myself. Can't stop the betrayal of my father's ghost, can't pretend this is anything but surrender. And it's breaking my heart at the same time Caligula Clemenza is filling it up, making me feel something for the first time since...

Since thirteen.

He figured me out, this clever little Clemenza. He knows exactly what I am. Even threw it in my face when we got back from the Obelisk, just to make me fuck him. Told me I was a coward.

He's more right than he knows.

But here and now, with him riding me so good, that tight little asshole milking me just right, I can't do anything but let Caligula take his pleasure. He's going faster now, finding the friction he needs, and I rock up to meet him, to push deeper, to find that sweet spot inside that makes him groan and throw his head back.

He rides me with a wild abandon, something in his eyes keeping me pinned in place while he does, so that all I can do is lie there and let him use me. God knows I've done it enough to him. A little payback might be good for him.

Might take that desperation out of his face.

I reach up to touch him, slide a hand over his cheek, a little worried at the intensity. "You okay?"

"Harder," he gasps out.

My back's getting sore, the stitches tugging at my skin, but I can only obey. I thrust hard up into him, that sweet knot gripping my dick like it never wants to let me go. I thrust into him again and again until he falls forward, one hand on the wall and the other on my chest as he braces himself.

He lets me fuck him like that until he's right on the edge, his cock drizzling and leaking all over my belly, and then he changes the pace again, slowing so he can lean down to my mouth, present his for more kissing.

I take the chance eagerly. I never knew kissing could be so addictive, but Caligula Clemenza is the most potent drug I've ever tried. My tongue slides into his mouth as he reaches back to pull my legs up, drive me deeper into him.

I've never felt so connected to another person in my life.

So close to him that I feel every heartbeat, every breath. The scent of our sweat and sex fills the air, and I want to bottle it, keep it with me forever. His skin is hot and slick under my hands as I grip his hips, his muscles bunching and relaxing with every movement. It's the sexiest thing I've ever felt.

He pulls away from my mouth just to say, "I'm close, Dami. I'm so close…"

My own orgasm is building too, a tight, hot coil at the base of my spine. My balls are drawing up. A tingling starts at the back of my thighs. I drop a hand to his dick and he arches back. It only takes a few tugs and then he's there, splashing ropes of cum all over my chest and stomach. I keep pumping into him until I empty myself, filling him with so much of my spunk that it's trickling out and making a mess of the sheets.

He collapses onto me, panting. And I hold him, stroking that soft hair while our breathing evens out. We roll over onto our sides eventually, and his lips find their way back to mine, kissing and kissing like we can't get enough of each other.

"Dami," he murmurs against my mouth at last. "Thank you."

"For what?"

"For teaching me so many valuable lessons."

I push him back a little, puzzled. "What do you mean?"

He smiles. But it's a private smile, not aimed at me. "Well, I'm definitely not a virgin anymore."

"Is that…okay?" I ask.

"Of course," he assures me. "I mean, it had to happen sooner or later, right? I had to lose my innocence eventually." I'm about to snort and tell him 'innocence' is not a word I associate with him, when he kisses me again. "I'm just glad it happened with you," he says after, his voice all soft and sweet.

I kiss him back, just as soft and sweet as he sounded. And partway through, I realize how screwed I really am.

Because I can't hurt him anymore. I can't even imagine it now. All those dark fantasies I used to have, they make my belly twist in disgust.

But that means I'll fail my father. He'll never be avenged.

So what does that make me?

"I should clean up," Caligula says.

"Yeah," I say vaguely. "Yeah, sure."

While he's in the bathroom, I wipe myself down with an old t-shirt, unwilling to get rid of his scent completely. But by the time he makes it back to bed, my mind has gone down too many rabbit holes to count.

"What's wrong, Dami?" he asks, sliding back into my arms. "You look worried."

I lie without thinking. I can't tell him what was going through my head, not before I figure my own shit out. "Ah, just everything. The Bratva. The guy hunting you. Your cousin. Whether they're the same, or—"

"Oh, Dami," he sighs, turning over in bed and pulling me close to big-spoon him. "We can worry about all that tomorrow. Right now, we should get some sleep."

He's right. Having him here in my arms, warm and willing, is the *only* fucking thing that matters right now. I reach back to turn off the light, and then snuggle my nose into the back of his neck and breathe him in.

Tomorrow. We can figure everything out tomorrow.

But when I wake in the morning, I'm alone in the bed again. I give a rueful grin, wondering at myself. He must be in the bathroom. I've gone pretty hard on his ass—literally—the last forty-eight hours. But when I listen, it's quiet in there. I get out of bed, wincing a little at the ache in my back, and knock softly on the door. "Hey. You okay?"

No response.

I open the door. It's not locked, and swings open to show an empty bathroom. Slightly alarmed now, I check the walk-in closet, and that's where something catches my eye.

The clothes. All those clothes I bought him, they're in a heap on the floor under where they used to be hanging in the closet, as though someone was looking through them quickly, discarding fast what they didn't need.

The coat is gone. The Tom Ford herringbone that he came with. And some of those sweaters the Benedettis sent, slim enough to wear under a coat. And the brown boots, and the jeans…

And other shit has gone, too. I don't know what—clothes aren't something I notice much—but there are more hangers than there are clothes dumped on the floor.

I pull on my robe and go straight downstairs. It's too early for even Rosa to be up, so the kitchen is dark and quiet. He's not there. But he has to be in the house. Security is still active.

He *has* to be in the house.

Right?

I head straight back to my bedroom and slam my finger down on the biometric reader that opens up the door to the viewing room. I haven't been in here for days, not since I let Caligula Clemenza out of the basement last time.

And now I see I should have put him right back down there as soon as he was healthy enough. Because when I scrub back through the footage of the last few hours, my bedroom door opens, and a slim figure emerges with a stuffed backpack.

He's wearing the long coat, jeans, and the brown boots. I switch cameras to watch him head down to the kitchen, where he methodically goes through the cupboards, grabbing protein bars and trail mix packets and a whole box of granola to throw into his bag.

He exits the kitchen and I pick him up again in the garage. He goes straight to the keypad and enters the code. The metal barricade rattles up, and the Clemenza hits stop when it's only a foot or so open. He shrugs off the backpack, throws it under, and rolls out after it. The door shudders down again, locking us all inside.

I have cameras on the outside of the house, too. But after Caligula Clemenza crosses the street diagonally and jogs off down the road, I lose sight of him.

I stare at the camera for another few seconds as I process what I've just seen. And then I raise my fist high over the desk and slam it down hard enough to shake the screens on the wall.

He played me.

He fucking *played* me.

I should have killed him when I had the chance. I

should have chained him to the wall in that basement and flayed the skin from his body an inch at a time over three hundred and sixty-five days. I should have—should have—

I slam my fist down, over and over, until one of the screens blacks out.

I'll find him again.

And this time, I won't hesitate to kill him.

CHAPTER 42
CALIGULA

I WAIT until Damiano Orsini is sleeping heavily and then I slide out of his arms. As usual, he doesn't stir. He sleeps like the dead, but I can hear him breathing.

He sleeps all through my packing of clothes. I don't know what I'd do if he woke.

A part of me maybe hopes he will. A part of me doesn't want to leave.

But I have to.

I can't trust Damiano any more than I could trust Uncle Tony or Daniel King or Jesse Foster. Lorenzo Benedetti would say they're all cut from the same cloth, and he'd be right.

It doesn't matter how Damiano's body makes mine feel. Doesn't matter that I can still feel his lips on mine, his cock buried in my ass.

I can't control him.

I saw it for myself at the Obelisk when he killed Grisha, but he was so useful with Daniel King that I overlooked it. But then I found out just how untrustworthy he really is.

I can't believe a damn thing he says.

So I need to go.

I make sure to pack as much dry food as I can. I still remember the cold, the hunger from those months on the streets. But this time, I have an option I didn't have before.

The Clemenza Loyalists. If I can find them, I might be able to claw back what little remains of our empire.

It means giving up safety. Comfort. Damiano does offer me those things, it's true, but only so long as he can't kill me. Once Luca D'Amato lifts the protection order on me—because of course he will, eventually—nothing is stopping my current protector from becoming my executioner.

And my Family is worth more to me than comfort and safety. My Family is worth the risk.

For the first time, I find myself in sympathy with Damiano Orsini's drive for vengeance, because once I find my people and re-establish myself, I plan to hunt down Tiberius Vicario and make him pay for all of this.

As for Dami…

I harden my heart. He'll have to explain to his Boss about the dead Bratva and the vanished Clemenza. Good fucking luck to him.

I head to the garage and key in the code I was careful to memorize when Dami punched it in, waiting for the gate to lift only just enough to let me out. The cold hits hard. Snow must be on the way soon. I just hope it holds off tonight, at least until I can get to one of the quieter subway stations I used to sleep in sometimes.

Once I'm out, I hit the code on the other side as well, so the door closes again. I wish nothing but the best for Rosa, Vito, even Sammy. I have no desire to see them murdered in their beds, so I won't leave them vulnerable.

As for Damiano Orsini, he's big enough to look after himself, so he has no need of my well-wishes.

I pull my backpack onto my shoulders and start jogging

slowly across the street before taking a right and heading deeper into Midtown.

I've only gone a few more yards when the first snowflake drifts down onto the sidewalk in front of me. It melts. The next ones don't.

I stop at the next intersection, bouncing on my toes to keep warm. I need to find shelter, and I need to find it *fast*, but it has to be somewhere Damiano won't think to look.

I could go back. I could creep back through the garage, unpack everything, crawl back into bed with Dami, into his warm embrace and his protection…

I'm paralyzed with indecision.

And then I remember: *he's a liar*. I can't trust him. And I *won't* go back into that fucking basement.

Just as I've made my decision, a white van comes down the street behind me and takes a left at the corner, cutting me off before I start walking across. I have to jerk back to avoid getting hit.

The side door rolls open.

I hear quick footsteps behind me, but a black bag goes over my head before I can turn to see who it is. There's a sharp sting in my arm, and I'm falling—no, hands are lifting me, moving me into the van—

And then there's nothing but darkness.

The Clemenza Family saga continues in
The Beast Who Broke Me

ALSO BY LEIGHTON GREENE

ROUGH LOVE SERIES

Learn the Rules

Obey the Rules

Break the Rules

Flying Free

FRIENDS OF FRIENDS SERIES

Winter Wonders

Taming Tristan

Star Spanked

Haunted Hearts

Champagne Charade

MORELLI FAMILY SERIES

Married to the Mobster

Beloved by the Boss

Heist of the Heart

Enticed by the Enemy

Seduced by a Sinner

Kissed by a Killer

Devoted to the Don

Vow of the Vigilante

WEST COAST MOBSTERS SERIES

His Lethal Desire

His Brutal Heart

His Fatal Love

His Sinful Need

His Guilty Pleasure

His Wicked Wants

ABOUT THE AUTHOR

Leighton lives with her partner and her cockatiel on the east coast of Australia. Keep in touch via her VIP Readers newsletter, by liking and following her Facebook Page, or joining her Facebook Group for fun and games with other fans—lurkers welcome!

www.leightongreene.com

Printed in Dunstable, United Kingdom

82371038R00214